Cecil County Public Library
301 Newark Ave.
Elkton, MD 21921

P9-BTM-289

TIER ONE WILD

ALSO BY DALTON FURY

Kill Bin Laden: A Delta Force Commander's Account of the Hunt for the World's Most Wanted Man

Black Site: A Delta Force Novel

TIER ONE WILD

A DELTA FORCE NOVEL

DALTON FURY

ST. MARTIN'S PRESS ✠ NEW YORK

This is a work of fiction. All of the characters, organizations, and events portrayed in this novel are either products of the author's imagination or are used fictitiously.

TIER ONE WILD: A DELTA FORCE NOVEL. Copyright © 2012 by Dalton Fury. All rights reserved. Printed in the United States of America. For information, address St. Martin's Press, 175 Fifth Avenue, New York, N.Y. 10010.

www.stmartins.com

Library of Congress Cataloging-in-Publication Data

Fury, Dalton.
  Tier One Wild : a Delta Force novel / Dalton Fury. — 1st ed.
     p. cm.
  ISBN 978-0-312-66838-9 (hardcover)
  ISBN 978-1-250-01856-4 (e-book)
 1. Soldiers—Fiction. 2. Terrorism—Prevention—United States—Fiction.
3. United States. Army. Delta Force—Fiction. 4. Americans—Pakistan—
Fiction. 5. Qaida (Organization)—Fiction. I. Title.
  PS3606.U795T54 2012
  813'.6—dc23

                                        2012028285

First Edition: October 2012

10 9 8 7 6 5 4 3 2 1

To the Eagles still fighting demons long after the drumbeat faded

and the guns have gone silent

ACKNOWLEDGMENTS

Kolt did most of the heavy lifting in *Black Site,* which for an informed reader—a student of *black* special ops—is easily the biggest hurdle to being absolutely sure that it could ever be anything more than fiction. You see, in special operations, like any other military unit, it's the sergeants that carry the heaviest load, not the Os.

Besides the Tsunami-size bad call Kolt "Racer" Raynor made in the Pakistani badlands, he spent most of his time working what we call "singleton" missions. He operated alone. Those kinds of ops that for one reason or another, someone reasoned that it made more tactical sense to send a single operator instead of a team to handle the job.

But the quickest route to burnout for any operator is back-to-back-to-back singleton ops. They are just inherently packed with stress, high blood pressure, self-doubt, and living a backstopped but shallow cover. And of course, nobody expected Racer to survive the *Black Site* mission. But he did.

Everyone knows Kolt was the luckiest son-of-a-bitch alive. Including Kolt.

In fact, he vowed to stiff-arm any future singleton ops. Just to stay sane, he needed mates. He needed like mindsets, someone to cover his six and pick up his slack. Can you blame him? It's been a heckuva long war on terror, and everyone has limits.

If you are still with me, after reading *Tier One Wild,* you know that Racer preferred a team. Without them covering for him, or providing covering fire, this Delta Force thriller series is dead on arrival.

With the first two books behind us, I ain't flapping when I say Kolt and I have more in common than I originally thought. We both hate operating alone. And we both have a ton of God-given vices. So it's a no-brainer that we both recognize that we are only at our best when working with team-mates. We're happiest when our Ranger buddies are there to keep us sharp. Safest when our mates are posted at the breach, porting the windows, or pulling high cover in the stairwell. Our critics might even say riding the coat-tails of more talented operators.

And just as it took a team of teams to track down Abu al-Amriki and the SA-24s, it took a mirror effort—a collective World Series attitude—to birth what you hold in your hands.

Operators don't leave ranks until they are ready to jack it in and retire to the house. And I am proud to say nobody left our team. The same commando-minded professionals that brought *Black Site* to life remained on the manifest for *Tier One Wild*. And with any book, or any mission, the support effort by anonymous pros behind the scenes can make or break the op. I am deeply grateful and exceptionally proud of the folks at St. Martin's Press and Trident Media Group whose work in the shadows made the main effort look good. Within specops, we call the *main effort* the assault force. Everyone else is support.

Leading our assault force once again was my editor and diehard New York Mets fan Marc Resnick. I am convinced that a pack of terrorists couldn't break his positive spirit, or his smile, or even get him to root for the Braves for a single inning. And even if they could, my superagent, Scott Miller of Trident, would be there in no time to make things right. Like many of you, there is a little tier one wild in Scott. With Marc, Scott, and me once again was the übertalented and savvy writer Mark Greaney, to whom I owe an enormous debt for his coaching, mentoring, and friendship. Even though Scott could handle any terrorist, Mark would still pile on like the Cleveland Browns' secondary. But make no mistake, there is no doubt that the only member of our assault force that we could have put on waivers to bring Kolt Raynor to life would have been me.

Besides the boys at work, nothing gets done without the support of family. And even though my wonderful wife and daughters aren't all that impressed by all this Dalton Fury stuff, they let it slide as long as it doesn't interfere with my day job. Keep it out of the house and all is good, but one thing is for sure. Let Kolt slip up and lose the support of the ladies in my house, and he is a dead man.

I'm often questioned if the stuff Kolt pulls off is real. Would Dalton Fury try to take down a hijacked airliner as it was taking off? Of course not, but I'm no Kolt Raynor.

And since ST6 smoked Bin Laden in mid–2011, I'm often asked if Delta Force really tells other people or troops that they are Navy SEALs to preserve their true identity or cover. Well, yes, I am a Navy SEAL. In fact, just because I don't surf, or sky shark you in free fall, or kick your ass at a bar and steal your girlfriend, as far as my cover for action is concerned, I'm the best darn Navy SEAL on target.

Of course, either you don't believe me, or I ain't sticking around long enough to play twenty questions. Just like on target.

Tier One Wild (1) Using common sense over process, getting away with more than the other guy, and possessing a bit of an attitude. (2) The mindset that all Tier One (Delta Force and SEAL Team 6) operators roll with, encompassing the idea that someone who is specially assessed and selected to serve in the ranks of a special missions unit (DF and ST6) has the mental and physical capacity to perform to a much higher standard, to accept more risk, to march to a different drummer, and to tell a general officer that he is full of shit (with slightly more tact but with absolutely no fear of retribution).

TIER ONE WILD

PROLOGUE

New Delhi, India

The dead lay throughout the first-class cabin. Their bodies stank in the still air.

Four men, two women. A Flight attendant. An air marshal. A man who had looked like he might start trouble. An Indian diplomat from the Punjab. A German woman who had been shot for screaming.

And one martyr.

Unlike the five dead nonbelievers, Marwan's body had not been dumped across the seats. No, his men had laid him gently on his back, his arms positioned across his chest, a clean starched napkin from a first-class dining cart draped over his face, the two running ends of his red headband just visible. Marwan had been the leader of the six-strong cell of Lashkar-e-Taiba fighters. He and his men had boarded this aircraft two days earlier dressed like businessmen returning from a telemarketing conference in Mumbai. Marwan had gone to the rear galley shortly after takeoff, while the rest of the passengers sat strapped into their seats, compliant like lambs chained to posts in the marketplace. He'd found the case left for him by a Jordanian brother who worked in food service at the Chatrapati Shivaji International Airport in Mumbai, and from it Marwan quietly and efficiently passed the Skorpion machine pistols out to his men. He donned the bulletproof vest left in the bag and slipped the hand grenade into his pocket, and then the seven Pakistani Lashkar-e-Taiba operatives rushed up the aisles and took over the plane.

Twenty-five seconds after they thought they had control, Marwan fell to the aisle dead, killed by a pistol shot to the back of the head, fired by an air marshal. The marshal was himself killed by Skorpion fire in the next moment, which immediately put Jellock in charge of an operation that still had not recovered from the death of its leader.

Jellock was not Marwan. He was scared and uncertain. He was tired and hot and sick of the strange food on the aircraft and the overflowing toilets and the bodies putrefying up in first class. The ballistic vest he now wore dug into his skin and weighed him down as he ran the length of the plane shouting orders.

In the past fifty-five hours he'd forced the 767's American flight crew to fly to New Delhi, then back to Mumbai, then to Bangalore, and now back to New Delhi. Jellock had been afraid to keep the aircraft in one place for too long while he waited for his demands to be met. In the meantime, the Indian government had stalled and his men had threatened and then killed passengers and crew.

He wished Marwan were here to tell him what to do, where to go, how to keep order among the other five men in the cell.

But Marwan was dead in first class, and the others looked to Jellock for direction while they bickered among themselves and beat on the passengers in frustration.

What do I do? This is taking too long!

The twenty-three-year-old's exhausted and stressed mind focused quickly. *Too long.* Yes! Too long they had been on the ground here in New Delhi. He felt the government's delays had been trickery, that he'd been played for a fool.

Too long.

Jellock stood, stormed into the cockpit, found the flight crew sleeping in their seats, and he screamed at them. "We leave New Delhi! We fly away!"

"Where?" asked the pilot wearily.

Jellock thought a moment. He needed a safe place. Someplace where the aircraft could remain for enough hours for him to get some rest. "Quetta!"

"Pakistan." The pilot said it as a groan. A statement of frustration.

"Yes!" Jellock screamed every word he said to the pilots, thinking it would make him appear authoritative.

The pilot shrugged. "When?"

"Now! Take off!"

"Son, you don't understand. We have to go through a preflight checklist and pull our maps for the route we—"

"Take off now or I kill a passenger!" Jellock turned to yell out into the cabin. "Mohammed!"

The pilot rubbed his eyes and reached for his case containing his maps and charts. "Okay! Okay. Just give me five minutes to—"

"One minute!" Jellock yelled, certain of the deceit of this nonbeliever. "In one minute we are moving to the runway or I kill one passenger every minute!"

"Three minutes! You've got to give us at least—"

"Two minutes! No more!"

"I need three!"

"You can have three, but I kill one passenger." He turned back to the cabin. "Mohammed! Bring me the first child you see!"

"All right! Calm down! We're moving in two!" shouted the pilot, before tuning out the terrorist and focusing on his aircraft.

ONE

The hazy night sky was cool three thousand feet above and aft of the Boeing 767, but Delta Force Major Kolt "Racer" Raynor perspired into his goggles. Rivulets of sweat ran down the back of his black Nomex suit as he hung under the taut canopy of his square parachute and focused on the scene below.

It had been nearly four years since he'd led other men into battle. He had been assessed as ready by both his superiors and his peers, and he felt ready, but still, he was human.

And this shit was scary as hell.

Two more canopies drifted down through the darkness near him. The three chutes were stacked—teammates Digger and Slapshot were strapped together in a tandem rig below and fifty feet ahead of Kolt, and Stitch was positioned slightly above and fifty feet behind.

All four men floated with the wind down toward their drop zone, a few hundred feet aft of the hijacked American Airlines flight.

Digger spoke into his radio from his position up front, hanging in front of Slapshot. "Hey, boss. That plane looks like it's ready to depart. There's no auxiliary power attached. Aft stairs are up, too."

"Guess they aren't gonna wait around for us to sneak up all ninja-like," Slapshot mumbled into his mic. The big man always injected humor when no one else was in the mood.

And Kolt was not in the mood. "Damn," he said.

Next Stitch came over the radio: "Back to me a bit, boss," and Racer immediately realized he had drifted a little too close to the men in front of him. Calmly he adjusted his toggles to remedy the error.

The plan had been to land and then link up with other Americans on the ground—CIA case officers and military types from the embassy here—and then they would decide how to proceed. They'd set their drop zone as a spot on the tarmac behind the hijacked aircraft, out of sight from the terminal, because the Agency boys on site had said TV cameras were positioned all over the terminal, and no one at Delta wanted the cameras to get a shot of a team of commandos dropping in from the sky at 0330 hours.

As he hung twenty-five hundred feet above the ground, Kolt eyed the plane, keeping it between his stack and the cameras.

He hoped like hell he and his mates would get a crack at taking the jet down before this was all over. He reasoned that, if the plane stayed put in New Delhi for just a few hours more, there was a decent chance he would get the order from the Joint Operations Center to hit the target.

But as he was thinking this, below his boots red and green indicator lights began blinking on the wingtips of the 767. Almost instantly the two Pratt & Whitney engines on the aircraft began to roar. Seconds later the nose of the craft turned slightly to the left, centering on the long runway that ran off to the west.

The 767 began to move forward as the engines pitched higher.

Kolt Raynor groaned in frustration. "You've got to be kidding."

Digger shouted into his radio, "Son of a bitch is rolling."

"Repositioning on the tarmac or heading to the runway?" Stitch asked from the back. He could not see past Racer's chute.

"Bet they're flying out of here. They've been doing a lot of erratic shit like that."

"Suggestions?" Kolt asked quickly into his mic. He knew to get the input of his sergeants at a critical moment like this.

Slapshot said, "There isn't much sense in linking up with officials if the hijacked plane isn't gonna hang around."

And then Stitch chimed in, "Racer, you have execute authority. Why don't we hit it?"

It was true, Raynor had pried execute authority from Colonel Webber, the head of Delta Force. This allowed Raynor, as the military commander at the scene, the flexibility to call for a hasty in-extremis takedown of the aircraft if he saw the opportunity to do so or if he felt the necessity to try, like if the terrorists, or "crows" in Delta parlance, started shooting hostages before official approval for Delta's mission came from the JOC.

Still, Kolt wasn't sure what Stitch was getting at. He keyed his mic. "*Hit it? While it's moving?*"

"We can land on the roof and head for the cockpit. I've got the harpoon. If we go in single file we can breach the escape hatch. If we increase our descent speed we can be inside before they go throttle-up."

"Have you guys done that before?" Kolt asked incredulously.

"Not on a moving aircraft, and only in training back at Bragg, boss," Slapshot answered. But he agreed with his fellow sergeant's assessment. "We aren't going to get another chance at this. If the plane isn't there, then the TV crews might see us, and if they film us dropping on the tarmac that will get back to the crows in the jet. Might just piss them off enough to kill some more passengers."

"Now or never," Stitch said. "What's the call, Racer?"

Kolt asked, "What about Digger?"

Now Digger chimed in. Though he was the youngest of the team and perhaps the most fit overall, he possessed one potential handicap to the operation.

Where his lower right leg used to be, he now wore a titanium prosthesis. Kolt could not imagine how he could run along the roof of a moving aircraft with a leg made out of metal.

"No sweat, boss. I've got this," Digger said. He sounded confident and eager.

Kolt's operational brain trust had spoken and their vote was unanimous. Still, this was his first hit since returning to the Unit just two months prior, and Colonel Webber had made it crystal clear to Raynor that he needed to change his ways. There was no room in the modern Delta Force for the Tier One Wild antics that had gotten him in hot water in the past, and Webber had reminded Kolt numerous times that he was on incredibly thin ice. Nevertheless, Kolt and his boys had been the alert squadron at Fort Bragg when this hostage crisis unfolded, so Kolt and his team had been called to bat.

Make your decision, Raynor! He said it to himself in a silent shout.

Three seconds later he pressed the push-to-talk button on his chest rig again. "Let's hit it." *Webber's gonna have my ass,* he thought, but right now he had *much* bigger fish to fry.

In the Joint Operations Center at Forward Operating Base Yukon in Bagram, Afghanistan, the chow hall, the gym, and the movie tent stood empty. Right now everyone with access was stacked at the back of the JOC watching the shocking footage displayed on a single large plasma screen at the front of the room. A Predator drone's night-vision camera caught the huge commercial aircraft moving slowly through the darkness toward the runway, and its satellite uplink broadcast the ghostly images to the screen at the JOC. Racer and his team were not in the picture, they were still high in the air on their descent, and their drop zone was out of the camera's current field of view.

The Agency guys at the airfield in New Delhi were on the other end of a Thuraya sat phone and their running commentary was piped through the speakers of the JOC. The CIA's liaison officer stood near Colonel Jeremy Webber, holding a phone to his ear and passing on additional information to the head of Delta Force.

The tension in the air infected everyone. All were frozen in amazement at the huge plasma monitor, referred to in the JOC as "Kill TV."

The men and women stood in rapt attention as the hijacked aircraft rolled steadily down the taxiway, clearly moving for takeoff on Runway 29. A few seconds later, the Predator downlink went fuzzy. The "eye in the sky" had blinked. It was a mechanical glitch that seemed to be common with that aerial asset at exactly those moments when clear observation was desperately needed.

The Kill TV feed came back up a moment later, just as the silhouetted figures of four men under three parachutes passed between the 767 and the camera's lens. Black hot figures flying through the air with the heat off their bodies trapped in the chutes above them, creating a faint umbrella shape.

"Holy shit. There they are!" exclaimed the operations sergeant major, breaking the silence that had fallen over the JOC. They should have been landing far back on the tarmac, but it looked to everyone at Bagram as if the Delta team were making for the runway itself. "What the hell are they doing?"

The three chutes sailed purposefully toward the plane on the ground, which meant only one thing to Colonel Jeremy Webber. The men were *not* continuing on to the drop zone on the now-empty tarmac.

No. It looked like . . .

Webber cocked his head slightly. "Racer is assaulting." He said it in a clipped voice that indicated to everyone in the room that he was pissed.

No one in the JOC was new to special operations or terrorist interdictions, but still many gasped in shock. Assaulting an aircraft as it sat at the end of the runway, seconds from takeoff?

Colonel Webber sat back in his chair. He *was* pissed, but he was not surprised. Kolt fucking Raynor, his man on the scene, had been a pseudo-insubordinate troop commander before he'd been kicked out of Delta four years ago. Now that he was back in the Unit, there was little reason to expect anything but pseudo-insubordination now, even with all Webber's "personal counseling" of his wayward major.

He stared silently at the downlink screen. Webber would have stopped Racer and the others if he had any control over this situation. But the Delta operators' audacious and daring actions effectively neutered any long-arm leadership—or micromanagement—since the JOC was 220 miles away from the action.

Colonel Webber cleared his throat and in a confident and booming voice said, "All right, we seem to have a common operating picture and are now in a current operation with operators on target. Push the QRF to the airspace and air-loiter twenty minutes out, spin up the extraction fixed-wing aircraft ASAP, and get me the SECDEF on the red line."

Immediately several of the staff in the JOC went from statues of stone to blurs of activity—the Quick Reaction Force choppers were ordered into the theater, the extraction aircraft were ordered ready, and secure comms with the Pentagon were established.

Webber's confident orders, tuned to just the right authoritative tenor by decades of command, sounded confident and certain, but that was just for public consumption.

Silently to himself the colonel breathed softly, "Dammit, Racer, you'd better not dick this up."

Even though they had not expected to drop right into combat, the four men six hundred feet above the aircraft were geared up for battle. Kolt "Racer"

Raynor and Master Sergeant Clay "Stitch" Vickery wore individual MC-4 HALO rigs while Master Sergeant Peter "Digger" Chambliss hung behind Master Sergeant Jason "Slapshot" Holcomb in a HALO tandem rig. These were not the best parachute rigs available to Delta, but they were the best rigs they had been able to grab as they raced onto the MC-130H Combat Talon II at the intermediate staging base at Masirah Air Base off the coast of Oman. As this was an in-extremis op, they only had time to bring in the best gear they could amass on the fly. All four operators wore the Ops-Core FAST ballistic helmet with infrared strobes activated and blinking on top. Under the helmet all wore dark brown Peltor ear protection and radio headsets. The team would be going in light protectionwise; three wore just chest plates, which would stop a frontal pistol or rifle round to their center mass; only Racer wore hard protection on both his chest and his back.

Each operator had a .40-caliber Glock 23 with a tan grip and a SureFire tactical light attached to a rail under its barrel. These pistols were secured in rigs on their chests, not on their hips. In the tight aisles of a commercial aircraft, the chest holsters allowed for faster deployment of the combat handguns than a belt rig. Only Slapshot and Stitch brought rifles along—each carried an HK416 strapped barrel-down on their left side. Extra ammo was secured in their chest rigs, which also held their MBITR MX radios in nylon side pouches.

The radios were wired to their Peltor headsets so that they could communicate effectively during the assault.

All four men were dressed in black flight suits with an American flag, subdued gray and black in color, on the left shoulder. On the right shoulder a call sign patch was affixed . . . a black border with a luminous tape letter/number combo. Kolt's read M11, as he was a troop commander in Mike Squadron. As a troop sergeant major of Mike, Slapshot was M12. Stitch and Digger were, respectively, team leader and second-in-command of Mike's Alpha team, so their patches read MA1 and MA2. Three of them were wearing desert tan and black Salomon trail shoes, while Kolt wore the same old tan leather combat boots he'd had since the invasion of Iraq nearly ten years earlier. The shoes were worn and torn, but he still loved them, old school though they were.

They had exited the MC-130 Talon II at twenty thousand feet wearing Gentex oxygen masks with a hose attached to a Twin 53 bailout bottle inside a pouch on the right hip. Once they descended below ten thousand feet they disconnected their masks and let them hang to the side. All wore thermal underwear and black balaclavas to maintain body heat during the descent. On their hands were black Mechanix M-Pact Covert gloves with plastic knuckle protectors, and digital altimeters were strapped to the back of each of their hands.

Each man also carried a pair of nine-banger flash-bang grenades and a personal first aid pouch with one-hand tourniquet rigs.

At four hundred feet above the target Slapshot, with Digger riding in the front of his rig, maneuvered to line up his approach angle to the rear of the 767, which was now turning off the taxiway and onto the runway. All Kolt and Stitch had to do was follow the red and green chemlites on the pack tray of their teammates to the target while maintaining safe separation. Racer, the least experienced jumper in the bunch, struggled to keep in formation with the other two chutes.

Kolt said, "Our spot is the long axis of the fuselage. We'll harpoon the escape hatch above the cockpit, depressurize the plane, and enter. We're going to have to do this fast and dirty before they take off. Once inside, haul ass aft and make friends in the rear. Remember, there are a hundred forty souls on board, plus at least six crows."

"One four zero souls, six assholes, roger," said Stitch.

"One-forty poor SOBs. Six bad guys. Got it," replied Digger.

"One-four-zero live. Six die. Then breakfast. Roger," said Slapshot, interjecting his trademark nonchalance into the tension.

"Boss, I have the harpoon," Stitch reminded his team leader.

To this Kolt replied, "Pull around to my left and take the base."

"Roger that," Stitch said, and seconds later he glided past his major, and then past the tandem team in front. He corrected back to the right and moved to the head of the line. Now it was Stitch's job to lead the others. He had red and green chemlites on the back of his pack as well, and the men behind him kept their eyes locked firmly on those lights as they neared the target.

Kolt struggled to keep his place in the stack as they neared the landing, but he managed to touch down on the slick aircraft roof just a few steps behind the others. He, Slapshot, and Stitch pulled their harness release pins and the three parachutes floated off the right side of the plane, just clearing the wing's edge before drifting softly to the tarmac.

All four men were prone on top of the aircraft now, and they fought to stay atop the slick and sloping surface, knowing they needed to get off the roof and inside the plane before the pilot applied takeoff thrust and jetted down the runway. Stitch and Kolt hugged the skin of the aircraft, something akin to balancing on a giant basketball, while Slapshot, still attached and lying on top of Digger, pulled the tandem chute's quick release to disconnect himself from his mate.

Inside the cockpit the two-man American flight crew had no idea that four Delta Force commandos were crawling toward the cockpit along the aircraft's fuselage. Both the pilot and copilot sat strapped to their seats with their headsets on, and they concentrated on the rushed takeoff sequence, manipulating the appropriate buttons.

The leader of the terrorists, the jittery man-child with the bulletproof vest who called himself Jellock, leaned into the cockpit. "One minute we are in air or boy die!"

The copilot held out a placating hand to the armed gunman, then turned to the captain. "We ready to go?"

"I have no idea," the pilot replied as he turned to the runway in front of him. "But we're outta here before they shoot that kid."

He reached for the throttle, and the copilot did the same.

TWO

The four operators moved forward in single file on top of the plane. Only two handholds jutted from the plane's surface, and with a single gloved hand each, Slapshot and Kolt tested every bit of tensile strength of an antenna blade the shape of a shark's fin while Digger held on to a strange-looking nozzle protruding up about five inches and set back seven feet from the escape hatch. The other hand was locked in a death grip around Stitch's right ankle.

Slapshot reached out to grab Digger's right ankle, but he stopped himself from doing so and instead reached over and latched on to Digger's left leg.

Stitch, at the head of the line, could feel the vicelike grip around his ankle as one of his mates held on tight. He assumed the others were doing the same to the men in front of them.

Without warning, the heavy whine of the engines behind them grew to a roar, and the aircraft moved forward with a jolt that made all four men press their gloved hands tight against the roof for purchase.

"She is taking off!" Stitch tried to yell it above the engine noise, but none of his mates heard him. At first the four operators struggled to stay glued to the aircraft body as the 767's thrust increased and it rolled forward into the darkness down the runway. But quickly they began crawling forward again, as fast as they could on the slick surface.

Because the plane had been refueled earlier at the terrorists' demands, Raynor and his men knew the takeoff speed for the heavy plane would be somewhere in the neighborhood of 180 knots. It was already at 10 knots, and Raynor couldn't key his radio mic for fear of falling off the aircraft. He yelled to Stitch in the front of the short line of operators. "Breach it!"

Now the entire team's survival depended on Stitch. He had less than forty seconds to get the job done, or he and his fellow operators would find themselves flying on the outside of the plane until they were whipped off to their deaths by the incredible wind.

All 767 jets are equipped with an emergency escape hatch above the cockpit. Formally referenced in the technical maintenance manuals as the Crew Compartment Overhead Hatch, the little door in the roof provides an emergency egress pathway for the plane's crew. It is not considered an entrance point and was never intended to provide access to anyone on the outside of the aircraft.

But Delta did not care what the aircraft designer's *intentions* were. *Their* intentions were what mattered now.

As the jet reached twenty knots' ground speed, Stitch leaned on his left side and reached into his chest rig to draw the harpoon device. He pulled it free, pressed the activation button with his right thumb, and lined it up two feet away at the center mass of the escape hatch. Given the distance, he couldn't miss.

Developed by a shrewd Delta assaulter, the harpoon was a simple CO_2 cartridge and a hollow tube the size of a large pickle that provided a quick and dirty way to depressurize an aircraft before an explosive breach through the side doors. Its capability was crucial in the event that the hijackers had booby-trapped all the plane's doors before the assault force arrived on the scene.

This time, though, the assault force consisted of just four men and there would be no explosive breaching of the side doors. Moreover, as cunning and conniving as Delta operators are, no one had ever envisioned harpooning the escape hatch after takeoff thrust had been applied and the plane sped down the runway toward liftoff.

Aircraft, as a general rule, do not take off after an assault has begun.

As the ground speed of the 767 passed sixty knots, Stitch pulled the trigger and the harpoon pierced the shiny metal as advertised, immediately initiating a slow depressurization of the cabin below. Stitch then tossed the firing mechanism over the edge of the speeding aircraft to get it out of the way.

• • •

With his left hand on the throttle, the copilot heard a loud noise through his headset, and saw the sharp black edge of a large dart protruding through the middle of the escape hatch, above and centered just behind the pilot and copilot. "What the . . ."

He snapped out of his momentary paralysis as the lead terrorist burst back into the cockpit.

Behind the menacing Skorpion machine pistol, the man's dark curly hair and deep brown skin tone stood in sharp contrast to his loose white shirt buttoned over his body armor.

"V one," the pilot said calmly, announcing that they had reached the speed at which they would need to continue to take off, even if there was an engine failure. The pilot ignored everything around him and concentrated on the runway ahead.

The terrorist who called himself Jellock said, "What was that noise?" The copilot did not answer. Another thud on the roof diverted the terrorist's eyes up to the escape hatch.

On the roof of the speeding jet, Stitch's job was only half finished. He needed to get the hatch open. With the plane now at a ground speed of ninety knots, he frantically dug into his chest rig and pulled out a six-inch explosive charge from a pouch. He peeled away the thin film covering the sticky tape with his teeth, and he slapped it on the hatch-locking mechanism. Quickly he turned his head away and detonated the charge.

Boom!

The explosion punctured the escape hatch and filled the cockpit with a misty gray haze. Jellock had been staring right at the hatch, so he was temporarily blinded by the flash. He screamed and raised his weapon with one hand and fired blindly into the cockpit while rubbing his eyes with his other hand. One of his rounds found a home in the left shoulder of the pilot, who spun in his seat, but remained upright in his safety harness.

Jellock raised his Skorpion toward the roof now and let loose another burst. The rounds ripped through the padded insulation and punctured the thin metal skin of the aircraft. Unsure of what was coming next and opting for the protection of his comrades, the Pakistani turned and fled the cockpit.

•   •   •

Stitch felt a sting in his left hand as he gripped the hatch edge and pulled him-self forward. An incredible burning in his pinkie finger that felt as if the hatch had been slammed shut on it. But he remained in control of his entire team's destiny, so he ignored the pain and struggled against the wind resistance and the forward thrust of the aircraft as he felt the jet's nose attitude increase at one hundred knots.

Without taking time to look inside, he reached through the opening and tossed a nine-banger behind the crew seats. Almost instantly a succession of nine bright and deafening explosions rocked the cockpit.

Disorienting the flight crew during takeoff was an unfortunate but neces-sary component of breaching a cockpit held by terrorists. Stitch just had to hope like hell the men flying the plane could overcome the effects of the blast and get the jet in the air without veering off to the left or right or running out of runway.

Stitch pulled himself face-first into the small hole right behind the last of the explosions, completely unaware that a .32-caliber round from the terror-ist's gun had severed his pinkie finger.

He tumbled six feet to the floor, landed half on the copilot and half on the main console. It hurt like hell, but he was relieved to be inside.

The wounded and disoriented pilot had handed off responsibilities to his copilot, and somehow the copilot managed to remain composed. He kept the aircraft straight on the runway, even though the flash-bang had all but blinded him. He had to get his ship airborne; there was no way he could back off the throttle and reject the takeoff at this point, there was not enough runway to prevent the fuel-laden craft from exploding in a fireball at the far edge of the airport grounds.

He guided his huge 767 into the air with steady hands that belied the chaos going on around him.

Scrambling to follow Stitch into the aircraft, Digger slid in headfirst with the same bit of pathetic acrobatics of his teammate.

Slapshot tumbled in behind them.

Digger and Stitch didn't wait around to be introduced to the pilots. The two operators gained their footing and exited the crew compartment door to begin clearing the aircraft, with their weapons out in front of them. The steep angle of the takeoff roll required them to move through the cabin as if they were running down a hill. Slapshot stayed where he was and reached up to help Kolt into the plane.

The aircraft's rear wheels left the runway and it rose at a ten-degree pitch and 190 knots. Kolt held on to the edge of the hatch for dear life, now pulling with all his might against the roaring air current. He pulled himself forward and in through the hatch, but as he did this, the jagged aircraft skin caught the cord running from his Peltor ear protection to his radio, yanking his earpro as well as his helmet off as he dropped to the floor. Kolt's goggles were attached to the helmet so he found himself without eye protection, either.

Raynor landed to the rear of the center console next to Slapshot, vaulted to his feet, and then leaned back down between the flight crew. He yelled to be heard over the roar of wind and engine noise from the hatch above.

"Lock the door behind us! Fly a runway heading! No banking! Level off as fast as you can!"

Even though the nine-banger's effects made hearing the black-clad commando nearly impossible, the American Airlines crew got the idea.

Kolt Raynor brought his Glock up as he raced out the cockpit doorway behind Slapshot. The pilot, though injured with a small ragged hole in his shoulder, unbuckled his harness, stood, then closed and locked the door. He then did his best to jam the escape hatch above back into place before reaching for the first-aid kit.

The four Delta men had studied the aircraft in great detail while en route from Fort Bragg, memorizing every inch and every feature. This wide-body 767-400 had two aisles in first class with a single row of large seats running down the center. The rows then continued past the forward galley, all the way back through the first coach cabin, to a central exit alley with lavatories. The two aisles then continued on through the rear coach cabin to the galley and lavs at the rear of the plane. Digger and Stitch raced down the right aisle of first class, clearing it as they ran forward. Kolt and Slapshot followed just behind and on the left side. The four assaulters passed the several dead bodies stowed in first class, then rushed through the forward lavatories and galley, and continued down the steep aisles on both sides of coach.

By the time Kolt made it into the coach cabin, terror had struck the passengers like a tidal wave. Wild animal-like screams and shrieks pierced his ears. The Delta operators knew all about panic and what to expect from innocent civilians on board a hijacked aircraft. The civilians, though terrorized and frantic, retained enough survival instincts to keep their heads down during the interdiction. Raynor and his boys knew that anyone brave enough to look up over the seat, for the first couple of seconds anyway, was very likely one of the bad guys.

All four Americans promoted the natural tendency of the innocents to stay out of the line of fire with angry shouts: "Get down! Get down! Get down!"

Slapshot sprinted down the left aisle in the forward coach cabin. He noticed a dark brown hand with a black machine pistol just above a headrest and took aim. He raised his HK rifle to eye level, placed the red dot of his optics an inch above the headrest, slipped his finger into the trigger guard and onto the taut trigger, and dropped the hammer twice on two subsonic 5.56 rounds. It was all muscle memory and he completed the action in under two seconds. Both hot copper bullets tore through the headrest just low of his aiming point, and entered the armed man's chest. The pistol fell to the cabin floor next to the Pakistani's body.

"One crow down," Slapshot said into his mic.

Delta kept moving.

Stitch had, unquestionably, the worst job of the team. He was the "runner." Armed only with a pistol in his right hand and a second pistol strapped to his chest, he raced down the right aisle, scanning intently, trying to separate normal sights from threat indicators. But his job as the runner was not to engage all the bad guys himself. No, his rush aft was designed to draw out the enemy. The three Delta men behind him knew to scan ahead to ID terrorists gunning for Stitch, the man spearheading their assault.

By now Stitch knew he'd lost a finger to enemy fire; his bloody left hand stung even through the painkilling effects of his adrenaline, but the appendage continued to function, so he ignored the pain and continued.

Suddenly his forward momentum stopped as he ran smack-dab into a punishing burst of .32-caliber rounds.

He hadn't even seen the shooter.

The bullets slammed squarely into the center of his chest plate armor. The impact stood him straight up and locked his knees momentarily before his instincts forced him to the deck.

The shooter then stood up, clearly thinking he would get a better angle on the American commando. Digger, in overwatch of Stitch's movement, placed his rifle's sights above the terrorist's red headband and squeezed off two rapid rounds. Both found their mark, and they blew blood and brain and bone straight up and onto the overhead compartment. The enemy dropped back into his seat like a bag of wet cement as those around him screamed.

"Two down," Digger announced.

Stitch regained his footing and continued down the aisle with his handgun. He moved so fast he almost missed one of the terrorists sitting on his right, but the man made it easy as he identified himself.

"*Allahu Akbar!*" he screamed as he rose with a machine pistol in his right hand and a young female passenger held close to him with his left. Stitch spun toward the noise and squeezed off a .40-caliber round almost instantly. The Pakistani's head snapped back, the Skorpion fell from his hands, and the woman wrestled out of the dead terrorist's death grip and into the arms of her husband in the next seat.

"Three crows down." Stitch kept moving.

Just then, on the left side of the plane, a dark-skinned man stood quickly in a window seat, shouting something incomprehensible. Both of his hands were thrust into the air as he stood and tried to get out into the aisle, shoving past those in the seats next to him. Raynor's Glock lined up on the man's forehead, and Raynor's finger took up the slack of the pistol's trigger safety as he prepared to shoot the man dead.

But the man's hands were empty.

He was a "squirter," a civilian panicked by the assault and trying to make a hopeless run for it.

A fraction of a second before he fired, Kolt recognized the man was not a terrorist, but as long as the man was up and moving and not in control of his actions, he was, most definitely, still a threat.

Kolt reached across two passengers and shoved the man back into his seat.

"Get down!"

Slapshot, moving down the left aisle facing aft, was a few yards ahead of Raynor. Out of the corner of his eye he saw a man lean out from the center exit aisle of the plane with a weapon in his hand. Kolt was dealing with the panicked passenger, and Stitch and Digger could not see the man from their position on the right side.

The terrorist ducked quickly back into the galley before Slapshot could fire.

The master sergeant shouted into his MBITR's mic as he kept his eyes focused on the corner. "Crow in the center galley!"

He continued moving aft, hunting for terrorist indicators.

Without his Peltors, Kolt didn't hear the call on the net, but it did not matter. He'd caught a fleeting glimpse of the man as he ducked around the corner. When Slapshot was held up for a moment with another squirter in the center cabin, Raynor leapfrogged his mate and made it to the galley, his eyes locked on the folding metal door of the lav. The terrorist would be inside; there was no indication that he'd retreated into the rear coach cabin.

Raynor did not hesitate. He sidestepped left into the galley area to clear the rest of the space, and here he inadvertently stomped down on a male steward's left penny loafer. Kolt looked at the young man cowering in a ball on the floor of the galley and the two made brief eye contact.

The kid smelled like he had shit his pants and his body shook uncontrollably.

Kolt reached down with his nonfiring hand and grabbed the collar of the kid's blazer. On the other side of the steward was the door to the lavatory concealing the Lashkar terrorist.

"Need your space," Kolt said. "Move toward the cockpit." But the young man remained still. Kolt had used the balance of his good manners on the squirter, so he yanked the kid by his collar and lifted him up, trying to force the steward out of his way.

"Don't move me!" the kid finally shouted in a panicked falsetto.

Raynor shouted, "Get your ass out of the—"

Dragging the kid all the way to his feet, Kolt finally saw it. A shine and movement of a wire attached to a drawer in the side cupboard. It was a shine and a movement that did not belong. The wire ended in a noose around the steward's neck and was clearly visible now, though Raynor had not checked for it an instant earlier.

As Kolt pushed the steward out of the galley, the kid's movement pulled the wire, which opened the drawer, which then fell to the floor. From the plastic drawer a small cylinder bounced out, a spring-loaded handle popped off, and then the cylinder rolled across the galley.

This, Kolt Raynor recognized instantly.

"Grenade!" he screamed at the top of his lungs.

The steward was clear; he had stumbled into the forward coach cabin and slammed straight into Slapshot, knocking the big operator back onto a passenger in his seat.

Raynor heard the lavatory door open. His senses in overdrive, he whipped his head a few degrees to the right before picking up the blur of a weapon's muzzle.

Kolt was going to take a hit from the grenade on the floor behind him, there was no way to avoid that. In that flash of an instant he told himself he would "eat" the grenade if he had to, but he was damn well not going to let some asshole Pakistani terrorist shithead shoot him.

Raynor opened his mouth to absorb the overpressure of the impending explosion, and he dropped to a prone position to get below the bulk of the grenade's shrapnel. While doing this, he opened fire on the lavatory door, blasting four .40-caliber rounds chest-high as he hit the deck, hoping like hell that most of the blast would go over him.

Between gunshots he heard shouts from both Digger and Stitch, plaintive cries for a passenger to "get the fuck down!"

An old woman appeared suddenly in the galley from the rear cabin; her hand was over her mouth and she was vomiting, desperately trying to make it to the bathroom to avoid embarrassment. Instead, she stumbled around the corner, saw Raynor on the floor facing her and firing into the lavatory.

She did not see the grenade on the floor behind him, but it would not have mattered if she had.

Kolt started to shout at her, but he was enveloped by white light and violent noise and indescribable pain.

THREE

Kolt Raynor fought through the pain and stared at the light ahead of him. It blinded him but he could not turn from it. He'd lost clarity, he'd lost the ability to discern what was real and what was a dream.

The flashlight flipped off and a group of men stood behind it. They wore black rain parkas and their faces were obscure in the darkness.

"Get up."

Kolt looked around, and he found himself sitting in the mud. He was not on an aircraft over New Delhi now; he was in the Smoky Mountains, straddling the Tennessee–North Carolina border.

He'd been walking for hours through rain and cold, the nylon straps of his pack dug into his body, and the bottoms of his feet burned like someone ten miles back had set fire to his boots and he'd just let them burn.

But he'd slipped and fallen into the muck a few minutes earlier, and he'd been sitting here in the rain ever since, fading into and then out of consciousness.

This walk in the woods was Relook, Kolt Raynor's return tryout with Delta. Kolt had been a respected Delta officer some time back, but almost four years earlier he'd been cashiered from the Unit in disgrace and declared persona non grata by his former mates.

That should have been the end of Kolt's career, but the previous autumn he'd been given a chance to redeem himself for his failures. A one-man, off-the-books op into Pakistan had shown the Delta brass that the former major still had the goods, so now he was getting his shot at returning to the fold.

Kolt thought Relook would be easy. A couple weeks of isolated land navigation with a heavy-ass rucksack strapped to his back, an intense but doable recheck with a couple of classroom shrinks, and a quick check-the-blocks commander's board where the current Delta leadership would throw him some softball questions before welcoming him back into the Unit with open arms. That was the way he remembered it going down all the times he had been cadre for other Relook candidates wishing to rejoin the ranks after leaving for one reason or another. Sure, one or two of those guys were denied a second shot, but those men were the exception, not the rule. The Unit wouldn't bother offering Relook if they didn't really want the operator back.

Still, Kolt knew he'd have to "go through the gates." Standards were standards.

But he quickly found out that the standards had changed. He was well aware that he was the first Delta operator ever offered a Relook, a second chance, after being dubbed persona non grata. In the ranks, even though guys came and went over the years, PNG was a lifetime sentence. Once that was decided, there weren't too many miracles that could remove the tag.

Except, possibly, if you did what Raynor had done in Pakistan the previous year. If you did *all* that, and somehow lived to tell about it, you might get a cautious invitation to come back home to Delta.

But things were different at this Relook. First, Kolt's two weeks in the woods humping the mountains were done with a rucksack thirty pounds heavier than any other second-chancer had ever been forced to carry. Second, he wasn't picked up each night and brought back to the barracks for hot chow and a hot shower. Instead he was forced to remain alone in the mountains. Third, as Kolt humped the mountains with a map and compass and checked in at each rendezvous point, the cadre member present acted odd. Kolt knew the majority of them, and he knew they were required to retain a professional image, to show no emotion other than a square-jawed poker face, but this wasn't formal selection and assessment for guys trying to earn an entry spot in Delta. This was Relook: a simple check of an experienced operator who had already proven his mettle in Delta's ranks. He figured the guys would give him a wink and a nod, maybe even give him some good-natured shit, stick a heavy rock in his ruck and tell him to drop it off at the next rendezvous point. Anything to show him they were happy he was coming back.

But no. It wasn't the same, and if Kolt sensed it on day one when his basic orders were to not be late, light, or out of uniform, by day three he *knew* this experience was going to suck.

By day eight he was positive. By day fourteen Kolt was wishing he had never taken Webber up on the opportunity.

Few men can cover forty miles a day for two weeks straight in the cold mountains and remain mentally and physically together, and Kolt was no different in this regard. The bottoms of both feet were missing two layers of skin. His three pairs of socks were covered in blood, as were the insides of his jungle boots. His back had been rubbed raw in three spots where the friction of his pack tortured him with every step. His shoulders screamed and his knees and shins were beaten to hell from the deadfall and rocky terrain. Raynor's four-year-old back and leg injuries throbbed and ached with each step.

"Raynor!" Kolt heard the yell just before a boot kicked him in the leg.

Kolt shook his head to clear his eyes. The men were closer now, they stood over him.

He rubbed his eyes as he tried to make out who the guy kneeling in front of him was. In a second he recognized him.

Wait. Yeah . . . I know this asshole.

He was a Unit psych, a shrink there to test him psychologically while the rest of the cadre tested him physically.

"Bring him to the trailer," he said, and the other men standing over Kolt lifted him up on his bloody feet and rushed him off the trail and down a little hill.

Here a small gravel parking lot sat in a clearing. A road ran from it off into the night.

Kolt was taken to a Winnebago trailer parked on the lot, and he was helped through the open door and pushed into a chair in front of a laptop on a table. The computer showed Kolt live on the left side of the screen. On the right side was a second window, and in it a teenage girl with short brown hair hiding her ears, and one of her eyes looked straight at him.

Her exposed eye was red from crying.

What the fuck is this? Kolt thought.

Behind Raynor, the shrink just nodded at the girl.

"My mother says you knew my father," she said.

Kolt looked at the psych behind him. No response. Kolt was near delirious with exhaustion, but he had not forgotten he was in Relook. He figured this was just part of the new standards. Play along, he figured. This was all some test that he'd need to pass.

"What's your name, young lady?" Kolt asked, trying to soften the situation, use his people skills, and stall for time.

"Kelly Lee. My father was Sergeant Spencer Lee. He was a medic."

Kolt's mouth opened in shock. *Jet?*

Jet had been killed in Pakistan four years ago. Raynor had met Jet's daughter once, and he did not believe this was her. He could not believe the damn shrinks would drag out the kid of a dead operator as part of some mind-game test.

Surely this was a trick.

"How is your mom? Laura, isn't it?" Kolt could feel the tension in the air. He needed to vet the girl to see if she really was Jet's daughter. If this was some sick test Delta had engineered to dick with Kolt, this girl not correcting Jet's wife's name would end the nonsense.

"No, my mother's name is Stephanie."

Shit.

"She said you made a mistake, Mr. Raynor. She said you got my daddy killed. She said it was all your fault."

Raynor looked back to the psych, whose eyes were locked on his. He turned back to the camera, and his voice wavered as he said, "Kelly . . . your dad was very brave. We were good friends." Kolt was still not sure if this was a test or if the girl on the screen was actually Jet's daughter. It had been close to five years since he had seen her at a squadron picnic.

"But you killed him. It is your fault. Why, Mr. Raynor?"

Kolt stiffened. *What the hell do I say to that?*

He didn't have kids, hadn't even married, as he was always too busy with the Army to ever give a woman the attention she certainly would demand. Many of his buddies handled married life okay, but Kolt had no illusions that he was ready for that level of commitment to something more than the military.

He looked up to the shrink, but the shrink just stared back blankly, his face impassive and ghostlike, illuminated as it was by the laptop's glow.

"I'm . . . I'm so sorry about your father. We were caught in a trap. It was a trap that I led us into. I failed your dad, I failed some other men who died that day, and I will spend the rest of my life trying to make amends for that. I know that doesn't take the pain away and it won't bring him back. I did mess up, Kelly. But your daddy died fighting for his country, for his family, and for his teammates. He didn't die in vain. He made a big difference." Kolt wasn't sure where to stop. He wanted to say so much more, but knew after a while Kelly wouldn't be hearing anything else he said.

The shrink turned the laptop away from Kolt. "Thank you, Kelly, we have to go now."

And with that, the psych closed the connection and Kelly Lee was gone.

Kolt sat in the chair, his shoulders slumped forward and his head hanging from exhaustion and despair. Behind him he heard the shrink leave the trailer, and another man entered.

Colonel Jeremy Webber, commander of Delta Force, sat down on the sofa across the table from Kolt.

Kolt quickly wiped tears from his tired eyes. He did not speak to his unit commander, knowing enough to give way to his superior.

Webber looked Kolt in the eye. "Our combat rules of engagement have changed somewhat since you were in. I need to know you are good to go with the new regs."

This was a surprise. There was no mention of Raynor's conversation with Jet's daughter.

Kolt composed himself and asked, "What's the change to the ROE, sir?"

"I need to know if you can drop the hammer on a man who possesses no imminent threat."

Kolt blinked in astonishment. He was being asked if he could, in effect, execute someone.

"Sir? Even if he isn't displaying hostile intent?"

"No threat, but someone who has been designated by presidential order as an enemy of the state."

Kolt responded quickly. "That is a significant change, sir. But if those are clear orders, then I'm in."

"They aren't at all clear, son, but those are the rules, and it is our job to follow those rules, murky though they may be."

Kolt hesitated. "'Capture or kill' has turned into . . . 'kill'?"

Webber nodded in the dim light of the trailer. "There are scenarios where that is the case. Can you do it? Can you order your men to do it?"

Raynor thought of the bad guys he'd been up against in his time. He thought about the mission in Pakistan that went bad, and he thought of the mission in Pakistan where he'd managed to redeem himself in the eyes of many.

But not in the eyes of Kelly Lee, Jet's daughter.

Kolt Raynor nodded. With a voice stronger than his body should have allowed, he said, "Yes, sir. I can do it. I will do it."

"You know you fucked up in Pakistan four years ago."

"Yes, sir."

"You know there will be people at JSOC who will never forgive you for that. Nothing you can do to change that, but you will have to work twice as hard as anyone else just to be seen as competent in the eyes of many."

"I'll work three times as hard. Just give me the opportunity to prove it to you."

Webber nodded thoughtfully. Then he extended a hand. "Welcome back to Delta, Kolt."

"Thank you, sir." Kolt reached out with a hand that was cracked and scratched and blackened with thick Appalachian soil.

Webber smiled. "Don't thank me. Be careful what you wish for, Racer. You've impressed me out here, but I'm easy. The boys will decide for themselves, and so will Kelly and the other orphaned kids from that fucked-up op in Pakistan. Besides, you'll be back in the shit before the scars from the black-site op heal."

"Wouldn't have it any other way, Colonel."

FOUR

The images from the last night of Relook melted away, and Kolt Raynor found himself once again on the floor of the galley of the 767 over New Delhi. Above him Slapshot's HK416 fired a burst into the rear cabin; hot brass ejected from it and bounced off of Kolt's face.

He felt blood running out of his nose, a burning sting high on his left thigh, and a dull ache in his back.

"Five crows down!" Slapshot shouted, then the sergeant reached a gloved hand down and grabbed Kolt by the shoulder strap of his chest rig. "You still with us, Racer?" he asked while scanning ahead for threats in the rear cabin.

A pair of double-taps from a Glock handgun cracked off to Raynor's right.

"One crow still up in the rear galley," Digger announced. He crouched on the other side of the center galley and fired his Glock again.

Kolt closed his hands on his pistol and climbed back to his feet on unsteady legs that were not ready for the weight. They wobbled a moment, but he continued forward on them, blood dripping off his chin now and his thigh burning with each movement of his body. He stepped over the terrorist who had taken four gunshot wounds to the chest and enough grenade shrapnel in the face and neck to make him all but unrecognizable as human. Kolt also stepped around the elderly passenger; she was facedown in the galley, lying still in blood and vomit.

Kolt pushed her out of his mind as he entered the rear coach cabin, firmly back in the fight now.

"Everybody down!" he shouted as he brought his pistol to eye level at the seated crowd before him.

The oxygen masks had dropped, and this, as well as smoke from the grenade's detonation, obscured the Delta men's view of the passengers and, more important, any terrorists back there with them.

On the other side of the aircraft Digger and Stitch made their way down the aisle, almost falling forward, as the plane was still in a steep climb attitude. They literally ran over a woman who had left her seat in panic after brain matter from one of the terrorists had splattered her shirt and neck. They stepped on her legs and back to get by, not worried in the least if they were hurting her.

"Stay down!"

Seconds later, at the rear of the plane, Stitch spun around into the galley. As the others approached, he spoke into his mic softly. "Galley clear, but I've got two closed lav doors."

"Wait one," said Raynor, then he instructed Slapshot and Digger to turn back around, climb back up the aisles, and cover the passengers.

Racer shouldered up to Stitch and each man fired several rounds into the two closed lavatory doors, both at chest height and at knee level. They opened their doors immediately after.

Stitch's lav was empty, but a Pakistani armed with a Skorpion machine pistol tumbled out at Kolt's feet. No need for an eye thump on this one, both men knew the man was dead.

Kolt pulled his radio from his vest and keyed the mic. "Five crows down. Safe the weapons and secure the pocket litter. Try to keep the rest of the passengers in their seats."

Kolt noticed the wound to Stitch's left hand as he turned to head back up the aisle.

By now the aircraft had leveled out, though Raynor was certain they were nowhere near a normal cruising altitude. He made his way alone back up the length of the airplane, passing Digger, who, as the medic, was checking the elderly woman who had walked into the grenade blast. She was gone, Kolt had no doubt, but it was Digger's job to be sure.

Raynor continued up through first class, passing the bodies of the men and women who had been dumped there by the terrorists long before his team's attack.

These were the men and women Kolt and his men had not been in time to save.

It wasn't his fault, he knew this. But they were just as dead, and as with the elderly woman by the center exits, he felt like shit about it.

Kolt lifted the flight attendant's phone, which would connect him to the cockpit. Soon an American voice answered.

"First Officer Freely here." The FO had to yell over the sound of air rushing at over two hundred miles an hour across the partially open escape hatch.

Kolt said, "Sir, we think we got them all. How many bad guys were there?"

"The flight attendants told us there were six terrorists."

"Then the cabin is secure. You do have some small fuselage breaches due to rifle fire."

There was a slight pause. Then the cabin door opened. Kolt stepped halfway into the cockpit.

The men wore sweat-soaked short-sleeved uniform shirts, open down to their waists to expose wet undershirts. Although only one of them was wounded, both men looked like shit. Raynor noticed they had managed to all but reseal the overhead hatch, though the breach still allowed some cold air and wind noise into the cockpit.

"Is she still airworthy?" Raynor asked.

It was the pilot who answered now. "If we keep her low and slow we should be okay. We need to put her down as soon as possible. Where to?"

"Back to New Delhi. There are friendlies there who will be ready for us." Then Kolt pointed to the blood and bandaging on the pilot's shoulder. "I'll get someone up here to check that out."

The pilot nodded. "We'll be on the ground in fifteen minutes. How are the passengers?"

"We lost one in the assault. Might be others injured."

That sank in a moment.

Kolt turned to leave, but the copilot called out to him. "Hey, buddy. Who *are* you guys?"

Raynor wiped his bloody nose with the back of his arm, then looked back up to the copilot. With a straight face he said, "New Delhi Airport Security."

The copilot just shrugged with a sly smile. "Well then . . . Namaste."

Kolt allowed himself a quick smile before heading back to the coach cabin to check with his men.

. . .

Raynor was surprised to see that the man Digger had shot in the rear cabin was not dead—not yet, anyway. There were two holes in his chest that Kolt could see. Digger knelt over him now, his right knee jammed in the terrorist's belly, checking him for any other weapons.

"How is this guy still alive?" Kolt asked in surprise.

"He had a shitty Paki-made soft armor vest on his chest. It slowed down the rounds, but didn't stop them."

"We land in ten to fifteen mikes," Raynor said to his mate as he looked down at the sucking chest wounds opening and closing on the terrorist's soiled white button-down shirt.

The Pakistani's eyes opened upon hearing Kolt's voice. "American, yes?"

Kolt knelt down next to Digger and looked at the man. "Yes."

The terrorist laughed through bloodstained lips. "You are *here*? You should be in your country. Soon we will strike at your heart."

Kolt knelt in closer, put his hand on Digger's shoulder. "What did that asshole just say?"

"Sounds like this crow might have some intel."

"Can you keep him alive?"

Digger shook his head. "Walter Reed himself couldn't keep this dude alive. He's got less than a minute. Sorry."

"I'm not," Kolt muttered cruelly. "Fuck him."

The man coughed. His fading voice was barely a whisper now. "Americans die. Many Americans die soon." The young man's eyelids softened but did not close. His pupils rose under them as his chest stopped moving.

Kolt wondered what he meant by that.

"Let me take a look at your thigh, boss," Digger said.

"It's fine. One of the flight crew took one to the shoulder. Check him out first."

Digger nodded, then headed to the cockpit to see to the wounded pilot.

Slapshot came over the MBITR radio a moment later. Kolt had turned the speaker on the radio up, since he'd lost his Peltors while surfing on the roof of the jet. Slapshot's voice was almost drowned out by the passengers on the flight, who, with heads still down, had begun clapping and cheering. "Has anybody seen Stitch's finger lying around?"

The wounded operator, at the rear of the plane now, spoke up next. "Forget it. Happened before we breached. It's probably still on airport grounds. Guess my second career as a piano teacher is out." He finished with a laugh.

Kolt doubted Stitch had ever sat in front of a piano in his life. It was gallows humor, and it helped for now, but Raynor knew that his teammate's wound was going to hurt like a bitch for a lot longer than the chuckles from the jokes about it would linger.

"Is that your third Purple Heart, Sergeant?"

"This is my fourth bleeder, actually, but whose counting?"

"You did good work today."

"Thanks, Racer. You, too. Nothing you could have done for that lady in the galley. She walked right into it."

Kolt just nodded. He wasn't so sure he hadn't fucked up that part of the op, but he would have a chance to make a full confession later during the after-action hot wash.

Kolt felt his satellite phone vibrate, and he knew it was the JOC calling. "Yeah?"

"It's Webber. Sitrep, over."

"Five crows KIA. One hostage dead in the assault. A couple of civilians wounded. Two eagles WIA."

"Their status?"

"I took some ball bearings in my leg from a booby-trapped grenade. And Stitch lost a finger."

"That's gonna keep you both up tonight, but that's a damn small price to pay for what you men just accomplished." A short pause from the colonel. "I was ready to roast your ass on an open fire as soon as this was over . . ." He paused. "But you made the right call, son. Fine job."

"Thank you, sir. Could have gone either way."

"Always the case in our line of work."

"Yes, sir."

Another pause. "Racer, we'll bring Stitch back home for treatment, but I need the rest of you to hang out back here at Bagram for a bit. That is, if your leg is okay."

Cecil County Public Library
301 Newark Ave.
Elkton, MD 21921

Kolt was still on alert status. If Webber wanted him to stay put, then some other situation was imminent. "Roger. Negligible wound, treat-and-release. What's up?"

"Might need you to head over to Libya in a day or two. Something's brewing and we've been asked to stand by."

Kolt cocked his head. "Libya, sir?"

FIVE

Cairo, Egypt

One could reasonably argue that Maadi is the greenest, quietest, and therefore most tranquil neighborhood of the otherwise loud and chaotic metropolis of Cairo, Egypt. It straddles the eastern bank of the Nile River, hence the lush vegetation, and it lies in the suburbs a dozen kilometers south of the city center, hence the relative serenity. The streets here are lined with trees and the high-rise apartment buildings, private homes, and commercial properties are surrounded by narrow lawns and trimmed shrubbery, a far cry from the gray-brown urban sprawl to the north and east.

Maadi is a first-class neighborhood, with real estate prices to match. The Maadi Yacht and Sports Club is the center of local culture and activity, and the neighborhood's streets are friendly and peaceful. This sense of serenity, however, helps hide the activity that had been going on for the past year within the walls of a large cargo transportation firm near the river. The company, Maadi Land and Sea Freight, Ltd., was occupied by men who were neither locals from Maadi nor Egyptians.

They were Libyans.

Some thirty former employees of the intelligence agencies of Colonel Muammar Gaddafi's government lived and worked within the walls of Maadi Land and Sea. To a man they were not in the country illegally. On the contrary, each and every one of these former spies and internal security officers had obtained travel documents out of Libya and into Egypt. These documents, however, were not obtained via proper consular channels. No, they had been purchased with bribes and extortion and even violence, because all of these men were wanted criminals, both at home and abroad.

Maadi Land and Sea Freight, Ltd., was a front company whose true purpose was to serve as a conduit moving equipment and matériel between Egypt and Libya in a clandestine fashion. It had been set up years earlier by Libya's spy service, the Haiat amn al Jamahiriya, the Jamahiriya Security Organization (or JSO), when Libya began exporting weapons to revolutions it supported and terrorists it bankrolled. But shortly after the revolution in Libya and the fall of Colonel Gaddafi, the company had been converted by surviving former members of the JSO into a for-profit enterprise. Maadi Land and Sea Freight, Ltd., opened as a turnkey operation so that the ring of ex-JSO operatives could stay in the business of the smuggling and sale of weapons from Libya, now lining their own personal coffers with the money earned from these transactions.

The leader of the entire criminal enterprise was a silver-haired but fit fifty-eight-year-old Libyan named Aref Saleh. Saleh had been one of Gaddafi's top spies for three decades before the fall of Tripoli, and much of his time outside of his home country had been spent in Egypt as the director of the Cairo branch of the Foreign Liaison Office of the JSO. In this role he ran a large group of agents in Egypt as well as in other nations around North Africa and the Middle East.

These contacts from his past provided him with business partners as well as a natural market for the weapons now for sale.

Saleh had organized the men under him, former members of the JSO, much like a real corporation. He had a marketing department that found clients for the Libyan arms, a shipping and logistics department that transported the Libyan arms to the end users, and a matériel procurement department that found the missing equipment and bought it from middlemen or else took it outright. He also had a robust corporate security office. While all of the thirty men working with him knew their way around a firearm, having all served in the military, ten of his employees were dedicated solely to security matters.

Aref Saleh and his company were always under threat, so they were always on guard. They lived on the property of Maadi Land and Sea, turning many of the offices into apartments and converting the building's previously only adequate security system into a virtual fortress with armed guards, security cameras, and motion detectors.

While Aref and his minions had had great success selling rifles and machine guns and ammunition and land mines, their highest-priced item was the surface-to-air missile. They had already sold SAMs in small quantities to several groups around the Middle East and Asia. On today's agenda, however, they would be meeting with two men who had traveled to Cairo from Yemen—senior leadership from al Qaeda in the Arabian Peninsula. AQAP were some of the biggest players on the block, because they had deep pockets, thanks to their benefactors in the Gulf States, and they outfitted fighters and operatives in several countries. Saleh's sales department's preliminary meetings with personnel from this organization gave them hope that today's meeting with these principals from Yemen would prove fruitful.

The secure nature of the Libyans' business meant that all meetings with potential clients were conducted off-site in any one of a number of safe houses throughout Cairo. Today's meeting with the men from Yemen was to be held in a private two-story home a kilometer from the Maadi Land and Sea compound, close to the Maadi Yacht and Sports Club. Four of Saleh's security men had gone early to the location to set up for the meeting. Four more would then fan out into the neighborhood to keep an eye out on the streets for any surveillance. And then, shortly before the AQ principals arrived, Saleh and his upper management team would themselves make the trip to the safe house in their armored and tinted Mercedes S600, a vehicle once owned by former Egyptian President Hosni Mubarak himself.

Normally Saleh arrived late to his sales meetings, as he did not care about keeping his clients waiting a few minutes. Mostly his customers were Third World rebels and the like, men well accustomed to inconvenience. An hour or two sitting in the safe house kitchen at a table drinking tea was hardly any real annoyance for men who lived in this world of discomfort. But today's prospective buyers were serious men fighting a serious cause and the several preliminary meetings with other members of their organization had shown Saleh and his people just how serious the Yemenis were about striking a deal. A potentially big deal.

For this reason, Aref Saleh would not keep them waiting. He would arrive first to show them respect.

The Al Qaeda men were in the market for Russian-made Igla-S shoulder-fired rockets, the most expensive item in the catalogue of the illegal Libyan arms organization.

Between himself and his staff, Saleh hoped he could sell as many as fifteen of the Igla-S's to al Qaeda in the Arabian Peninsula, and they had even arranged for that number to be ready to ship from a secret warehouse in Tripoli to Benghazi, a Libyan port, in advance of this meeting. At $450,000 each, a sale of this magnitude would garner his operation upwards of $7 million, as well as pave the way for more sales in the future to AQAP.

Shortly before noon a small car pulled up in front of the safe house on Street Fourteen around the corner from the Maadi Yacht and Sports Club. Two men climbed out of the vehicle, and then the driver rolled off to find parking on the tree-lined road. The men were watched by no fewer than a half dozen sets of eyes from many angles up and down the street. The guests were both young, in their thirties, and they both wore simple Western clothing and prayer caps. Their beards were dark and midlength, and they both looked like fit and healthy young men, perhaps individuals who worked in some trade that required manual labor.

They walked up to the front door of the safe house and it opened as soon as they stepped onto the stoop.

In the foyer of the home, the two men from Yemen were met with smiles by four men in business suits. Aref Saleh and three of his armed guards then greeted their prospective clients with handshakes and gestures of blessings, and then the two men were politely but carefully frisked for weapons or listening devices by waving a detection wand over their bodies. Within moments they were taken into a Western-style sitting room, and tea was poured for Saleh and his guests while the guards spread out into the corners of the room.

Saleh sat on a sofa across from the two men, who had seated themselves in armchairs. The shorter of the two young al Qaeda men said, "We were told to call you Idriss."

Saleh nodded with a smile. "That is correct. And I am told you are Miguel. Interesting choice for a name."

Miguel only said, "And this is my superior. You may call him Haroom."

Aref Saleh turned to Haroom and said, "I look forward to doing business with you, my friend."

The other man nodded, indicating he understood, but he did not speak.

"Will you remain silent, friend?"

Haroom did not answer, but Miguel answered for him. "You can do your business with me directly."

Saleh nodded politely. And with a smile he said, "Very well, then. How may I help you two brothers?" The Libyan was not fazed in the least that one of the men would remain silent for the meeting. Saleh had dealt with men like this for a quarter century, and a necessary part of dealing with terrorists and revolutionaries was their odd organizational structures and their often overly dramatic personalities.

Miguel began explaining how his organization had a need for several of the Igla-S missiles that the Libyans claimed to possess, and he hoped that they could begin a long business relationship with this organization located here in Cairo.

While his subordinate spoke, Haroom remained silent. He would speak if he had to, but it would reveal more about him than he would like the Libyans to know. Because even though Haroom spoke Yemeni Arabic quite well, and he understood the dialect the Libyan was speaking, he was not himself a native speaker of Arabic, not of any dialect of the language at all. He was, instead, a native speaker of English, and he spoke it with a northern California dialect.

Haroom's real name was David Wade Doyle, but he was more commonly known within the upper echelon of AQAP by the name Daoud al-Amriki, or "David the American."

David had been a member of al Qaeda for over ten years, and a senior operational commander for the past four years. His last operation, in western Pakistan the previous autumn, had led to the deaths of several American military and CIA personnel, but in the end David's mission had failed.

He was determined that his new mission, for which he would need the missiles on offer by the Libyan in front of him, would *not* fail.

Thirty-year-old David Doyle was born in Kelseyville, California, one hundred miles north of San Francisco. His parents were farmers and trappers, and Doyle grew up outdoors. His parents were also atheist, so David had had no connection with religion until the family moved to San Francisco when he was sixteen in order for his mother to begin treatment for breast cancer.

They moved into an apartment building and young David began hanging out with the three boys who lived next door, the children of immigrants from

Yemen. Soon enough he even began venturing into the mosque with the men of the family. He was taken in by the culture and the faith and the kinship he felt with those there, so when his mother died and his father decided to head back north, the seventeen-year-old Californian dropped out of high school and traveled with the immigrant family back home to Yemen on vacation.

The family returned home to California, but David Doyle never did.

He converted to Islam when he was seventeen, and he spent years learning Arabic and studying the Koran. The mosque he attended in Sana'a was among the most radical in the country, and he himself became radicalized by the teachings of the imam.

When the USS *Cole* was attacked in port in nearby Aden, Doyle felt nothing but happiness at the deaths of seventeen American sailors, and he wanted to take part in his own act against the nation of his birth.

He began training in al Qaeda camps in the interior of the country and it was here, on September 11, 2001, where he learned about 9/11, referred to among al Qaeda personnel as the Planes Operation. He and the other young men in training cheered and prayed, and then they headed toward Afghanistan to help with the resistance.

Doyle was in Peshawar, Pakistan, when Afghanistan fell, recovering from shrapnel wounds to the stomach he received in Jalalabad. He returned to Yemen soon after to continue his recovery. Here he returned to his mosque, and spent the balance of his time either in training or in teahouses watching the news.

He killed his first American in Iraq, not Afghanistan. He'd come after the initial invasion and, at a distance of forty yards, he put a burst from his RPK into the helmet of a Marine, a fresh-faced lance corporal no older than Doyle himself. He felt no repulsion for his act, he only wanted to be certain that his comrades saw him do it.

He then spent years in and out of Iraq and in and out of Afghanistan, in combat, on recon missions, and planting bombs. Eventually his knowledge of English made him a valuable al Qaeda asset and they moved him away from the danger of the combat zones, sending him to camps in Pakistan to help train the Taliban. Soon he was taken in by AQ leadership to be cultivated as an operational commander.

It was his own plan that he'd acted out the previous year in Pakistan at the black-site prison the Americans operated there. His failure in the Khyber Pass could well have resulted in his execution by the leadership of al Qaeda in the Arabian Peninsula, but instead he'd been given a chance to redeem himself through jihad and martyrdom on a new, bold mission.

And this time he would not fail.

And now, as he sat in his comfortable armchair in this beautiful home in Maadi, David Doyle was very aware that, in a perfect world, he would get his fucking missiles and he would kill this fucking Libyan bastard in front of him.

It was a necessary evil that Doyle found himself working with ex–Libyan intelligence officers. He had no respect for these greedy and evil men.

Muammar Gaddafi had been no friend to the cause for which Doyle had devoted his life. Libya had even accepted al Qaeda prisoners from the United States in 2004 for rendition and torture. All so the United States could get intelligence against AQ, and all so Gaddafi could garner favor from the powerful and angry Americans.

No, Doyle had no respect for JSO men, they may have been Muslims but that meant nothing to him in and of itself. They were not devout, and they would not stick their necks out for the cause. They had served their master until his death and they had served themselves in the year since.

They were no better than the many infidels Doyle had killed—these Libyan fuckers would probably not even give him a discount for his purchases.

Doyle saw that the charismatic smile of the silver-haired man in the business suit had faded while Miguel talked. Idriss did not look at Miguel; no, he looked at Doyle. Looking him over, Doyle thought he could detect evidence of recent surgery on the man's feline-like face. Perhaps the former JSO leader had had some facial reconstructive surgery to help hide his true identity from the authorities.

The American al Qaeda commander knew more about Idriss than he was letting on. Doyle would not have traveled to Cairo with only one confederate and put himself at the mercy of this man's organization with nothing more than hope that he would get his missiles. No, Doyle knew all about this man and his enterprise. The former spy and enemy of Islam was a bastard, and David Doyle was disgusted to be in his presence.

· · ·

For his part, Aref Saleh just stared at the silent bearded man while Miguel spoke. Haroom did not mask the malevolence he felt toward Saleh, and after a minute of the angry glare, Saleh interrupted Miguel by speaking directly to Haroom. "I see it in your eyes, brother. You judge me for what I do. You judge me for what I did for Libya."

David Doyle said nothing.

"I have great respect for you and your cause. I have provided many of your fellow mujahideen with weapons at prices that were below my expenses."

Doyle did not believe this for a second, but he did not challenge the statement.

The Libyan stared for a long time before saying, "Still, young brother, I would ask you to refrain from your overt malevolence. You are a guest here in my home."

Doyle did not speak. Neither did he change his demeanor.

Finally Saleh broke the staring contest with a shrug and a smile. He looked to his men in the room with him. "Very well, my Yemeni brother. As you wish. Give me your evil look. I am a gentleman, however. I will take your money and not subject you to the same wicked stare. If I did not need to be friends with Colonel Gaddafi to work for him, I certainly do not need to be friends with you to take your money."

Doyle spoke now for the first time. "And I do not need to be friends with you, Mr. Saleh, to purchase your goods."

Upon hearing his real surname, Aref Saleh sat up straighter in his chair. His faint and insincere smile disappeared.

"I do not know your accent, young brother, but you are not a Yemini. It appears that you come from a land where a man has no problem with intemperance. You have contacts who have uncovered my identity. I am impressed. But you put me in a difficult position by announcing that you know who I am. You would do well to hold your tongue. Absolute trust is another component that is not necessary in order for us to do business, but I will not work with someone whose malice I take as a direct threat."

"I do not need to trust you, either." Doyle's Arabic betrayed him as a nonnative speaker, but not necessarily as an American. "I only need to know how to find you if you double-cross me." He smiled slowly. "And now that you know I can do just that, we can proceed."

Saleh's bushy eyebrows rose. Behind him, two of his guards stepped forward, ready for a fight. Miguel started to stand from his chair.

Saleh stopped them all by raising his hand. He addressed the man with the odd accent.

"Do you really believe you hold all the advantages here, brother Haroom?"

"No. I am unarmed, as is my colleague. I only attempt to level the playing field by letting you know that my organization has identified you, so that if you attempt to trick me—"

"Yes, yes. Your people can find me."

"Exactly."

Saleh wiggled his fingers and his men moved back into the corners of the room, though they remained on guard. He said, "Very well. Our mutually assured destruction has been established. I hope all this work on your part indicates that you are prepared to make a purchase."

"I would like nothing more."

After a moment's more consideration, Saleh called out to men in the next room. Within seconds two men entered. They wore business suits, but instead of briefcases they hefted a green wooden crate between them. It was over five feet long but narrow, not more than two feet wide and deep. They placed it on the floor next to the two men from Yemen.

Saleh said, "I give you one of the most lethal portable air defense systems ever made. The Igla-S portable antiaircraft missile complex, or Igla-S PAAMC. *Igla* is a Russian word that means 'needle.'"

Al-Amriki knew all about the Igla, but he allowed Saleh to make his sales pitch.

"The weapon has a three- to four-kilometer vertical range, and it possesses high jamming immunity due to its impeccable infrared target-acquisition system. It has a contact and a proximity fuse, and a powerful warhead. It is small enough that one could, with some difficulty, carry two on his back, or a half dozen of the launchers along with missiles and power sources in the average two-door hatchback."

The AQ men knelt over the weapon and scanned the markings and the serial number, even the writing on the wooden case. Doyle found what he was looking for immediately, the shipping label. The consignee was the Central Organization of Industry and Purchase in Libya, and the airport of destination was the Tripoli International Airport. Inscribed also on the case was *2006. Box 88 of 243.* He'd been told by al Qaeda spies with contacts in the Libyan Defense community to look for these markings. If Saleh were trying to peddle counterfeit weapons, he would not necessarily know to replicate the authentic shipping labels and crate stamps.

After a minute of handling the weapon—the missile was not seated in the launch tube and the power source was not attached, so there was no chance of an accidental discharge in the well-appointed living room—the two men from AQAP sat back down in their chairs and faced Aref Saleh. The Libyan could see that the mood had lightened perceptibly. These terrorist commanders were, at the end of the day, just stupid boys, Aref determined after witnessing their reverence when running their fingers over the weapon system.

"So," he said. "Do you have any questions I can answer?"

The one called Haroom said, "I will need some proof that they work as advertised."

"Proof?" asked Saleh with genuine confusion. "I think you just need to check the lot numbers against the missing—"

"I *believe* they are authentic Libyan arms. Of that I have no doubt. But you have told us they are easy to operate. Is this true? I mean to say, can a quickly trained operator fire one as easily as you say he can?"

"Of course. The instructions are barely two pages in length."

Doyle shrugged, said, "I want to fire one. At an aircraft."

Saleh waved his hand in the air. "That is ridiculous."

Doyle then said, "I will purchase one launcher. You will help us find a suitable location to fire it. A suitable target. If this test goes well, we will buy sixty missiles from you."

"*Sixty?*" Saleh said it in disbelief. This was four times the number he had hoped for.

"That is correct."

The Libyan thought the man was toying with him. "I don't have time for games. You were vetted by my people as a legitimate representative of your organization, so I agreed to meet with you, but I will now ask you to please leave."

"We will pay four hundred thousand dollars each for sixty weapons."

The Libyan cocked his head, tried to read the man across the table. Finally he said softly, "You are serious."

David Doyle leaned forward. "Contingent on the successful test-firing of one weapon against a commercial aircraft."

Saleh said, as much to himself as to his customers, "Twenty-four million dollars."

Haroom corrected him. "We will pay for the test SAM, as well. So, twenty-four million four hundred thousand."

"I see," said Saleh, his voice registering his amazement. "I think this can be arranged with some effort and research."

For a chance at $24 million, Aref Saleh would find these boys a damn airplane to blow out of the sky.

SIX

Tripoli, Libya

Dr. Renny Marris had been in this line of work long enough that he should have felt the eyes on him, but he felt nothing but the warmth of the Mediterranean sun on his face as he stepped out of the massive Corinthian Bab Africa Hotel, just two blocks from the Mediterranean seashore. It was just past eleven a.m. and he had been hard at work with neither food nor drink since daybreak, so he decided to get out of his dark suit and into the bustling streets for lunch, even if he'd have to bring some of his work along with him.

Marris walked past the taxi stand in front of the hotel and then continued on foot up the steps to the parking garage. Over his shoulder he wore a worn canvas messenger bag that bulged with files and folders full of his work. He knew better than to take these documents out of his suite, but time was short and he had a lot to do, so he allowed himself this transgression with barely a moment's thought.

Marris was a man who lived more in his work than in the world around him.

He slid into the driver's seat of his two-door Mazda with some effort. He was a big man, a shade over six feet tall and well over two hundred pounds, much of it a thick middle that seemed to spread more and more each month since he'd reached the age of fifty, five years prior.

The burly Canadian drove out of the hotel grounds, then headed east through thick midday traffic on the palm-tree-lined Al Kurnish Road. The blue waters of the Med were on his left, and on his right was the Medina, the old city. A massive array of tightly packed whitewashed buildings and narrow streets and alleys that covered several square kilometers, it had begun as an ancient settlement by the Phoenicians in the seventh century, and now comprised just a tiny tip of Tripoli's wide oceanfront.

Though he was not a particularly fit man, he was not worried about venturing out among the locals. Apart from the petty crime rife in many Third World cities, Tripoli, Libya, was safe enough for most of the thousands of Westerners living and working there, now one year after the overthrow and death of Colonel Muammar Qaddafi.

It was safe enough for *most* Westerners. But it was not safe at all for Dr. Renny Marris.

He was blissfully unaware of any danger. He'd been wrapped up in his duties of late, and he'd been lulled into such a comfortable relationship with Tripoli, working here for a year with no major personal security problems, that his mind did not wander into the realm of threat perception.

As he turned into the Medina, behind him a pair of vans followed him closely.

Another car followed these two.

Oblivious to his long tail, Marris drove on, deeper into the shadows of the tight streets and alleyways of the Old City.

Many of the roads did not have street signs, but Renny knew where he was going. He loved the hustle and bustle of the Third World, the Arab world, and he'd found this little hidden courtyard café populated by locals and intrepid expats some months back while meeting with a shadowy contact. He'd returned every week or two since. He enjoyed the food, the atmosphere, the feeling that he could leave his office or his busy hotel suite full of computers and fax machines and sat phones and disappear into the belly of ancient North Africa in just a matter of minutes.

But he was wrong. He was hardly disappearing.

Dr. Renny Marris was a lead investigator for the United Nations, and he was a natural for the position, as he possessed a PhD in mechanical engineering and a reputation as being an ardent pacifist. Young Dr. Marris had served several stints working for aid agencies and human rights groups around the world, becoming an expert in land mine eradication in the 1980s. In the nineties he branched out into stopping the illegal trade of other forms of conventional weaponry. Now, into the second decade of the new century, he had been working in the field of antiproliferation of conventional weapons and weapons of mass destruction for over two decades.

He'd spent his career in Ethiopia, the Congo, the Balkans, the former Soviet satellite states, Iraq, and Central America.

But these days, ground zero for a man in Marris's field was Libya.

As the rebellion against the Gaddafi regime intensified, heavily guarded defense depots were abandoned by soldiers fleeing for their lives. Many of these soldiers took valuable weapons with them, and many of the rebels plundered the abandoned depots clean of the remaining war booty as soon as they could.

While the revolution was still in full swing, Dr. Marris and the UN arrived in-country to look for evidence of the chemical weapons Gaddafi was rumored to have produced and stockpiled over the years. But the Canadian inspector and his team found no evidence of a chemical program. This was good news, but it was followed quickly by bad news. Renny and his team heard rumors of the disappearance of conventional weapons in mind-boggling quantities. They began moving across the country, even as battles still raged, attempting to secure loose tank shells, land mines, artillery pieces, and shoulder-fired surface-to-air missiles.

It was these SAMs that produced the biggest threat to the world at large. The missing high-tech Russian-made Igla-S shoulder-fired rocket (its NATO designation was the SA-24 Grinch) was a terrorist's dream weapon; a single shooter with a single rocket and a single tube, a weapon system that weighed just over forty pounds, could take down a 747 full of passengers flying at ten thousand feet.

And hundreds of these weapon systems were missing around the nation.

Marris's investigation had led to the capture of many of the lost missiles. Poorly organized gangs had taken some of them, and others were stolen by individuals who were caught when they tried to sell them on the crude black market that had developed. The new weapons bazaar of Tripoli was unorganized and insecure, and Marris and his team had scooped up tons of dangerous contraband with ease.

Other munitions were intercepted by Egyptian or Tunisian officials over the border or by U.S. or other Western powers on the open seas.

But a few months back all parties had been given a grim reminder of the high stakes of this game of cat and mouse. One of the dangerous Iglas-S systems had slipped through the grasp of all the entities trying to recover them. The SAM was bought and sold and transported, and then bought and sold and transported again. And then an Airbus A330 owned by Indonesia's national carrier, Garuda Indonesia, had been shot down shortly after takeoff in Jakarta, killing all 266 aboard.

Dr. Renny Marris himself had arrived at the scene of the crash site within twenty-four hours, there to see if Libyan munitions were involved. He confirmed this by forensic testing on the impact point of the missile, and it was soon determined that the Indonesian terrorist group Jemaah Islamiyah had been responsible for the unspeakable crime.

That much of Gaddafi's conventional weaponry had been stolen was not news around the world. At first there was panic around the globe with the news that up to twenty thousand surface-to-air missiles had been stolen and were on the loose. But as many of these and other arms had been recovered, the story died down.

And there were no chemical or nuclear or biological weapons involved, which greatly affected the sex appeal of the news story. The Jakarta incident was front-page news for a few days, but then the story faded as the media minimized the continued threat.

But while it was true that the majority of the weapons were back under the control of the Libyans in power, or had never been stolen in the first place, or had been scooped up by Western parties once they were in transit out of Libya, Dr. Marris and his staff knew that these were the low-hanging fruit. There still remained in excess of a thousand missing Igla-S's and enough artillery shells to fuel IEDs around conflict zones for fifty years.

So Marris left the low-hanging fruit to the Americans or the Libyans or whoever else wanted to get involved, and he stayed in Tripoli, working the hard cases.

Within the last month he had discovered that, along with other arms traders who had poured into the nation after the revolution, a tight-knit organization made up of former members of the JSO, Gaddafi's external intelligence service, were behind the bulk of the smuggling. These spies had survived the rebellion by using their tradecraft and now they were either in hiding in Libya or over the border in Egypt or Tunisia or Algeria, facilitating the sale of all types of conventional weaponry that had been hidden around North Africa after their government's downfall.

Marris' efforts were bringing him closer and closer to the JSO ring's leadership.

His staff worked at his downtown office, but most days he stayed in his suite at the Corinthian, sat in front of his laptop, and reported via webcam to the UN in New York or conducted online meetings with government officials or Human Rights Watch or sat for interviews with Western news organizations. As the pace of his investigation increased, he found himself in higher demand.

An investigation such as the one Marris and his team had been involved in would, of course, draw attention from the criminals as well. And it was no surprise that a couple of his investigators had been roughed up in the past month. But to Renny this was good news. It meant he was getting closer to a breakthrough, closer to the JSO men who were, as far as Marris was concerned, much more afraid of him than he was of them.

Once again, Dr. Renny Marris was dead wrong.

He pulled into a parking lot near the Old British Consulate, in the center of the Old City, and he hefted himself and then his satchel out of his car. He crossed the street and entered his destination, and soon found a table at the large bustling courtyard café.

Marris sat in the quietest corner of the courtyard and ordered a lunch of skewered lamb and rice along with a cup of strong coffee. He opened his satchel and arranged a sheaf of papers in front of him, and then began reading, losing himself in his data.

He had a videoconference with New York this afternoon. In the meeting he would update UN leadership about a recent snag in his investigation. One of his confidential informants, a general in the Libyan army, had gone missing. Marris felt certain the man had lost his nerve and broken off contact, so scared was he about possible reprisals by the JSO.

It was a setback, no question. Marris had relied on the general's cooperation, and now that the man had disappeared, Marris would need to find new access into the shadowy organization of ex-spies controlling the export of illegal weapons out of the nation.

This new access would not come without a great cost in bribes, and he needed the UN to foot the bill. So now he read up on the facts and figures he would use this afternoon in his case to the UN so they would give him the money he needed to retool his inquiries.

Renny's food came and he ate it while he worked. He ordered a second coffee after his meal, and he sipped while he continued to read the reports before him.

While working, even while working out in the open like this, Renny took no notice of his surroundings. He had not a clue of his own personal security.

It was only when he looked up from his work to rub his eyes that he noticed a young, well-dressed black man sitting across from him at his table.

The man offered a toothy grin and an extended hand. "Dr. Marris. Good to see you again. Donald Meriwether, from the conference in Bruges last September. You are looking well." The man spoke English with an American accent.

Renny *had* been to a conference in Bruges the previous September, but he did not remember this man. Still, he took the man's hand and shook it. "Nice to see you. Meriwether, is it?"

"That's right."

"Yes." Marris, suddenly aware that much of the paperwork in front of him was highly confidential, began stacking the sheets as if he were about to leave.

"Can I buy you another coffee?" the American asked.

"Oh . . . thank you, but I need to get back to work. Um . . . I am sorry. Bruges is a bit of a blur. I can't say I remember meeting you. What do you do?"

"Much the same as yourself, at the moment. In fact, I'd love a couple minutes of your time to chat about a topic of mutual interest. Maybe we could step over to the lounge?" Just off the courtyard was a dark room full of cushions and low tables. Here men sat in the dimness and smoked from hookahs and drank tea and coffee.

"Why?" asked Renny Marris, on guard now.

"Please. I'd appreciate a quick word." The man stood, beckoned Marris to follow.

By the time they had settled into the tobacco-scented cushions in the dimly lit long and narrow lounge, the Canadian weapons expert had determined he had not, in fact, met this man in Bruges. He had also decided that this was no chance meeting. This man would be some sort of American agent—CIA or military intelligence or something along those lines.

He groaned inwardly. He had few hard and fast rules, but he had made one, an ironclad oath to himself that he would have neither contact with nor connections to the American government.

The CIA had been running around Libya on the same mission as Marris and his team for the past several months. They had had some successes, successes Marris chalked up to the easy-picking variety. But in this work the CIA had ruffled more than a few feathers along the way.

Marris had worked around CIA and other intelligence agencies in all the places in which he'd plied his trade for the past thirty years and, as far as the Canadian peacenik was concerned, American intelligence was an enemy who, for their own benefit, occasionally worked toward the same goal as did the good guys.

Marris asked the man in front of him, "Why don't you just tell me who you are?"

The young man said, "I read your article last month in *Foreign Policy*. Very interesting."

Marris adopted a skeptical, slightly sarcastic tone. "Would you like my autograph? No? I asked who you are."

The American's comfortable smile dropped off. "I'm with the U.S. Embassy."

Renny Marris did not blink. "You are CIA."

The black man did not blink, either. Instead he just repeated, "With the embassy."

"What do you want?"

"Associates of mine are big fans of yours."

Renny clutched the strap of his bag tighter. "I am certainly not doing what I do so that I can generate fans in American intelligence. The proliferation of U.S. weapons is tenfold more harmful to the world than these Libyan arms."

"Agree to disagree," said the American, displaying no outward reaction to the insult. "Look. I'm not here to tell you about everyone who loves your work. I'm here to tell you about a few who do not."

"Who?"

"The JSO guys you have been tracking."

"How do you know who I am tracking? Do you have spies in my operation?"

"We have feelers in *their* organization, same as you. And we have learned something recently. They know about your investigation, and they know you are close to identifying their leadership. That puts you in the crosshairs."

"And?"

"We want to help you out of the crosshairs."

Marris laughed, a touch of anger along with it. "I do not need a babysitter from the CIA watching over me. And I certainly am not going to be recruited by you. You want to control conventional weaponry so that you will have the biggest guns on the block. That isn't peace. That is force. That is domination. *I* work for the good of all mankind, which means I don't work with or for America."

"'The good of all mankind'?" The American chuckled and clapped his hands together. "That was a fabulous speech, Doc. I bet that goes over well at the UN or at UC Berkeley or pretty much anywhere in Europe. But, brother, you are in Tripoli at the moment, and 'all mankind' around here isn't so appreciative of your efforts. Look, we are glad you are here and doing what you are doing. But that's us. The two vans that followed you here into the Old City and the three goons in the lime-green four-door outside the café are a subset of mankind who don't take kindly to your nosy nature."

Marris looked out toward the courtyard for a long moment. Only a sliver of the street was visible through the entrance of the café. "I don't see them."

"You will when you go outside. Big guys in bad blue suits, one eyebrow each. You need to start opening your eyes when you leave the sanctity of the Corinthian."

"I've been followed before. It is part of my work. You followed me here yourself, did you not?"

"I did," the man conceded. "But not to slide a knife across your throat. You need to take my word for it. Tripoli is not safe for you anymore. Not safe for you *or* your investigators."

Marris swatted away the comment with an annoyed hand, but the American continued his pitch.

"You are doing good work, but you could be doing more good. If you had a little more money, more physical and capital assets helping you out. We want to get the rest of the loose munitions off the market. Just like you."

Marris just rolled his eyes. "Do you think you are the first American spy to try this pitch on me?"

"I know that I am not. I am, however, the first to tell you this while in a position to protect you from immediate harm."

"Are you threatening me?"

"Warning you. Know the difference. They will kill you. The guys out front or men just like them."

"It sure sounds like a threat."

"It is an informed observation, Doc."

The Canadian finished the dregs of his coffee, all but slammed the little cup back on the plastic table. "I don't want to see you again."

"It might be safer for you if you did. I think I will just follow you around for a while. For your own good."

Marris looked back over his shoulder at the crowd in the courtyard café. There were easily seventy-five people there, all male. "Mr. Meriwether. I am calling you that because I do not know what else to call you, not because I am so naive that I think you gave me your real name. All I have to do is shout out to the room, in Arabic, in French, or probably even in English, that you are an operative of the CIA, and then, I am quite certain, you will be otherwise engaged from following me through the streets for the rest of the day. Maybe for the rest of your life."

The African-American did not seem fazed by the threat at all. Instead he just smiled. "My real name is Curtis. And you might want to think first about how badly you want to draw even more attention to yourself right now, because I have friends who can get me out of any jam I might get into today. You . . . on the other hand, only have me."

Renny Marris did not speak. Instead he collected his satchel, stood from his thick cushion, and headed back through the courtyard café toward his car.

The big Canadian made it back to the parking lot by the Old British Consulate. The early afternoon pedestrian traffic had tapered off to almost nothing, so after he unlocked the door to his car and looked back over his shoulder, he had no problem picking out the black American crossing the street toward him.

He tossed his bag in the backseat angrily.

Curtis called to him as he approached. "Dr. Marris? One more quick thing."

Renny sat down in his car. He reached to close the door but first said, "No! I told you! I do not want to talk to you."

"Then don't talk. Just listen." Curtis grabbed the door and held it open.

"I certainly do not want to listen to anything you have to say." Marris fought for the door. He found Curtis surprisingly strong.

"All right, then. Don't listen. Just look." The CIA man pulled a small mirror from his microfiber sport coat. It had a telescoping arm on the back of it, and this Curtis extended to its full length.

"What's that?" Marris asked.

Curtis did not answer. Instead, he just said, "Don't leave home without it." He held the arm and lowered the mirror to the dusty cement, just outside the passenger door, and he angled the mirror to reflect just under the car.

Marris leaned out of the car and looked down at the reflection. An odd device was attached to the bottom of his car. A cylinder the size and shape of a coffee thermos. It was wrapped in gray electrical tape and a coiled insulated wire ran out of one end and disappeared off the edge of the mirror.

"What is *that*?"

Curtis replied, "Surely, Renny, a man with your expertise can recognize a car bomb when he sees one."

"How . . . how did you . . ."

"How did I know? An associate of mine saw the three men in the green four-door attach it five minutes ago. My associate took pictures—we can review them back at the embassy. Fortunately, they didn't have time to rig a pressure plate under the driver's seat, they just wired it to your ignition system."

"No," the Canadian said with a quavering voice.

"No? Look at it!" Curtis held the mirror steady and Marris looked down at it again. "Have you had your nose stuck so deep in those briefing reports and technical manuals of yours that you've lost the ability to ID a real weapon when you see one?"

Marris looked at the American. "No . . ." He said it with reservation, but then he shook his head forcefully. "No. It's a trick. A cheap, cruel, patently obvious scheme to get me to jump into the arms of you, the CIA, like you are my only hope. You put that there to scare me."

Curtis shook his head. "We didn't do it, and we *are* your only hope."

Marris held his car key up in his right hand. "I'm going to turn the ignition, Curtis. You are bluffing."

"If you turn that key, you and I are both going to be barbecue. The local medical examiner is not going to know where your charred remains stop and mine start."

That sank in a moment, and the Canadian lowered his hand and slowly climbed out of his car. "I still think this is a CIA trick, but I do not know if the bomb is real or not. You might be just cynical enough to plant an actual device." He grabbed his messenger bag out of the back of the car. "I want that thing off my vehicle, and I want my vehicle towed back to the Corinthian."

Curtis just said, "Call the JSO. We didn't do it, so we aren't undoing it. We *are* offering you the safety of the embassy. You need to come with me."

Marris just shook his head and turned toward the street. "Good-bye, Curtis."

"You walk away and you will be dead in a day."

Dr. Renny Marris did not respond. Instead he crossed the street through angry traffic.

Curtis stood there in the little lot, watching him go. On the far side of the road, the bearded Canadian turned to the south, then disappeared into the warrenlike market stalls of the Old City.

Seconds later three Arab men in blue suits followed him into the alley from the street.

Curtis spoke softly to himself. "One day, nothing. More like one hour." He pulled his mobile phone from his pocket and dialed a local number.

An American voice answered on the other end. "Yeah?"

"Are you at the Corinthian?"

"Affirmative. We are in Tripwire's suite. We're photographing everything in place so we can put it back like we found it."

"Don't bother. Scoop it all up. Everything. Clear the place out." Curtis paused to watch two more men enter the alleyway, walking like they had someplace to be.

Curtis said, "Tripwire will not be back."

SEVEN

Dr. Renny Marris walked north through a narrow alleyway, moving against the flow of the few passersby strolling in the hot afternoon. He knew he would not find a taxi back to the hotel here, he'd have to leg it all the way back to Al Kurnish Road.

He worried he would not get back to his suite at the Corinthian in time for his afternoon interview, but that was not his only worry at the moment. The bomb on the bottom of his car had not rattled him so much at first, but now he found the palms of his hands sweating and his heart beating harder and faster than normal. He also found himself looking back over his shoulder from time to time, nervously scanning the crowd.

While he still thought it likely the CIA had planted the device, he did have to admit that it was not beyond the realm of possibility that someone affiliated with the ex-JSO officers running the arms-smuggling enterprise might indeed be after him. They were serious criminals, no question about that, so it was likely they were dangerous, as well.

Dr. Marris knew only the larger roads of the Old City, and now, forced to go on foot to hunt for a cab, he found himself utterly lost. After a minute of twists and turns, he looked up and caught a glimpse of the minaret of the Ben Saber Mosque behind him on his left, and this told him he was headed in the right direction.

But the road dead-ended and the small shops were just little kiosk shelters and did not have exits on the other side.

Marris turned back around and retraced his steps.

Just before veering to the right to head up another dark alleyway, he noticed the three men for the first time. Just as Curtis had claimed, they wore bad blue suits and they had bushy eyebrows.

Renny Marris turned away and walked faster.

Even though the adrenaline from finding a bomb under his car was coursing through his thick body, he discovered a new sensation within him, a fear that came with the realization that Curtis may have been telling the truth.

Deep here in the Medina, the afternoon foot traffic was almost nonexistent, with the return of the workday after lunch. He headed up a narrow alleyway lined on both sides with small kiosks selling hand tools and copperware. Other than a few shopkeepers who were focused on their own business, Renny Marris found himself alone.

As the alleyway ended in a T, he chanced a glance back over his shoulder. The three men were still there, closer now than before. He turned to the right and followed a path up a hill, thinking that might bring him back closer to the main road, and he picked up the pace. As he walked he fumbled through his satchel for his mobile phone. With his thumb trembling from adrenaline, he dialed the number for his office. The afternoon heat seemed to grow by the second, his shirt was wet from sweat under his coat, and cold rivulets of perspiration ran down his lower back into his trousers. He walked even faster now, and even thought of breaking into a run, but he was too self-conscious to do so.

"Bonjour, Dr. Marris. Where are you? We just called your suite and no one picked up."

"Listen carefully, Amelia. I'm in the Old City. I think I am being followed."

"It's probably just the police. They follow our investigators all the time. They are perfectly harmless, you know that."

Before Marris could answer, he walked past a shop selling local clothing. At the front door was a large full-length mirror, and he used this to look back behind him. The three men in the blue suits, their jackets unbuttoned now, had closed to within fifteen meters.

"Oh, God." He wasn't being followed from a distance. These men were not trying to stay back or in the shadows, they were doing nothing to remain undetected.

It was almost as if they were hunting him.

"You sound like you are walking. Where is your car?" Amelia asked, a worried tone in her voice now.

"I . . . I left it . . . Can you send a car for me now?"

"Dr. Marris . . . if you really feel like you are in danger, you need to get to a place with many people around."

The Canadian had just made a left to head up another small alley. It felt to him like this direction would take him closer to the coastal road. He could not be far from Al Kurnish now, he reasoned, and he knew there would be hundreds of people, locals and tourists alike, walking and driving there. There he would be safe, but for now the alleyway wound to the right, and it was covered by a long arched roof. It was essentially a tunnel, as there was no light from the sky, only lamps outside of the few shops in this dark and quiet part of the Medina.

Marris had no choice but to continue on. The men were too close behind him. He heard their footsteps echo in the passage.

"Shit. Shit. Shit."

"Dr. Marris?" Amelia asked, more tension in her voice now.

"I—I do not know where I am. Call the police. Tell them I am in the Old City. Tell them to please hurry."

"That's a very big place. Tell me what you see." Amelia was nearly frantic now, following the fear in her boss's voice.

Marris lowered the phone from his ear. He could see now that this passage was another dead end. With a quivering thumb, he hung up his phone and slid it into his front pocket. Then he turned slowly around to face the men following him.

He would talk to them. He would diffuse this situation.

Marris saw the three men standing there, facing him, with no attempt on their part to avoid detection. They were ten meters away at most. Their suits strained against their big bodies, and their ties hung loose around their thick necks. As before, their coats were open.

In Arabic tinged with fear, Dr. Renny Marris asked, "May I help you, my friends?"

As one, the three men reached into their coats.

Marris only saw the hilts of the three knives before he started running.

A paint store on his left had an open storefront, and the middle-aged

Canadian ran inside, stumbling over a tall stack of paint cans, sending the display crashing to the floor. He ran behind the little counter, pushed past the proprietor of the shop, and here he found a curtain that led to the back of the store.

Mercifully, this shop had a rear exit, and Dr. Marris slammed his shoulder into the tin door and stumbled out into a tiny back alley only two meters wide. He ran now, no worries of embarrassment to slow him down, and he found himself to be surprisingly fast when motivated by a team of knife-wielding assassins. He heard the three men close behind him in the alley, and he screamed in fear.

He rushed headlong into another covered passage, the ceilings arched and blackened with hundreds of years of torch smoke. He glanced back over his shoulder as he stumbled, already out of breath after running no more than thirty seconds.

He saw the knives again, but this time it was not just the hilts; the blades were out of the men's jackets. They were long and curved, and they swung through the air as the three men ran toward him.

Murder in broad daylight, Renny thought, and his heart felt as if it would explode from terror. He had no weapon of his own, he was a pacifist, after all, so his only chance at survival was to run for his life.

Frantic, Marris stumbled around the corner, but found it to be yet another pedestrian cul de sac, a dead end. He tried to spin around in the direction of his killers in the hope he could rush past them before they could plunge a knife into his chest.

But Marris tripped as he spun. He brought his arms up to break his fall, but a strong hand reached out from a recessed doorway and grabbed him by the collar, catching him before he hit the pavement.

The hand pulled him into the darkness of the doorway. Marris landed on his back and a figure stepped over him quickly, a man in local dress—an open Holi cloak over a dirty brown T-shirt and local blue jeans, sunglasses, and a cream-colored head wrap concealing all of his face not obscured by his five o'clock shadow. He moved quickly, heading out into the tiny alleyway.

Marris shouted a warning to the man. "Watch out! They have knives!"

"No shit," Kolt Raynor said to himself as he stepped quickly into the passage.

Kolt did not pull his weapon, a Glock 23, hidden in a Thunderwear holster hidden in his jeans, just above his crotch. As he faced the approaching men, his hand hovered there, between his legs, but he did not reach into his waistband and draw the pistol.

Not yet, anyway.

Kolt would have loved to just pull his handgun and waste the three assholes in front of him, but gunfire in the Old City of Tripoli would ensure more gunfire, and he would do everything in his power to avoid that. On these types of low-vis operations, weapons were only used as a last resort. Standard operating procedure on a mission like this was to keep himself and his team as low-profile as humanly possible, so as not to create a political shitstorm for the United States. But keeping this action low-pro was easier said than done, seeing as how this extraction involved pulling Tripwire from the clutches of death.

"Bonjour!" Kolt said to the three men with a smile, and he offered a handshake to the closest man. He had no real illusions that his conversational jujitsu would stop this fight before it started, but he had seen some quick and oddly timed hellos confuse enemies for a few precious seconds in the past, so he figured it was worth a shot.

The center goon was closest. At a six-foot distance, the man ignored the offered hand and took one fast step forward. At the same time he raised the eight-inch blade over his right shoulder like a hammer.

Kolt saw this, and he knew that his training in Brazilian jujitsu would have to be better than his skills at making friends.

Kolt half stepped to the left, raised his left hand, and caught the man's right wrist from behind as the knife arced downward. Kolt's left hand forced the knife hand on and maintained the momentum as his right hand reached up and over his taller opponent's head. Kolt grabbed the man by the back of the head and forced him on, as Kolt's left hand directed the man's knife to the rear. As a second attacker, the man on Kolt's left, lunged forward, Kolt caught him unawares by directing the center man's knife straight into his thigh as he approached.

The first assailant let go of his knife and it remained embedded high in his partner's leg, three inches deep.

A bloodcurdling scream filled the covered passage.

Raynor remained in contact with the center assassin, his right hand still controlling the man's head and his left hand on the man's wrist. He pushed the wrist skyward behind the man's back, forcing the Libyan's head toward the ground while stepping left to keep the man's body between him and the third attacker. Only a somersault or a flip by the assassin would have prevented his shoulder from dislocating or his arm from breaking at the elbow joint, but the man just shouted and struggled against Kolt's grip.

Three seconds after the fight started, Kolt heard the Libyan's arm snap and felt the humerus pop from the scapula.

It was a sickening sound that he'd heard before.

The Libyan in the center of the trio dropped to the ground and rolled in agony as Kolt Raynor's earpiece came alive with Slapshot's voice. "Racer, this is Slapshot, two crows down."

Kolt was in combat himself, and in no position to execute effective command and control over his teammate at the moment. Slapshot was covering the entry to the alley fifty meters up the street, and Kolt had no idea who he had neutralized or why.

Kolt figured Slapshot must have used his suppressed 9mm pistol to take down the two men just up the street, otherwise the pistol's report would have echoed through the Medina.

At that instant it occurred to Raynor that he had forgotten his own silencer, having left it in the safe house. Not ten minutes earlier, Racer, Slapshot, and Digger had been waiting in the nearby safe house watching *Bachelor Party Vegas* on the tube when the call from the CIA's chief of station came in. This rushed them out the door, and Raynor forgot his "can."

In-extremis assault mode is a come-as-you-are party, and sometimes things get left behind.

Kolt had no time to dwell on the fact that his can was on the coffee table at the safe house, because two large arms suddenly appeared below his waist and wrapped around his knees. He looked down and saw that the man he had stabbed in the leg was now on the ground behind him and trying to pull him down. Kolt tried to keep his balance, but as he looked back up, the third man sent a roundhouse right fist to Kolt's chin. The punch buckled him like a folding knife. Kolt fell to his left side and tumbled on top of the wounded man on the ground. There he reached over and grabbed the knife handle and jammed it in his attacker's leg down to the copper hilt.

Both of the Libyans now lying in the stone alley with him screamed in pain and writhed in agony.

Kolt recovered from the punch to the face and went to the guard, lying on his back, up on his palms, with his feet facing the only assassin still on his feet.

The last man standing slashed wildly at Kolt's feet with his long knife, striking the sole of his tennis shoes twice, but not breaking through to his skin. The man tried to circle around, but Kolt countered this maneuver by rotating his body, keeping one leg up at all times as a deterrent.

As the attacker lunged forward to plunge the knife into the back of Raynor's calf, Kolt kicked the thug's left knee with all his strength, locking it straight and throwing the man off balance. Kolt hooked his left instep around the attacker's right knee and pulled as he maintained pressure on the attacker's left knee.

Kolt instinctively spread his legs, taking the full brunt of the attacker's 220-pound body against his chest and stomach, allowing the thug to take the mount. Kolt also heard another radio call from Slapshot in his earpiece, but he was too focused on his own problems to copy the message.

The attacker was now on top and he immediately went for Kolt's throat with both hands. Kolt thought to go for an arm bar. As a longtime student of Gracie jujitsu, Raynor was comfortable on his back with the man above him, but he knew he needed to sink a submission hold fast.

More bad guys could be just around the corner, and an arm bar, even executed properly, wouldn't do the job fast enough.

So Kolt reached up with his right hand and trapped his attacker's left in place on his chest as the man tightened his right hand's grip on Kolt's neck. Kolt reached up with his left hand and found his attacker's right elbow. He applied pressure to the elbow to draw his attacker's attention, and then quickly jammed the man's left forearm against the man's own chest. This was exactly what Kolt wanted, an opening to apply a triangle choke.

Kolt brought his right foot high over his attacker's left shoulder and slammed it down on the side of the big Libyan's neck. The attacker panicked, reacting exactly as Kolt had expected, and yanked his right arm away from Kolt's neck. Raynor immediately shifted his weight again, this time to bring his left leg up over his attacker's right shoulder and lock the instep of his right foot behind the knee joint of his left leg. Kolt was in total control and he could feel his attacker's flight impulses kick in.

The triangle choke was too loose, and the attacker continued to struggle, his bald head turning wildly from side to side. This told Kolt that he hadn't executed the choke correctly, so he sank the triangle leg lock deeper and lifted the attacker's right arm into the air, essentially cutting off the man's airway.

Kolt held the man's elbow with his left hand and kept the attacker's arm locked straight by controlling the wrist area of the man's suit sleeve with his right hand. Kolt squeezed harder. When sparring with his mates, if the choke was fully seated, Raynor could expect his opponent to tap out within a half second or risk losing consciousness. *Tap or nap,* they called it. But this time, Raynor would not be letting go. Kolt arched his back, raised his hips slightly, while driving his legs downward through the goon's shoulders. After seven seconds, the man momentarily froze as his oxygen flow was cut off.

Then he went limp. No more resistance, no more threat.

The fight was over, and Kolt let the dead weight of the man fall to his side. He was probably dead, Raynor knew, but there was no sense in taking time to check.

"Racer, did you read my last? Acknowledge." It was Slapshot again. Kolt knew he must have missed something during the fight for his life. He hoped it wasn't too important.

He looked up to find himself staring at the business end of an AK-47. Behind it was a bearded man in a suit much like those of the three men who lay on the ground around him.

Kolt knew he was a dead man—there was no way the man could miss from that short distance.

The bearded man pulled the trigger, and Kolt watched the muzzle of the AK tilt abruptly downward. Raynor flinched on the cool alley stones, but immediately he knew he had not been shot.

The weapon had not fired. The shooter experienced a failure to fire and had jerked the trigger.

Lucky fucking day.

Still on his back, Kolt reached into his pants and gripped his Glock 23. He slipped it from the concealed holster, and in his frenzy he snagged it momentarily on his pants zipper, all the while watching the gunman manipulate his rifle.

Kolt brought his gun up and pointed it at the man behind the Kalashnikov. Raynor's hand shook uncontrollably. *Breathe.* He reached up with his left hand to take an operator's grip on his Glock and steady his front site. *Shit. This is going to be loud.*

The shooter racked a fresh round into the chamber of the AK, and he raised it frantically at the armed man on the ground in front of him.

Kolt's fingertip broke the four-pound trigger on his pistol once, somehow hoping one round fired would be quieter than a controlled pair. The .40-caliber round tore through the formally dressed man's rust-colored necktie, freezing him upright for a second as the rifle dropped from his hands.

The gunman fell forward and his forehead smashed into the pavement only feet from Kolt's head.

With all four of the JSO goons down, Kolt looked into the alcove where he had left Dr. Marris. The dark alcove was empty.

Just then a call came into his earpiece. It was Slapshot. "I've got Tripwire. Do you want us back there?"

"Negative. I'm coming to you. Digger, are you receiving?"

"Crystal, boss. That sounded like your Glock. You good to go?"

"Need some new shoes and a little more mat time, but I'm good," Kolt answered, breathing heavily into his covert mic and already mentally conducting his personal hot wash of his performance.

"Understood."

Raynor left the four men behind in the dirty passage. One of the three was clearly dead. Another was probably a goner, too. And neither of the others would be leaving that passage under his own power.

Shit. So much for low-vis. Time to run like hell.

EIGHT

Kolt headed back up the passage and then into a seedy market area. He ran past two men lying facedown and unmoving on the stone ground; both had short-barreled Kalashnikovs near their bodies. These would be the crows Slapshot had dropped. He then found Slapshot and Marris just up the street, tucked into a small kiosk in a larger alleyway. Though deep in the shade of a mosque's minaret, Dr. Marris was covered in sweat. Slapshot looked relaxed, as always.

Raynor pulled Tripwire up to his feet. "Let's go! We'll get you out of here."

"You . . . you two just killed all those men."

Kolt recognized, from the sound of Tripwire's voice and the glazed look in his eyes, that he was in shock.

"They're okay. They're just resting."

"Wha—who are you?"

"Right now I'm your best friend, but that could change in a snap. This way. I have a car."

"I'm not going with you. You are American. CIA?"

"We'll discuss it when we get you someplace safe." The two Americans started walking, but Marris lagged back.

"I don't want to go."

Kolt had no plans to spend another thirty seconds in this alley. "With due respect, Doctor, I don't give a shit. I was ordered to get you out of here. I neglected to ask my superiors if I needed your approval to save your life."

"And if I refuse? What? Will you shoot me?"

Raynor sighed. "Yeah, but just in the leg."

"You gonna carry him, boss?" asked Slapshot.

"Why do you think I brought you along?"

To Marris, the Americans seemed absolutely serious. He stood and walked quickly with them up the street. He was still in shock, and therefore somewhat compliant, but Kolt knew the shock would soon wear off.

As they turned into a larger road, a car shot out of a darkened garage, then stopped in the alleyway right alongside them.

"Get in back," Raynor ordered Marris.

"No. I want to find a taxi."

"*This* is your taxi, Doctor," Raynor said, and he shoved the big man inside.

Slapshot had already climbed into the backseat, and Digger was behind the wheel.

Dr. Marris tried to climb back out of the open door, but Kolt shoved in next to him, effectively pinning him between the two operators.

"I want out of here!" Marris yelled.

But Kolt ignored him, and shouted to Digger behind the wheel. "We're up! Primary War RV!"

"Roger." The car took off on the narrow streets of the Old City.

"Did you hear me?" Marris continued. "I said I don't want to go with you!"

Kolt shouted at the man who was now pressed against him. "Listen! I have to keep you alive. That is my job. But I don't have to keep you happy. You are coming with us to the embassy."

Marris reached over Raynor and grabbed at the door latch.

Kolt elbowed Marris hard in the face.

"Ahhh!" the Canadian screamed as he cradled his nose in his fingertips. "You broke my nose!"

"No, I didn't."

Marris held his nose with both hands. His lip dripped blood. "How can you be sure?"

"Because I know what it sounds like when I break someone's nose. You'll be fine."

On the main road out of the Medina, the car lurched to a stop just short of the Al Kornish Road. The three men in the back rocked forward as one, with the loss of the car's forward momentum.

The front passenger door opened and Curtis climbed in. They were moving again even before he shut the door.

Curtis turned to the backseat, saw Marris bleeding from the nose just as one of the JSOC operators placed a black hood on his head, just over his eyes so he could still breathe and talk. It was Delta SOP to protect the identity of the operators during the exfil, but Curtis clearly did not understand this treatment of his VIP.

"What the hell are you doing? That's not necessary!"

Kolt shrugged but said nothing. The hood stayed on.

Curtis looked angrily at Racer and Slapshot for an explanation, but when none came he turned his attention to Marris and said, "Dr. Marris, I know at the moment you might be a little miffed, but—"

"A little miffed? These two monsters just killed several men right in front of me."

Curtis again looked to the Americans in the backseat, a flash of surprise and anger on his face now. But he recovered enough to give an explanation to Tripwire. "Your life was in danger."

"*My* life! *My* life! I did not ask them to take so many lives on my behalf! I could have talked my way out of this. Or your men could have used pepper spray or rubber bullets or . . ."

While Tripwire talked, Slapshot laughed aloud on his right. "'Pepper spray,'" he mimicked.

On Tripwire's left, Kolt Raynor scanned out the window for threats, and he called up to the CIA man in the front seat. "We can drop him off at the next corner if you like."

Curtis just shook his head. "Shut your mouth and do your job."

Kolt kept looking out the window. In front of him, Digger glanced in the rearview, making eye contact with his boss. Kolt saw that the young operator was waiting to see how he handled this.

Kolt said, "Mr. Meriwether, we just took care of a major problem for you. But you are making a bigger one for yourself now. You have three seconds to apologize for that last remark or it is going to get awful crowded in that front seat."

Meriwether stared at the tough-looking JSOC officer. He was about to respond, but Slapshot looked out the back window and immediately said, "Boss?"

Kolt followed his teammate's eyes. In the thick traffic of the Al Kurnish

Road a pair of similar-looking rust-colored vans changed lanes, one in front of the other.

"The Econolines?"

"Just a hunch," admitted Slapshot.

Kolt instantly forgot about his pissing match with Curtis. He focused on the two big vehicles, watched them as they wove through slower-moving traffic. The rear van blew past a police crossing guard at a traffic circle who was trying to get him to stop. Kolt had been well trained in mobile countersurveillance, and he knew what that meant.

The two vans were doing whatever it took to stay close to one another, and to stay on his tail.

"Good hunch," he said to Slapshot, before leaning over to Digger behind the wheel. "Alternate rally point, and don't take the scenic route."

"Got it."

Up front, Curtis was still a little flustered by Racer's threat. He looked slowly around at the three military men. "What's going on? Is somebody tailing us?"

Kolt was more focused on the vans behind him, but he answered, "Yep."

"Okay." Curtis nodded. He was prepared for this possibility. "Let's get him to the embassy."

"Negative," replied Raynor.

"What the hell do you mean, 'negative'? This is my op and if I say we take him to the embassy, you sons of bitches will damn well comply!" He looked at Digger. "Make a left up here and then another left on—"

Digger said nothing, he only turned right at the intersection. Nobody was taking orders from CIA anymore on this op.

"What the fuck?" shouted the CIA man.

Kolt said, "Look, ace. Not trying to tell you how to run your extraction, but don't you think there is a chance those dudes in those two trucks eight car lengths—" He turned and checked the positioning of the force following them. "Check that . . . *six* car lengths back, just might have a single cell phone between them? And do you think there is a chance these guys could scare up some confederates to set up an ambush at one of the bottlenecks between here and the front gate of the embassy?"

Curtis opened his mouth to reply, but Raynor continued. "We head south, keep the twists and turns unpredictable, keep our tail guessing. They won't be able to call up a blocking force from their buddies in the police or army."

Digger made a quick turn to the left now, and everyone in the car leaned hard to the right.

"But . . . where are we going?" Curtis asked.

"South. We have an alternate means of extraction that will pick us up."

The black CIA man shook his head. "No. South is desert. We get out in the open and they will have a chopper on your little rally point inside of ten minutes. The JSO has people inside the police and the air force. You three guys and your peashooters are going to be outmatched by a Hind with rocket pods."

Kolt shrugged. Looked at Marris and then at Curtis. "Then we'll need to disappear in five minutes, won't we?"

Slapshot chuckled and then said, "Before we turn into pumpkins."

Curtis looked utterly confused.

Kolt said, "Relax. We have air assets en route. We know what we're doing. We're frequent flyers."

"Why the hell do I not know about these air assets?" Curtis asked.

Kolt nodded. "Not a clue. Take that up with your office." Then he looked around the car, began eyeing Dr. Marris. "Tripwire looks like he's about a deuce and a half. What are you, Curtis? 'Bout one-sixty-five soaking wet?"

Curtis recognized the reason behind the question. He just said softly, "Oh, God."

Digger's slick driving lost the two vans before he made it out of the congestion of the city, but Kolt had no illusions that the men in the vehicles had not reported to their superiors that the fleeing UN inspector and his protection force were heading out of town to the south.

They sped southeast on Ayn Zarah Road, passing fruit orchards and undeveloped land on both sides of the blacktop. Their tires kicked up dust that seemed to increase the farther they fled from the center of Tripoli.

Soon Digger made a hard left off of Ayn Zarah and onto a narrow paved road. As he cleared the intersection, a VW bus pulled out of a grove of fruit trees and rolled into the street behind him. The minibus stopped in the lane, effectively blocking any traffic off of Ayn Zarah. Two men climbed out of the VW and went around to the back, where they lifted the rear engine access panel of the vehicle.

"Bad guys?" Digger asked.

"Negative. They work for the airlines," Kolt answered as he keyed his radio's mic to make a commo check with the blocking force.

Digger floored it on the straight and empty road, raced a quarter mile up to the east, and then slowed and parked the car there so as to block both lanes of traffic.

"Hold it here!" Kolt instructed.

"What are we doing?" Curtis asked now, but Raynor held up a hand to listen to a radio transmission in his earpiece.

"Thirty seconds out," said a small voice in his ear.

"Roger that," Kolt said in response to the call, and then he transmitted to the men up the road pretending to work on their VW bus. "Blocker One, we secure?"

"You're clear for now," came the reply from one of the men up the road.

These men were from Air Cell, a unit of secret air assets operated by the United States government and available for clandestine work around the world. Air Cell had pulled Kolt and his mates out of a jam or two in his time in the Unit, and he trusted the pilots and support crew to get him out of his current predicament.

Marris started to ask again just what the hell was going on when a small blue and white high-winged single-engine aircraft appeared over the top of the VW bus up the road. It touched down on the empty road seconds later. It barely slowed after its wheels hit the pavement; instead it raced all the way up to the five men in the car blocking any traffic from the east, and then turned around, aiming its nose again to the west.

Over the loud buzz of the propeller, Raynor heard a transmission from Blocker One. "Unfriendlies inbound from the north! Two vans, hauling ass. ETA one mike."

Kolt shouted to the car, "Shit. Bad guys will be here in one minute. Everyone double-time it on board the plane!"

Curtis and Slapshot did not need any prodding; they leapt from the car and climbed in back of the impossibly tight cabin of the plane.

Kolt pulled Marris from the car, but he would not walk forward. "I'll guide you," Raynor said as he pushed on the bigger man, but Marris did not budge. He was still hooded, and still in a noncompliant mood.

"Get in, Dr. Marris," said Raynor, his hand tight on Marris's jacket. Tight enough to insinuate that he would be dragged aboard the aircraft if he did not get in on his own power. The big man did not fight the American this time; he stumbled forward and then climbed into the aircraft, and Digger followed and strapped in next to him.

Kolt himself sat in the tiny copilot seat of the plane. He put on the headset stowed in front of him and spoke into the mic quickly. "Eleven hundred pounds, plus or minus fifty. We gonna be too heavy?"

"I'll get us out of here," the silver-haired pilot responded in his mic, and then he pushed the throttle all the way to 100 percent power.

Kolt pulled the little cabin door shut.

This Argentine-made Aero Boero AB-180 was ideal for STOL (short take-off and landing) work. It was a lightweight tail-dragger specially customized for clandestine duties, with a larger engine and a smaller gas tank.

With a total of six tiny seats, including the pilot's, this mission was barely within the envelope for the aircraft's capabilities.

The AB-180 picked up speed quickly, but as far as Raynor was concerned, they were getting dangerously close to the VW bus blocking their path ahead.

And just when Kolt felt confident that they would make it into the air and over the bus, the two rust-colored vans raced into the road in front of the VW. The enemy vehicles had made their way around the parked bus by driving right through the fruit orchard. They barreled down on the approaching single-engine aircraft, dust kicking up around their tires.

Behind the vans, the Air Cell support men darted into the orchard, leaving the VW right were it was parked. There was nothing more these two men could do but extricate themselves from the scene.

As the vans approached, the pilot spoke into his mic. "Somebody wants to play chicken."

Kolt, asked, "What's the plan, old-timer?"

The pilot did not move his hand from the throttle or turn his head toward the question. "I've got to fly this baby, so I'm going to keep my eyes open, but you might want to shut yours. This is going to be a might close."

Raynor sank back in the chair and fastened his seat belt. He realized he was growing tired of dramatic air travel.

But he did not close his eyes. When the first of the vans and the nose of the AB-180 were less than one hundred feet from one another, the pilot pulled back on his stick, then drew it to the right. The plane's nose lifted skyward and then the aircraft's wings banked hard to the right. The plane climbed slowly into the air, and seemed to hang over the edge of the roadway and the orchard to the north of the road.

The two vans shot by to the left of the aircraft, the first one missing the low tail of the plane by fewer than eight feet.

Digger called from the back with nervous laughter, "I'm getting too old for this shit."

In the copilot's seat, Kolt, a decade older than Digger, blew out a long sigh of relief.

The Air Cell pilot turned the plane to the southeast, and within minutes they were flying at five thousand feet over a landscape of desolate desert.

Unsure of who was sitting next to him, the hooded Canadian asked Slapshot, "What are you going to do with me now?"

"No idea, partner. Ask the tour director." Slapshot placed a headset over Marris's head and positioned the mic in front of his mouth. He put the push-to-talk button in Marris's hand. "Press down and speak. All set!"

Marris keyed the mic and transmitted. "Where are we going?"

Curtis replied into his headset's mic, reasserting his authority over the operation. He did his best to control his heavy breathing before speaking. "We are going to an airport nearby where we will climb aboard a larger aircraft. It will take you wherever you want to go."

"I want to go back to Tripoli."

Curtis sighed. "Except there. How about you take a vacation? We'll fly you to Toronto. Once you get home you can come right back here if that's what you want. But, just so you know, we are talking to our friends in your government there, as well as in the UN, and we will stress to them how dangerous it has become for you in Libya. You might have a little trouble getting back in."

"You Americans are all bastards."

"We are the bastards who just saved your life. Do your work from home. Please don't stop. But try and keep from getting slashed to pieces for a while. The U.S. government is very fond of you, and we'd hate to lose you."

"Fuck you, Curtis."

Curtis pulled off his headset and concentrated on looking out the window at the horizon. He got nauseous on small planes, and needed to focus his attention on not spewing his lunch across the cabin.

They landed at Nanur Airport forty-five minutes later. The airfield was in the desert some two hundred kilometers southeast of Tripoli, and was in use by U.S. military and intelligence assets under agreement with the new government. As they touched down on the runway they saw a pair of aircraft on the tarmac waiting for them. A chic CIA Gulfstream business jet for Curtis and Marris and a dramatically less chic Air Force C-130 for the three Delta operators.

Kolt knew leaving a half dozen dead and wounded behind would make life extremely difficult for American intelligence here in Tripoli. Curtis's job just became exponentially harder, but Kolt and his team had had no choice but to wipe out the would-be assassins, and Kolt and his team had no choice but to exfil the country immediately after so doing.

The six-seat tail-dragger shut down its engine, Kolt slapped the Air Cell stunt pilot on the back for a job well done, and then he climbed out of the AB-180 and legged it a few hundred yards across the tarmac with his teammates to his awaiting C-130.

As he started up the ramp into the Hercules he saw Curtis jogging over to talk to him. Kolt sent Digger and Slapshot into the cargo hold to get strapped in for the long flight back to Bragg, and he waited for the CIA man to make it over.

Curtis stuck a hand out and Kolt shook it. "Sorry I snapped at you back there. I was wound up pretty tight."

"It's forgotten." It wasn't, not really, but Kolt had been working on his attitude lately, and it seemed like the professional thing to say.

Curtis then asked, "Was the deadly force unavoidable?"

Raynor did not hesitate. "Yes."

Curtis stared back at Raynor through mirrored aviator sunglasses. "It's going to make things tough for us. Half dozen goons down. It's not going to look to anyone like a UN official made a run for it on his own. Parties are going to know CIA was involved."

Kolt shrugged. "It couldn't be avoided. You handed me shit and bread and I made the best-tasting shit sandwich I could with the time you gave me in the kitchen."

Curtis did not smile at the metaphor. Kolt just looked at his own reflection in the man's aviators.

Curtis said, "It's going to make an incident."

"If you're looking for help to soften your cable traffic to Langley, I'm the wrong guy, Curtis. Bottom line: Tripwire is alive."

Curtis was becoming more combative. "Yeah, but you were supposed to keep it low-key."

"Maybe it would have been more low-key if Marris was dead in the street because we *didn't* engage those assassins."

Curtis said, "I just need to know you had no other options."

Kolt wanted to snap back at the guy. He wanted to say that he had told him twice that it *was* his only option, and if Curtis wanted to second-guess men risking themselves for his operation, maybe next time Curtis should either come up with a better plan or else do the dangerous shit himself.

But that was the old Kolt. The new Kolt held his tongue. But he also held the CIA man's stare. After the staring contest continued for a few more seconds, he asked, "Was there anything else?"

"No."

Kolt turned away and headed up the ramp of the C-130 without another word.

Digger, Slapshot, and Kolt sat next to one another on the webbed seats attached to the fuselage of the Hercules. A group of conventional soldiers, engineers who had been working on infrastructure projects in Libya, sat toward the front of the cargo hold dressed in desert camo, chatting among themselves about their impending leave. The young men all stared at the hairy men in local clothing sitting in back near the ramp, wondering who the hell they were.

The three Delta men did not engage the others in conversation.

"Hey, boss?" Slapshot called out over the whine of the four big Pratt & Whitneys as the plane began taxiing toward the runway.

"Yeah?"

"Just once, I'd freakin' *love* to rescue some hot blonde with a big rack who is so full of appreciation that she can't keep her hands off of me."

Kolt smiled, leaned back against the cold and hard fuselage. Draped his turban over his eyes and shut them tight for the flight home. "You should have joined the SEALs. *They* get all the flashy gigs."

NINE

Fort Bragg, just west of Fayetteville, North Carolina, is named for Braxton Bragg, a nineteenth-century North Carolina native who graduated from West Point, fought in the Second Seminole War and the Mexican–American War, and served as a general in the Confederate Army in the Civil War.

The base reaches into four counties of central North Carolina and it is the longtime home of the 82nd Airborne Division as well as the U.S. Army Special Forces (Green Berets) and many other units. But Bragg is most known for the numerous super-secret organizations that operate in the shadows. They pockmark the rolling hills throughout the 251 square miles of government-owned property.

And somewhere out there, tucked into a relatively tiny portion of those 251 square miles, lies the home of Delta Force.

As Delta Force began its initial activation process in the late 1970s, it acquired the "Stockade," a former military detention facility located on the north post. They remained there till the mid-eighties, when they moved to their current location northwest of the main post and most definitely off the beaten path. A Unit member can drive to work and barely see another soldier. A Delta operator can go throughout his workweek on base without seeing any 82nd Airborne or Special Forces personnel, even if he's running in the backwoods and in the numerous training and maneuver areas.

Unit guys refer to their facility as "the compound" or "the building." Those on the outside sometimes call the fenced-in complex the "Red Roof

Inn" due to the dark-maroon/red-colored roofing on the buildings, or "where the Hardy Boys live," applying one of the many nicknames the men of Delta Force use for their facility. "He's behind the fence," they say when referring to someone who has entered Delta's ranks and has seemingly fallen off the earth.

The compound is secluded and set back off the passing roads, hidden by tall trees and man-made earthen berms. The buildings and property there contain dental and medical facilities, a chow hall, a gym, firing ranges, obstacle courses, an ASP (ammo supply point), motorcycle trails, close-quarters-battle shoot houses, an Olympic-sized pool, basketball and racquetball courts, and a climbing wall. It's a civilization all its own, and a motivated operator can remain there for months without ever leaving the grounds.

Armed guards, dressed in professional uniforms, work the gates and patrol the perimeter. Many are retired Vietnam vets and all are honored to be guarding the unit compound. Most of these men stay on the job twenty years or more and know everyone in the compound by name and face.

On his first day back at Bragg after his exploits overseas, Kolt Raynor sat on a gurney in the infirmary, his olive-drab flight suit pulled down around his ankles.

He'd spent the previous ten minutes facedown, pants off, ass on display, while Doc Markham pulled week-old grenade shrapnel from his right thigh.

But that bit of unpleasantness was over now, and he was in no real pain, as the doc had given him a local injection to numb the meat in his leg before he went digging for the ball bearings that had shown up on an X-ray. He'd then stitched him up, and now Racer was seated in his underwear while the doc finished dressing the tiny wounds.

Doc Markham was new. He was a few years younger than the thirty-eight-year-old major, and he'd come along since Kolt's first stint in Delta. But the young man spoke in a commanding voice. "From the looks of the scars on you, Major Raynor, I'm going to guess this isn't the first time you've had someone in the medical profession tell you how lucky you are to be alive."

Kolt smiled. "I've heard that from people in other professions, as well."

"Well, you took nine pieces of shrapnel into the thigh. Two blew right on out the side of your leg. I've removed the seven that didn't make exit wounds, but I sure wish you had come right back after this happened instead of lollygagging wherever the hell you went in the five days since catching this grenade blast. You're lucky we don't have a nasty infection to deal with."

The doc knew about New Delhi and Racer's involvement, from the weekly command staff meeting as well as the compound's robust rumor mill. But he knew nothing about Tripoli. That op had been too black for dissemination to the support staff. As far as he knew, Kolt had been hanging out at a cathouse in France for the past week.

Kolt just said, "I got a little held up on the way home."

The doc smiled a smile that gave Kolt the indication that he understood now—Racer hadn't been lollygagging anywhere just so that his wounds could get infected. He did not say anything more, but instead inspected the old bruises in the middle of Raynor's back. "You took some more frag to your plate, didn't you?"

"I did."

"Thank God for body armor."

Raynor chuckled. "I do so on a daily basis."

Doc Markham looked at Racer's chart. "Well, let's see. A concussion and cranial lacerations last fall, a broken back and three gunshot wounds four years ago, and a half dozen more visits to the doctor for broken bones and frags over the past dozen years . . . I can't do much else for you but ask you to make sure there isn't a next time . . . but since you won't listen to me on that, please make an effort to get back here and get treatment a bit quicker . . . if at all possible."

Kolt knew the guy was just doing his job, and his job entailed reading his operators the riot act about taking care of their bodies. The old Kolt might have said something cute but smart-alecky. But the new Kolt, the kinder, gentler man that he was trying to be, just said, "You got it, Doc. Appreciate you fixing me up."

"That's what they pay me for, Major. Change the dressing on your thigh in a couple of days and come back in a week so I can take one more look."

"You got it. See you then."

Five minutes later Racer limped out of the infirmary on his way to the SCIF—the Secret Compartmented Intelligence Facility—the intelligence center of the compound. Whenever he found the time, Kolt liked to drop in and see what was going on in the world that might affect him and his troops.

Kolt's day had begun that morning with a hot wash over the in-extremis retaking of the American Airlines jet in India and the in-extremis Tripoli rescue of the United Nations weapons inspector. A hot wash was an after-action conference with all parties involved in the action, a meeting where all the details are discussed and the outcome of the event is evaluated. These forums can be brutal and intense when determining if mistakes have been made, and often the harshest critic in the room is the operator whose actions or judgment comes under scrutiny.

This morning's hot wash had been no different, except for the fact that there were two major actions under review, and Major Kolt Raynor was at the center of both of them. It had been a long and intense morning for Kolt, but he'd come out of it relatively unscathed. Colonel Webber had listened to everyone's accounts of both ops, and he made it clear that he supported his major's decisions in both incidents. Webber had been impressed with Kolt's focus after his long hiatus, though he was not at all surprised by his willingness to accept risk—for himself as well as his men. That was the Kolt everyone at Delta remembered from his first stint in the Unit.

The colonel couldn't argue with the decision to assault the 747 from the roof, reasoning that the hijackers were heading to Pakistan, where they could easily escape after killing everyone on board.

The fact that Raynor did not know they were heading to Pakistan only slightly affected Webber's assessment. The major had to make a quick decision, and that decision had saved lives.

Webber also recognized the necessity of using lethal means in Libya when the three men following Tripwire turned into six men trying to kill him. And the colonel found the major's split-second decision to extract Tripwire from Tripoli with the fixed-wing Air Cell asset during daylight hours was most impressive.

Of course, neither op had been perfectly executed, and Kolt and his team were typically self-critical and thorough. A hostage was killed on Kolt's watch in New Delhi, and a nonsuppressed handgun led to compromising the CIA's overarching mission in Tripoli. Webber didn't have to say much. He was mainly in "receive" mode. But given how both ops were seat-of-the pants missions with absolutely zero prior planning time, and probably more fitting for three assault teams instead of just one, Webber figured his men had done a damn fine job, and he would absorb any heat from Washington that came their way.

Raynor knew Webber was his champion here in the Unit, at least until the next op.

Kolt's return to Delta had been a positive experience overall, but, just as he had during his first time in the troop, he did have his detractors. People seemed to either love Kolt or hate him. During his first stint in Delta, those who weren't in Kolt's fan club admitted that he was one of the hardest-working guys in the compound, but they also said he was a hardheaded son of a bitch and, for an officer, took the Tier One Wild tag a little too much to the extreme.

The intervening years and the mileage that went along with them had affected him, there was no doubt about that. Kolt considered himself even harder-working than before, with much more to prove than during his first stint here. But now he was determined to change his image—to take that extra breath before speaking or that extra moment to empathize with the other person's point of view.

Kolt had always listened to his sergeants. Years ago he had walked into the Unit from the Rangers knowing good and well that he was on the far left of the learning curve, and each and every man he commanded would know more than he about every last aspect of the job. Kolt was not one to argue with the "men in the know"—Delta's sergeants. He knew he didn't have to know more than his men to lead them, but he did need to know how to manage his team. But Kolt hated bureaucracy, and those times when he felt his hands were tied by regs or bullshit orders—thus putting his men or his mission in danger—Kolt Raynor historically had been the first one to push back against the system.

More often than not, Kolt simply ignored the red tape and marched to his own drummer, driven by his own instincts. This had gotten him into trouble, and it had labeled him around the compound as the officer with the shortest fuse in the Unit. That this intensity was for his men and his mission was a mitigating factor, but this did not get him off the hook completely.

Something else that had always irked Raynor's detractors during his first time in Delta was the fact that his best friend, Josh Timble, had been perhaps the most respected active duty officer in the organization. Timble had taken Raynor under his wing from the start. TJ ran interference for Racer with Delta leadership when his mouth went too far or his talents did not go far enough.

And there was one more thing. Even after all the bad shit that had happened to Racer, most guys in the building still thought he was the luckiest son of a bitch alive. The New Delhi hit was one of the biggest Delta successes in a decade, and the fact that Raynor caught the op less than two months after being reinstated gave many in the building the sense that life was not fair.

The news media were all over the New Delhi hijacking, of course, pushing "unnamed sources" inside the military and intelligence communities to come clean about which unit had saved the day. Passengers reported American accents for the black-clad and armed commandos, but the government was uncharacteristically tight-lipped about the operation—a lesson learned after all the hype following the bin Laden kill. So, with little to go on but speculation, virtually all of the media had proclaimed that the vaunted SEAL Team 6 had done the deed in the skies over New Delhi.

Kolt and the rest of Delta just laughed this off. Nobody around the Unit benefited from publicity. ST6 could have the attention, for all they were concerned. The men at the compound knew what they had accomplished. There would be an impressive plaque erected next to plaques commemorating other successful ops carried out by Delta, and maybe even a historical diorama built in the long corridor of the compound known as the Spine.

Visiting VIPs would marvel at it, operators would generally ignore it.

Despite his overall success in the past week, Kolt found himself in a sour mood today. He was glad to get the last bits of New Delhi out of his leg, and he was happy to have returned from two dangerous missions with all of his men. But the death of the elderly woman had him second-guessing his actions.

The loss of the lady, a seventy-four-year-old Dutch woman as it turned out, who had rushed to the bathroom as the grenade went off, was a black eye on the otherwise stellar mission. Most agreed that the poor lady had felt the quite understandable urge to get to the lavatory so as not to vomit in public, and in her panic she acted on this impulse despite all that was going on around her.

The woman's death had made him morose and angry.

As Raynor headed through the Spine toward the SCIF, he saw Benji, an old-timer master sergeant from another squadron, walking in the other direction. They shook hands.

"Welcome home, Racer."

"Good to be back."

"Some guys get all the luck, huh?" Benji said it with a smile.

Benji used to be one of TJ's men, but now his team was led by thirty-five-year-old Major Rick Mahoney, code named Gangster. Gangster had let it be known around the compound that he thought Kolt Raynor was an asshole and allowing him to return to Delta was a mistake. But unlike Gangster, Benji and

Kolt always got along, so the remark about his lucky streak did not bother Raynor at all. He just said, "Good to see you, brother."

"You, too. Heard about your butt. Doc Markham take a look at it yet?"

"It was my thigh, but yeah. He fished out the foreign bodies. I'm one hundred percent me again."

"That's good. You guys have two more weeks on alert. I hope it's nice and quiet for you."

Kolt said, "With the OPTEMPO running off the charts looking for those missing SAMs, anything can happen at any time. I was just heading down to the SCIF to see if they've got any new blips on the radar."

Benji chuckled. "You don't think they'll let you know if something comes up?"

"Sure, my beeper will go off, but you know me. I'm all about gaming the system. If I get an early heads-up, maybe I can be better prepared."

Benji nodded.

Just then Tackle came up the hall. Tackle was, like Benji, one of Gangster's men. At thirty-nine, he was another of the old-guard master sergeants in the Unit and, like Gangster, he had never been one of Raynor's biggest fans. "Hey, Racer," Tackle said, "word is you got your ass blown off by a grenade."

Benji smiled, either not picking up on his teammate's snide tone or, more likely, just ignoring it.

Kolt sighed. "Thigh."

Tackle said, "You getting a Purple Heart for those scratches?"

"Not up to me, but I hope not."

Tackle shrugged. "Whatever. Anyway, we take over alert status from you guys soon. How 'bout keeping your bullets in your mag until you get your downtime?"

Raynor said, "Again, not up to me."

Tackle kept moving up the Spine.

Benji said, "There is a little jealousy about you scoring those two hits back-to-back like that. You get it, right? Guys go half a year without any fun and then you walk into the compound, and within eight weeks you are crawling on the roof of a plane during takeoff."

"Yeah, I get it," Kolt said, knowing that Benji was glossing over the other reasons he wasn't popular among some men in the compound.

• • •

A few minutes later Kolt saw Clay "Stitch" Vickery in the Grimes Library off the chow hall. The library, named after Delta's first command sergeant major, William "Country" Grimes, was stocked with every possible book on unconventional warfare, terrorism, and the like.

Stitch was hard to miss. He was six-foot-three, with a barrel chest. He drew his code name from his early Operator Training Course teammates. During a hot wash after a live-fire night helo raid training exercise, he was asked to explain his actions when he entered the room where the hostages were held. He simply said, "I stitched the bad guys and saved the good guys." Everyone burst out in laughter and he was knighted with the code name.

Kolt knew men like Stitch were hard to come by in Delta, where the average operator was five feet eleven inches and one hundred eighty pounds. His thick build easily filled a doorway, with his cantaloupe-shaped shoulders practically touching either side of the doorjamb. His tall frame had him looking down on most others and bumping his head on the overhead compartment when experiencing the cramped surroundings of international air travel or an up-armored Humvee.

Stitch was a good assaulter, but an even better sniper. He was entirely comfortable operating alone, had been blessed with an eagle eye, and he truly embraced the balance of art and science required of the best snipers in the world. He had decided not to stay in an assault troop, but instead to stick with the recce troop track and become an "advanced assaulter," a term snipers liked to call themselves once they graduated from an assault troop to a recce troop. The obvious dig being that anyone could be an assaulter, but it took a lot more skill, dedication, and training to become a Unit sniper.

As with all Delta men, his brawn was only a part of the equation. His brain was fine-tuned to his lethal craft. He had been instrumental in designing a custom 7.62mm round that could penetrate level IV ballistic cockpit glass and retain its trajectory, ensuring the pilot remained safe but the hijacker next to him went down hard.

But Stitch's devotion to the Unit came with a heavy price. His first wife had run off with a major in the 82nd Airborne, and his second wife had simply realized her husband was more married to the Unit than to her, and she packed her bags when he was in Afghanistan in 2006.

Since then Clay Vickery had pretty much sworn off women, so it was no surprise when Kolt found him sitting alone in the Grimes Library when he should have been at home having someone kiss his boo-boo.

While Stitch used his bandaged left hand to flip the page of a thick hardback, Racer walked up to him and asked, "Did you find a book about operating with only nine digits?"

The big man looked up at Kolt and smiled. "Welcome back, boss. Heard you and the guys made a wrong turn on the way home, ended up in Tripoli."

"We did, indeed. Sorry you couldn't join us, but it worked out pretty good without you. Your big ass wouldn't have fit in the extraction aircraft."

"I'd have legged it out of the AO for the chance to tag along. I heard it got a little hairy."

Kolt changed the subject. "How does it feel?" he asked, nodding to the man's hand.

"Burns like a mother, but it's getting better." He opened and closed his index finger. "Trigger finger's workin' fine, boss."

"Good." Kolt slapped him on the back. "You'll be needing it soon enough, I expect."

Stitch smiled. "I doubt that. Haven't you heard the news? ST6 is getting all the hits. We don't even exist."

Kolt laughed. "They can have the limelight, as long as we get the action."

Just then a female voice came over the intercom. Raynor recognized Joyce, Colonel Webber's secretary. "Major Raynor, call 4005. Major Raynor, 4005."

It was Webber's office extension. Kolt grabbed the phone off the wall next to him and dialed while Stitch looked on.

"It's Raynor, sir."

"In my office, ASAP."

"On the way." Raynor exchanged a look with Stitch and then turned to head toward Webber's office.

"If you're not out in an hour can I have your locker, boss?" Stitch teased from behind, but Kolt was too concerned to respond.

When Kolt stepped into Webber's office he saw that Monk, a master sergeant from the other squadron, was already sitting in front of Webber's desk. Monk nodded and said, "How's the ass, Race?"

Kolt smiled, more concerned with whatever Webber wanted to talk to them about, but he indulged Monk. "Upper thigh. Let's not start the ass rumor."

"That ship sailed long ago, Major."

"Great," Kolt said with a sigh.

Webber sat down behind his desk. "I wanted to let you guys know first. The CIA and FBI finally have an ID on Daoud al-Amriki."

This was big news. The year before, al-Amriki had held several Delta operators hostage, including TJ, Racer's best friend. He had also led a team of al Qaeda operatives in Pakistan to take over a CIA-run black site in order to turn the tide of the Afghan War.

For the past seven months little was known around Delta about the man other than what TJ had been able to ferret out in his twenty or so debriefings with U.S. military and intelligence investigators.

"Who is he?" asked Racer.

Webber had a printed page on his desk in front of him, but he didn't look at it. "His name is David Wade Doyle. He is thirty years old, originally from Kelseyville, California."

Monk asked, "What the hell was he doing with AQ in Pakistan?"

"Unknown. But it is thought he is now an operational commander for al Qaeda in the Arabian Peninsula."

"Shit. Not the first time an American has made it into AQ, but I've never heard of any of them as hands-on as this guy was in Pakistan. Do we have intel about where he is now?"

"Not really. FBI had learned he moved to Yemen when he was a teenager to convert to Islam. They don't think he's been back to the States since. Still . . . they are making the rounds, interviewing anyone he knows in the U.S. CIA's got people working all his known contacts in other countries, as well."

Raynor shook his head. "He wouldn't retrace his steps. Wherever he is right now, he's far from anyone who will finger him to the FBI."

"I agree."

"Does TJ know about this?"

"TJ was the one who confirmed the ID."

"How?"

"From a photograph, an old photograph. The British army picked a guy up in Basra, Iraq, back in 2003. He spoke perfect English and managed to convince the Brits he was a freelance reporter, so they let him go. Wasn't long before other prisoners talked about an American AQ fighter they had met. As you can imagine, the Tommys were pissed they'd let this guy slip through their fingers, but he must have left the theater, and the story was forgotten. MI6 didn't know anything about him. But with all the hunting around for Daoud al-Amriki in the past few months, an ex–British army sergeant who was in Basra in '03 and now works in their foreign ministry remembered the story, made some calls, and a picture appeared. TJ confirmed it immediately, so then the FBI started digging around domestically, trying like hell to find out who the guy was."

"Needle in a haystack," said Monk.

"Pretty much. But finally State found a passport photo of a guy about the same age who went to Yemen back in 1998, and the two faces matched. David Doyle became Daoud al-Amriki."

"Nice," muttered Kolt. He didn't think that should have taken seven months.

Webber continued, "TJ thinks we haven't heard the last of this Doyle/ Amriki, and I'm inclined to agree with that assessment. The kid left a good life to go over there and live like a scorpion in the desert all those years. He is a true believer."

"He's a son of a bitch," Kolt said through gritted teeth.

"He is that, too," agreed Webber.

"Any chance we're going to be sent after him?" Monk asked.

Webber stood up from his desk. His two operators followed suit. "In a perfect world, hell, yes. But you guys know the deal, it could go to the SEALs. It's up to the CG. Now that they've ID'd him, maybe they will be able to flush him out of wherever he is before his next play gets off the ground. That is, unless we are too late."

Kolt knew he and his men would turn into pumpkins in two weeks and if the hit went to Delta after that, he'd likely be listening to Monk, Benji, Tackle, and Gangster over a satellite radio from the squadron classroom.

Kolt left Webber's office a few minutes later. He decided he'd call TJ on his way home, maybe invite his old friend over for pizza. Kolt knew TJ would want someone to talk to right now, and Kolt could provide that for his friend, if nothing else.

TEN

That evening Lieutenant Colonel Josh Timble turned his red F-350 Super Duty pickup onto a farm road a few miles north of Fort Bragg. With his wipers beating warm rainwater off his windshield, he drove past row after row of chicken coops covered with corrugated roofing, and then pulled to a stop next to a beat-up black Chevy Silverado outside of a dilapidated trailer that sat in a copse of mature pecan trees.

Kolt's truck.

Josh and Kolt had moved into this little trailer together after Kolt joined the Unit as a newly minted operator nearly a decade earlier. They'd shared many good times here over the years, and Josh reminisced back to those days as he turned off his engine and his headlights and just sat there looking around at the place.

It was a dump, no doubt about it, but it had always been a dump, and with rent only two hundred bucks a month, the two friends never complained.

TJ found it surreal to be here again, looking through the rain-swept windshield at his old home. For three years he had been a prisoner of war in Pakistan, and he'd spent many nights chained to a wall or a cot or locked behind an iron door, and he'd thought of this place, and of his friend Kolt Raynor.

Not all of TJ's thoughts about Kolt had been good. It was Kolt's mistake that had gotten TJ captured in Pakistan, after all. But any animosity TJ had felt in those first months of captivity had faded away with time, and he knew Kolt had done everything in his power to make amends for his mistake.

Josh did not blame Kolt for what had happened.

Not anymore.

The months since coming home from Pakistan had been difficult. Timble had only returned to Delta a month prior, and he was not back in his former position. He was no longer operational, his three tough years as a POW had taken a heavy toll, and although his body had recovered to a large extent in the months since coming home, he was in no way ready for operational status with Delta. Instead, he now worked in RDI, Research and Development Integration. It was Lieutenant Colonel Timble's job, along with many others, to find the next top sniper rifle, or GPS device, or armored vehicle, or lightweight body armor; any piece of kit that would help frontline Delta operators perform their difficult duties.

The work was vital to the success of Delta, but it wasn't on the sharp edge, and for a man like TJ, it was a hell of a letdown from the excitement and importance of his former job—leading America's Tier One operators into battle.

Now he spent his days working with approved vendors, all of whom had signed a nondisclosure agreement to get access to the Unit. His fellow RDI colleagues were other broken and busted Delta assaulters and snipers. It was a grim place for men who had spent their adult lives as fine-tuned physical and mental specimens. The men of RDI felt as if they were a million miles away from their old jobs, even though the Unit's operators were just across the hall.

Josh missed his old life, and he longed to return to operational status.

Kolt Raynor opened his door to find TJ standing in the rain with a large pizza and a six-pack of beer. The two men had seen each other around the compound and had eaten lunch together in the chow hall a few times, but both had been too busy to spend much time together in the short time since TJ had returned to work.

"Good to see you," Kolt said.

TJ came in, shook off the rain, and tossed a cold beer to Kolt. "Nice to see *you* back home in one piece, Kolt. I hear you have been a busy boy."

"It's been an interesting few days, to say the least."

Josh sat down on the old lumpy couch and Kolt sank into a cracked burgundy leatherette chair as he broke open the lid of the can.

TJ smiled while looking around. "Love what you've done with the place, brother."

Kolt shrugged. "We did such a fine job with the interior decoration all those years ago, I've seen no reason to update it."

TJ laughed as he watched Kolt power-chug the beer, squeeze the can, and toss it into the kitchen sink, just a few feet away from where he sat in the living room. Then both men dug into the pizza. Between bites Timble said, "You got banged up in New Delhi?"

"It was nothing. Stitch got the worst of it, but he couldn't be happier with how things turned out."

"You guys are rock stars at the compound."

Raynor just smiled. Then he changed the subject. "You heard about the hostage killed in the takedown?"

"Yeah," said TJ. "That was unfortunate."

Kolt just shook his head. "Should have seen the setup. I should have fucking *known* there would be a trap."

"You did your best. Your best is better than ninety-nine-point-nine-nine percent of the rest of the world. Your best is better than most any guy in the troop. But your best wasn't good enough to help that woman."

"I don't know. I'm not sure I still have it," Kolt said.

TJ kept eating while he talked. "Look, Racer, I don't know the details, but word in the building is that you had about three seconds to process what you were seeing with that plane about to take off. Nobody else would have risked landing on the roof and taking down a moving aircraft."

Kolt cut him off. "Was it worth it?"

"Stop whining. You are a leader. Leadership is your job. You had to drive the risk. You went off your instincts, an old lady bought it, but you saved hundreds. You did your job."

Kolt nodded. One thing Kolt appreciated about Josh during their years serving together was that Josh always told Kolt what he needed to hear, not what he wanted to hear.

Josh asked, "Did you learn from the experience?"

"I did."

"Good," said TJ. And just like that, the matter was put to rest. "So, tell me about Tripoli."

Kolt hesitated. Started to speak but stopped himself. Then with a nervous smile he said, "You know how it is, man. I can't go into much of that."

Timble nodded. "You were there, and now you're home. Is that about it?"

Kolt shook his head. "I was *somewhere,* and now I'm home." He saw that Timble hated being on the outside. "I'm sorry. You know there is nothing I'd rather do than go through every last bit of the hot wash with you. But I can't."

"I know you can't. Shit. It's tough being in RDI. It's like kissing your sister."

"Your sister is hot," Kolt said, an attempt to lighten the mood. It worked for a couple of seconds.

"You know what I mean. I hate being on the outside. All I know about New Delhi I got from some of the gossip around the building. I know Stitch lost a finger and I know you got some frag in your ass. I know most of the Unit thinks you are a fucking hero for what you guys managed to pull off, and I know that a couple of the guys, guys who didn't like you in the first place, think you fucked up again and got that Dutch lady killed."

Kolt just grunted. The speed and the quality of the gossip around the compound never ceased to amaze him.

TJ continued, "I also know that pretty much everyone in the building, myself included, thinks you are the luckiest son of a bitch in history for getting two SECDEF-level hits just weeks after returning to service."

Raynor smiled at this. It gave him a little pleasure to think of some of the other Unit guys stewing in their juices about him getting the primo role in a couple of Delta's biggest ops of the last year.

Kolt chuckled now. "What do you mean, 'on the outside'? You sound pretty well dialed in."

"I wish. You know there are few secrets that haven't made their way down the Spine. But it's not the same as being operational."

"You'll be operational again," Kolt said.

"I'm working on it."

"You still look like you need to gain some weight."

"Yeah, that's what they tell me. Been working out, running, eating like a pig. It will happen." He took a big, dramatic bite of pepperoni pizza.

"I know it will, brother. Keep it up. You look better every time I see you."

"Thanks." Then he got around to the reason he came over tonight. "Did Webber tell you about al-Amriki?"

"Yeah, he did. And we got the target brief from intel this afternoon. David Wade Doyle. How does it feel to know his true identity after all this time?"

"It's a step in the right direction, I guess. But we should have blown this guy's ass up with a Hellfire months ago. This personality is not getting the attention he deserves. We need to go after Doyle until he's roadkill."

"Preaching to the choir, man. No telling what he's up to now."

TJ seemed to think it over a moment. "Something big. I can feel it. He will pull out all the stops after his failure in Pakistan. He's going to throw a Hail Mary."

"You may be right. Hopefully the CIA will get a spike on him and send us out to take him down." Kolt smiled. "Maybe you'll be back with us by then. Who knows? You might get a second dance with that asshole."

TJ nodded, and then they ate in silence for another minute.

Finally, Raynor looked down at his watch. "Shit. I've got to run. Meeting the boys at the range for some low-light shooting at 2200. You want to come along, get some trigger time?"

TJ stood up. "I'd love to, but I've got an appointment with a vendor first thing in the morning."

"Nice," said Raynor. He did not mean to sound patronizing, but he couldn't help it. He followed with, "Are we getting some new cool shit?"

"Hopefully. With any luck I'll be back in the squadron before it's issued." As he headed for the door he said, "And Kolt?"

"Yeah?"

"Might be time to think about getting an apartment."

"And leave all this behind? Are you kidding?"

TJ just shook his head and walked out to his truck.

ELEVEN

Mykonos, Greece, had been chosen by Aref Saleh and Daoud al-Amriki as the location for the test of the Igla-S surface-to-air missile. Aref Saleh traveled to Greece often to meet with contacts there, and he had transported rifle and machine gun ammo into Greece from Libya on two earlier occasions without trouble. But he wanted to keep his access and his contacts here intact, even after the sale to the AQAP operatives, so he developed a plan that would get himself and his clients into and then out of the country without compromising his established means.

Saleh, al-Amriki, and Miguel did not travel to Greece directly. Instead they flew to Turkey under false Egyptian passports, and then they used former JSO assets who worked in the human smuggling trade to take them by boat from the Turkish coast, first to the Greek island of Ikaria.

And then, on the second night, they traveled by speedboat to Mykonos.

Before leaving Cairo they shipped one completely disassembled Igla-S system secreted in several large crates of motorcycle and scooter parts directly to a freight forwarder in Mykonos. It was decided that, if the three men were captured trying to sneak into Greece, they would be expelled with little fanfare, as North Africans attempting to get into Europe is far from a unique event. But three men with Egyptian passports caught attempting to get into the EU while transporting shoulder-fired surface-to-air missiles would ensure than none of them would ever see beyond the walls of a Greek prison, so the weapon traveled separately.

Once in Mykonos, Saleh sent an agent of his living there to pick up the crates from the forwarder at the airport. Saleh was prepared to sacrifice one of his agents in Greece on this operation, but not himself.

His agent returned to the parking lot of a restaurant a mile from Saleh's safe house. Saleh, al-Amriki, and Miguel were not there waiting for him. They were, instead, watching the parking lot and the two-lane coastal road that led to it from their rented house in the hills above.

The agent was alone, he had not been followed, and he had the crates with him. After letting the man sit and wait for an hour, Saleh drove down to the parking lot, took the boxes with the Igla-S, and returned with them to the safe house.

Committing such a bold criminal act as the shooting down of an aircraft meant the three men would have to arrange for a hasty escape after the fact, and Saleh, al-Amriki, and Miguel had worked this out well in advance of their test of the weapon system. They had their getaway ready in the form of a Uniesse Marine forty-two-foot open powerboat. It was owned by the Turkish smugglers and had made the Aegean crossing many times in the past. Saleh and his men had anchored it in a rocky cove just minutes from the airport.

The three men decided to engage their target in daylight. This would, as long as they remained out of sight, lessen the chance that witnesses would report an ascending plume of fire from a missile shortly before the plane went down. There was no chance whatsoever that this SAM attack would go undiscovered; the wreckage would give many telltale clues that the passenger plane had been shot down. But Amriki, Miguel, and Saleh wanted to delay this inevitability as long as possible.

At least long enough for them to get out of Mykonos.

A day of scouting by Amriki and Miguel led them to a small hillock shielded on three sides by sheer rocky cliffs. The site afforded them a view of the airport to the north, as well as quick access to a road that led to the beaches to the south.

It was a perfect spot to ambush a plane as it passed by, low and slow, after taking off from Mykonos.

The three men spent the night in the safe house, and then breakfasted on the veranda facing Paradise Beach. Every few minutes an aircraft would take off and fly overhead, and then bank over the bay before disappearing into the bright sky.

At noon Saleh went to the boat, and the two AQAP men returned to the hillock in a two-door Fiat. They took the Igla from the trunk, and they prepared themselves for the test-fire.

When they were ready and comfortable that no one was close by on the hillside, they chose a departing Airbus A319 as their victim. There was neither political nor strategic justification in the choice; the Airbus was merely a target of opportunity. As it turned out, it was a Lufthansa medium-haul flight that flew a Mykonos-to-Athens route five days a week. It was not a particularly large aircraft, but it would do for their test.

The plane could have been carrying 124 passengers, but it was a Wednesday, the slowest day of the week for the route, so only 84 passengers and 6 crew members were on board as it rolled down Runway 16, gaining takeoff speed in the hot Greek summer sun.

Two minutes later it passed by the launch site, and al-Amriki leveled the weapon at the departing jet, holding it high with the grip stock and his shoulder. The white aircraft was his initial aiming point, but he refined it to the blue and gold tail, putting the glass aiming reticule between the two engines on the departing plane.

He heard the hum indicating that the warhead had found its heat source in the sky.

"*Allahu Akhbar,*" Daoud al-Amriki said, and he pressed the trigger.

Immediately the rocket fired out of the launch tube, then its internal propellant ignited, and with a roar it arced into the sky. Doyle had fired RPGs several times and even a captured American antitank weapon in Afghanistan once, but he had never fired a shoulder-launched SAM. The rocket was nearly the length of the launcher itself, but as it rose it turned into a tiny pinprick in the sky ahead of a line of wispy gray smoke. The missile seemed to streak high above the flight path of the aircraft for a second, but then it angled sharply back down.

Impact between the missile and the tail of the Airbus took place just six seconds after Daoud al-Amriki pressed the launch trigger.

The Lufthansa flight was no more than three thousand feet in the air, passing over Agrari Beach on the southern side of the island. The pilot had just begun a gentle bank to the west when his craft was hit from behind by the missile. With its fuel tanks more than half full for the flight to Athens, and with the low altitude and the full power of the engines, the Airbus A319 did not stand a chance.

A fluff of brown and white smoke behind the Lufthansa flight was visible from the ground. The two men on the hillock just stood and watched. The sound of the explosion, a sharp crack and a low boom, made its way to them several seconds later. By then the Airbus had changed its flight path; it banked hard to the west, its climbing nose went level with the earth and then tipped down.

Ninety-six seconds later the burning jet crashed nose-down into the crystalline sea four miles southwest of the island of Delos.

There were no survivors.

Miguel and al-Amriki drove calmly but purposefully to a secluded spot near Paradise Beach, where they climbed aboard a dinghy with Aref Saleh at the motor. The three men raced to their speedboat, which was anchored a quarter mile offshore. No one paid any attention to them; the holidaygoers at the beach watched the smoke in the distance and discussed what had happened three thousand feet above their heads just minutes earlier. Most had seen the plane go down, many had watched its portside wing erupt into a fireball, and a few had even seen the initial explosion of the port engine.

But none could definitively say they'd seen a fast-moving missile rise from the hills behind them and hit the plane.

The forty-two-foot powerboat with the three men on board raced due east in order to put as many miles as possible between the men and their crime, but by afternoon it had adopted a southerly route and slowed somewhat so as not to draw attention.

They arrived at Fourni Island around midnight. They were close to Turkey, but still in Greece, so they anchored in a tiny natural harbor to wait out the rest of the morning and the light of day. Fourni had been a haven for pirates for centuries due to its high cliffs and this made it easy for the men to avoid detection.

That evening, after darkness returned, they finished their escape, heading east into Turkish waters.

They docked in Didim, a Turkish seaside resort, just before one in the morning on the second day after the destruction of the Lufthansa flight. Within minutes of climbing off the boat they were in a minivan, heading for the interior of the country, and at eleven o'clock the next morning they were on separate flights, Saleh to Cairo, and al-Amriki and Miguel to Sana'a.

Daoud al-Amriki's people in Dubai executed the first wire transfer into Saleh's account before the end of business two days later, and by the end of the week the Libyans were readying their logistics means to move the weapons from Libya to Egypt, and then on to Dubai.

All parties were extremely satisfied with the arrangements.

Kolt Raynor was called into Colonel Webber's office by his secretary on the public address system. Kolt had been spending his time since returning to the compound from overseas reading the daily intel summaries of potential threat locations and personalities and reviewing hot washes from past operations conducted in Iraq and Afghanistan that took place after he had been declared persona non grata and tossed from Delta. He'd also put the finishing touches on the award recommendations he was submitting for Stitch, Digger, and Slapshot for the New Delhi hijacking op. None of the boys needed another valor award, nor did they even want one, but Webber had suggested it and Kolt knew they deserved it.

While Kolt sat on his ass in the office, the sergeants worked on their commando skills. Running the O-courses, busting plates on the flat range, tweaking their HK416s' zero, and generally putting in the solid day's work expected of a Tier One operator at home station.

"Kolt," Webber said as soon as the major entered his office. "It has been confirmed that the Lufthansa jet that went down in the Aegean Sea the other day was shot down by a MANPAD."

Kolt breathed out a frustrated sigh. He knew it. The Jakarta SAM in the spring, and now this.

"Authorities on the scene say the evidence indicates that, as we might all expect, this was one of the SA-24s missing from Libyan arms depots."

Kolt asked, "So will the White House step up the hunt to get the rest of the MANPADs back?" To Kolt it was a no-brainer. They should have been working on this every waking moment.

The colonel said, "Not in time to help the ninety passengers and crew who died off Mykonos."

"Is anyone taking credit?"

"Sure. AQ, Taliban spokespeople, Greek separatists, Turkish nationalists in Greece."

"The usual suspects."

"Yes."

"Is the Agency leaning on anyone in particular?" Kolt asked.

"Not yet. They are digging through old message traffic. Looking into all the bad actors. But while that's going on, you are going back to work."

Kolt's eyebrows rose in surprise.

Webber said, "Racer, I need you to lead an Advance Force Operations cell in Cairo. The CIA guy you helped out in Tripoli, Myron Curtis, is there, and he's got a line on an organization of ex-JSO men who, he thinks, have been brokering the sale of the Libyan SA-24s."

"Are we deploying with execute authority?"

Webber shook his head. "Negative. Not yet, anyway. You will help with determining atmospherics, building the target folder for a potential hit. He will likely want you to do some clandestine recce, but you'll need to get approval for that from me. Curtis and his team have been in Cairo for a few days, and they're having trouble getting the personnel from the local CIA station. They are pretty busy with political and social events in Egypt these days."

Kolt had done this sort of thing before. Recce, surveillance, watching, and waiting. Using a high-powered telephoto lens instead of a high-powered rifle.

"This case officer, Curtis? I figured I'd be the last guy he would ask for."

"He didn't ask for you. He and others at CIA were pissed about how it went down in Tripoli. It's gotten all the way up to the White House that the JSOC team that came to help with the evacuation of Tripwire had itchy trigger fingers, and only the deft work of CIA kept it from turning into an international incident between us and the new government in Libya."

Kolt just gritted his teeth. *Assholes.* Then he asked, "Then why *are* you sending me to Cairo?"

"Because Curtis wants an AFO cell. You are on alert status, so you go. I am satisfied with the work you did in Tripoli, and am not about to change the batting order around here because some case officer thought you didn't show enough restraint in dealing with a street full of assassins."

"Thank you, sir."

Webber remained stone-faced. "Thank me by not fucking up in Cairo. Curtis is running the show on this, and he doesn't like you, so be on your best behavior and mind your manners. You remember the talk we had before you completed Relook?"

Kolt knew Webber was referring to the conversation in which Webber told Kolt that he would be judged twice as hard as he had during his first time in Delta.

"I think about it every day," Kolt said softly. He didn't like Curtis much, but he did not have to like him to work with him.

"Good. You leave tomorrow night on covered air."

"Yes, sir. I'm taking Digger and Slapshot?"

"Yes. And one more. You know Hawk from training cell?"

"No, sir." Kolt hated admitting he didn't know someone in the Unit, but since his return he'd been all but overwhelmed with training and executing his ops. "Commo guy?"

"Hawk has some language and other assets that might be beneficial for the recce in Cairo. You could do worse."

"Sounds perfect."

Webber then moved on to other matters. There would be a full briefing later in the afternoon for Kolt and a couple of guys from Intel about the situation in Cairo, and then the four Unit members would assemble gear and fly out the next evening on a CIA Gulfstream.

That evening, after the briefing and a couple hours of assembling their gear for the Cairo operation, Kolt and Peter "Digger" Chambliss drove together off base for dinner at Huske Hardware House Brewery in downtown Fayetteville. It would be their last American meal for a while, which was not as much of an issue for Kolt as it was for Digger, who, at twenty-seven, was the youngest operator in the squadron. He bemoaned the fact that he wouldn't get a decent burger and fries in Egypt.

Huske's was all but packed. It was a favorite joint for both 82nd troopers and Green Berets from nearby Fort Bragg, so the century-old multifloor brick building wasn't exactly known as the place to cradle a grudge. It was owned and operated by the Collinses, a husband-and-wife team who always met their patrons with a welcoming smile. Josh Collins was somewhat of a local celebrity himself. As a former Army boxer and Army Ranger who saw plenty of combat action in his day, he could tell by the looks on the faces of his patrons which guys had come back from the wars in Iraq and Afghanistan.

And Collins was well read in to Kolt's reputation.

Kolt sipped his beer and looked across the table at Sergeant Chambliss. Digger was six feet tall and had nearly shoulder-length wavy blond hair. He looked a bit like a California surfer, though he hailed from Ohio. Even though Digger was young, Kolt recognized the incredible hunger in the man that Raynor himself was known for when he joined the Unit.

Four years earlier, when Peter Chambliss had been a member of 5th Special Forces Group, his Humvee had detonated a land mine on a rocky Afghanistan road in Kunar Province. The vehicle flipped in the explosion, tossing Sergeant Chambliss like a rag doll inside. After the dust settled he checked his wounds, and the twenty-three-year-old Green Beret found his left leg below the knee held on only by the torn fabric of his BDUs.

He was medevaced out and shipped to Ramstein and then to D.C. and then home to Ohio for surgery and rehab. It was a life-threatening injury that he survived, and it was a life-changing injury that he was determined to overcome.

One year to the week after losing his leg in Afghanistan he was redeployed to Afghanistan, back with 5th Group and now the proud owner of a state-of-the-art prosthetic limb.

And two years after returning to 5th Group, he became a member of Delta, the first amputee ever assessed and selected.

Digger had stuck an ARMY STRONG bumper sticker on the poly-fiber shinbone of the device, and he never passed up an opportunity to make light of his situation.

Digger may have had some optional after-market parts installed on his body, but Kolt Raynor knew this kid had the heart of a lion and the never-surrender mind-set of a Delta operator.

Parachuting down toward the hijacked American Airlines flight in New Delhi, Kolt had momentarily questioned Digger's capabilities, and then, in the next ten minutes, Digger had gone on to execute his role flawlessly during the interdiction.

Kolt would never question the man, or his artificial limb, again, although he would make Digger wear his "old-school" artificial leg in Cairo for OPSEC reasons. This second prosthetic had been purchased from a clinic in Iraq and it was made with the equipment and materials one would find in the Middle East, and Digger donned it from time to time when it fit his cover status.

In some locations where Delta operated in a clandestine fashion, the ARMY STRONG bumper sticker just wouldn't do.

Between bites of his dinner Digger began telling Kolt a story about his first combat jump as a Ranger. Kolt had heard the tale four or five times in the two and a half months he'd known Sergeant Chambliss, so his eyes drifted off the sergeant and onto a young woman who came through the door. She was nice-looking, mid-twenties, with dark hair and eyes, and a body that made it clear she knew her way around the gym. She was also unescorted, though she appeared to be looking around the bar for a friend.

Although Kolt considered her more pretty than drop-dead gorgeous, the girl fascinated him. He thought he saw a hint of Asian ancestry in her dark shoulder-length hair and slight facial features, and he found her searching, intelligent eyes hard to look away from.

"Boss? You with me?"

"What?" Kolt looked back to Digger. "Sorry."

"You gonna finish those fries?"

"Be my guest," Raynor said, and he dumped them on Digger's plate. He looked back toward the entrance for the girl, but instead he found her standing at his table, looking directly at him.

Kolt raised his eyebrows in surprise. "Hi."

"Major Raynor?"

Any fleeting thoughts Kolt may have had that his rugged good looks had caused this attractive young lady to pick him out of the crowd evaporated in an instant.

"Never heard of him."

The girl's almond eyes widened now, and she turned her attention to Digger. It was clear she knew she had just committed a violation of operational security. Kolt was a major in the U.S. Army, but in Huske's, or any other civilian establishment, he was anything but a soldier.

Digger took the edge off. "Boss, she's with us."

She put out a hand. "Cindy Bird."

He shook it. "Hello, Cindy Bird." He kept looking at her, careful to keep his eyes locked on her eyes, lest they wander south to her body. Even with Digger's heads-up, he had no idea who this girl was or what she wanted with him. "This seat's yours," Digger said as he leaned over and pulled a stool back from the table.

"I look forward to working with you, sir," she said as she sat down, still addressing Kolt.

"Working with me on what?"

She leaned forward toward Kolt now to speak in a softer, more secure tone. "I'm very sorry. Colonel Webber didn't tell you?"

Kolt figured it out, but more slowly than he would have liked. His mouth curved into a slight smile before he said, "*You* must be Hawk."

"Yes, sir. Is there a problem?"

"None at all, Sergeant. I'm just surprised."

"Surprised at what, sir?"

Kolt did not want to say he was surprised that the training cell sergeant he was taking to Cairo in his AFO cell was female, and a good-looking female, at that.

So he just said, "I'm surprised Colonel Webber has a sense of humor."

Bird got it. "He didn't tell you that your cover in Cairo included a wife, did he?"

"That must have slipped his mind." He looked at Digger now as if to say, *You son of a bitch . . . you knew all along.*

"Swear to God, boss. I had no idea you didn't know her already."

Kolt noticed now, by the way she plopped down in the booth next to Digger, that she was not quite as ladylike as he had first imagined. He could see the tomboy and the youth in her actions.

"How old are you, Hawk?"

"I'll be twenty-five in September, sir."

"And what month is it now?"

"Umm . . . July."

"So then that makes you twenty-four."

"Yes."

Kolt smiled, shook his head. "Sorry about my initial reaction. I don't want you to get the impression that I don't respect the program. We should have seen the potential a long time ago. We're lucky to have the few of you that make it. On top of that, Colonel Webber speaks highly of your talents."

Cindy Bird smiled broadly. Kolt thought back to what Webber had said about Hawk's assets. He tried not to roll his eyes, and he also had to force himself not to look at some of those assets now.

He then remembered something else Webber had said. "You have some language?"

"Yes. Egyptian Arabic. Not fluent yet, but I'm taking night classes at Methodist. I'm somewhat conversational. Not sure if that will help."

"It sure as hell won't hurt," Kolt said. "Okay, Hawk. I have somewhere to be first thing in the morning, but we'll dig into this at 0900. Meet us in the SCIF."

"Looking forward to it, sir."

Kolt reached for his wallet to pay the check. "First thing, stop calling me 'sir.' It's Racer, or boss. Second, why did you feel the need to come find me off post?"

"Oh, sorry, sir. I mean boss. I'm here to meet my boyfriend. He's in Fifth Group. Apparently he's running late. SOP for most Green Berets." She winked at Digger, who was an ex–Green Beret. To Kolt she said, "I just recognized your face from pictures I've seen around the squadron lounge. Those are some great shots from the old days. Spear Runner and Gauge Front must have been incredible experiences. I love checking out the history of the Unit."

Digger laughed. "The old days."

Kolt groaned. "Hope you didn't miss the one of me and Teddy when we took San Juan Hill?"

Hawk looked confused for a moment. "I don't think I saw that. San Juan Hill? I'm not familiar with that . . ."

Then it dawned on her, and she smiled. "Teddy Roosevelt, sir?"

Kolt nodded.

"So that makes you, what, about a hundred and thirty-five? You don't look it."

"Not a day over one-twenty," Digger said as he finished his beer.

TWELVE

Immediately after returning to the Middle East on the heels of their successful test-fire in Greece, al-Amriki and Miguel went to Sana'a, the capital of Yemen. Here they lay low in a safe house belonging to a local cell of al Qaeda in the Arabian Peninsula. They remained inside the walled building, behind closed doors and shuttered windows, and they hunkered down in case any track-backs from the Greek shoot-down led investigators in their direction.

They stayed in communication with their confederates and associates by using a runner from the local cell, sending the man out to various Internet café's throughout the city with messages to pass on to other cutouts who, in turn, communicated with members of Aref Saleh's trading network in Cairo and AQ banks in Dubai, ensuring that the money was received by the smugglers and the "product" was on its way and well cared for while under sail.

The SAMs would travel to Dubai, in the United Arab Emirates, and there an agent would divide them into four shipments of fifteen crates each. They would then travel independently via air cargo to Paris, where an agent would arrange for them to continue on to their final destination.

The man in Dubai and the man in Paris were agents of al Qaeda, but the receiving agent at the final destination was a member of another organization. He was the weak link in the chain, but he had been tested with some dummy cargos and had handled everything in an acceptable fashion.

This had all been arranged in advance by Daoud al-Amriki himself, after months of planning and using dozens of cutouts.

Amriki's operation was being funded out of an al Qaeda account kept flush with cash by benefactors in the Gulf States. The operation that he was undertaking had been one of the last wishes of Anwar al-Awlaki, the former regional commander of AQ in Yemen. Awlaki had been killed by a U.S. drone shortly after giving the order that al-Amriki should get whatever resources he required for his secret mission, no questions asked. This green light had resulted in al-Amriki gaining access to tens of millions of dollars to buy weapons and secure training, as well as a look at data on a thumb drive: dossiers on AQ operatives around the globe who were available for his mission.

The thumb drive came to Daoud with six men, al Qaeda security enforcers who were ordered never to let the data out of their sight. David used a laptop computer to view the information over a number of days. He went through the dossiers, picked his operatives, found his support cells, and developed his plan of action.

Then the thumb drive, the six men, and the laptop Daoud had used to view the data all left.

Al-Amriki picked the best men available for his mission, beginning with the operative here in the Sana'a safe house with him. Miguel was not his partner's real name. No, Amriki's partner was Waleed Nayef, a thirty-four year-old Kuwaiti and the son of an executive of NBK, the National Bank of Kuwait.

Nayef had been born in Kuwait City, and he lived a childhood typical of a wealthy family in the oil-rich state. But at the age of twelve he had been traveling with his family on vacation in New York when Saddam Hussein invaded his homeland from the north. His family was allowed to remain in the United States, living with friends in New York's Upper West Side, until the crisis passed.

Due in part to contacts made in the city while his nation was under occupation by Iraq, Waleed's father took a job as director of the NBK branch in New York after the war. Young Nayef lived in Manhattan until he was seventeen, learning English along the way, and then his father was transferred back home.

Waleed attended the University of Kuwait and it was there he watched al Jazeera television with rapt attention as the United States invaded Afghanistan in 2001. Around the same time he became radicalized at a mosque in Kuwait City by an influential Iraqi cleric. When this imam returned home and was then killed during the invasion of Iraq in the spring of 2003, Waleed Nayef and several other young Kuwaitis immediately headed north to Baghdad to join the resistance there.

Nayef was smart and hardworking and incredibly motivated, so it was no time at all before he became a member of al Qaeda in Iraq, then led by Abu Musab al-Zarqawi.

Zarqawi was killed by American Forces in 2006 and Nayef was injured weeks later. He returned to Kuwait to recover, and here his influential father realized for the first time that his son had become an Islamist fighter, though he had no idea that Waleed was an up-and-coming operative in a branch of Osama bin Laden's organization.

After Waleed's recovery his father arranged for him to return to the United States, hoping this would somehow cure him of his radical thoughts. Waleed agreed to go, promising his father he had no further intentions of warring against the country where he had spent much of his youth. In fact, Nayef only agreed to the journey because he knew it would make him more valuable to al Qaeda.

As soon as he had fully recovered from his wounds, he traveled to North Carolina to attend graduate school at Duke University.

During the three years he lived in North Carolina, Waleed was immersed in American life and culture and language. At the same time, through contacts on the Internet, he once again became involved with al Qaeda, this time allying himself with Anwar al-Awlaki, the New Mexican–born operational commander of al Qaeda in the Arabian Peninsula. For these three years Waleed did nothing more than post anti-American invective on Web sites and message boards, while attending school to obtain his master's degree in civil engineering. But his secret life and not his academic life was his true priority—the young man knew that his future was in the Middle East, not in the United States.

In 2009 thirty-one-year-old Waleed Nayef traveled to Yemen and joined al Qaeda in the Arabian Peninsula, the most powerful branch of the al Qaeda organization. He became a key operative within months, traveling to his home country of Kuwait, the United Arab Emirates, and Europe. He worked high-level operations in the banking sector, transferring money between accounts and meeting with high-profile and high-income supporters of his organization to appeal for donations and sponsorship of projects AQAP was overseeing around the globe. The work was difficult but not dangerous, as he did not operate with a gun in his hand or plant bombs in the roadside against Western forces, as he had done in Iraq. But his operational activity meant that he had to employ intricate espionage tradecraft in all of his dealings. He worked undercover, using a great number of legends and falsified documents, remaining on the lookout for surveillance teams on his trail, and he took intricate measures to avoid electronic eavesdropping of his telephone or e-mails.

In short, in just a few years, Waleed Nayef had become one of al Qaeda's top spies and one of JSOC's top faceless priorities. His official targeting title by the United States was "AQ Facilitator."

But even though his job was important and his operations crucial to the success of his new organization, he had long sought something more from his missions. When he was brought in by AQAP leadership and told that he had been selected to join a new operation, he jumped at the chance to work on a mission that, he had been promised, would kill thousands of infidels and greatly affect the West's ability to fight against Islam.

He was then introduced to David Doyle, the man he knew as Daoud al-Amriki. This was some months prior to their traveling together to Egypt and then to Greece and, at first, Nayef and Amriki shared a mutual distrust of one another. But al-Amriki had slowly begun to rely on the operative he knew as Miguel, and even more slowly he read him in on the mission to come. And Nayef came to respect the American converter to Islam.

The Kuwaiti national was amazed by the full scope of the American operative's plan. Amriki chose Miguel to be the second-in-command of the mission. Once the action began, Nayef would operate separately from Daoud, and he would be in charge of his own unit of fighters. But his assistance in the training phase would be equally crucial to the operation's success.

THIRTEEN

On their seventh day in Sana'a, Miguel and al-Amriki were contacted by AQAP leadership and told to gather their belongings, sanitize their safe house, and come to a meeting at a nearby storefront. Here they were met by two men in a four-wheel drive Jeep, and they were driven out of the city. Even though Amriki and Miguel were high-ranking members of the organization, once they passed the last military checkpoint, twenty kilometers outside the capital, they were hooded so they could not see the route they were taking to their destination.

They drove on a series of progressively worsening roads, al-Amriki could tell this by the bumping and jarring of the vehicle's suspension. They stopped for gas and then continued on. Al-Amriki realized they were heading southeast, from the warmth of the sun on the back of his neck. This was no surprise to him, as AQAP held much territory in the southeastern region of Yemen. This was al Qaeda country, and though that should have been comforting to an AQ operative, here American drones monitored the traffic on the roadways. At any moment, he knew, he could end up just like Anwar al-Awlaki, Abu Mussab al-Zarqawi, and any one of hundreds of other al Qaeda members who had been taken out by the U.S. from the skies above.

He, and Nayef next to him, did their best to put this fear out of their minds, and they journeyed on to the south with their faces covered.

After six hours of travel they arrived in Al Kawd on the northern shore of the Arabian Sea, some thirty-five miles northeast of Aden. Fighters from al

Qaeda in the Arabian Peninsula had taken the town the year before after pushing Yemeni government forces out of the area, declaring the region to be an Islamic emirate, and they had spent the intervening months expanding their territory. In many towns and villages, such as nearby Zinjibar and Jaar to the north, AQAP held a tight grip on much of the province of Abyan.

The main threat to the al Qaeda fighters here was no longer the Yemeni military, as the government in Aden had pulled most of its forces out of the area.

No, Predator and Reaper drones operated by the United States served as the biggest danger to the leadership of the terrorist organization. Over thirty drone strikes in the province in the last year alone had killed scores of fighters.

They spent the night at a small walled home there, and then, at first light, they traveled north in the back of a different vehicle than the one they had used the day before.

Al-Amriki and Miguel were taken north to the village of Al Hisn, and then they were instructed to climb onto the back of a mule cart. The driver of the cart spoke little as he transported them on a dirt road to the west.

There were no trucks passing on the road, but the surface was not in such bad condition. Al-Amriki did not understand why he and Miguel were riding in the back of a slow-moving donkey cart. He asked the cart driver, and the man pointed toward a bright clear sky without saying another word.

Miguel leaned over to Doyle. "Drones," he said, which was plain enough to Amriki, but it seemed somewhat paranoid to think the CIA flying overhead targeted every vehicle in the province. Doyle presumed a Hellfire missile would be at least as effective on a donkey cart as it would on a pickup truck, so he did not see the point in this level of subterfuge.

They were not targeted and ninety minutes later they found themselves approaching a small hamlet on the banks of Wadi Bana, a wide gulch just south of a mountain range that rose from the brown earth like the arthritic spine of a starving cow. The cart pulled into the small rustic village and then stopped. They were asked to climb out and then an al Qaeda commander in the Arabian Peninsula recognized by al-Amriki and Nayef appeared in a darkened doorway, and he beckoned the men to join him under a thatch awning.

"*A salaam aleikum,*" said the man.

"*Wa aleikum a salaam,*" replied the new arrivals.

"Welcome to your new home, brothers."

Al-Amriki looked around him in the village. Goats and children ambled in the road, old men and women in burkas milled about.

"Where is the base?" Al-Amriki asked.

"*This* is the base," the commander said. "The American drones fly overhead, and they see this as just a small village on the banks of the wadi. But, my brothers, it is much more than this. Look carefully."

Daoud did as instructed, and soon he saw. Between the rustic stone buildings, motorcycles were hidden under brown tarps. The building's roofs were similarly covered with brown canvas, creating tentlike firing positions on the roofs from which armed men peered down, covering the roads with their weapons and scanning the skies with binoculars.

A long barn just ahead next to a corral filled with barnyard animals was missing one of its walls. Across a stretch of dirt and sand what appeared to be a nondescript building stood, but al-Amriki realized that it was a solid baked-brick structure, in front of which were stacked row upon row of tractor tires painted brown. In front of the tires was a long line of what al-Amriki recognized to be wooden target stands.

He knew now he was looking at a firing range; men could fire from under the cover of the barn and not be seen from the air.

As he walked with Miguel and the AQ commander, he was shown obstacle courses disguised in the twists and turns of a small market, a bomb-making factory in a pair of simple buildings with a covered walkway between them, a garrison that held forty armed men and their gear that was actually more than a dozen one-room homes with adjoining portals in the walls, and an underground armory built into a hillside and reinforced with sandbags, cement, and rebar.

The American AQ operative had been to secret bases here in Yemen, as well as in Pakistan, Somalia, Eritrea, and Lebanon. But he had never seen anyplace like the one in which he now stood.

Al-Amriki looked out across the complex. "It looks just like a normal village."

"It does, and to the drones in the sky, that is exactly what it is. We have a mosque, fifty-four individual homes, a market, a madrassa. Even livestock and children and women. From the air it appears as if the roads in our complex are connected to the roads of Al Hisn, but in actuality they are not. We have checkpoints to prevent anyone from venturing anywhere near here other than those who are allowed entrance."

"And what about security in the base?"

"Twenty armed sentries at any one time. We have them on the roofs, as well as on the hillsides on all points of the compass, but they carry radios instead of rifles. The drones have strong eyes. We have heavy machine gun emplacements, as well."

"And where will my men be billeted?" asked al-Amriki.

"In the clinic on the far edge of the village, closest to the wadi. You and your men will be protected by both Allah and the Red Crescent on the roof."

"And our training?"

"Will take place in the larger structures, as well as down in the wadi in the narrow cuts of earth that will block out a clear view from above."

"I am very impressed. You have thought of everything."

The older man nodded without emotion. "The reach and strength of the Americans has only made us more powerful, brother. We have lost many Shahid along the way, but those of us who have survived the Americans for ten years are mightier than we would have been without this challenge."

The twelve operatives who would join al-Amriki and Miguel on their mission trickled in over the course of the next day. In ones and twos they came into the village in mule carts, each time thinking they were just stopping here for a moment before heading to some walled military complex farther up in the hills to the north. Quickly they were escorted into the small white clinic building, where they met al-Amriki and Miguel, the two men who would lead them on an operation that they knew nothing about.

On his second night in the village, al-Amriki assembled all of his hand-picked operatives in the largest room in the clinic. They sat on cots or stood along the walls illuminated by candlelight, the few small windows in the structure covered with canvas. In the village around them, sentries were told to keep a watchful eye over the new students.

David Doyle, aka Daoud al-Amriki, addressed his operatives while standing at the front wall. "Men. You are brave to join this mission. You have been promised that you will meet danger and death along the way, and still you have agreed to come with us. But danger and death will lead you to paradise, where you will be rewarded for your proud sacrifice.

"Paradise, my brothers, is in your future. Now your training begins. Our target is the West, so as soon as this meeting is concluded, we will begin living as Westerners. We will shave our beards, we will dress in Western clothing, eat Western food, tell Western jokes. We will each be given a new identity and documents to support this new identity. We will have e-mail addresses, phone numbers, and other things so that our legends will stand up to all but the most directed scrutiny."

It was clear by the reactions in the room, even under the dim lighting, that the order to shave their beards and act like infidels was an unpleasant surprise.

"Blaspheme?" asked one man, a twenty-five-year-old muscular Pakistani with a long angular nose.

"Regrettably, yes. But we will be forgiven our transgressions in paradise, I swear it."

"What is our mission?" asked a twenty-two-year-old UK citizen with Saudi heritage.

Doyle did not want to tell them any more, but he knew these men were devout soldiers of Allah, and they were clearly pained by news of this transformation that they were about to undertake. He could not jeopardize their devotion to his mission, so he decided to give them a taste of the operation to come.

"I will not tell you everything yet. You will not learn the full scope of the operation until you prove that you are capable of contributing to its success. But I will tell you that our destination and our target is the United States, and our goal is a body blow to the West. We will kill thousands, we will disrupt their ability to make business and to make war, and we will bring them to their knees. Inshallah, we will tear down the American government and see that it is replaced by a government that weakens all of their so-called democratic institutions."

"How?" someone asked.

Al-Amriki smiled. "We will do this by becoming wolves in sheep's clothing, and then entering the center of the flock."

The operatives smiled in the flickering candlelight, their hearts strengthened by their new leader's words.

"Now . . . my brothers . . . my wolves. Go change into your sheep's clothing. Read the papers you will be handed that show you your new identities. Learn every last bit of it. Memorize it. Turn into the person you will pretend to be.

"Each and every one of you speaks English. Use your English, beginning now." Daoud al-Amriki, David Wade Doyle, switched effortlessly into his mother tongue to finish. "I want only English spoken between the fourteen of us.

"Soon Miguel and I will interview you, one at a time. You will have adopted the legend you have been handed, and I want to believe this legend. When you pass this test you will be given more information, and then you will be tested on this. There will be much work in the coming days, but remember, every day we are here will be another day closer to our jihad."

Al-Amriki was pleased with the reactions on the men's faces. These were all educated young men, many had themselves led al Qaeda operations. These were not mindless gunmen who would do as they were told, running into the enemy's cannon fire if ordered to do so. These were not fools in a Waziristan market, ready to pick up an AK and charge an Abrams tank because some *malik* with a smooth tongue spouted off a few verses of the Koran. No, each and every one of these twelve men had served and served well for years; they had fought on the front lines and they had penetrated deep into enemy territory. There was not a man here who had risked less than David Doyle himself to prove his fidelity to the cause.

Four of them were Pakistanis who'd grown up with the language and had gone to school in the United Kingdom, two more were Turks who learned English to study in the UK. Two were Iraqis who'd learned the language and then served in and around American troops for years as translators. And three of the men, just like Doyle's assistant commander Miguel, had studied in universities in the United States and spoke fair to good English. These three men were from Oman, Yemen, and Morocco.

Al-Amriki and Miguel had developed a curriculum for their time here in the Wadi Bana camp. Each of the twelve operatives-in-training would have to pass a course to prove that they could blend into American society. In addition to the changes to their hair, clothing had been purchased online from various sources by support personnel of this mission. University T-shirts, blue jeans, American-style tennis shoes, and baseball caps would be worn at all times inside the buildings, though outdoors they would wear local dress to hide their mission from the drones.

Each one of the operatives would live and breathe his legend here in the camp. This tiny speck of flatland at the edge of the wadi in southern Yemen would become, at first light tomorrow morning, a virtual college town.

Daoud al-Amriki had failed before, for reasons he still did not understand.

But he had thought of everything this time.

He would not fail again.

FOURTEEN

The flight from Fort Bragg to Cairo took all night. The CIA Gulfstream raced over the north Atlantic, landed to refuel at Ramstein Air Base in Germany, and then climbed back into the dark skies to continue on toward Egypt.

Other than a couple hours of shut-eye, for the duration of the trip the AFO cell led by Major Kolt Raynor worked in the dim cabin of the Gulfstream. The team pored over laptops loaded with FalconView, a DOD mapping software that gave them a bird's-eye view of the AO, much like a higher-resolution Google Maps, though, unlike Google Maps, it also provided them with powerful mapping and analytical tools that helped them "see" the area before going there in person. They created their own maps of choke points and bottlenecks near the important locations, like the safe house and target areas relayed to JSOC by the CIA personnel already on the ground in Cairo.

They also studied the material given to them before departure by the intel folks at Bragg. This electronic folder contained schematics of the safe houses in and around Cairo, as well as the logistical assets available to them—cars, vans, boats, motorcycles—and the stores of equipment such as guns, ammo, food, water, and batteries cached at each location. Kolt and his three subordinates looked over the size and layout of each safe house and noted where they would park cars and stow their own gear. They even discussed escape routes and rally points in the case of an assault on their hide.

Kolt and Slapshot were very much accustomed to this work; both men had taken part in numerous AFO cells in their careers in a wide variety of locations. Digger was new to this sort of operation, other than the previous week's lightning-fast, in-and-out op in Tripoli, but he did have an impressive résumé of combat and counterterror ops under his belt, many of which had been extremely dicey.

Hawk had done one brief stint of AFO cell duty herself the previous year in Libya. She had been involved with Operation Red Baron—covert work with the CIA to locate Gaddafi in Tripoli. She had been on the ground in his hometown of Sirte at a joint safe house when the deposed leader made a run for it. She tried to go along to the ambush site with CIA assets in order to ID Gaddafi, but the agency men there with her would not allow it, as adding a female to that chaos seemed like an incredibly bad idea. It was not because she couldn't handle what she would see, it was, instead, because the lack of law and order likely would have affected the rebels, keeping them from acting like gentlemen during the flurry of celebration after Muammar's capture and killing.

Kolt had learned this and more about Hawk first thing that morning, when he dropped in on the shrink's office at the compound and asked for a look at Sergeant Bird's file. As the officer in charge of the AFO cell, it was well within his purview to dig into every detail of the men—or in this case woman—he would be taking with him on the upcoming operation.

He'd learned, in his hour or so thumbing through her records, that Cindy Bird was the only girl in the family, with five brothers. Dad, an Army man, had coached her brothers in Little League sports, football, basketball, and baseball. Cindy had two soft hands and could dribble the basketball with either hand at an early age. Football was out, so she stood on the sidelines throughout high school in a short skirt atop sleek fast-running legs, pom-poms, and an often-fake smile as she tried to motivate the Friday night crowd.

But as a kid, baseball had been her favorite sport. She played for her dad, on the field right next to her brothers at times, and could throw the ball from deep center to home plate without hitting the cutoff. The boys always stole the glory spots in the infield, so she took to the outfield, with an uncanny ability to detect how far and where the ball was going as soon as it came off the bat. She circled the grass in her spikes like a bird of prey, and rarely did she let a ball drop.

One day her dad told her she was more of a "Hawk" than just any "Bird" after she robbed a dangerous hitter of a walk-off home run, and the nickname stuck.

Living with five brothers, three of whom wrestled in a youth program and another who studied tae kwon do, as well as an Army father, she learned how to handle herself at a young age. She rolled around the backyard or living room with the men in the house as they tried to practice submission moves on her or each other constantly after school.

Her dad had introduced all the kids to handguns at an early age to protect them and ensure they understood how to use the two home-defense pistols stored in the house. Cindy was a natural shooter, something her dad said likely explained how she was able to track those fly balls so easily. She outshot her brothers, which was all it took for them to elect to ride bikes or play a game of pickup football on the weekends as opposed to going to the range with their dad and sister.

Despite her cheerleading days and a stint on the freshman homecoming court, Cindy Bird wasn't much into dressing up. She was the type of girl who would wear an old pair of jeans and a T-shirt every day if she could. She was always topped with a ball cap over a ponytail, and most of the boys in town were more interested in the looser girls in cleavage tees and tanks and high cutoff jeans, so she garnered little attention.

In 2003, in the middle of her senior year of high school, her father died in Iraq. The Army told her mother that he went quickly, but word around the unofficial wives' channel was he suffered badly until he bled out during a heated firefight in Fallujah.

Her dad's death changed everything in the life of Cindy Bird.

Cindy went on to college, studying to become an environmental engineer. She struggled through all four years, demotivated by the loss of her father and the nagging emptiness inside her. Her mother remarried quickly, which bothered Cindy. She tried to make the best of it for her mom's sake and sucked it up and, despite this hardship, she managed to graduate with a respectable B average.

Somehow the career path she had chosen no longer seemed desirable to her. She had taken her dad's death very hard, and recalled the camaraderie and passion he had experienced in the Army. Her older brothers had told her their dad had been in some Special Forces unit, but she could not picture her gentle father as the "snake-eater" type. Still, it did strike her as odd that she rarely saw him in uniform and he always seemed to sport long hair and a thick mustache most of the year. She also realized she did not see him much after 9/11, but she was too busy with her girlfriends, high school gossip, and memory-making, and not all that bummed that Dad wasn't around to quiz her on her whereabouts when she came in late on Saturday nights.

Cindy had no idea that her father, Michael Leland Bird, had been the only Delta Force squadron commander ever lost in battle. His code name was "MLB"—a play on his actual initials, but more tied to his love for baseball. His men called him "Major League Ballplayer."

In 2008, shortly after graduating from college, Cindy enlisted in the Army. The recruiters tried to talk her into going straight to Officer Candidate School, since she had a four-year degree. But she remembered her father had been enlisted before he became an officer—a "Mustang," they called it—and he had always said his time in the trenches as a soldier made him a better officer and leader.

Cindy Bird became a "74D," a chemical, biological, radiological, and nuclear (CBRN) specialist, and she was stationed in Fort Riley, Kansas, though she spent a full year deployed to Iraq.

In early 2010, Sergeant Cindy Bird received a phone call at battalion headquarters from a man claiming to be a recruiter for a special unit. She hadn't ever heard of such a thing. He asked her if she had received the recruiting letter in the mail earlier in the week. She had, but had only read through it quickly and discarded it as junk mail. The recruiter was very professional and took a few minutes to recite Cindy's qualifications back to her, almost as if he were checking to see if it was the correct Cindy Bird. Born in northern Virginia, lived for nine years in Fayetteville, North Carolina, attended North Carolina State, five brothers, etc. The recruiter never mentioned her father. It seemed a little odd to Cindy that the recruiter's last comment was, "We'd be honored if you assessed for our organization."

Cindy received PCS (permanent change of station) orders to Fort Bragg and reassignment to the 43rd Personnel Support Battalion. She had done well so far as a 74D, taking her job very seriously. But it was starting to bore her, so the phone call from the mysterious recruiter intrigued her. Besides, she had seen pretty much everything Fort Riley, Kansas, had to offer.

Cindy Bird was one of a dozen women brought together to assess for a new compartmented subunit within Delta. Not to become female operators but rather to simply help out when a woman's touch was needed. The program had been Colonel Webber's idea. As a young captain in Delta, he had written a classified thesis on the benefits of women in the covert world. His paper argued that a woman can get away with murder compared to a man, and even though his proposal followed closely on the heels of 9/11, few in the National Security Council at the time were willing to break one of the unwritten rules of warfare—no women in combat. Ironically, one of Webber's visionary superiors in Delta back then, Mike Leland Bird, thought the idea was brilliant.

After more than ten years of war in Afghanistan and Iraq, a sea change in attitude occurred at the highest levels. Colonel Webber dusted off his paper and it quickly hit the President's nightstand. Green-lighted by POTUS, Webber sent out his recruiters to find the best females available to assess in a pilot program. After thirty days of whirlwind assessment, which took the candidates from San Diego, to Chicago, to Dallas, to Denver, and ultimately to Washington, D.C., to test their mettle, only Bird made it as far as the commander's board. Cindy "Hawk" Bird was a test case. The odds were stacked against her in an elite all-male organization. She was put in training cell on a probationary basis.

Webber told her the job was hers to lose.

Cindy "Hawk" bird was officially welcomed into the Unit in 2011. She finished her six-month training as Raynor was laid up in Walter Reed healing from his secret mission in Pakistan.

Now, with a year in Delta Force, she was the only female in the training cell.

During the long flight to Cairo, Raynor and his AFO cell spent time going over their cover credentials for the operation to come. They would need to know their legends like the backs of their hands, so they took turns quizzing each other throughout the flight.

Kolt and Cindy were Frank and Carrie Tomlinson, a well-to-do Canadian couple on their honeymoon in Egypt, their sights set on seeing the Great Pyramid. They had brought clothes that looked like something a Western couple might pick out to wear to the Middle East, and they had wedding rings and guidebooks, and they'd even brought along cell phones loaded with names and numbers for contacts back in Canada.

Digger and Slapshot held passports and documentation backing up their legends as Mike Terry and Dean Kirkland, two freelance journalists in town looking to chronicle daily life in the city after the departure of Hosni Mubarak the year before. The new government was a complete mess and riots in the streets were commonplace, so it was no great stretch to imagine the pair as intrepid freelancers looking for a story.

The audiovisual equipment "Mike and Dean" would be lugging through the city in support of Curtis's operation would look like perfectly natural accessories for reporters, and they both carried business cards inscribed with real, if hastily created, Web pages that showed photography and bylined articles by both men. Their backstop was shallow, but as long as they weren't rolled up by the wrong people and stayed in their circle under questioning, they would be fine.

The Gulfstream landed in Cairo just before 0500 hours, and then pulled to a painted box on the tarmac. A pair of black Range Rovers rolled up alongside the plane. The CIA flight crew lowered the stairs and Kolt, Slapshot, and Cindy deplaned, each carrying two big rucksacks of gear. Digger wheeled a large black Pelican hard case behind him.

Myron Curtis and four other men piled out of the two vehicles. Curtis marched quickly up to the AFO cell and then, with a look of surprise on his face, he just said, "Racer."

He did not seem overly pleased.

"Curtis," replied Kolt in a flat greeting.

It was clear the thirty-five-year-old African-American had not expected the same group of operators who'd worked with him in Libya a week earlier to be the ones assigned to his operation in Egypt. He just shook his head slowly. "I'd always heard Delta was a small outfit, but I had no idea there were only three of you motherfuckers." Curtis must have seen Cindy, but he did not put together that she was part of the team.

Raynor smiled a fake smile. "I guess you just got lucky twice. You've met Digger."

"Not formally." Curtis shook Digger's hand perfunctorily, clearly annoyed that he would be working with this particular outfit on this mission.

"And the big guy is Slapshot."

The two men nodded at one another, but Curtis was already reaching his hand out to Cindy now. His face lightened.

"And this is Hawk," said Raynor.

"You are . . . you are in Delta?"

Cindy nodded, pushing windblown hair out of her eyes with one hand while accepting Curtis's hand with the other.

"A pleasure, Miss Hawk."

In a professional tone she said, "It's just Hawk, sir."

Curtis smiled. "And it's just Myron, Hawk."

Raynor groaned to himself.

Curtis introduced Denton and Buckley to the team, two bearded men Kolt took immediately as CIA paramilitary operations goons from their Special Activities Division, though they looked to Kolt like they'd just come out of Central Casting. Then he presented Murphy and Wychowski, two men Kolt took for case officers. They also looked like clichés to Kolt. They were rounder and less road-hardened than their SAD counterparts, less tan, and better dressed. Next to the paramilitary guys they looked like blow-dried network weathermen.

With the introductions out of the way, everyone climbed into the two Range Rovers, and they left the grounds of the airport.

FIFTEEN

The safe house chosen by Curtis and his team for this operation was on the eastern side of Maadi on Ahmed Kamel Street, just a few kilometers from their target location. It was in a two-story office building that had an empty ground floor and a second-floor office suite rented out by the CIA and staffed to look like a small travel agency. A back door behind the counter led to additional office space, a warren of small rooms, each converted into living quarters and meeting spaces. There were five rooms in all, each with a door to a narrow hallway. A single bathroom was at one end of the hall and a well-stocked kitchen sat at the other.

As soon as Kolt climbed out of the SUV in front of the safe house, he began evaluating the security situation his team would face here. Immediately he found problems. He stood in front of the building, looked past the small, gated lot where they had parked their Land Rovers, and he saw two high-rise buildings under construction. Dozens of open and dark cement floors looked back down on their position. To a man like Raynor, each and every nook and cranny was a perfect place to position watchers with binoculars or spotting scopes or even a sniper team.

Kolt was also quick to notice the antenna farm on the roof of his safe house, a dead giveaway for trained enemy operators.

Kolt went inside, took the stairs to the travel agency, and then passed through the rear door to the safe house. Here he checked the rooms and hallways. He noticed cases of Stella beer, the local brew, stacked waist-high in a corner of the kitchen. The windows of the two rooms had a view over a back alleyway, and he saw thirty-round AK magazines and binoculars in the windowsills, and Kalashnikovs propped against the walls under them.

It was a typical CIA setup, and Kolt did not like it one bit.

He'd learned in the intel report on the flight over that by day the small travel agency in front of this clandestine dormitory kept up appearances that they booked vacations for whoever came through the door. In actuality no one did come through the door, as the travel agency was not exactly easy to find, nor was it particularly energetic in its marketing. The staff who worked in the office were a small team of well-paid and vetted Egyptian support personnel from outside of the city who were never more than a step or two away from HK MP5 submachine guns hidden under their desks.

At night when the travel agency was closed, a SAD officer covered the lower floor of the building and a second officer manned the top of the stairs, just outside the door of the travel agency. Both of these men carried HK MP7s under their jackets and HK pistols on their hips inside their waistbands. As far as Kolt was concerned, these two men would be able to ward off some limited threats to the building, but this really wasn't a lot of firepower in the case of a real attack. Kolt figured their presence provided more of a chance for compromise than they were worth, as anyone looking through the ground-floor windows would see white Westerners inside, and that news was sure to spread across the neighborhood like wildfire.

After Raynor finished his eval of the site, Curtis called everyone together. They congregated in one of the small rooms to begin their initial briefing.

Myron Curtis took the floor, but Kolt first expressed his reservations about the safe house's setup in his typical direct language. "Your cover for status here sucks."

Curtis cocked his head in surprise. "We sweep for bugs daily and there is code access on the front door. We've got armed security day and night. That's all we need. Look, Mr. Operator, you aren't in Afghanistan. If we had an A-team on the roof armed to the teeth we would get noticed by the wrong crowd."

"I get that, Curtis," Kolt said. "But you're missing my point. Because we *aren't* in Afghanistan, your three antennas on the roof need to be camouflaged. Try local TV antennas; yours scream 'American spy.'"

DALTON FURY

Kolt continued his dressing-down. "Your Alamo kits in the two window-sills are visible from the high-rises to the north, and the two gorillas pacing the stairs and halls with the lights on all night will attract more attention than we need."

Curtis shrugged. "What you see is what you get, Racer. We've had NOC personnel, nonofficial cover operators, working out of this location since before the revolution with no issues."

Kolt did not like it, but this safe house was a pretty average CIA setup, considering Egypt was an ally of the U.S. If they had been somewhere where the locals were considered hostile to the United States, they might be less obvious. He understood he couldn't just order up whatever type of coverage on the safe house that he wanted, much as he would like to. Kolt was a guest, not the MFIC.

Raynor very much preferred to be the motherfucker in charge.

And, by the looks of it, so did Myron Curtis.

Kolt and his team then pulled up chairs around a small desk with a laptop on it, and Curtis sat at the desk, his stool turned around to face the others. Murphy and Wychowski stood in back by the door, and the two SAD men wandered off to their room to crash after a full night of guard duty.

"All right, people," Curtis began. "I've brought you here to Cairo because we suspect a location here of being a transit hub for a portion of Libya's missing SAMs. We have tracked former officers of the Haiat amn al Jama-hiriya, that's the Jamahiriya Security Organization, to one particular address, and I think it is possible they are using this location to store and repackage the munitions before sending them on to their clients."

Hawk took a few notes, Digger and Slapshot just sat in their chairs with their arms crossed.

"We know the ex-Libyan security officers have caches across Libya and Egypt where they are storing as many as seven hundred SA-24 systems, all with viable missiles. With the possible exception of a missing nuke, these loose MANPADs on the world's stage represent the worst imaginable proliferation issue the United States could possibly face."

Curtis pulled up a digital image on his laptop. It was a head shot, apparently taken for official Libyan credentials, of a middle-aged dark-haired man with thick jowls and a heavy brow. "This is Aref Saleh, Gaddafi's former JSO director here in Cairo. We believe he is at the center of the smuggling operation. In fact, we are referring to the enterprise now as the Aref Saleh Organization."

Kolt leaned forward to get a closer look. In the briefs he'd received on the Libyan MANPAD situation, there were only mentions of involvement by ex–Gaddafi intelligence operatives. That Curtis had a name and a face meant to Kolt that either this intel was brand-new or Myron Curtis had not bothered to forward it back to Langley for distribution.

Curtis pulled a new image up on his laptop now. Kolt and his Advance Force Operations cell all stood up from their chairs and leaned in. They found themselves looking at a satellite photo of a leafy neighborhood spotted with tall buildings. Raynor recognized from a few reference points that the neighborhood represented on the screen was their current location here in Maadi.

"This is us," Curtis said, tapping on a building with the tip of his pen. "Now, moving over here to the west, along the eastern bank of the Nile, you see these buildings here." He scrolled the satellite image over and zoomed in on a long, low building separated from a square, taller structure, both surrounded by a parking lot. By zooming in again Curtis revealed a fence around the complex, protecting the two buildings on three sides from the large Kornish al Nile and two smaller residential streets. On the fourth side of the building was the Nile River itself. "This complex here is the warehouse and offices of Maadi Land and Sea Freight, Ltd. We are calling the warehouse here at the northern part of the property location Rhine, and the three-story office building here at the south location Stone. According to intel reports, Maadi Land and Sea is run by ex-members of the Jamahiriya Security Organization. Saleh's men. We think it is very possible the missing SA-24s brokered by Saleh are brought via boat up the Nile or truck from the west from those hidden caches in Libya and Egypt, stored in the warehouse at Maadi Land and Sea, before then flying out of Cairo or, when moved in larger quantities, traveling overland to seaports."

Hawk asked, "Why don't you just let the Egyptian police know? Have them roll up the Libyans."

"Reasonable question. Number one, we don't know how good our intel is. It's from a reliable source, but it's nowhere near one hundred percent. Number two, if this *is* Saleh's shipping point to his customers, there's a good bet they are paying off local officials to look the other way. We can't risk compromising our operation by just sending up a flare to the Egyptians. If Saleh and his boys scatter, we'll just have to start all over. Our best bet is to find out who is involved, confirm the existence of the SAMs here in Cairo, and shut this transfer point down."

Hawk nodded.

"We've been here three days already. Our surveillance in that time has revealed the same group of men coming and going from the building. We haven't gotten eyes on Saleh, so we don't think this is his actual base of operations, but the men we have seen might well be JSO operatives. We've managed to ID a second location these guys own in the neighborhood, a private residence nearby on Ibrahim Khedr Street, and I have secured an apartment near there for the purposes of static surveillance, but so far it looks like a dry hole, as we haven't seen any activity there.

"We *have* tailed Saleh's men to malls, we've seen them go to restaurants and venture into and out of other public places. We assume they aren't just kicking back and enjoying themselves. We think they are on the job."

Kolt said, "Clandestine meetings. Brush passes. Dead drops."

Curtis nodded. "That's what we figure. But I don't have the assets here to tail all these subjects. Every one of my team has been close enough to the subjects that, if we just go plop down in a restaurant next to them or follow them into a shoe store, we are going to get ID'd in seconds."

Slapshot said, "If you feel that way, your recce assets are likely burned already. Why the need to get so close?"

"We're looking for Saleh himself, or any known personality from JSO, and they've made themselves hard to ID. JSO did an outstanding job of destroying personnel records in the dying days of the Gaddafi regime, so, other than a few top guys of the ex–spy agency, we are all but flying blind on IDing their men."

Kolt asked, "Where did your intel come from?"

"About the JSO's involvement in the SAM smuggling? Much of it came from Tripwire."

Kolt was surprised. The last time he saw Dr. Renny Marris he did not seem like he was about to start sharing his secrets with the Central Intelligence Agency.

And something else did not make sense to Kolt. As Curtis began speaking again, Raynor interrupted. "If Saleh and his people knew Tripwire was on to them, which they obviously did if they targeted him for termination, why did they not close up shop here and relocate when he escaped?"

"They identified Tripwire through his source in their organization. But this source did not know about Maadi Land and Sea."

"How do you know this?"

"The same crew that went after Tripwire, the crew you and your colleagues . . ."—he struggled to find the word—"disabled . . . also killed an officer in Libya's new army. A general named Younis."

"So?"

"So this General Younis was Tripwire's informant. Younis originally worked with the JSO, helping them take possession of caches of SA-24s. He used army assets to move shipments of missiles to port in Benghazi, and he was paid handsomely for it. But someone on his staff tipped off Marris, and Marris approached Younis. Fearing he was going to take the fall for every plane that got blown out of the sky for the next two decades, the general told Marris what he knew about the Aref Saleh Organization."

"And then?"

Curtis shrugged. "We speculate Marris told his superiors at the UN, and then someone at the UN informed on Younis to Saleh's organization." Curtis shrugged. "It happens. The UN isn't exactly known for keeping secrets. Anyway, the general was pulled out of his Toyota Land Cruiser in front of his dentist's office, tortured for two days in a disused air raid shelter in Tripoli, and then sliced and diced to bits in a threshing machine at a farm twelve klicks south of the city."

"Jesus," Hawk mumbled.

"Libya has excellent torturers. We feel certain the general told them about his contact with Marris, and that's why Marris was targeted. But even though the general knew some of the players in Saleh's group, and even though he knew the locations of some of the caches in Libya, he did not know anything about Saleh's operation here in Cairo, so the Libyans knew he could not have told the UN about that. They figured they were safe."

Kolt said, "Curtis, I am getting the impression that the only reason you had us roll Tripwire out of Libya was so that you could rifle through his papers."

Myron Curtis smiled a sly smile. "What can I say, Racer? On that day in

Tripoli, there were a lot of winners. It was my call to save Tripwire, and my call to scoop up the files in his office before the JSO got there to take a look at everything the UN knew about them. Still, we didn't hit a home run that day. If you and your boys hadn't shot up the Old City like it was Dodge City, we might have had time to raid the caches near Tripoli and take some of the missiles off the market."

Kolt sighed. If Curtis had been on the scene in the Old City when those long blades came out, Kolt had no doubt in his mind that the CIA man would have been screaming for his best buddies in Delta Force to waste everything that moved in a three-block radius.

But Raynor let it go. He was going to have to work with this guy, after all. "So, if you didn't learn about Maadi Land and Sea from Tripwire, what led you here?"

Curtis strummed his fingers on the desk. It seemed to Raynor like the CIA man preferred to hold his cards close to his chest. But after a moment he said, "I'm no Renny Marris, but I was in Libya trying to track down weapons myself. I found out about a shipment of SAMs in the port in Benghazi that sailed to Cairo, but I missed it here by a couple of days. The size of the shipment led me to believe they would travel by container ship, and not aircraft, to the end purchaser, so I went up to Port Said and found a bill of lading that matched my intel on the travel of the SAMs. But again, I missed the cargo itself. Langley is looking for the boat even as we speak.

"The bill of lading said the cargo was Egyptian machine parts heading to Slovenia, but I knew the cargo came from Libya, not Egypt, and everybody knows that Libya only exports two things to Europe, oil and immigrants. Anyway, I followed the paper trail and found out the company that paid for the shipment was a shell with a post box here in Maadi. I came here, watched a guy picking up some mail at the box, and trailed him back to his car. He came back to Maadi Land and Sea, so I looked into that name in our database. That company had been tied to Libyan external security by Langley in the past. After a couple of days of surveillance around Land and Sea we began to suspect this to be a transfer point for some of the weapons. The property has shady guys coming and going, a lot of warehouse space, and a lot of security."

Raynor then asked, "How big a shipment of missiles are on that boat that left Port Said?"

"Big. Very big. From the size of it we think there could be as many as fifty."

"*Fifty* SAMs! And you let it get away?"

Curtis shrugged. "Sue me, dude. I had two guys and next to no assets. There are teams, just like mine, spread all over the globe trying to prevent the proliferation of Libyan munitions, and I got closer than they did. Don't worry. We'll find the SAMs, hopefully while still on open water, and we'll get the SAMs off the market."

Raynor sighed. He'd been saddled with missions that were poorly supported, and he'd bitched and moaned about that in his past. He was not going to judge Curtis for less-than-stellar results when dealing with the same bureaucratic BS that Kolt had complained about for years. Curtis had come to Cairo short on personnel and short on resources, and he managed not only to find the Libyans but to track one of their shipments to the port and ID the vessel.

"Okay. How can we help you?" Kolt asked.

"I have two case officers with me, plus the two SAD paramilitary guys for security. That's not enough warm bodies to accomplish what I need to accomplish. The local station is up to their eyeballs in the political cluster fuck that is Egypt these days; they only had a couple of young case officers they are loaning me for surveillance from time to time. So I ordered up you guys to bolster the investigation."

"What are you doing now surveillance-wise?"

"Right now we have covert video of the entrance to Maadi Land and Sea. The camera is mounted in a tree across the street in a private garden. We monitor the feed here, and it shows us what comes and what goes. I rotate one of my men out into the little parks in the neighborhood, and we use the feed at the front gate so we can tail subjects leaving when possible. What we need from you is as much intel on the physical property of Maadi Land and Sea as we can get. Maadi is a community with a lot of expats, so a husband-and-wife couple walking the streets aren't going to stick out the way my guys do. A couple of tourists wandering the sights of Cairo will melt into the surroundings easily. Even if the Libyans get lucky and you are seen more than once, assuming it's in public places, it won't be a big deal."

"What about us?" asked Digger.

Kolt answered before Curtis. He didn't need the CIA man command-and-controlling his operators' every move. "Surveillance and support and on-call close-target recce."

"Sounds like a blast," said Digger.

Curtis did not like Kolt answering for him. "That plus hopefully we'll get the okay to have you guys do your ninja routine and infiltrate the warehouse, that's objective Rhine, and get a look at what's inside."

Raynor shook his head. "Let's not get ahead of ourselves here. One step at a time."

Curtis stood, indicating the end of the briefing. "Of course, Racer. Of course."

SIXTEEN

The next morning Kolt and Cindy drove their rented Daewoo four-door sedan on the Kornish al Nile, the Nile river road that passed by the wall in front
of Maadi Land and Sea Freight, Ltd. The two Americans could see the top
two floors of the office building behind the wall, but the warehouse itself was
out of view. They did get a glimpse of a gatehouse at the front of the building
with a uniformed man behind the glass.

"This isn't good enough," Kolt said. "We're going to have to go foxtrot."

Hawk agreed. "On foot it is."

They found a place to park a few blocks south of their target, and activated the covert 360-degree cameras that provided live feed into their cell
phones. If anyone tampered with their car, they'd know about it.

They then strolled back up the Kornish al Nile, turning into a small green
space on the far side of the busy street from Maadi Land and Sea. They spent a
few minutes staring into the shops through the large windows. They weren't
eyeballing the sale items, but studying the opposite side of the street through
the reflection of the window glass. Focusing directly on the target area would
easily be picked up by a trained team of countersurveillance, and although
they would be able to assess the skills of the enemy over time, for right now
they needed to give their adversary the benefit of the doubt.

They took a few pictures of each other here, trying to get the front gate
in the frame, though there was not much they could tell from street level.

As they strolled hand in hand out of the park, Hawk noticed an eight-story apartment building to the east of them. "I bet the balconies on those higher floors would get us what we need."

Raynor nodded, and they headed that way.

Real estate agent Sharif Farouk whipped his seven-year old Mercedes coupe off Kornish al Nile and into the lot of one of the nine condominium buildings in Maadi that bore a sign in the lobby with his cell phone number. Anytime he had vacancies available in a building he always posted a sign, even if passersby in the market for a $3,000-a-month unfurnished condo were few and far between.

The woman who'd called him less than an hour before was Canadian; she explained that she and her husband were here on their honeymoon and had been so taken with the lushness and tranquillity of Maadi that they were considering leasing a home here.

Sharif was all too happy to cancel a lunch meeting and shoot across the city to meet with the Canadians.

He found the polite young woman attractive and her rudimentary command of his language equally adorable. Her dark hair, slight Asian eyes, and bright smile had him captivated from the moment he shook her hand in the foyer of the building, a forgettable eight-story structure with electrical issues and twenty-five percent vacancy stats that were seriously cutting into Farouk's monthly commission.

Though he found the wife lovely, Sharif's impression of the husband was that he was cold and impersonal. Other than a limp handshake, Frank Tomlinson just stared out the window of the lobby and then stood quietly with his hands in his pockets as his wife asked Sharif about the neighborhood during the ride up the elevator. Sharif got the impression that Mrs. Carrie Tomlinson was in the driver's seat as far as wanting a second home in Egypt.

Mr. Tomlinson looked like he'd rather be anywhere else on earth.

Sharif switched to English for the tour of the penthouse unit with a view of the river. He regularly showed homes to expatriates in Maadi, so, along with English, he was required to know French and a smattering of German for his job. As they went from room to room, Mr. Frank Tomlinson wandered off to the long balcony and stood outside, staring morosely at the Nile. Seeing this as an opportunity to both deflect the wife from noticing the water damage in the inlaid parquet flooring in the dining room and simultaneously winning over the husband who, Sharif assumed, held the purse strings in the relation-ship, he followed Frank outside and beckoned Carrie to follow.

"You see? It is a very beautiful view. The sunsets here are amazing."

Mrs. Tomlinson gushed and hugged her husband, and Mr. Tomlinson did little more than snort.

Soon, Sharif and Carrie were back inside looking over the master bed-room and the master bath and the two small bedrooms that Sharif angrily noted smelled like mold had crept in from the neighboring unit, where a leak in the water line had gone unnoticed by maintenance for weeks because the condo was unoccupied.

Soon they were back in the lobby downstairs, Carrie had brochures of the property and the business card of the real estate agent, and then Sharif Farouk walked the beautiful and chatty Carrie and the brooding Frank back out into the hot summer sun, having no illusions that he would ever hear from them again.

"Wow, Frank," Hawk said as they headed back to their car. "I guess I married a jackass."

Kolt just smiled as he walked, aware that the agent might still be watch-ing them. Softly he said, "Well, Hawk, I've never had another operator squeeze my butt cheek in the middle of an op before."

"No?"

"Not that I recall, anyway."

"Yeah, maybe that was a little much. I was trying to lighten the mood, but I think it made Sharif a little uncomfortable."

Kolt let her off easy. "No worries, the less I said, the more he would focus on you. I needed some privacy."

"How did you do?" she asked.

Kolt did not answer till they got into the car. As he pulled back onto the Kornish al Nile he replied, "Video and stills of the entire complex, tag num-bers on most of the vehicles in the parking lot, shots of the sentries and their gear, and close-ups on a couple of upper-management-looking types who were standing on the veranda smoking."

"Awesome," she said, "but I thought we were going to emplace the vehi-cle observation point to get that footage."

Kolt hesitated before saying, "Is that what you learned in San Diego?

Half the work here is instinct, Hawk. Not high-tech. By-the-book streetcraft isn't always the answer."

Cindy nodded.

"You did pretty good, though. You were in character. You sensed what I needed from you and you kept that guy occupied. Nice work."

"Thanks, Frank," she said with a grin. "A piece of cake. Pretty much exactly the type of ops we went through in training."

"They don't all go down that easily," Kolt warned her.

Cindy said, "Racer, when I kissed you, I put my hand on that scar on your scalp. Mind if I ask how you got that?"

"Not at all. Mind if I don't answer?" he said without looking at her.

Kolt thought back to the previous year and the hit on the Sandcastle near Peshawar. He'd wear a tattered scar on the back of his head for the rest of his days to help him remember that day. His hair covered it, but when he got his annual military cut for his Department of the Army official photo it would show for a couple of weeks.

"Guess not. It's just that we may need to cook up a story in case I am asked about it. I *am* your wife, after all."

Racer said, "You hit me with a frying pan."

"Screw you," she said with a laugh. "Do I look like the type who would hit someone with a frying pan?"

"More like a double-tap to the forehead."

"Thanks . . . I think."

Slapshot and Digger perspired under the hot midday sun as they sailed up the Nile on a small wooden sailboat called a *felucca*. They both wore white gallabiyas, traditional dress for Egyptian males consisting of a long, loose-fitting shirt.

They needed to get a good look at the complex from the riverside. Digger knew how to sail from childhood vacations in Lake Michigan, and Slapshot was school-trained on everything from a paddleboat up to a thirty-seven-foot 370 Justice, the largest Boston Whaler on the market, having spent several weeks in Key West with the rest of his team years ago in preparation for a secret hostage rescue in South America that was ultimately shelved when one of the American hostages was killed and the administration lost its nerve.

The two men, both in traditional clothing and skillfully sailing by in an old wooden boat, would attract much less scrutiny than a couple of obvious Westerners in a motorboat skulking just offshore.

As they headed past the three-story office building on the southern portion of the walled complex, Digger manned the sails while Slapshot used a mini HD camera hidden in a basket to get images of the rooftop, the grounds between the water and the walls, and the parking lot in between. They counted three guards, men in jeans and short-sleeved shirts carrying MISRs, the local brand of the Russian AK-47. One man at the fence on the riverbank held binoculars in his hand. He brought the optics up to his eyes and quickly focused on the sailboat passing by.

Digger and Slapshot just looked away, and the camera kept recording.

They noticed four trailers parked next to one another in the rear parking lot on the north side of the warehouse. They suspected this meant the loading bay was right there but out of view. They also noticed the fence came down into the waterline of the river, and a fifteen-meter pier jutted out into the river.

But there was no indication of what was inside the facility itself, either in the warehouse or the office building.

They opted against a second pass, instead continuing upriver to a landing point a few hundred yards away. Here they called Murphy, one of the CIA case officers, who came and picked them up.

SEVENTEEN

By early evening, all four members of the JSOC team had returned to the safe house. Curtis and his two men had spent a mostly fruitless day attempting mobile surveillance of some men who had spent a few hours outside of the walls of Maadi Land and Sea.

Kolt brought his team into the conference room and Curtis came in a moment later. Kolt said, "We took a look at Rhine and Stone from both sides, and there is definitely something up. Whatever is going on inside those buildings is a hell of a lot more important than some shipping concern. With all these security goons on the outside of the buildings, it's guaranteed they've got guns on the inside, too. They are most definitely protecting something or someone."

"Something like Libyan arms," Curtis said confidently.

"Maybe," allowed Kolt. "But it's too early to know that for sure." He could see Curtis's mind was already made up about what was going on inside the walls of the shipping company. He would not let himself fall into group-think without further analysis of the target. It was a dangerous mistake that he was determined to avoid.

Raynor said, "I scrolled through our recce photos of both the black side and the white side. We have fair-quality shots of two older cats, could be the MFICs, at objective Stone. You need to take a look."

If Curtis was impressed, he hid it well. "Any chance you guys were burned by getting too close?"

"No chance."

Curtis looked to Digger and Slapshot now. The two men shook their heads. Neither of them was particularly thrilled about getting second-guessed by CIA.

Myron Curtis next turned the lights down in the room and sat in front of the laptop attached to the large monitor on the desk. He took the SD cards handed to him by Racer, containing the snaps they'd taken while casing Rhine/Stone. He slipped one of them into a port on the side of the laptop. In seconds he was scrolling through photos from Racer's camera, shots taken in the tiny park across the street from Maadi Land and Sea, and then from a higher angle. These were the pictures taken from the balcony of the condominium tower.

The camera's magnification was impressive, as was Racer's ability to keep the instrument steady. One after another, photos scrolled across the screen showing the warehouse, the office building, the parking lot, and several vehicles parked there. By using the zoom feature on the software, Curtis was able to zero in on individual license plates on a row of luxury cars by Stone—the office building—and get good close looks at men on the roof and partial shots of men on the balcony on the south side of the property.

He then put in the SD card from Digger's camera. He clicked through the images taken at water level from the bow of the felucca.

He moved quickly through the images, he said he would scan them intently later, but he stopped suddenly on a pair of men standing together on the balcony, the same two Raynor had captured from the other side.

Curtis zoomed in tight on the men. One of them was turned away slightly from the Nile River, as he had been in the dozen other shots that included him. But the other man, fortyish and nice-looking, with slick black hair and narrow eyeglasses, seemed to be looking straight into the camera's lens. "Well, I'll be damned," Myron Curtis said.

"You know him?" asked Slapshot.

"Not socially, no. But I know who he is. This is Ashraf Afifi. He was, until the fall of the Gaddafi regime, deputy director of JSO operations in North Africa. He had a reputation as something of a playboy in Tripoli. They say he actually nailed Gaddafi's wife."

Hawk remarked, "The colonel's wife? Sounds like he has brass balls, too."

"Holy shit," agreed Digger. "So the bravery of our targets is not in question."

Raynor smiled at the comments.

Curtis kept talking. "Everybody thought he was dead, killed in the last year's uprising. In the three days we've had the remote cam up at Rhine, he has, most definitely, *not* come out of that property, unless he was in one of the vehicles with tinted windows. They have a Mercedes and a BMW with smoked glass."

Curtis thought for a moment, happy that they had finally ID'd a former JSO employee here in Cairo, but confused by this revelation. "We assumed only lower-level men, foot soldiers and logisticians, would be working here in Maadi, as our link analysis indicates that this is just a storage and shipping facility for all their shit. We'll have to double back on the intel to see what this means."

Slapshot leaned forward with his arms crossed and said, "Curtis, I'm probably the dumbest guy in this room, but to me it means maybe your intel about this just being a shipping warehouse is wrong."

Kolt spit some tobacco juice into an empty water bottle. It was a good point. Despite his aw-shucks manner, Slapshot was nobody's fool.

Curtis bristled. "Anything is possible, but like I said, we have yet to ID Saleh, and we know he is a hands-on son of a bitch. He is a wanted man in Libya, and we know he has been in Libya, but the prospect of him moving into and out of the country at will seems pretty implausible to us."

Kolt said, "The other guy in the picture. No chance that's Saleh, is there?"

Curtis looked again, briefly, and said, "Can't see his face. We don't have any reference shots of the back of his head."

Raynor stared down Curtis while he thought, *Just asking, smartass.*

They spent the next few minutes going over the rest of the photos. Finally Curtis said, "Next on the agenda. While you guys . . ."—he looked at Hawk with a wink—"and girls . . . were outside Maadi Land and Sea, we spent the day tailing a couple of the other personalities. Just after noon three possible Saleh Organization men went by objective Chalice, a second JSO property a kilometer from Rhine/Stone, on Ibrahim Khedr Street. Two men went inside while a third stayed behind the wheel of the C-Class Mercedes that delivered everyone, and he parked out front. They were only there about twenty minutes, the driver outside was attentive enough, and our resources were thin, so we could not get any closer."

Raynor cocked his head. "No need to get closer in that situation. Any idea what they were doing there?"

Curtis all but waved away Raynor's comment. "Nothing important. It's just an unoccupied two-story brick home, not far at all from Maadi Land and Sea. It's also owned by the same front group, so we checked it out, but it's a dry hole."

"How do you know that? Did you go inside?"

"No, but it's empty."

"But you just said some dudes went there today."

"They just dropped by. Did not stay long."

"What, for cookies and milk? Guys like that don't just drop by for no reason."

"Relax Racer, it's nothing."

Kolt pressed him. "Why don't you have audio out there? Bugging Maadi Land and Sea is a bitch, but if the Ibrahim Khedr house is just a house with no security, can't your guys get in there and tech it up with remote surveillance?"

"Trust me, Raynor. It's not that easy. In Libya, these guys swept for bugs each and every day at all their properties. There is no reason to assume the same would not hold true here."

"Aren't your mics better than their sweepers?"

Curtis shrugged. "We had a pretty good understanding of the technology Libyan intelligence used in electronic surveillance countermeasures, so I'd like to think we have the ability to put in something they couldn't detect. But we can't say for sure these ex–Libyan intel guys aren't getting their tech equipment from better manufacturers than they had access to in the old days. For all we know they might have detection means we can't fool. We cannot allow this op to be compromised by Saleh's goons turning up a bug."

Kolt shook his head. "That doesn't make sense, Curtis. If they had that high-speed shit in there, then they wouldn't need all the overt goons with guns."

Curtis snapped, "We aren't taking that chance. They find a single bug and the entire operation will be compromised. We are too close to risk that."

"Look, what about something stand-off, like laser mics? We brought a couple. We can use the apartment across from Chalice and try it out."

Curtis shook his head. "We don't use those. They suck."

Kolt shrugged. "They are better than nothing, which is what you are getting right now. The laser microphones pick up sounds inside a location by detecting vibrations on window glass that could then be converted to synthesized speech. Or some techno shit like that."

"We have a remote cam on Chalice in the apartment, just like at Rhine/Stone. If somebody shows up there for any length of time we'll head over there and check it out. But in three days there has been exactly twenty minutes of action at that location. We are going to focus on Maadi Land and Sea. *That's* where the action is."

Kolt was not going to let this go. "What if those men went by today to inventory the munitions they have stored there? Look, we've got the kit and the personnel," Kolt said. "Stupid not to give it a shot."

"Racer," the CIA man insisted, "you and your team are going to focus on Maadi Land and Sea."

Curtis was clearly getting annoyed at all the second-guessing from the team he assumed was there just to do his bidding. But Kolt had done the circle jerk with agency folks before and was not one to back down from a confrontation, especially when it involved a mission as important as this. "Why?"

Curtis looked at Raynor for a long time. Then he shrugged. "When we learned about this house, our first assumption was that perhaps Saleh, or maybe one of his top lieutenants, was using it as a residence. That's why we set up surveillance. But I don't think Saleh is here in Cairo, and if he is, he's probably in Stone. We'll continue to do spot checks on objective Chalice, but we're not nugging that place with twenty-four-hour surveillance, because no one is living there, and we know they aren't storing missiles there."

"How the hell do you know that?"

Now Curtis shouted back at Raynor. "They have an eight-thousand-square-foot warehouse two klicks away that is protected with walls, cams, and guns! Why the fuck would they stick the SA-24s in an unoccupied building in a residential neighborhood?"

It was obvious to Raynor that Curtis did not like having his assumptions questioned. It was SOP in Delta that, if an assaulter or sniper thought the officer's assumptions were shit, he sure better speak up about it. Myron Curtis obviously didn't have thick skin. He was in charge. It was everyone else's job to shut the hell up and take orders.

Kolt said, "Okay, Curtis. I understand. You pushed a deployment order through because you thought ordering up some JSOC operators would give you your own little squad of dumb asses who would come over and follow your orders without question. Am I right?"

Curtis glared at Raynor, and softly he said, "And then, in a cruel twist of fate, I get you."

The meeting broke up a moment later, and Kolt's team began filing back to the two rooms in the back of the safe house reserved for them. But Kolt lagged behind in the meeting room to talk to Curtis. He wanted to toss the guy out the second-floor window, but he fought the urge, and decided to try and right this ship before it completely capsized.

"Curtis, there is too much at stake here for you and me to get into a pissing match. It's not about your authority or my authority. It's about getting those damn missiles off the market."

"Don't patronize me, Racer. There is nobody who wants that more than me."

"I believe you. But you aren't going to get it done like this. Look, I've got no problem with cutting out a level or two of the bullshit layers of bureaucracy in order to complete my mission, and it looks to me you roll the same way."

The younger man just nodded.

"But you are walking on a razor's edge with this op. Your security is shit, you aren't sharing crucial intel with Langley, and it looks to me like you had us come over here to hang around until we somehow get the go-ahead to hit the warehouse. It doesn't work like that, Curtis. We have to get some real indicators, some actionable intel that says there are munitions at objective Rhine, before the JSOC commanding general will even consider us going in there."

Curtis said, "I know that. I know we can't get into Rhine without proof that the Libyans have munitions. But I'll get the proof, and when I do, I need you and your team ready to hit it. You need to concentrate on knowing that property like the back of your hand."

Kolt sighed. "If we get the hit, we'll execute the hit. But we aren't hitting shit without authority from my boss at Bragg. In the meantime, let us help you. We're not just shooters. We probably have more experience tailing targets than your guys."

"These Libyans are good. I saw what happened in Tripoli with Saleh's men there, I can't let an overzealous operator—"

"'Overzealous'? That's a big word, Curtis. You learn that in case officer school?"

Curtis paused a long time. Finally he said, "I know all about you, Major Kolt Raynor. I know what happened in Pakistan in '09."

Raynor's jaw tightened. He leaned closer to Curtis and spoke slowly now. "You don't know shit, and you need to think very carefully about the next fucking word that comes out of your mouth."

Curtis nodded with a cruel smile. "I had friends at Langley look into you. You are a piece of work, Raynor. You have a track record of leaving body bags wherever you go. I just might need a gunslinger or two on this mission, if it comes down to it, so I'm not going to send you home. But for now you are a loose cannon and a danger to this op. You want to conduct surveillance on Chalice? Fine, go ahead. That will keep you out of my hair. Me and my team will find intel linking Saleh or the munitions to Maadi Land and Sea, and then I'll send you—correction—*JSOC* will send you in to blow some shit up and to kill some sons of bitches. You might want to focus on getting ready for that."

Raynor turned and left the room without another word.

When Kolt returned to the room he was sharing with Cindy, he sat down on his bunk to pull off his boots.

She faced him, sitting on her own little bunk and firing up her secure laptop. "What's the deal with you two guys?"

"No deal. We met a couple weeks ago."

"And something bad happened?"

"Only to the bad guys. I guess Curtis doesn't see it that way."

"Am I going to have to be the referee between you two?" she asked jokingly.

Kolt did not like the inference. He was pissed about Curtis, pissed about the potential for this operation to fail, and he did not like being teased by the pilot program girl from training. He was in charge here, and she was getting a bit too relaxed with their banter. "No, Hawk. You will not."

To her credit, Cindy immediately realized she'd gone too far teasing about a serious situation. "Sorry, boss. I was out of line."

"Not a problem. Stay focused on the mission, Carrie."

"Yes, sir. I mean . . . right, Frank."

The Delta personnel spent the next day doing more recce of Rhine and Stone and setting up the laser mics in the apartment across the street from Chalice. Much of their surveillance work was tedious and much of it was repetitive, but Kolt knew that they would need much more intel on the locations. One had a tendency to make dangerous assumptions with a single look at a target. It would take multiple recons to understand the daily patterns inside the walls of Maadi Land and Sea.

So Digger and Slapshot sailed by in a felucca for a second time at mid-morning and a third time in late afternoon. Raynor and Hawk did their honeymoon routine again. They hired an English-speaking tour guide to take them around the neighborhoods of Cairo so they could take pictures with their high-end camera equipment. At their direction he drove them over the Ring Road Bridge spanning the Nile, and then south on the Cairo-Aswan road. Here, in a wide spot of greenery along the river, they stopped and ate a picnic lunch while their guide ate his lunch back at the car. Kolt took his camera, attached a 400mm lens, and took more than one hundred pictures of the target location across a hundred yards of blue water.

As they added to their target folder, the target was beginning to look more and more difficult to take down. Armed men, motion lights, fences, open ground to cover.

The AFO cell recognized that the hit, if it came, was going to be a real bitch.

EIGHTEEN

In the late afternoon two flights arrived at Cairo International Airport within minutes of one another: an Egypt Air flight from Beirut and an Olympic Air flight from Athens. From among the hundreds of passengers disembarking from the two aircraft, seven men converged just past customs control. They ranged in age from thirty-three to forty-four, they all wore fine tailored suits, and their luggage was minimal. They all climbed into a single minibus at curbside pickup. From there they were driven through traffic-clogged streets to the Hotel Sofitel Cairo Maadi Towers and Casino.

The seven men took keys to four suites, all on the ninth floor. From their balconies they had views of the pyramids in the distance, but they instead pulled the draperies closed in their rooms and slipped NE PAS DÉRANGER cards in their key locks.

They took no calls and held no meetings that evening.

They were not businessmen; they were Quds Force, Army of the Guardians of the Islamic Revolution.

They were spies of the Iranian Revolutionary Guard.

One of the seven was the deputy director of the organization, and the other six men were his security force. Each and every one of them had military special operations experience. They had worked missions in Iraq and Afghanistan and Lebanon and Syria, and they had come to Egypt, for want of a better explanation, so their boss could do some shopping.

The leader of their group was here to meet with Aref Saleh, formerly of the employ of Colonel Muammar Gaddafi, to purchase weapons, but for now they would wait here in their hotel until given further instructions by the shadowy arms merchant.

The Russian-made Igla-S missiles that he had for sale were worth the inconvenience.

Iran had shoulder-fire SAMs galore. Igla-S's as well as others. But the Iranians weren't looking to increase their own armaments stores. Instead, they were gift-shopping. The SAMs they would acquire here in Egypt could be traced back to Libya, not Iran, so they created real plausible deniability.

The mandate of Quds Force was, in part, to build underground Islamic organizations throughout the world.

They were here to secure the purchase of twenty Igla-S systems to deliver them to Hezbollah in Lebanon. The Lebanese themselves could have arranged this, but the Iranians were working as cutouts as well as benefactors to Hezbollah, so they were here instead of the Lebanese.

In the al Qaeda base disguised as a village near Wadi Bana in southern Yemen, a soft knock at a wooden door echoed in a baked brick room. David Doyle, clean-shaven and with his brown hair cut short and spiked, stood looking out a tiny bare window, his back to the door. A simple aluminum table sat in the middle of the room, and around it were three chairs.

Miguel sat at one of the chairs with a notepad and a pen in front of him. At the sound of the knock he called out in excellent English, "Come in."

David Doyle joined his second-in-command at the table now.

The door opened and a dark-complexioned man with short hair and trim sideburns entered slowly. He wore baggy cargo shorts with sandals, and a sweatshirt that made him perspire in the still air.

"Good morning," he said to the men on the other side of the table. His voice was tentative.

"Good morning," said David Doyle. "Please, have a seat. This won't take long."

The man sat in an aluminum chair that scraped the brick flooring as he scooted forward. Thin beads of sweat streamed from his temples; he wiped his face with the forearm of his white sweatshirt. The garment bore the orange silhouette of the head of a longhorn steer and the word TEXAS above it.

"How's it going?" asked Miguel.

"I'm fine, thank you. How are you?" the man asked, his accent thick but his English easily understood.

Miguel did not answer. Instead, Doyle took over the questioning. "What is your name?"

"Jaza Hussein, but everybody calls me Jerry."

"Where are you from?"

"I'm originally from Pakistan, but now—"

"What do you do, Jerry?"

Jerry smiled, pinched the front of his UT sweatshirt. "I'm working on my master's in public policy at UT in Austin."

"Are you, now?"

"Yes." He hesitated, then said, "Yep." His second try sounded more natural, less stilted and formal.

"That's cool, Jerry. I hear that's a nice town."

Jerry nodded quickly, spoke quickly. His nerves showed. "Great town. Got a little flat right off of Guadelupe Street."

"A *what* off of Guadelupe?"

"An . . . an apartment?"

"*I'm* asking *you*."

"An apartment. Yes. In my country we call them flats, but here in the States we—"

"I understand," said Doyle.

Miguel looked down at the papers in his hand. "I had a friend who went to UT. I visited him once."

Jerry's eyes widened slightly, but he nodded and smiled. "Cool."

Miguel then looked up from his papers. "I forgot, what does everyone at UT Austin call that stretch of Guadelupe there by the campus?"

Jerry's eyes narrowed in thought. They looked off to the side slightly. Then back to his interviewers. "Yes. That is referred to as . . . 'the drag.'"

Doyle said, "You don't sound too sure about that, Jimmy."

The interviewee smiled nervously. "Jerry. It's Jerry. And, yes, I *am* certain. It is called the drag."

"What was the name of the guy who shot all those people from the clock tower?"

Now there was no hesitation. Jerry was emboldened. "Whitman. A total motherfucking asshole." He said it as if it were all part of the man's name.

Doyle and Miguel looked the man over for a moment more. Finally Doyle said, "Well done, my friend."

The operative across from them smiled, his chest filled with pride. But Doyle then said, "But it needs to be a lot better."

Jerry said, "It will be, David. I promise."

"Good."

"Very well. Leave us, and send in the next student."

Jerry stood with a nod and a slight bow and left the room. As he shut the door Miguel said, "Not bad for one day of study. That guy is Pakistani. Never been to the U.S. Never been to the UK."

Doyle was a tougher instructor. He said, "He's got the language, and he's coming along on the facts quickly enough, but he has to get rid of the nerves. The objective isn't to make these men into Americans, it is to make them into foreign students *in* America. I don't give a damn if a cheeseburger makes him puke, I just want him to act comfortable when questioned."

"It has only been one day, David. He will be fine. They will *all* be fine."

Doyle just grunted. His entire operation depended on his operators' ability to blend into the fabric of the United States.

There was a fresh knock at the door.

"Come in," said Miguel.

It went on like this for the entire morning. These were just the initial interviews, the easy ones. Over the next few days Doyle and Miguel planned to put each of the men through several more, each different from and more difficult than the last. The two leaders would play the role of busybodies sitting next to the men on a bus, then they would be curious and suspicious citizens, racially profiling the men and challenging them on what they were doing near an airport.

Finally, Doyle would pose as a police officer, and he would pull the men over in their car, one at a time, and question them against their documents.

Each of the twelve operatives had memorized stacks of material relating to their legends, and Doyle would make certain they knew every last line of it. He would also make sure they could recite it back while relaxed, while exhausted, while scared, and while angry.

This, and their ability to press a trigger that launched a missile that would kill hundreds of infidels, and to repeat this action over and over and over, would determine their ability to carry out the mission.

NINETEEN

Slapshot and Digger had spent the hours since dawn swapping thirty-minute shifts watching location Chalice from their hide—ten feet back from the ground-floor bedroom window of the flat across the street and fifty yards west of the Saleh property.

Slapshot was on duty now, seated in the chair in the darkened room, his head covered in a dark brown sheet and his arms resting on the table in front of him on either side of the Schmidt of Bender variable power spotter's scope resting there. He made no sudden movements that could be seen by anyone either on the street or in any windows in the neighborhood.

To the right of the scope on the table was the laser microphone. To use the device, he would have to open the bedroom window ten feet in front of him a crack by sliding out of his position, and then low-crawling across the floor to the window, and then opening the window slowly and carefully before retracing his movements back to his chair.

Neither he nor Digger had detected any countersurveillance in the area, but they weren't taking any chances. Their SOP for this type of surveillance determined their actions.

The CIA men, however, were not as careful.

Twice the day before, Murphy and Wychowski dropped in on the hide; both times they entered from the back of the building, not on Ibrahim Khedr, and they kept the lights off throughout the one-bedroom apartment. Still, Digger and Slapshot admonished the men for making too much noise, noise that could not have been heard from the street, but possibly could have been detected from adjoining flats in the building.

Both times the CIA men rolled their eyes at the over-the-top OPSEC protocols of the high-strung Hardy Boys, and both times Digger and Slapshot stuck to their guns and told the Agency men to either get the hell out or shut the fuck up.

At ten o'clock on the nose, two black SUVs that Slapshot recognized as belonging to the Aref Saleh Organization pulled up to the curb in front of objective Chalice. In total eight men climbed out of the trucks, and the drivers pulled back out into the light traffic and disappeared up the road, back in the direction of Maadi Land and Sea.

The eight men walked straight up the steps to the entrance of the home and went inside.

"Heads up." Slapshot penciled the time into the log after calling out softly to Digger, who was lounging on the bed in the dark behind him. "Looks like something's about to go down."

"Fuckin' finally," Digger said, then he rolled slowly off the bed and headed over to the table. He sat behind the laser microphone, woke the laptop attached to it back up with a swipe of his finger across the track pad, and slipped the attached headphones over his ears.

While he was doing all this, Slapshot low-crawled to the window and cracked it open. It took him a minute to make it back to the desk, and by the time he returned, Digger was receiving broken transmissions from inside the house across the street.

"Anything?" asked Slapshot.

"Yeah. Garbled Arabic. I'm recording."

"I'll push it to Racer. Maybe Curtis or one of his guys can translate the audio feed."

Ten minutes after the Aref Saleh Organization men arrived at the home on Ibrahim Khedr, all was silent in the house. Whatever was going on with the eight men inside, it did not involve talking in any one of the front rooms where Digger could beat his laser's focal point off the window and back to his receiver. So far, the laser mike was worthless.

Just before ten-thirty, however, Slaphshot moved his eye out of the spotter's scope so that he could take a sip of lukewarm tea from a mug. The entire act was slow and deliberate and covered by the brown sheet over him. Before he nestled his eye back in the rubber eye cup of the scope he looked out the window and saw a beige Range Rover pulling up a block east of Chalice in front of a luxury apartment building. This in itself was not unusual, cars came and went on this residential street with mind-numbing regularity, but when no one climbed out of the Range Rover after half a minute Slapshot directed his spotter scope on the vehicle and took a closer look.

Inside, two men sat in the front seats, their eyes directed up the street to the west.

Seconds after this a second vehicle, this one a two-door Honda Civic, pulled to the curb to the west of Chalice, within fifty feet of Slapshot's position. He did not need his Schmidt of Bender scope to look into this vehicle. He could clearly see two men sitting there, looking down the street to the east.

"Who are these guys?" he asked softly. "Check this plate number."

Digger pulled off his headphones—he wasn't receiving anything in them anyway—and followed Slapshot's eyes to the car just below them outside. Slapshot then directed him to the other car, across the street and on their right. Slowly and purposefully Digger lifted a set of binoculars off the table and looked through them.

After a few seconds he remarked. "They are new."

"You're right. They don't look like Saleh's men."

"No, they don't."

Digger ran his finger down the list of license plate numbers Curtis's team had tied to the Aref Saleh Organization. No hit. "New kids on the block, bro."

Just then the doors opened on both of the new vehicles on the street. All four men climbed out, and then shut the doors behind them quietly. They fanned out, one man on each sidewalk, both on the north side and the south side of the street. Two men to the east of Chalice, two men to the west of Chalice. They began walking around the area, looking from the sidewalk into the windows of the buildings around them, taking their time.

Slapshot spoke even more softly than before. "These guys are thorough. Better than Saleh's men."

"Damn right," Digger said, using his binoculars to get an extremely close look at one of the men directly in front of his overwatch. "And these are gorillas. Not intelligence desk jockeys, like Saleh's guys."

Slapshot agreed. "All of them are printing concealed weapons. Security goons. Doubt any of them have ever sat behind a desk in their lives."

"I'll call Racer and let him know it's getting hot out here. These guys obviously are working an advance. Something is going down."

The men in the street all had black curly hair and short, trim, beards. All four of them were in their twenties or thirties, and their loose-fitting suits had bulges at the hips and under the arms, where pistols and submachine guns were, no doubt, stored for quick retrieval.

Slapshot asked, "Wonder who the client is?"

"Unless these guys are lost, or just window-shopping, we'll know soon."

After three minutes of scanning by the four men in the street, another Land Rover SUV pulled up in front of objective Chalice. Slapshot looked through his glass and saw a big driver and a big passenger in the front. A single passenger sat in the backseat. There was a conversation that lasted several seconds among them all. The Americans in overwatch wondered if one of the security men already on the street was communicating with the three in the SUV via radio earpieces, but Slapshot did not move his scope to check.

Finally the front passenger got out of the SUV and opened the back door. As the man climbed out, two of the four security men who had been watching the street collapsed on their protectee and followed him up the stairs, their hands inside their jackets, their heads on a swivel.

The man at the center of this scrum looked a couple years older than the others, and he was clearly in charge. But he was not a personality Slapshot recognized.

Digger had already lifted the camera with the 400mm zoom lens. He snapped dozens of rapid digital shots of the men, focusing on the man in charge, still careful to not make any sudden movements that could be detected from the street.

In seconds the men disappeared inside the two-story home and Digger went back to the laser mic.

Slapshot went off glass and focused his naked eye closely on the man right in front of their position.

The man had been leaning against the thin trunk of a tree that grew alongside the road, and his eyes had been scanning the street to the west. But while Slapshot monitored him, the security man pushed off the tree and stood erect, his eyes alert and his body language on guard.

Slaphsot said, "Shit. Something has got the sentry on this side spooked."

Digger said, "I'm getting faint chatter. They must be in the foyer of the house. I don't have line of sight on the window there. Need them to move into another room."

The black BMW tied to the Aref Saleh Organization pulled up the street from that direction and turned into the garage of Chalice.

"You getting pictures?" asked Slapshot.

"Gonna try," replied Digger. "All depends on whether or not they leave that garage door open for a few seconds."

But Slapshot was not listening. Instead, he watched the sentry in front of him lift a radio from his pocket and put it to his mouth.

The man's eyes were still fixed on something to the west. Slapshot slowly leaned forward, looking out the window to the left.

He couldn't see anything without getting up, and he was *not* going to run the risk of compromise by doing that.

Suddenly he had an idea about what was going on. He sat back down quickly. "No. Please no." He grabbed the phone and pushed the button to connect him with Curtis.

Curtis answered on the first ring. "Yeah."

"Are you or one of your guys bumpered on Ibrahim Khedr Street right now?"

"Negative. I'm at the safe house, and they are both here with me."

"What about the Cairo Station guys that are helping out?"

"They are tailing a black BMW that left Maadi Land and Sea ten minutes ago."

Slapshot sighed. "You got comms with them?"

"Sure, what's up?"

"We've got a black Beemer at Chalice, and one of the detail guys for another force just spiked on something suspicious down the street. What's the plate number of the one they are on?"

"Shit. I don't know. *What* detail guys at Chalice? *What* other force?"

"There is a full protective detail here in the street. More dialed in than the Saleh Organization yo-yos. Can you do us a huge favor and get your boys to scram? And while you are at it, please tell them if they crash the party of our target again while we are in an active OP that we will shoot them ourselves." He followed this with, "Sir."

"They aren't *my* boys, soldier. They belong to Cairo Station."

"They belong to Langley. Like you. Sir."

Curtis hesitated before saying, "I'll call them off." He hung up the phone.

Slapshot looked back to the security man in the street. He was on his radio now, no doubt collapsing the rest of his team.

The American in the dark ten feet back from the window whispered hopeful instructions to the man: "No, dude, it's cool. Just some dumb-ass white guys out for a Sunday drive. Your boss is fine, no need to be security guy of the month, just let him go on with the meeting."

Digger was now monitoring the security man to the east. "Looks like they are bugging out."

"Son of a bitch," said Slapshot as he watched the scene. The front door of Chalice opened, and the two men there shouldered up with the VIP exiting the door. Together they all walked purposefully but calmly to their SUV parked on the curb. The security men weren't hauling ass, they clearly were not convinced they had been compromised, but apparently the leader of this VIP's protection detail thought the anomaly with the fair-skinned men showing up behind their host at just this moment was worthy of calling off the meeting.

Within seconds the SUV and the two cars that had arrived with it had all driven off to the west.

A minute later the BMW from the Saleh Organization's motor pool rolled back out of the garage and drove off to the east.

"Did you get anything at all?" Slapshot asked.

"Background noise. They must have been hugging each other in an entry hall the whole time or something."

"That thing is a piece of shit," Slapshot said. He then picked up the phone and called Curtis back. He said, "They are gone."

"Dammit. Any idea who this other entity was?"

"We have pictures," he answered. "But no joy on the audio capture. Would have been nice to hear that meeting."

Twenty minutes later Raynor was on the phone to Curtis. He and Cindy had spent the morning on a Nile day cruise that took them, along with a big group of gawking Westerners, twice past Maadi Land and Sea. Frank and Carrie Tomlinson were completely invisible as they took photographs of the security lighting in the back of Rhine, as well as pictures of the gate to the pier that jutted out from the back of the property.

They were now back in their car, with Hawk doing the driving. Raynor said to Curtis, "I hear your boys were burned at Chalice."

Curtis replied angrily, "You don't know that for sure."

"My guys say so. So . . . yeah, I *do* know it for sure."

"They aren't my boys. I told you, I took what I could get from Cairo Station. They tailed a car with tinted windows. They tried a bit too hard to get a look at the driver of the car when he pulled into the garage, and that spooked this other entity at the scene. Shit happens, Racer."

"That's sloppy as hell, Curtis, and you know it. Spy School 101."

Curtis countered quickly, "Look, we aren't even sure there was any meeting happening."

Kolt said, "C'mon, man, a full PSD, advance on the location, SUVs, radios, printed concealed weapons, even tinted windows. What about that doesn't scream 'bad guys getting together for a powwow' to you?"

"All I'm saying is we can't be certain. They didn't get any audio."

Kolt took that as a slight on him but he ate it. He had been the one who recommended the laser microphone. "Let's just assume this was a meeting. If they didn't finish, they'll either try for another meeting or skip town. Did the BMW go back to Rhine/Stone after leaving Chalice?"

A pause. Curtis wanted to keep the op compartmented as much as possible. He did not like revealing *anything* about his mission to Raynor. Finally he said, "Yes, it did."

Kolt sighed. "I'm going to ask you one more time to include us on these tails. We can bumper up and swap out more often with four more on surveillance and at least two more vehicles. You need us, Curtis, before this entire thing goes south. We're not just here to kick doors."

A longer pause now. "Okay. Not today, but okay."

"Dammit, dude! You are—"

"Look!" said Curtis. "I don't have anything for you to follow right now. Come back here and I'll send you and your little girlfriend on the next run."

Kolt just disconnected the call.

"I heard that," Hawk said.

"Yeah. Remind me to kick his ass before this is all over."

"You'll have to get in line, boss."

TWENTY

That evening, while Curtis was paying a visit to Cairo Station to let them know about the potentially burned team and beg for some more bodies, preferably some with better tradecraft, Raynor called Webber on the satellite phone. It was 1415 hours back at Bragg.

"Do you know anything about the chief of base out here, this Curtis guy?" Kolt asked.

"I've checked around. The sergeant major says Langley loves him and our CIA liaison says he gets results."

"Really? What results?"

"He's a bit of a cowboy, but he is a hell of a dogged investigator. He's an egghead, though. No military experience."

Kolt wanted to chime in, *No shit,* but he held his tongue.

"Graduated from Cornell. Masters in poly sci. French and Arabic minors."

"Any *real-world* results?" Kolt could not hold his tongue for that.

"He's reined in some SA-24s, and he's taken tons of other munitions off the market. Last spring in Tripoli he shut down a gang of smugglers with two railroad cars full of land mines heading south into Central Africa. Langley was thanked by several governments for the work that this guy and his team accomplished. What's the problem?"

Kolt said, "Well, that's great, but his OPSEC and his PERSEC suck. We're not up against some bandits running a boxcar of toe-poppers into Chad.

These Libyans are well connected and sophisticated. And whoever that was at the meeting today was world-class."

Webber's tone stiffened a little. "Look, We didn't send you over to pull guard duty. I get it if you don't like the layout of his safe house. I will back you if you pull up stakes and grab your own house for you and your team to bunk in. But when it comes to the recce that you were sent there to do, *he's* the one running the op. Chances are, he sees this as his opportunity to get ahead at the Agency, and he sees you potentially getting in his way. So what else is new about those guys? You need to deal with it."

"I understand. But when we—"

Webber interrupted. "You need to work with Myron Curtis and his team. Help him build the target folder for that location. Make it happen. End of story."

"Yes, sir."

Webber hung up and Slapshot came into the commo room. "I heard half of that. I can guess how it went."

Kolt smiled, took a pouch of Redman passed from his teammate. "Webber wants me to be the big boy in the room."

"That sucks," said Slapshot with a chuckle.

"You're telling me. Curtis said he'd roll us into the surveillance plan tomorrow. I'll just hold him to that."

"Me and Dig?"

"Sorry, bro. Back to Chalice."

"That's okay. You think we'll get the hit before we pack up and go home?"

"I don't know. It's too sketchy, still. I wish we had some clue as to who those men were at Chalice today."

"Same here. Curtis didn't recognize them, but he's running the pictures up to Cairo Station."

"Send the pics to the intel shop at the Unit. You never know."

"Done."

Kolt stood and headed for the bedroom. "I've got second watch. Going to catch a couple hours of rack."

"*Hasta mañana*, boss."

Hawk came out of the bathroom of the safe house and stepped back into the room she shared with Racer. Kolt was in his boxers, climbing onto the top bunk. She looked him over. Her eyes focused on his left leg. "I see the bandages on your thigh where you caught the frag. But that other scar is older. Bigger, too. You got shot in the leg?"

Kolt nodded as he flipped onto the mattress. "You sure ask a lot of questions."

"Damn, boss," she said as she noticed a second wound below his knee. "Twice?"

Raynor said, "Twice on the leg. Once on the foot."

"AK?" she asked.

"Is there any other?" he confirmed with another nod.

"Close-range?"

Kolt thought back to the dry streambed in Pakistan where he'd been stitched by the Taliban fighter. He'd been no more than eight or ten feet away. "About as close as we are right now, I imagine," Kolt responded.

And then Cindy responded in a way that set her apart from nearly every other female on planet earth. "That's awesome."

Kolt laughed hard at that. She was the first female in the training cell, and even though the jury was still out around the command on how beneficial the pilot program had been, he could see that she was cut from a different cloth.

"Freak," he said. "Stick around long enough, and you'll get some enemy-administered tattoos of your own."

"I'm not going anywhere. I love this job."

Cindy flipped off the lights, then crawled into her bottom bunk.

Kolt said, "I met your dad. Never served under him, but Webber loved the guy."

Cindy smiled. "Yeah, me, too."

"He's why you joined?"

"Isn't all that in my file?"

Kolt smiled. "What makes you think I read your file?"

She paused before replying. "You have been thorough with every other piece of kit you've taken along on this op. I watched you clean your weapon, triple-check the freqs on all the radios, check the fuel levels in the op cars, change out the fuzzy dice, and everything else."

"Surely you don't think I just consider you another piece of gear."

"No, boss. Just saying that I don't believe for a second you would have taken me if you didn't know everything about me worth knowing first."

Before Kolt could answer, Hawk added, "If I had the same access as you, I'd have read *your* file before coming on this op."

Kolt adjusted his body to where his thigh wound wasn't pressing against the thin mattress. Then he admitted, "I did read your file, yes."

"Well, since *I* haven't read *your* file, can you tell me why *you* joined Delta?"

Kolt thought it over. The psychs had asked him just that, many years ago. But no one in the Unit had asked him since. The guys in the Unit either figured they knew why you were there, or else they didn't give a shit.

Kolt smiled, the expression hidden from Cindy in the dark.

Bunking with a female was different than bunking with a male, for more reasons than Raynor had initially imagined.

He said, "I did it for the college money."

"Yeah, whatever."

"I don't know. I've about forgotten. Serve my country, same as everyone. I also did it to prove to myself that I could." He paused. "Also same as everyone, I guess."

"That's it?" she asked. She didn't seem satisfied with his answer. Since she was a female, Kolt wondered if it was the length of his answer that she didn't like.

He obliged her. "After I enlisted and I went through Ranger School, I kept thinking some RI would grab me by the arm and tell me, *Get your ass out of here. You aren't Ranger material.* But they never did, and I made it. A couple years later, I got pulled aside and was told to jump fences to the officer corps, so I hit the books pretty hard. While I was in school, I kept expecting some professor to pull me aside and say, *Sorry, son. The university is not for you. Why don't you go back to the enlisted ranks?* But that never happened, either, and they handed me a commission of infantry. And then, all the way through tryouts for the Unit, I kept waiting for one of the cadre to pull me aside and say, *Thanks for playing, Captain, but the Rangers are expecting you back Monday morning.* Again, it never happened, and I made it through."

It was quiet in the room for over a minute. "I guess you know I was PNG for a while."

"Yes," she said. He could hear the discomfort in her voice with admitting that she knew.

"Well, for the three years I was out, I blamed myself, yeah, but I also figured everyone who ever thought I was worth a shit was wrong. I found myself blaming them for . . . encouraging me forward. So when I got the chance to come back to the Unit, I would not have done it if it were just about me. But by then . . ." He struggled for the words. He'd never even talked to the psychs like this. "By then I knew that I had to help others. I did my best, and that got me back in. Still, every day I feel like I've got something to prove. I see men all over the compound who've accomplished more, worked harder, faced greater adversity. I am damned lucky to be here, and lucky to serve with them."

"Shit, boss. I don't buy that. You are a legend."

Kolt shrugged. "No, I'm lucky, the legends are dead. I'd prefer to remain just another guy on the team this time around."

"Medals for the dead, right, boss?"

It was a Delta slogan. No one in the Unit gave a damn about a medal. The dead were deserving of honor. Those living were just doing their jobs. Besides, only after shit went bad on target did anyone do anything to earn a medal. Executed as planned, there would be no reason for medals. Even so, Kolt was surprised Hawk even knew of the slogan.

"Medals for the dead."

Cindy changed the subject slightly. "My boyfriend, Troy, went through selection and assessment last year, but he got yanked on Bloody Thursday. Couldn't hack it. Since then he's had a stick up his butt about the Unit. He'd freak if he knew I was a member."

"It's not for everyone," Kolt said, more to be polite than to enter into a new topic of conversation.

"Guess not. He's got the raw materials to be a hell of an assaulter, but he just jacked it in. I don't know why, he doesn't say."

"I can think of about a thousand reasons why someone would jack it in. It's designed so only the most motivated or the most insane make it. The Army psychs weed out the nut jobs before they get that far, and the Delta psychs double-check the Army psychs. It's a pretty good system for making sure the right kind of people make it in. Nothing wrong with your boyfriend for giving it a shot. He is in the ninety-eighth percentile."

"I don't know," she said. Clearly she was bothered by his failure.

Kolt shook his head in disbelief. "Fifth Group isn't badass enough for you? Damn. Maybe you are just impossible to please."

She laughed out of politeness, but Kolt sensed that she was thinking that over.

He asked, "Where does he think you are right now?"

"Temporary duty at Aberdeen to attend the Field Management of Chemical and Biological Casualties course."

"TDY at Aberdeen makes sense. Gotta keep those NBC skills up," Kolt said sarcastically.

"You know what they say about you, Racer?" Cindy asked, turning the subject back to him.

"Something along the lines of 'effort takes no talent,' I would guess."

"You heard that one?"

"I've been hearing it most of my life."

"I think it's a compliment. Besides, I've heard you did some stuff that you couldn't do just by being an eager beaver."

"I've been around long enough to know I earned some of the criticism. I can understand where they are coming from. TJ pulled my ass out of a couple of fires over the years."

"Do you think Lieutenant Colonel Timble will return to operational status?"

"I guarantee he will. And if you hear anybody say that he won't, kick their ass for me."

"Will do."

"Hawk, we need to go to sleep."

"Roger, boss. Another day of honeymoon fun tomorrow."

"You know it."

TWENTY-ONE

Day and night, the training in the village compound near Wadi Bana continued.

Many of the indoor aspects of the training took place during the evenings, when the al Qaeda drone spotters in the hills around the villages were at a disadvantage to the night-vision capabilities of the Predators, Reapers, and Global Hawk UAVs that crisscrossed the skies high above Yemen. Doyle and his men would use the nighttime to sit inside and study maps of the U.S., read tomes of documents about aircraft and airports and timetables, and for each man to learn more specific information for his legend. They also pored over driving laws and customs, and the procedure for mundane tasks like renting hotel rooms, purchasing bus fare, and buying a chicken sandwich at Burger King.

The physical training occurred during the daylight hours, when drones could be spotted, though Doyle still kept his men under some degree of cover that shielded their actions from the skies. The men did PT and worked on hand-to-hand combat in the makeshift gyms, they trained with firearms on the partially covered range, and they practiced with the Igla-S system, using mock-up devices made out of mortar shells and dead car batteries and grip and trigger mechanisms removed from rocket-propelled grenade launchers.

The models looked odd, but they rested on the shoulder and they used modified iron sights made from tin, and the weight, at just over seventeen kilograms, was almost exact. The men had to pull them quickly from the backs of cars and from boxes and even from holes in the ground and then get them on their shoulders and aim them. They had to run with them, climb ladders with them, and even though they did not have an actual SA-24 there in the village, they studied the schematics of the weapon and watched videos on YouTube until late in the night to familiarize themselves with the missile system.

Doyle pushed them relentlessly, and after a few days of this, he selected four men out of the twelve. He told these men that they had earned a special place in the mission, right alongside David himself. Their training during the day would be done away from the other men of the cell, on the far side of the village. Here, Doyle had a twenty-foot-long steel intermodal transport-shipping container brought up from the wharf in Mukalla City on the coast. Without explaining the reasoning behind this, he then had it painted the same color as the sandstone buildings of the village, and placed four feet in the air on bricks. He blocked off the rear half of the container with sandbags, and then stacked wooden ammo crates along one wall of the container, leaving a space eight feet wide, seven feet tall, and ten feet deep.

David brought his four cell members to the front of the crate and opened the steel door. "Our part of this mission, my brothers, will require the most discipline. The hardest part will not be the act of firing the surface-to-air rockets, No, it will be waiting for our moment of jihad. All five of us must spend much time in a place just like this. We will train by sleeping here."

One of the men looked at Doyle. "All of us? Sleeping in this little space?"

"Yes. Our role in the attack will be the most important, but it will also be the most dangerous. Where we are going there will be much security, so we will hide in a space much like this walled-off container. Here we will wait, and I do not know how long. Perhaps just overnight, but perhaps longer. Only our faith will get us through this."

"What are we waiting for?"

Doyle smiled, squeezed the Iraqi's shoulder. He looked directly at the young man but addressed then all. "For the perfect moment. When it is time for our attack, we will leap out of our hiding place, quickly arrange ourselves and our weapons, and all fire simultaneously. We must practice relentlessly to do this quickly, quietly, and perfectly, because we will only have one opportunity."

And with that David and the four confused cell members all crammed into the small space. He pulled the door shut and locked them in. They had to sleep with their knees in their chests, shoulder to shoulder, through the heat of the steel box.

It was miserable, but David promised them all paradise for their efforts.

During the day, while other cell members spent time on other tasks, David and his men trained on quickly opening the container's door, and then leaping to the ground with their rifles around their necks. Once on the ground, they each pulled a launcher from the container, shouldered the heavy device, and aimed it at a point in the sky.

Over and over again he and his men practiced their quick escape from the container and their quick preparation to fire.

At first it took the five of them a minute and a half to accomplish this, much of the time wasted by getting in one another's way trying to slide the missile launchers on the floor of the container and then struggling with getting them on their shoulders. But as they progressed they became more efficient. David ordered the men out of the container two at a time, with the second pair helping the first to shoulder their weapons. Then, while the first pair moved away from the doorway of the container and aimed their tubes, the second pair leapt down, and David helped them both with their Igla-S's. These two men lined up with the first pair as David leapt down the four feet and managed his own preparations. When he was ready he shouldered up to the others and gave the order to fire.

After several hours of repetition of this, the five men had their time down to forty-six seconds, roughly half the time of their initial attempts.

David was pleased with the progress, but he wanted it done faster. He knew something the others did not.

Their target would have, literally, hundreds of security assets around him, and this security would envelop David and his four men almost as soon as they revealed themselves.

Doyle decided he would have to shave at least fifteen seconds more off of the process if his mission was to be certain of success.

Because in order to kill the President of the United States, David knew, every last second would count.

Two days after Myron Curtis told Kolt Raynor that his AFO cell would be able to take part in the mobile surveillance, he finally kept his word. Curtis hung up from a call with Murphy and Wychowski in the commo room, and then leaned into the kitchen, where Racer and Hawk were eating a late lunch of rice and beans.

"Okay, you're up. Shake a leg."

Kolt looked up from his plate. "What's up?"

"The rabbit Mercedes S600 just left Maadi Land and Sea. Murphy and Wychowski are tailing it, but it's heading into the city, and Cairo Station doesn't have anyone to spare. We need another vehicle to help with the coverage."

Raynor and Bird were moving before Curtis finished speaking. They had backpacks loaded in the hallway, with keys and mobile phones resting on top of them. They scooped these items up as they ran out of the safe house.

Hawk got behind the wheel of their two-door Renault and Racer climbed into the passenger seat, and they headed out of the front gate of the parking lot and then northeast into the city. Kolt plugged in the external GPS antenna and waited fifteen seconds for the icon on the laptop screen to come to life against the satellite photo of their area of operations before establishing comms with Murphy to coordinate their movements. Soon Hawk was bumpered a few blocks away when the Mercedes pulled into a parking garage at a shopping mall in Heliopolis.

Murphy notified Racer that he and Wychowski weren't going in.

Kolt said, "You want us to try a foot-follow?"

"Negative, Racer. We don't know how many are in the car. Let's stay safe for now and wait till they head out."

Kolt did not like this, but he also did not want to press his luck on their first run. They repositioned across the street from the CIA team in hopes of gaining the follow when the rabbit vehicle departed.

At six p.m., the Mercedes left the shopping mall and Kolt and Hawk immediately took the lead in the two-car surveillance set. They followed at a safe distance as the black luxury car with the tinted windows headed north. Twice they passed off coverage to Murphy and Wychowski in the beige Renault two-door, but each time they rotated back up after a few minutes, overtook the CIA men, and accepted the lead again.

After a long drive in heavy traffic, Hawk passed the Mercedes two lanes over and took up the surveillance in her visor mirror. The rabbit took a turn to head into Garden City and the CIA team followed as Hawk and Racer took the next turn to catch up by a different route. The Mercedes S passed by the U.S. Embassy, and then they turned onto the Kornish al Nile, the same road as Maadi Land and Sea Freight, Ltd., though they were several miles north of the JSO compound.

The Mercedes pulled into the Kempinski Hotel parking lot, and the CIA Renault kept heading up the Kornish. Murphy phoned Kolt and Hawk to pass the word.

Cindy said, "It's 1830 hours. My guess is they are there for dinner."

"Swing around and park. It's got to be a monster lot. We can monitor the Mercedes while they are inside."

Cindy did as Kolt instructed, pulling the vehicle far from where she saw the Mercedes parking. But by the time she put the vehicle in park, they both saw a man halfway to a side entrance of the hotel.

Kolt leaned forward, squinting. "Is that . . ."

"It's Afifi," Cindy said. "The guy Slapshot got the picture of on the balcony of Stone the other day."

"He's by himself," Kolt remarked.

But Cindy was not listening. Instead, she was a blur of movement on his left. She turned off the ignition, tossed the keys in Kolt's lap, and said, "You're up!"

With no shred of grace or glamour, she then crawled over her seat and into the backseat of the car. She dug around into her backpack for several seconds, then pulled out a small black cocktail dress, a pair of medium heels, and a new packet of panty hose.

"What the hell do you think you're doing?" Kolt asked while maintaining visual out the window.

She undid her hair clip and let her black locks fall freely down to her shoulders and in front of her face.

"Putting on my sexy. Are you blind?"

"You are not going in there alone. It's too risky."

"Boss, we're still just guessing at all this. We need some fresh intel."

"Hang on, I'll go with you," Kolt said.

"Racer, I can do this one better alone."

Raynor stared at her in the rearview mirror. He knew she was right. They really needed eyes inside and in the parking lot.

She looked at him in the mirror for a second before pulling off her top. "No peeking, please."

Raynor forced his eyes back to the entrance of the Kempinski, knowing that he needed to make sure Afifi did not leave.

After a moment he decided he needed to check on his colleague. Her dress was on now, sort of, and she was sliding one beautiful, tanned, and incredibly toned leg into her panty hose.

"Are we going to talk about what you're about to do?"

"I'm going to walk in there like I own the place and belly up to the bar. I'll be discreet, no drama."

Kolt replied, "Not dressed like that, you're not."

"Really, Frank? You are telling me how to dress?"

"Yes. You are going to attract too much attention like that." Raynor began to turn away.

"Why?" Hawk asked.

"I need to spell it out for you?"

"I'd like that very much," she said with a little smirk.

"Sorry, Hawk. I wouldn't give you the satisfaction."

She was putting her heels on now. "Look. I won't draw attention. I'm not going in to get next to him, and I'm not going to do anything obvious. I go in. I have a drink. I walk out."

"I'm not sure about this," Kolt admitted.

"It's my ass," Cindy said.

"No, if you get burned, it's *my* ass."

"I won't get burned. If you're worried that much, you better get around to the black side and cover the service entrance, because I'm heading to the bar and will monitor the front."

Cindy climbed out of the car and headed toward the front entrance with a small handbag that seemed to appear from thin air, but most likely came out of her backpack. While Raynor watched her walk away, she flipped her hair up, then grabbed the sides of her dress near her hips and tugged it to remove the wrinkles across her rear end.

Kolt shook his head in disbelief, put the car in gear, and headed around back.

•   •   •

She came out just fifteen minutes later, and called Raynor to come back around to pick her up. He did so, and they headed back out into the Saturday afternoon traffic on the Kornish al Nile.

"Tell me you didn't give him your phone number," he said.

"You're funny. No, I didn't, but I did learn that the bartender in the lobby makes a gin and tonic that will knock you on your ass, and I learned that you and I have a date."

"What?"

"Afifi had a drink with a woman. They were all over each other. Then he got a phone call. I heard him repeat it back. He has to go to the Sofitel back down in Maadi. It sounded to me like it was business, he's been ordered to meet someone there for dinner."

"Did he say who?"

"If he did, I didn't pick it up. My Arabic isn't that great. I can tell you from the tone of his voice after he hung up that he was pissed, and so was his date. I figure we can get there first and plop down in the lobby for a drink."

"Did he scope you in there?"

"Negative. One hundred percent certain. Possible his date did, but she's not going to the Sofitel."

Kolt thought it over. "Okay, I'll pull over and you can drive, I need to stow the laptop and radio."

"You also need to change clothes, boss."

"Right, although I don't think I can pull off the transformation you just made."

Hawk said, "I'll tell Murphy what we're doing."

They arrived at the Hotel Sofitel Maadi Cairo Towers and Casino shortly before seven, with Kolt behind the wheel again, having switched back out with Hawk for the appearance of their cover. Immediately a valet appeared at Raynor's driver's-side window. Kolt put the car in park and stepped out.

"Your keys, sir?" the man said in English. Kolt had not been to very many luxury restaurants in his life, and he therefore had next to no experience with valet parking. It went against his normal sense of OPSEC to hand the keys to his vehicle over to some stranger and then let him take the vehicle to some unknown location. But he was in character, he was newlywed Frank

Tomlinson, so Kolt handed over his best means of quick escape to some slick-haired kid with a disingenuous smile.

Fuck, thought Kolt.

They headed inside and directly to the bar off the beautiful lobby. Kolt was a little overwhelmed with the place, but he retained the presence of mind to pull Cindy's barstool out for her, and she put her hand behind his head, pulled him closer, and kissed him on the mouth for his chivalry.

When he pulled away their eyes stayed locked, until Kolt finally turned away, sat down, and then brushed nonexistent dust from his pants at the knee.

He wondered what her Green Beret boyfriend would think about that, but he did not dwell on it for too long.

They looked into each other's eyes as they sipped their drinks, showed affection by holding hands and touching one another, but Kolt found the conversation mindlessly boring. Cindy struggled to find new things to discuss to keep the dialogue going. This was not an easy task, because so many topics that would have interested them both and would have made for easy chitchat were absolutely off the table. Subjects like the newest in commo gear and rifle slings and Army leave policies and who the special missions unit selection board was considering to replace Webber as the next Delta commander would be obvious breaches of their cover.

So instead Cindy talked about her cat.

After a few hours of this over the past three days, Kolt felt like he knew more about Sparkle's personality than he did about his own.

It was an effective tactic, Raynor had to admit. She was animated and happy when she talked about the damn cat, she looked perfectly natural in her cover for action. Kolt did his best not to look bored, and he let her talk easily 90 percent of the time. He just sat there smiling, nodding, and looking around the room, while his younger "wife" went on and on about hairballs and kitty litter.

He felt comfortable that their cover was solid.

While she was in the middle of one of her cat stories, Afifi entered the lobby talking on his mobile phone. A look from Raynor conveyed to Hawk that their man was in the building, but she continued on with her story.

Much to their surprise, though, the Libyan sat down at the bar just a few empty seats down from them, and continued talking on his phone. He paused his conversation only to order a single-malt scotch, and as he turned away from the bartender to regard the room behind him, his eyes stopped at Cindy.

He looked her up and down lasciviously, with no care or concern that her "husband" was seated right next to her.

Kolt slipped his mobile phone out of his pocket, activated the microphone, and began recording Afifi's phone conversation for later analysis. He placed his phone on the bar with the speaker turned toward the man, who was only just now turning away from the good-looking woman in the black cocktail dress.

Soon Raynor noticed a pair of men entering the lobby from the stairwell. They wore suits and ties, but they had hard faces and cold eyes. They looked around the room, regarding every person, every doorway, every shadow.

Kolt knew they were security. He thought he recognized one of the men from the photos Digger had taken at Chalice the other day.

Kolt glanced back to Hawk. He was determined that these men would not "make" him. He would not give them any evidence whatsoever that he was anything other than an indulgent newlywed listening to the tales of his hot but slightly goofy wife.

After a few minutes he had evidence that his efforts were paying off. The two men at the staircase came out into the room now, and two more men, not quite carbon copies of the first pair but close enough, came out of the elevator and assumed positions in the lobby area with nice fields of view.

Raynor sipped his draft beer and took over the conversation for a moment, focusing all his attention on Hawk, because he suspected these men were an advance detail for a VIP, and he wanted his cover perfectly established before the VIP appeared.

He told a story about a dog he'd had as a child, making up most of the details to stretch it out.

It seemed to take forever, but finally Afifi got off of his phone and went to a small private room in the dining room behind the bar. The elevator opened shortly thereafter, and two more goons, similar to the four already in the lobby, stepped out, leading an older man through the lobby and into the restaurant. Kolt did not dare watch them to see where they headed once inside, but when he did glance back it appeared they had entered the same room as Afifi.

The four security men who'd placed themselves in the lobby came closer to the restaurant. Two wandered over to the gift shop and pretended to read magazines there, and two more came to the bar, sat at stools on Hawk's right, and ordered fruit juice.

Even though they were young men in their twenties, they took no interest in Cindy whatsoever.

These characters were disciplined, Raynor noted. Plus, he figured, they probably got their share of ass when they weren't on the job.

Kolt still had his phone recording, though he wondered how much of Afifi's conversation he'd managed to pick up with him and Hawk chatting so much closer to the mic. He reached to turn it off, but the two men at the bar started talking to one another while they scanned the lobby and the patrons of the restaurant.

It was foreign, that's all Kolt could tell. He hoped Cindy could understand some of their conversation. He looked at her for some sign that she was listening while she was talking, but immediately he saw something in her eyes.

She stopped talking for a moment.

Kolt took over the conversation, but even he stopped when she silently mouthed something to him with wide eyes. Kolt knew their every move was broadcast in the mirror behind the liquor bottles on the wall. The last thing they needed was for her to look suspicious to the security goons. Kolt tried to give her that look, a look that said, *Don't dick this up now.*

The look did not register. She started to mouth it a second time, but Kolt reached over, placed his hand behind her head, and pulled her close. He kissed her neck, then moved his lips toward her left ear.

"Honey, whisper in my ear. Be cool."

Cindy knew right away she'd messed that up and faked a giggle to recover. She turned in to rub her cheek against Kolt's and whispered.

"Farsi."

Kolt showed no expression. He just nodded and smiled, and willed her to calm down. He placed his hand on hers on the bar, and then he asked for the check.

Farsi, he thought.

Iranians.

Shit.

He kept his smile as he paid cash for the drinks, and he reached for his glass to kill the rest of his beer. As he brought the drink to his lips he saw four men in gray suits enter the lobby, heading for the restaurant.

Raynor recognized Aref Saleh from his photos, even though he could tell the man had had some work done on his face.

Quickly Kolt turned to Cindy. "Shall we?"

Her eyes were on Saleh, as well, but Kolt's attention diverted hers before his goons noticed.

Seconds later Frank and Carrie were heading out the door.

"Sorry about that," Cindy said after the valet brought them their car and they headed off back to the safe house. "I lost my head for a second."

Kolt nodded. Getting excited like that was a rookie mistake. But she was, in fact, something of a rookie. He said, "You got away with it. Are you certain about the language?"

"Yes. I didn't understand what they were saying. But I recognized the sound of it."

Kolt saw that she was pretty agitated about this discovery and he understood why. If these seven men were Iranian, then that meant they were not some band of rogue freedom fighters or some terrorist outfit. No, the men at the Sofitel meeting with a personality from the JSO arms ring would be Iranian intelligence agents of some sort.

It upped the scale of these proceedings.

Cindy asked, "You are sure that was Saleh?"

"Yep," Kolt said. "Curtis is going to wet himself with excitement."

"But what do Iranians need with Saleh's SAMs? They must have thousands of MANPADS."

Kolt nodded slowly while he drove. "Curtis can confirm it, but I suspect these guys are going to be with Quds Force. They are a special unit of the Iranian Republican Guard in charge of extraterritorial operations. They will pass the shoulder-fired missiles out to every asshole on the planet that wants to knock down an American or an Israeli plane."

"Wonderful," Cindy said.

They made it back to the safe house just before nine, and Curtis and his men were waiting for them in the commo room.

"Did you get anything?" Curtis asked.

Kolt noticed that Curtis's eyes were on Cindy in her dress, but he answered the question as if he were the one being addressed. "Yep. Positive ID on Saleh. Afifi, as well."

"Hot damn." Curtis stood from his chair and high-fived Murphy and Wychowski. He then looked back to Raynor. "Who did he meet with?"

Kolt reached into his pocket and pulled out his mobile phone. He tossed it across the little room. "How's your Farsi?"

"Dammit. Iranian?"

"'Fraid so. Got some conversation between a couple of them. Seven men in total. One VIP, along with a six-strong, exceptionally well-trained security detail."

Curtis thought over the implications. "These Iranians are going to be Quds Force of the Republican Guard. We've heard rumblings about them nosing around in Tripoli trying to get MANPADS. Dammit," Curtis repeated. "I'll need to let Langley know. We are not going to let a team of Quds operatives waltz out of Cairo with a trailer full of MANPADS. They want these SAMs so they can give them to third parties. They can bring down aircraft without it being tied back to Iran. They'll pass them off to their proxy goons in the Sadr militia in Iraq or to Hezbollah in Lebanon, or to God knows who else, God knows *where* else."

Kolt said, "Spare us the lesson in geopolitics. Combating Iranian influence has been one of JSOC's top priorities since '06. Quds guys know how to fight, and those Libyans are going to know how to disappear. If the Egyptian Army tries this on their own it will be a mess. Plus, we've got to assume there are Egyptian government officials who will tip off Saleh."

Then Kolt added, "The Quds men are billeted at the Sofitel. That seemed pretty obvious."

Curtis thought this over. "Langley can easily find out which rooms were rented out by an entourage of seven men. I'll see if I can get operations to send over an electronic surveillance/wire tap team to get in there and drop some bugs. This ought to warrant that level of attention from Langley."

Murphy said, "When we get that location bugged, we'll need someone here in the commo room who can do real-time translations."

"We *will* need another terp," confirmed Curtis. "Get a Farsi terp from Cairo Station, stat. If they have a guy vetted who speaks Arabic and Farsi, that would be ideal."

"I don't recommend that," Kolt said.

"Don't sweat it, Racer. Cairo Station will have someone that they've been using for years."

"Do it right and send tonight's audio file to Langley. Maybe they can get someone who speaks Farsi here with the audio team. We start pulling support staff from the embassy . . . that's going to get around."

Curtis shrugged. He seemed to reconsider.

Feeling that his harsh comments about the unvetted Arabic terp may have sunk in, Kolt eased up. "Just be careful about who you bring into our operation. Think OPSEC first, okay?"

Now Curtis smiled. "Don't you worry, Racer. I'll talk to Langley about getting a crew on the way, and you and yours can sleep safe and snug in your beds tonight."

TWENTY-TWO

The Vezarat-e Ettela'at va Amniyat-e Keshvar, or VEVAK, is the Ministry of Intelligence and National Security of the Islamic Republic of Iran. Iran had long recruited agents in the U.S. Embassy in Cairo Egypt. Most of the day-to-day running of the assets was done by an Iranian officer working under diplomatic cover as a commercial affairs officer in the Iranian Embassy of Egypt at 12 Rifaa Street in Cairo. Majid Dalwan, the director of Egypt's VEVAK office, spent his days recruiting new contacts as well as tending to established agents, each working in diplomatic offices across the city.

By no means had Dalwan's network of agents here managed to seriously compromise the American Embassy, but they had managed to achieve a toehold on some sectors of operations.

One of VEVAK network's toeholds was a fifty-six-year-old Egyptian translation support officer in the U.S. Embassy named Hamdy el Nasr. The man had served as an English translator for years for the Mubarak government before taking his current position at the U.S. Embassy. Now, in his administrative role, he found himself in charge of organizing the translation needs of several departments of the embassy.

Dalwan had made gentle contact with el Nasr a year earlier, and he'd found the man to be receptive to offers of small amounts of cash for small bits of intelligence. He had twice stolen documents from his embassy, and he had given the VEVAK officer at the Iranian Embassy information on Farsi speakers who worked with the Americans locally.

His product had not been terribly useful to date, so months ago Majid Dalwan passed the embassy employee off to one of his underlings. He had not personally spoken to el Nasr since then, so he was surprised to find his under-performing agent on the other end of the line when his office phone rang just after nine in the morning.

"Good morning, my friend," said Majid. "It is not like you to contact me. Is there a problem?"

"No. None at all. I wondered if we could have a chat in response to the e-mail I received from your office the other day."

Dalwan thought it over for just a moment. He had ordered his officers to put out feelers to local agents in the Iranian community. Dalwan had been noti-fied by the Republican Guard that they would have Quds personnel operating in the city for a few days, and Dalwan had been instructed to keep an ear out for any uptick in chatter by American, Israeli, or Egyptian intelligence organiza-tions that might indicate one of these agencies had knowledge of the Iranians in the city. So VEVAK had sent a general e-mail out to their contacts asking them to get in touch if there were any rumors or out-of-the-ordinary happenings.

So this call from an administrative officer in the U.S. Embassy in relation to the e-mail filled Dalwan with instant curiosity.

Dalwan made a decision. He had been doing this long enough, and he knew that this agent was solid enough, that he felt a face-to-face meeting was warranted.

"Let's meet at the usual place."

"Yes," said el Nasr. "I think that would be in order."

Majid Dalwan kept his expectations low as he and Hamdy el Nasr sipped tea at a nearly empty café a block east of Tahrir Square. He kept the conversation pleasant and light while he made sure el Nasr had not brought a tail. This took some time, but finally, when they were alone in the café, Dalwan leaned for-ward to his agent.

"What news do you bring me?"

"This morning I found out we have hired a Farsi translator on a one-week contract basis."

Dalwan looked at his agent. So much excitement in the older man's eyes, yet this news meant nothing to the Iranian spy except that he had just wasted his morning on a fruitless trip to Tahrir Square.

"Someone in the embassy needs a Farsi speaker. *That* is why I am here?"

"There is more."

"I certainly hope there is. Who has requested the duties of this contract employee?"

"I don't have the ability to see who requisitioned him. I only know because I arrange payment of interpreters and translators, and this man, an old colleague, called me asking about an advance."

"Then what is it that you find so exciting?"

"I have no record of him being hired for work this week. We have no need of a Farsi speaker at this time. Plus, the rate he claims to have been offered is very high. This indicated to me my old colleague is cleared for the highest security clearance."

Majid Dalwan ran his fingertips along his trim mustache. "Maybe he needed to translate love letters from the ambassador to his Persian girlfriend, and they will pay him in cash. Maybe he is—"

"I am certain he is working with the CIA."

Dalwan cocked his head. "How do you know?"

"The local CIA station at the embassy has their own language experts. They do not need to contract them. So this man will not be working for the CIA at the local station. But this is an emergency contract at a very high rate of pay. To me it looks as if it entails overnight work, as well. Probably twenty-four hours a day on site at a location."

Now we are getting somewhere, thought Dalwan. He had no idea what the Quds Force men were doing in Cairo, and he did not care, unless it got in the way of one of his VEVAK ops. But if a group of American spies in town under nonofficial cover suddenly needed a Farsi translator for 24/7 on-site work . . . well, this sounded like a surveillance operation, and it sounded to Dalwan like his Quds colleagues were burned.

This was definitely worth passing on to the Republican Guard to inform their Quds agents. It might even earn Dalwan some kudos with his nation's military.

"This man that they are hiring, what can you tell me about him?"

"He is Egyptian, but he lived in Iran in the seventies. He is a university professor here in Cairo, and he has the required security clearances for intelligence work with Americans."

"And you have his home address?"

El Nasr said, "I do. He called me personally about the advance. I told him I will look into it for him, and I am meeting him for lunch. From the conversation we had I assume he will be going to his contract job after this."

"Excellent, my friend. You have done well by bringing this to my attention."

"Would it be imprudent for me to ask how I will be rewarded?"

"Not at all, I think you deserve double the usual rate for your product."

Majid Dalwan smiled.

At the AQAP village near Wadi Bana, Charles wiped sweat from his forehead and looked into his rearview mirror.

"Charles" was a Saudi whose real name was Mustafa. He sat in the front seat of a Toyota pickup truck, his hands on the steering wheel. Next to him was "Nick," a Pakistani named Nawaz. They sat silently, parked under an awning of one of the barracks.

David Doyle walked up to the driver's-side window and knocked on it with a radio.

Charles rolled down the window and looked to the leader of the cell.

"Afternoon," said Doyle.

"Hello, Officer."

"Do you have any idea how fast you were going?"

"I am sorry. I do not know."

"You were doing forty-eight in a thirty-five."

"I am sorry." Charles started to reach into his back pocket for his driver's license.

"Don't you fucking move!" David screamed, and he pulled a pistol from the holster on his belt. "Show me your hands, motherfucker!"

Charles raised his hands quickly. "I am sorry! I am sorry."

David pointed the loaded gun across Charles and at the chest of Nick now. "You, too, you piece of shit. Hands up!"

Doyle then pulled both men out of the car and frisked them with their hands on the hood of the Toyota. As he did this the rest of the group stood around inside the building and watched the action under the awning through large open windows.

When the frisking was finished, when Charles and Nick were allowed back in their vehicle and told to drive on, David ended the exercise. He turned to the group watching through the windows and said, "My brothers. Through it all you must remember to smile. People *smile* in America. It means nothing. They will still do you harm, but if you are not smiling at them all the time, then they will not trust you."

It went on like this for hours until, finally, every member of the force could obey all the commands and answer all the questions of a normal traffic stop by American law enforcement.

After this protracted lesson of the day, David and his four subunit members joined him at the container for more practice getting down to the ground and ready to fire. He'd gotten their time down to thirty-nine seconds, more or less consistently, but he pushed his men even harder.

They would only have a few more days before it was time to begin their journey to America, and he needed them ready.

Iranian intelligence officer Majid Dalwan contacted his counterparts in the Republican Guard, and by noon the Quds security men at the Sofitel knew a potential compromise of their operation had occurred. They were waiting outside the restaurant where Dalwan lunched with the interpreter, and then followed him in three vehicles at a distance. With two men in a car, and two more men on two motorcycles, they followed him out of Garden City and then south.

The interpreter parked his car in the garage at the Museum of Egyptian Antiquities and the surveillance team fanned out, expecting him to go inside.

But as soon as he climbed out of his vehicle, a black Range Rover pulled out of a nearby space and rolled up next to him. The Iranian professor climbed into the SUV and they headed out of the parking garage while the Quds officers scrambled to reorganize their mobile coverage.

The Range Rover headed south, and the Iranians backed off farther now, monitoring for any countersurveillance put up by the opposition. They called in two more motorcycles, bringing to five the number of vehicles tailing the interpreter now.

Within minutes they felt confident they were tailing a vehicle operated by intelligence operatives. The black SUV turned down side streets, raced through intersections as the lights changed, and changed lanes over and over, searching for a tail.

But the Quds men had been doing this sort of work for a long time, and they managed to keep one vehicle in sight of their target through all the countermeasures.

After three in the afternoon the SUV rolled into the gates of a small fenced office building in eastern Maadi. The single biker with visual on the Range Rover rolled on by while the other vehicles backed off.

Fifteen minutes later two Quds officers walked through the unfinished construction of a high-rise apartment building across the street from the safe house. They took stairs to the fourth floor, and then stood back in the shadows, looking over the building in front of them. Several cars were lined up behind the fence next to a single door to the lobby. There were neither signs nor security out front.

One of the Quds men settled down in the construction with a pair of binoculars and a mobile phone, while the other returned to the Sofitel.

By midafternoon the Iranians had established that a team of American operatives, likely not local CIA spies from their embassy, were operating a safe house in Cairo and working an operation that required Farsi translation.

They'd have to contact Iran for further instructions, and they would warn the Aref Saleh Organization that there had, almost certainly, been a serious compromise of the operation.

Aref Saleh slipped his satellite phone back onto its charging cradle and leaned back in his chair. It was perfectly quiet in his simple but functional office on the third floor of Maadi Land and Sea Freight, Ltd., on Kornish al Nile.

He strummed his fingers slowly on the blotter in front of him, thinking about the distressing call he had just received. Saleh was a good businessman, and he knew better than to argue with a customer, but he had just spent twenty minutes arguing with the leader of the Iranian contingent here in town to meet with him.

The man had admonished Saleh and his organization, claiming that the Quds Force operatives had been compromised here in the city due to the poor security measures put in place by the JSO. When Aref questioned him on this further, the Iranian explained that they had tracked a Farsi speaker to a CIA safe house in Saleh's neighborhood.

The fifty-eight-year-old Libyan had snapped back that these were tenuous grounds on which to place blame. If American intelligence was here in the city monitoring the Iranians, then, as far as Saleh was concerned, that was the Iranians' fault, and that was the Iranians' problem.

Saleh did not think there was a chance his operation had been discovered. He had paid agents in the Egyptian police, military, and government, just as he had in Libya, who would warn him if an operation against him were in place. Even if American intelligence were somehow onto his scent, Saleh did not think they would be operating without some level of participation by their allies in the Egyptian government. And *his* Egyptian government allies, Saleh had no doubt in his mind, would pass word on to him.

No, the Iranian fools had made a mistake, they had brought American agents along with them to the city, *they* were the ones under surveillance.

Not him.

An initial sale of Igla-S shoulder-fired missiles had been made to the Quds Force operatives weeks earlier; the man who had come from Tehran with six security officers for his protection was here to negotiate a second purchase of the goods. The meeting had been timed to coincide with the delivery of the first shipment so that these men would be here in town to assure that nothing went wrong.

Well, something had gone wrong. Saleh snorted as he thought of this. *Shiite thugs.* They were here to make a second purchase, yes, but also to intimidate him with their presence.

And *they* brought American spies.

Saleh did not know what they would do about this threat from America, but he told the Iranians, in no uncertain terms, that they needed to stay away from him. He did not need the Americans learning about him or his operation.

Late this afternoon the Igla-S weapons would arrive from the Libyan desert, and then late tonight they would ship out, following the orders of the Iranians.

Once this was done, Saleh decided, he would leave Cairo for a while. Maybe permanently. He would leave his shipping concern here to handle the goods physically, but he would relocate his offices for his own personal security. Not back to Tripoli, no. Perhaps to Beirut. Yes. He could pay off members of Hezbollah, and he would work from there.

Beirut was lovely in the fall and, unlike Cairo, it was free of American spies.

TWENTY-THREE

Kolt Raynor and his team had spent the majority of the day conducting mobile surveillance around the Sofitel in preparation for the arrival of the technical surveillance team from Langley the following morning. They returned to the safe house at 1630, eager for an hour's rest before heading back to the hotel for an evening sitting in their vehicles watching to see if the Quds Force operatives ventured out.

Kolt first popped his head in the comms room to let Curtis know they were back, then he headed into the kitchen for a bottle of water. As he did so he almost bumped into a thin man in his sixties who was opening the refrigerator door to peek inside.

"Good afternoon," the man said in accented English.

Kolt just looked at the man, then turned away and headed back into the hallway without returning the greeting. He stuck his head back into the comms room. "Curtis. A word, please."

The two men stepped out of the travel agency and headed down the stairs into the empty lobby of the building. Once there, Kolt turned on the CIA man quickly. "Who the *fuck* is that?"

"Jesus. Calm down, dude. He's the terp."

"What the hell is he doing here?"

"He's fully vetted by Cairo Station."

"He's local?"

"That's right. He's the best guy in town with clearance."

"I told you to stay away from Cairo Station on this."

Curtis stood his ground. "But I don't work for you, Major! Look, I know better than to farm this off to some untested Persian egghead who translates pamphlets for the U.S. Chamber of Commerce or some shit. This guy is a vetted agent. He's worked with us since the late eighties."

"That's great," said Kolt. "But you pull a guy into an NOC safe house who is getting paid by the local station, and it can create a paper trail or raise questions around the embassy. I've seen it happen."

Curtis started pacing the empty lobby. "You've seen it all, haven't you, Rambo? Well, let me remind you, it's my op. I know what I'm doing."

"I don't give a shit whose op it is, Curtis. I am responsible for my people and I sure as shit will not put them in danger because of some bureaucratic fuckup."

"What do you want me to do? He knows where the safe house is. It won't do any good to send him home now." Curtis clapped his hands together. "I've got it! Let's shoot him. Will that work for you? You've been here, what, five days, and you haven't killed anybody? Let's go fix that right now. We just pop a cap in that motherfucker and call it a day."

At that moment Kolt wanted to shoot Myron Curtis. But instead he said, "The terp can stay. PERSEC at this place is your problem. This place is getting too crowded. Me and my team are outta here."

"Oh, for God's sake, Racer."

"I'm serious. We'll find another locale and head out."

Kolt moved his team to a second safe house in under an hour. It was close to the Nile but five klicks south of Curtis's location. It was also near Cairo's metro's north-south line, which could be convenient, as well.

These digs weren't nearly as nice as the travel agency location, but they seemed a hell of a lot more secure. A simple house in a neighborhood with other white people walking around amid the local Arab population, a wall, a gate, a two-car garage, and several large, empty, dusty rooms.

Sleeping bags had been tossed in one of the bedrooms, but Kolt and Cindy opted for a ten-by-ten room with local-style twin beds. There was also a big living room with rugs on the floor, a kitchen stocked with canned food and dried food and a frightening array of molded, rotten, and otherwise nasty items in the refrigerator.

These safe houses were set up and maintained by the local CIA station. Cairo had been a hotbed of CIA activity since the revolution over a year earlier and Raynor decided it was no great surprise that personnel at CIA Station Cairo had been stretched pretty thin of late.

It didn't look like anyone had been in to check on this safe house in half a year.

But Kolt had his team in place, and he was satisfied that their position was secure. He and Slapshot had just established satellite comms with JSOC back at Fort Bragg when Kolt's mobile phone vibrated in his pocket.

He looked down and saw that it was Myron Curtis.

"Yeah?"

"It's Curtis."

"What?" Kolt was not going to engage the man in small talk.

"Thirty-five minutes ago a tractor-trailer rolled through the gates of Maadi Land and Sea."

"Bringing something or about to take something away?"

"The trailer was riding low. Definitely full, or close to it. It turned right at the gate, heading for the loading dock. We saw it on the live feed, so Murphy headed over there in time to hear the sounds of work at the loading bays of location Rhine. The trailer left three minutes ago, and it appeared to be empty. Murphy says the location is quiet at the moment."

Kolt thought it over.

Curtis said, "We are thinking maybe the Iranians worked out a deal for immediate delivery. The weapons are here in Rhine. I bet the Quds guys are going to drive the goods out themselves. They'll go up to Port Said, deliver them to a covered ship, and then take them through the Suez to Iran or up to Beirut. They can load up and go at any time."

Kolt knew that Curtis was still making assumptions, but the likelihood his assumptions were correct seemed to be increasing. Even though the Iranians were supposed to check out of the hotel in two days they could not assume they would not leave early, or the goods would not leave on their own sometime in the next forty-eight hours.

"Okay," he said. "I will contact my command and request authorization to hit Maadi Land and Sea tonight."

"Sooner the better."

"We're not going to do it in daylight."

Curtis just said, "Hey, I don't know ninja shit. You do. Just get the hit."

Kolt made the call to Webber, explained the situation carefully, and warned that if the SAMs were, in fact, in that warehouse, they might leave at any time. He suggested they either go after the Quds Force operatives at the Sofitel or hit Maadi Land and Sea.

Raynor further stressed that he and his team would have a difficult, if not impossible, time finding the munitions once those munitions left Maadi, so, whatever they were ordered to do, they needed to do it tonight.

Then Raynor called Slapshot and Digger together, and he briefed them that they might, just might, be heading into target areas Rhine and Stone very soon.

Kolt willed his sat phone to chirp. Finally, at just after 1900, it did. As expected, it was Webber. "Raynor, listen carefully. You are a 'no go' on the Iranians at their location at the Sofitel."

"Understood," he said. He had no illusions that he and his team would be sent in to the Sofitel Hotel to roll up a cell of Iranian spies.

Shit like that only happened in training or in the movies.

Then Webber said, "But you do have execute authority at objective Rhine. You may enter the warehouse for the purpose of identifying the SA-24s or any other Libyan munitions you may find there. That's it. This is a low-vis assault. No gunfights. If you engage, it better be a life-or-death call."

"Yes, sir."

"This is not authorization to enter the office building, objective Stone. We are talking about the warehouse only." Webber was going out of his way to stress this, Raynor noted. Apparently someone, somewhere, maybe the President himself, was worried about offending Egypt with a big shoot-'em-up in Cairo.

"And if we hit the jackpot?" Kolt asked, knowing he might be pushing it.

"If you get inside and ID the weapons, then yes, Racer, if possible, destroy them in place."

The Secretary of Defense wanted these missiles out of action, if and only if it could be done in a surgical fashion with no political snafus like Libyans in Egypt dead by the hands of American commandos.

But still, Raynor felt like he was being sent on half a mission. "Sir, we cannot know for sure there are weapons at Rhine at this time. We do know, however, that the offices of Maadi Land and Sea contain the leadership of the Aref Saleh Organization. If we can make entry there, we can capture or kill—"

Webber interrupted over the crackling connection. "Negative! You do not have authorization to hit the building on the southern portion of the property. You are to steer clear of all combatants. Maintain your cover. I can't have you risking four good operators to this. You don't have the numbers to actively handle that many bad guys. Are we clear on that?"

Kolt nodded to himself. Even this limited hit was a hell of a lot better than doing nothing. He repeated his mission for Webber's benefit. "Roger, sir. Soft and quiet. If we find the weapons at Rhine, then we can go loud in order to render safe."

"That is correct. That is the extent of your command authority. If you come in contact with combatants you may, obviously, use lethal force. You may not, and I am going to repeat this for you Raynor, you may not enter the office complex in order to engage Libyan nationals housed there. They have not been designated as a hostile force."

"Understood, sir."

"Racer. Make your own luck. Bring everyone home."

"Yes, sir."

The AFO cell spent the evening building their assault plan. Slapshot took the lead on this, as he had served the longest in the Unit, and Raynor knew to defer to him. Kolt and Digger asked questions, made suggestions, and Hawk took notes. She would not be involved in the assault, but she *would* be involved.

Slapshot said, "Hitting from the riverside is the way to go, boss. Looks like two patrolling sentries plus the same number on the roof of the office. Four total who could have eyes on the rear of the property at any one time. That's not nothing, but there is fair cover at several points between the pier and the loading dock of the warehouse. Best we take advantage of them."

Kolt nodded. "I like it."

They determined Racer, Slaphsot, and Digger would use a small locally procured dinghy with a 110-horsepower engine to land at the pier at 0330, when the guard force would be the least alert and the sliver of moon would be nearing its lowest point to the horizon before dawn. The three men would use night-observation devices to make their way from the pier, where they would use bolt cutters to cut through the fence at the waterline. They would then make their way up through the fifteen meters of low vegetation on the northwest corner of the property, cross twenty meters of asphalt parking lot where they would have to concern themselves with a couple of patrolling sentries and exposure to the roof of the office building and the pair of static guards stationed there.

Once they made their way to the warehouse, they would make entry either at the loading dock on the north side or, if that was not feasible, they would come around to the east side and go through the main entrance.

Slapshot and Raynor would go inside to find, photograph, and then rig the weapons with small blocks of C-4 explosive. Meanwhile, Digger would remain concealed outside to watch the exfiltration route.

They talked for some time about the size of the secondary explosions, but ultimately decided that, as long as there were a manageable number of SAMs present, the blast of the detonation would be confined to the warehouse of Maadi Land and Sea.

The men would make their way back to the boat and drift downriver before detonating the C-4 in a chain reaction, destroying the tubes, power sources, and warheads.

While this was all happening Hawk would be parked several blocks up on the Kornish al Nile. If the team ran into trouble and found themselves unable to make it back to the dinghy, they could exfiltrate on the northeast side of objectives Rhine-Stone and attempt to make it over the wall and out into the neighborhood. Hawk would swoop in and pick them up at their war RV, and they would hightail it out of the area.

The plan sounded clean and efficient, which meant to Kolt it sounded like it was too good to be true. He fully expected snags in their operation: a sentry who wasn't where he was supposed to be, or a member of the JSO leadership on the balcony with an early morning nicotine fit, or a sweeping flashlight that did not follow the rules and keep sweeping in the same direction.

"What's up, boss?" Slapshot asked. "Your mouth says it's a go, but your expression is telling me something else."

"Two things. One, I'm not entirely confident that the Agency fellas haven't been burned already. Second, this could get ugly quick. It's definitely high-risk here, guys."

"Not like you to worry about the risk, Racer. We've got this," Slapshot quickly said.

"It's not you guys. I don't know," Kolt said, looking around at the others.

"Do I need to leave?" Cindy asked, sensing she was the problem.

"No, Hawk. You're good. Actually, it's your guys' kids," Kolt said, looking at Slapshot and Digger.

Digger said, "We all know the risks. I'm here because of my kids, not despite them. I fight so they might not have to." This was said with a tinge of irritation.

"Ditto!" Slapshot added.

"Got it. Feel better just getting it off my chest. We'll either come back with our shield or on it," Kolt said.

"Damn right," said Digger.

Still, Kolt knew they had to make their plan as organized as possible in advance of the execution of it, otherwise the snags and snafus would increase tenfold.

Raynor stood from the table. "I like it," he told the team. "Let's make it happen."

At thirty minutes short of midnight Kolt traveled alone north on Cairo's main north-south metro line. He wore Western clothing that fit in perfectly with what virtually all the male locals were wearing on the train, and his tinted glasses covered most portions of his face not obscured by his short beard. He moved with the crowd, and drew no attention whatsoever.

He climbed off the train at the Hadayeq El-Maadi, and stepped out onto the street. Within seconds a beat-up-looking half-yellow, half-primer two-door Toyota pulled up and he climbed in.

"So you guys are a go, huh?" Myron Curtis said from behind the wheel as he headed off into traffic.

No one else was in the car.

"Yes. 0330 hours," Raynor confirmed.

"I'm glad you're going to destroy the SA-24s, but I wish you were also going in to arrest Saleh and his men."

Kolt had a brief mental image of him and his two mates flex-cuffing fifteen or so international criminals, and then somehow sneaking them out of the country. "JSOC wrote this op with the real world in mind. What you are talking about is fantasyland."

"Maybe so, but Saleh is going to just go to ground and keep transferring weapons to rogue nations and terrorists."

"Job security for you, I guess. We'll find him again. Seriously, if the SA-24s are in the warehouse, we'll destroy them, which will prevent the transfer to the Iranians, which will prevent the transfer to Lebanon, Iraq, and Afghanistan. We're just going to have to be satisfied with that for now."

Curtis shrugged. "Hey, you know me. I'm hard to please. Want to do one last drive-by of the target?"

"Uhhh . . . Negative, Curtis," Kolt answered with a tint of sarcasm. *This guy is a loose cannon.*

"Your guy still in the area?" Raynor asked.

"Yeah. He hasn't seen any activity since the last report."

"Good. What about the Quds Force goons?"

Curtis replied, "We have eyes on. I've got a man at the Sofitel watching them."

"What, down in the lobby?"

Curtis did not answer.

"What exactly does 'eyes on' mean, Curtis?"

"Well . . . if they are up in their rooms, then no, we don't have eyes on. But we've got a guy making sure they don't leave."

"Your man has eyes on his martini, more like it," Raynor said. "Your men are too close to the X. If they haven't been burned already, then they will be once things get interesting. Pull your surveillance off Rhine and Stone at H-10 mikes, and pull the guy out of the Sofitel at 0330, H-hour."

H-Hour, like D-Day, signified the beginning of an operation.

Curtis nodded as he made a turnaround at a traffic circle and began heading back for the metro station.

Kolt then said, "You, too. I want you to unass your safe house. Tonight."

The CIA man seemed surprised by this. He shook his head. "Nobody is going to find us."

"Look, man. You are less than two klicks from the target location. If we hit Rhine and blow a shipment of SAMs, it's going to be a big fucking deal. Everybody in Maadi will be running around saying Israeli or American spies are in the neighborhood. Your antenna farm and front travel agency won't survive the first knock at the door. Trust me on this, I've seen a bit of the Arab street."

"Of course you have, Rambo."

Raynor ignored him. "You'll wake up tomorrow to find two dozen kids on the sidewalk out in front of your place pointing up at your window and jumping up and down."

Curtis started to argue back, it was his way, after all, but he stopped himself. Something about Raynor's imagery sank in. After a moment he said, "We've got a place in El Salam City. Way up to the northeast. Ten or twelve miles from Maadi."

Kolt nodded. "I looked it over on FalconView on the flight in. I think that's a great choice. You'll need to steer clear of Maadi completely after this. No drive-bys. Your cables to Langley can wait. We can get a better damage assessment from CNN than from you taking snapshots of the rubble from the Kornish al Nile."

Curtis chuckled and nodded. He said, "Okay, Mother. We will sterilize the safe house, and get out of there by the time your team hits the building. And as always, I appreciate your concern for my well-being."

"I don't give a shit about your well-being. You can get hit by a bus once this op is over, for all I care. Just not till we get the SAMs dealt with."

"Fair enough."

"Thank you," Kolt said, officially crossing Myron Curtis and his team of well-educated but bumbling case officers off of his list of worries.

"You're welcome," said Curtis, as he pulled to a stop back in front of the Hadayeq El-Maadi station. "Now go find those SAMs and blow them to kingdom come."

"Yep," Kolt said as he stepped out onto the street. *Hope you enjoy yourself from the comfort of your new condo, partner.*

At the Hotel Sofitel Cairo Maadi Towers and Casino, the CIA case officer from Cairo Station assigned to watch the suspected Iranian Quds Force personnel rolled onto his side and fluffed the fleece jacket that he was using as a pillow.

As far as he was concerned, he'd done damn fine work tonight, and he deserved a couple hours of shut-eye. He'd positioned himself in the lobby at eight p.m., taking over for another man from the local station. Shortly after this, five of the seven target subjects came down from their rooms and headed into the gift shop off the lobby. The case officer had positioned himself close enough to hear one of the Iranians speak in English to the attendant there, explaining that two of their party had fallen ill with a stomachache and asking about a remedy.

As one of the Iranians paid for the over-the-counter medicine and then took it upstairs, the rest of the group entered the restaurant Le Clovis and were seated at a large table within view of the lobby. When their colleague returned, the five enjoyed a long, late, and relaxed dinner in the restaurant. And then, around midnight, the five men headed up to their rooms, shaking hands with each other. On the way through the lobby to the elevator, one of their party had spoken English to the bellman, telling him they would be leaving in the morning and arranging for someone to come collect their bags at eight-thirty.

Then the men climbed into elevators and went up.

The case officer's job had been to watch the men and make certain they did not leave the hotel. Once he had convinced himself they were in for the night, he left the Sofitel and returned to his car, where he lowered the seat and fell soundly to sleep.

He slept through the few comings and goings in the parking lot, and he slept as hotel security escorted a disgruntled gambler back to his vehicle. It was the kind of sloppy CIA fieldcraft that Kolt had lost sleep over.

And he slept through one more event of interest. Five men, each with a suitcase and a carry-on, entered the covered lot from the hotel's stairwell at two a.m. They climbed into a black Mahindro Scorpio SUV, and rolled slowly and quietly out of the hotel grounds.

TWENTY-FOUR

At 0230 hours Racer was back with his team at their safe house on Gamel Abd El Nasir. Digger and Slapshot had already taken the dinghy to the water's edge, just a few blocks to the west of their location. They had secreted it in some high reeds and anchored it in knee-deep water. From here it would be a journey of twenty minutes at low power to reach the property of Maadi Land and Sea Freight, Ltd., a mile north of their position on the same shore.

Now the two sergeants were checking their kit to make sure they had everything for the hit. They wore dark brown local garb, and they sat at the table in the tiny kitchen looking over satellite images of the property along with color photographs taken during their close-target recces of the past few days.

Raynor was in the back room with Hawk, sitting on a bunk next to her with his laptop in his lap. They were using FalconView and recon photos to help them find the best point downriver where she could gain access to the water's edge in the van and still remain away from concentrations of civilians or police. They finally found a spot, nearly a half mile from the target location, just before a slow turn in the river that might have exposed them to anyone on the Ring Road Bridge.

After picking out a couple of alternate access points to the river, Kolt got up from the bunk and checked his MP7 PDW rifle.

"Racer?" Hawk said.

"Yeah?"

"You are going to encounter a significant amount of security in that complex."

"Ya think?" He said it playfully, but his mind was 100 percent on mission.

"You could use another gun in this."

He stopped what he was doing and looked up at her. "Out of the question, Hawk. You are not an operator. Uh, I mean, listen, this isn't about your abilities. I know you can handle yourself, I'm not questioning that. I—"

"Well, sir, I'm glad you corrected yourself. I am not an operator. But just because I don't have a dick doesn't mean my gun on target wouldn't be a good thing if it goes loud."

"Sorry, Hawk. Not going to happen. You're an important contingency on this one. If we go to plan B, I need to know you are there to help us out."

She nodded. "Right, boss," she said, but she was thinking she could help the men out better if she was in there with them when the shit hit the fan.

"We leave in five." Raynor hefted his chest rig of magazines and his soft armor and headed out the door.

"Shit," Cindy Bird said to the empty room.

As much as he hated to admit that Racer was right, Curtis knew moving to another safe house before the hit on the target took place was a good call. He wished he had thought of it first. He knew he would not get it all sanitized before H-Hour, but that wasn't the point. He wanted to get his ass, and the asses of his men, out of the location before all of Maadi was rocked with emergency sirens and engulfed in flashing lights.

To that end he had everyone working on getting as much packed up as possible. Murphy and Wychowski stacked duffel bags and backpacks at the top of the staircase. Denton had backed the panel truck up in the gated parking lot next to the Range Rover and he and Buckley were finishing up loading all the guns and ammo into crates in their room.

Curtis made a final call on the sat phone before disconnecting it from the roof antenna and putting it in one of the many padded Pelican cases lying around. He then took a moment to check his watch. Racer and his team would be hitting objective Rhine in half an hour. He needed to pick up the pace if they were going to be rolling before then.

Curtis grabbed an empty backpack off of a shelf and began stuffing it with gear.

●   ●   ●

While Buckley broke down the Alamo kits of rifles, mags, and binos positioned in the windows, Denton hefted four big duffels of gear and headed up the hall. He exited the travel agency and then crossed the landing to the stairs, taking them down to the darkened lobby.

At the front door he glanced out the small window, making certain the parking lot was empty except for the panel truck and the SUV, and also making sure the electronic gate was closed. After doing this, he opened the door and headed out to load the bags. A warm breeze blew trash from the construction site across the street, over the dark two-lane road, and through the openings in the fence around the parking lot. The CIA SAD officer packed the gear in the back of the panel truck and then headed back into the building to grab two more armloads of duffels.

He pressed the key code at the front door to the building and the locks popped open. As he pushed open the heavy door, his head snapped forward, and his body tumbled into the lobby to the stairs, his legs still outside the door. His body twitched for a few seconds, but soon he stilled.

Denton had been shot through the skull by a suppressed Dragunov sniper rifle from the fifth floor of the lot across the street. The bullet had exited his forehead and taken a small portion of his brain with it.

As this all happened, the electronic gate access to the small parking lot began to open silently. As soon as there was a foot of separation between the two gate doors, a black figure pushed through the rest of the way. As he did so he let the remote control for the gate fall from his hands. His Libyan associates had been given the remote by the security company who designed it, and then they had passed it on to his team.

It had served its purpose, but now the Iranian needed both of his hands to operate his weapon.

The man in black, along with four more men dressed in black behind him, sprinted across the parking lot toward the door left propped open by the dead American. Here they vaulted the body and entered the lobby. The first three men crouched at the bottom of the open staircase, their weapons trained on the landing above, and the other two men rolled Denton's body back outside before shutting the door.

All four Iranian Quds Force operatives headed up the stairs quietly, their eyes scanning for targets in the dimness.

• • •

The Delta AFO cell drove west toward the site of their hidden dinghy in the shallows of the Nile River. Hawk was behind the wheel, a blue veil covering her face and hair, and an MP7 with its stock collapsed hung under her right arm.

Raynor sat in the back with Slapshot and Digger. They would darken their faces with black waterproof camo paint at the very last moment before climbing onto the boat, but for now he and the others kept their faces clean.

As they rode in silence Kolt grabbed his mobile phone from inside his duffel on the floor next to him. He announced to the van, "I'm going to double-check that Curtis and his team are out the door."

He punched Curtis's number, and listened to the phone make the connection.

"We're pulling up to the dinghy," Hawk said softly from the front seat, and the van slowed and stopped in the parking lot of a shuttered boathouse along the water.

"Come on, Curtis," Kolt muttered softly. Slapshot and Digger were pulling the long gallabiyas off their bodies, revealing the black Nomex, black canvas, and quick-release buckles underneath.

Curtis did not answer.

Kolt looked down to his watch.

Suddenly he had a very bad feeling.

"Hawk," Kolt barked. "You have Murphy's cell number saved on your phone?"

"Roger, why?"

"Call him, Curtis isn't answering."

It rang six times before Hawk looked back at Kolt and shook her head no.

"Shit!" Kolt said as he looked out the window. He didn't need this. But something didn't feel right. He knew Murphy had been staring at Hawk's ass since day one. Not answering her phone call was a hell of an indicator.

"Back to the safe house on Ahmed Kamel Street. As quick as you can get us there."

Digger asked, "You don't think they got hit, do you?"

Kolt shook his head, but the look on his face did not match the gesture. He tried the call again. "I don't know. If we get there and they are fine, or they are already gone, then we can be back here in twenty minutes."

As they neared Ahmed Kamel Street, the team saw a large number of locals out in the street for this time of night. They seemed to be looking around.

Hawk said, "Looks like something just happened in this neighborhood."

Digger added, "They all heard something, but they don't know where it went down."

"Park in the mouth to the back alleyway," Kolt said. "We don't need any spectators as we approach, and I don't want any snipers in the high-rise construction to take a potshot at us."

With that Hawk killed the van's headlights and, a few seconds later, turned into the alley that led behind the safe house building. At Raynor's direction, they parked two blocks from the back door of the property. Kolt said, "Foxtrot from here. Back entrance. Quiet and careful. No one knows we're coming."

The rest of the team nodded as one.

Kolt and Cindy began heading up one side of the alley, Digger and Slapshot across from them.

The back door to the building was secure, and all the lights were off downstairs. Kolt knelt down and took a quick look through the window next to the rear door, and he saw a body on the staircase. *Shit.* Quickly he slipped across the window to the other side, and motioned for Slapshot to unlock and open the door.

Slapshot pulled a pair of keys out and reached across the glass to the lock.

Seconds later the back door opened and Kolt moved into the downstairs lobby, his rifle high, his back moving sideways along the rear wall to the west. Digger moved in right behind him and followed the wall to the east, keeping himself out of view up the staircase ahead of him. Slapshot and Hawk moved in behind them—Slapshot following Kolt all the way around on the left and Hawk going in Digger's direction.

There was blood all over the floor in front of the front door. Kolt and Slapshot noticed this, but they kept moving.

Once they cleared the downstairs rooms, they moved upstairs in silence and near-complete darkness. The little light that filtered in from the lobby's windows revealed that the man on the stairs was Buckley, one of the SAD officers. Digger knelt to check his pulse, but in seconds he looked up at Raynor and shook his head. The stairs were covered in blood around Buckley's body, but Kolt and the others did not take time to look for his wounds before continuing cautiously up the staircase.

They found the door to the travel agency wide open, and the lights off. They slipped into the office silently, moving low, their weapons trained on the open door to the safe house in back. As they went behind the counter, they found Murphy. There was no point in Digger checking for a pulse. The man's eyes were wide open in death.

Their tactical train entered the hallway of the safe house and they cleared the kitchen, finding it empty, but bullet holes and blood smears told of a recent fight here. In the first bedroom they found Wychowski facedown in a pool of blood.

Digger checked his pulse, but he was dead.

The rest of the rooms were empty, just the way they had looked the day before when Raynor and his men had vacated them.

The team formed at the bathroom at the end of the hall. Kolt reached forward with one hand and pulled the latch.

As he opened the door, he felt the resistance of something pushing against it. He flashed the flashlight on his rifle's barrel quickly, illuminating the room before him, and he saw a scene of utter carnage.

A man head-to-toe in black was facedown next to the toilet; blood had spurted from an artery across the walls and mirror of the small bathroom.

And Myron Curtis was sitting on the floor next to the dead Iranian. His back was against the wall under the towel rack by the shower. The rack had been bent almost in half and the towel was wrapped tightly around Curtis's upper leg.

It was soaked in blood.

Curtis's eyes had been closed when Kolt flashed the light, and Kolt thought the CIA man had bled out. He called Digger forward, and the medic entered the bathroom and knelt over Curtis. The young Delta operator started to reach to check for a pulse but the CIA man lifted a pistol up weakly from under the bloody towel.

Digger pulled it out of the man's hands as he called out, "Boss?"

Kolt shut himself and Digger in the bathroom with Curtis and flipped on the lights. He checked the thigh wound along with Digger by carefully removing the towel. Instantly dark blood pumped from the hole in Curtis's pants. The thick string tourniquet Curtis had applied wasn't getting it done.

"That does *not* look good," Curtis announced in a tired and hoarse whisper.

Instantly the medic pulled a tourniquet out of his chest rig and wrapped it above the wound, cinching it tight, almost into Curtis's crotch.

"Ahhh!" Myron Curtis groaned as Digger cut off the field-expedient tourniquet Curtis had applied. Then he recovered and looked at Kolt. "Everybody else?" he asked.

Raynor just nodded his head. "We haven't found Denton. But there is enough blood in the lobby by the door. I expect his body is out in the parking lot. We're gonna check."

"Son of a bitch." Curtis winced again as Digger shoved Curlex into the wound down to the bone. Then he said, "They came from nowhere, I swear to God. I heard a crash in the travel agency, something breaking. I yelled out to Murphy, but he didn't answer." Curtis closed his eyes as he talked. It had happened not fifteen minutes earlier but he seemed to have to concentrate to remember the details. "Then those fuckers just came pouring up the hall."

"I got hit early, but I took this guy down." He motioned to the dead man five feet away on the other side of the toilet. "I heard Wychowski get shot. Buckley dumped a whole magazine at them and they seemed like they were backing off. He went after them, or out to look for Denton, or something." Curtis groaned weakly. "I heard them shouting in Farsi. It's the Quds Force guys, no doubt about it." He winced again. "Motherfuckers."

"Digger, check the dead guy for pocket litter," Kolt ordered, and Digger scooted over to frisk the dead man. "How many, Curtis?"

"Enemy? I . . . I don't know. Five? Six, maybe, including this one."

"Where's your terp?"

Curtis looked at Raynor with confusion. Then he put his head back against the wall and shrugged his shoulders. "Done in by a fuckin' terp." He shook his head back and forth like he couldn't believe it. "He was vetted, too!"

"Some are better than others." Raynor flipped off the overhead light and opened the door. In a whisper he spoke to the entire team. "Listen up. No way to know if there are observers across the street or even if the hitters are hanging out for a smoke in the parking lot. We know the alley is clear, so we go out the way we came in. But first we find Denton."

Curtis said, "I need to call Cairo Station."

Kolt shook his head. "We'll get to it. First priority is making sure we don't have an AMCIT hostage on our hands." An American citizen hostage, especially an employee of the CIA, would just pour gas on the fire that this incident had already become. "Second priority is getting the hell away from the safe house."

"But—"

"Curtis, you need to trust me on this."

Myron Curtis closed his eyes. "It's your show, Racer. I'm dead anyway."

"Stop whining, you're not dead yet," said Digger. He'd finished with the tourniquet. He looked up to Raynor. "What about the intel, boss?"

Kolt nodded and said, "Look, Curtis, we can't do anything for your men. We'll have to leave them behind. But what needs to be destroyed here in the safe house?"

"There is a black Pelican box with the secure laptops, phones, and our creds already packed. It has a red cross painted on the top."

"Okay, Slap, find it and grab it. Drop a thermite on any gear you can't carry out of here," Kolt said.

"We'll need to carry him out," Digger said, still tending to Curtis's wound.

Kolt nodded, slung his MP7 across his back, and, along with Digger, they hefted Myron Curtis over Raynor's shoulder.

They moved slowly down the hallway and out of the travel agency, and even more slowly down the stairs. Slapshot located the Pelican box while Hawk led the way, followed by Kolt carrying Curtis, and Digger at the rear. In the lobby Hawk looked out the front window.

"Denton," she said, then turned away. "He's done. Part of his head is gone."

At the rear doorway, Kolt lowered the wounded man, checked on him briefly, and said, "Slapshot?"

Slapshot had returned with the Pelican case, which he passed off to Digger. "Got him, boss." Kolt needed to be in charge of their escape, something that would be exponentially more difficult while carrying a man on his back. The bigger operator hefted the CIA man confidently and securely back.

The door to the rear alley of the safe house opened quietly, and then Hawk spun out, her rifle trained on the darkness, but she did not actuate the weapon light. Raynor followed her out the door. Slapshot was the third operator into the alley, heavily laden with a man slung over his shoulder.

And Digger brought up the rear.

They headed up the alley at a brisk walk, their muzzles sweeping the windows on both sides as well as the exit of the passage just ahead. Soon the Americans were back in their panel truck, heading north toward downtown

Cairo. As they drove, Curtis mumbled again that someone needed to call Cairo Station immediately.

Then he passed out.

Kolt asked, "How is he?"

Digger looked up. Blood shone on his latex gloves all the way up to his wrists. "He's got a bad bleeder. Hard to tell. Needs a hospital."

"How soon?"

Digger cocked his head. "How soon? What do you mean?"

"I mean, how bad is it?"

"I . . . I don't . . ." The young Delta sergeant did not understand. "Fuck, Racer, it's a clipped femoral. Those are never good, why?"

"I need to know if he can last an hour before getting any more medical attention."

Digger answered slowly, "His golden hour already started. I've got the bleeding stopped. I can't sedate him or his BP might drop too low. He's in a world of hurt, and it won't get better on its own."

"Can he make it another hour?"

Digger shrugged. "Boss, only the Lord knows. Not my call. My medical advice is he needs higher care ASAP."

Kolt nodded. He weighed the options. It was his call and he knew it. He was torn between saving Curtis or saving thousands if they took care of the SAMs. Either way, there were no guarantees for Curtis. But they might never have intel this good on the missiles again.

Kolt crawled quickly to the front of the van. He leaned up to Hawk and said, "Back to the dinghy."

She cocked her head. She could not believe what she'd heard. But Kolt just nodded at her and turned away.

Cindy made the next left.

"What's up, boss?" Slapshot asked. He assumed they would be heading straight for the U.S. Embassy in Garden City.

But Kolt said, "Listen up. If the Iranians know we're here, it's safe to assume the Libyans do, too. We can contact Webber, but going to JSOC to request a full assault team is a nonstarter. Besides, the Libyans aren't going to wait around for that. They will be out of the city by sunrise."

Slapshot shook his head. "Let's *not* do that."

Digger agreed. "No need for those company guys to have died for nothing."

Kolt was way ahead of them. "Okay. I just want to make sure we are all in for the right reasons."

They all nodded in unison. Kolt looked hardest at Cindy. He had to be sure she was good with it, too.

"We're going to hit Maadi Land and Sea right now with what we've got. Still no authority to enter anything more than the warehouse, but we can do that."

It was quiet for a moment, until Kolt said what was on everyone's mind. "More than ever, this hit needs to be delicate. But if we screw this up, attract the attention of the Libyan nationals, and this hit turns into a block party, never forget that you have the right to use lethal force to save your life or your mate's."

"We know the rules," said Slapshot.

The Delta men weren't targeting personalities or hunting humans on this one, but they knew it was a distinct possibility that things could get messy in a hurry, and none of them were disappointed on that score. Not after seeing five CIA men gunned down in cold blood.

Hawk had been concentrating on driving, but now she blurted out, "Racer, there are only three of you. You will need me to—"

"Yeah," interrupted Kolt. "We *will* need you to come along."

Slapshot leaned close to Kolt. "Is she ready for this?" he asked. It wasn't a sexist comment, more a questioning of the specific training she had received as a member of the Operational Support Division.

"I don't know." Then Kolt said with a tint of sarcasm, "It's her or Curtis here."

"I'm ready," she said. Her voice was not as confident as it could have been, but she was definitely resolute about going.

Kolt said, "We change up the hit. We'll split into two teams. Digger and Slapshot from the water, no change. Me and Hawk take the main entrance at the east. Simultaneous. Stay on comms. All four head for the warehouse, try to get under the guards. Suppressors and inside voices, although I'm not going to pretend we're going to make it with stealth alone."

The rest of the team said, "Understood."

TWENTY-FIVE

They returned to the dinghy at 0350, twenty minutes late for their designated H-hour. Hawk parked in the boathouse parking lot and took off her veil.

Curtis had awakened. In the dim light of the back of the van, Raynor crawled past Digger and Slapshot and knelt over the injured CIA man. "How you doing, man?"

The CIA man's voice was stronger than before. "I'm shot, Racer. How do you think I'm doing? Where are we?"

"Listen. I need you to hang in there. We have one chance to fix things. Right now. We don't do this tonight, Saleh and his men will pull up stakes, and the Quds Force will slip away with the SAMs. I know you don't want that."

Curtis looked up at Racer. "I'm listening."

"It's obvious the Agency has somehow been compromised. If we drop you off anywhere that Cairo Station knows about, then Saleh's people will know men made it out of the safe house. They'll be ready for us. On top of that, if we call JSOC or Langley right now, they will pull the plug on this hit. We have their intent, we're on the ground, and it's our call."

Curtis blinked hard. "Are you saying what I think you are saying?"

"What I'm saying is . . . my medic tells me you can hold on for an hour. That's enough time for us to get in and out of there, and then get you some better medical care."

"Holy shit," said Curtis. He looked down at the wound in his leg and the tourniquet on it. "I'll lose the leg, won't I?"

"No," said Kolt. "I mean . . . I don't think so. I've seen men wear a tourniquet for three, even four hours, and still keep the limb."

"You're bullshitting me."

Kolt wasn't, but he also was not as certain as he tried to make himself sound. "Look. I don't know for sure. I don't know you'll make it. I just know we can get the damn SAMs out of the hands of the Iranians. I need you to let me do that."

Curtis squinted away a new volley of pain. "You're going to do it anyway."

Kolt nodded. "Yeah, probably, but I'd like your blessing."

The black CIA officer smiled a thin smile, and sweat on his brow ran down his temples. "Fuck. It's the right fucking call. I sure as shit would do it to you."

Kolt smiled in response, but immediately his face rehardened into stone. "We'll be back to the van in an hour, or else we won't be back at all."

Curtis nodded. "Leave me a pistol. If you guys don't make it and they head out into the neighborhood to look for your ride . . . well . . . I'm not letting those sons of bitches take me alive." His words were slurred a bit, but he was still in command of his senses.

Kolt nodded. It was a bit dramatic, even for the circumstances. But he'd do as Curtis asked. "Slapshot, pass me one of those frags from the glove box."

Slapshot opened the small door and pulled out one of three fragmentation grenades. The safety and pull-pin were taped to prevent accidental detonation. He passed it to Digger, and Digger handed it to Kolt. As Kolt passed it to the wounded CIA officer, he said, "Digger tells me you are going to wish you were dead in a little while. You need to suck up the pain and ride it out. But if they come for you, *this* you don't have to aim. Don't let them take you alive."

Curtis nodded. It was clear he was already in agony. "Get the fuck out of here and go get those SAMs before I blow us all up."

Digger and Slapshot rolled out of their wooden boat and into the water just fifty yards from the dock behind Maadi Land and Sea, but they held on to the small craft and they let the current of the Nile River push them along, closer to their destination. They kept their weapons and C-4 in the boat, but even with the weight of the extra magazines, they had little trouble staying upright as they bobbed in the swift current alongside their boat.

Once they arrived near the pier that protruded a dozen meters into the river, they grabbed hold. While Digger held the boat and one of the small pilings, Slapshot wrapped a rope already affixed to the rusted bow cleat of the dinghy around the piling, and then hitched it back to the boat. Even with the significant current, the boat would only drift under the dock and stay there until the two Delta men needed it again.

Slapshot was first out of the water. He raised a handheld NOD monocular and checked the immediate area to the best of his ability by peering over the wooden decking, then heaved himself quietly out of the water and rolled onto the deck. Quickly he moved forward a few feet, then came to a crouch behind a cluster of wooden mooring pylons extending out of the water. His NOD was whited out when he faced the bright exterior lighting of the office building, but when he turned to the warehouse he was able to see a single armed sentry walking a route near the northern portion of the metal structure.

He decided quickly that, as long as no one flashed the pier with a spotlight and as long as he and his mate were careful not to let themselves be silhouetted from the lights of a passing boat, they would remain invisible until they got to the gate in the metal fence.

Digger appeared behind Slapshot a moment later, and the two dripping-wet men moved toward the gate without exchanging a word.

On the Kornish al Nile, Major Kolt Raynor walked quickly along the dark sidewalk a half block south of the entrance to Maadi Land and Sea Freight, Ltd. He had changed clothes; now he wore a black turtleneck and dark jeans, and his footfalls were softened by black running shoes. His hands were empty, and across his back he'd slung a small black duffel bag.

He stayed tight against the trees in front of the fence, keeping himself shielded from the gatehouse just ahead as he came closer to it.

"One minute," came Slapshot's voice in Kolt's earpiece. Raynor just nodded to himself as he checked up and down the street to make certain the area was quiet. It was after four in the morning; there was little risk of passersby happening upon the scene.

Across the street and on the other side of the entrance to Maadi Land and Sea Freight, Cindy Bird staggered slightly on the sidewalk. She wore a black tank top that showed a hint of her cleavage and muscular bare arms, and dark blue jeans. Her hair was strewn across her face. She was crying openly, using the back of her arm every few yards to wipe hair and tears from her eyes as her thick sobs echoed on the quiet street.

A white woman with bare arms and partially bared breasts stumbling and weeping down a predawn street in Cairo. It grabbed the attention of the sentry at the front gate of the shipping concern, to say the least.

She stepped onto the tree-lined sidewalk and up toward the freestanding gatehouse next to the driveway.

A suspicious guard with a heavy mustache and angry eyes stared at her while fingering the MP5 sub gun on his chest. He picked his walkie-talkie off the table in front of him and brought it to his mouth.

"*La mo'axza*," she said. *Pardon me.* It was not the customary Muslim greeting, but it showed the man that the woman spoke Arabic.

He took the walkie-talkie away from his mouth and hooked it back to the strap of his weapon and, with his hand still on the grip of his submachine gun, he watched her from the shack.

Cindy wiped tears from her eyes and smiled meekly at the guard. The man noticed her easy demeanor, but even more he noticed her bare shoulders. His eyebrows rose slightly, even as his eyes remained dark. "What do you want?"

In Arabic Cindy replied, "Yacht Club? Is this the Yacht Club?"

The guard shook his head, and his hand lowered from his rifle. "No."

"Yacht Club?" she asked again.

Now the guard stepped out of the shack and pointed up the street in the direction of the Yacht Club.

"I have been attacked, I need help," Cindy said in Arabic, bursting into a fresh bout of sobs after doing so.

The guard hesitated, and then brought his walkie-talkie back to his mouth.

As the guard pressed the talk button on the side of his radio, Kolt Raynor appeared behind him, having slipped through the darkness along the gate. As Cindy watched, Kolt grabbed the guard from behind as he slapped a tight rear naked choke to cut the guard's airway. After three seconds of trying to shake Kolt off, the guard's knees gave, and the Egyptian jolted forward, his eyes fluttering. Cindy half caught them both as they fell, and then she and Raynor rolled the unconscious man back into the guard shack.

Hawk pressed the button to open the gate, and by the time she stepped out of the shack Raynor had both MP7s out of his bag. Hawk took one, along with a small shoulder pack with six extra magazines of 4.6mm ammo, and her interteam radio and earpiece.

"Why are you still crying?" Kolt asked as he did a brass check on his Glock.

"I don't know, I've never seen a man killed like that. He was staring straight at me," Cindy said, wiping the tears with her left sleeve.

"Okay, first off, he's not dead. Second, get your shit together."

The gate closed automatically behind Raynor.

"I know, I know," Cindy quickly said. "I'm good. Really, I am."

"Look, this could get real ugly in the next few minutes. Guns kill. You saw that back at the Agency house. Decide right now if you have my six, or head back to the van. Your call."

"No, no, Kolt. I'm okay. I'm over it. First-game jitters, I guess."

"Okay. I need your head on a swivel in there. How about opening that gate again?"

As the gate opened the second time, Raynor slung his HK around his neck along with his backpack full of magazines. He passed the sentry's radio to Hawk and drew his suppressed Glock. She turned the volume low and attached it to her weapon's sling up near her ear, and then extended the stock on the MP7.

The two ran forward into Maadi Land and Sea, with Raynor leading the way with his silenced pistol.

Digger and Slapshot made short work of the metal gate between the pier and the property of Maadi Land and Sea. With their handheld NVGs they could make out both the static and the patrolling sentries, so they timed the noisiest part of their cutting of the metal links for when the guards were farthest away. Digger snapped links with his bolt cutters while his mate held the gate to minimize rattle, and when they had a large enough opening from the bottom of the gate up to peel it back to allow a man to slide through, they stopped and pushed their bodies and equipment into the grounds of the Libyans' property.

As a sentry closed on their position, both men fast-crawled up the reedy embankment to a low concrete retaining wall around a small drainage pipe. This gave them cover from the three sentries in the back of the warehouse property, but a guard on the roof of the three-story office building would be able to see them here if he shone a flashlight on them.

A set of cement steps cut through the center of the property, ahead and twenty-five yards to the right of the two Delta operators. They led to the parking lot behind the warehouse, and by utilizing them they could continue up the hill to the warehouse wall.

But in looking over their surveillance photos they'd noticed devices along the walkway that looked like they might be motion detectors. So the men pivoted to the left, moved low through the weeds, and then headed up toward the warehouse.

Slowly and carefully, and with one eye on the patrolling sentries in the distance.

They almost made it.

They hit the parking lot twenty yards from the wall of the warehouse, and then a bright white light on the roof of the low building flashed on, illuminating them like they were center stage on Broadway. Their night-observation devices whited out, and they flipped them up on their helmets to see. Behind them, their shadows reached all the way into the Nile. Neither man waited around to see if the motion-activated light would be noticed by the security forces at the rear of the property or not. They both sprinted toward the wall of the warehouse.

Digger had been keeping track of the nearest sentry—the man with the Kalashnikov was at the northwest corner of the warehouse near the loading bay. The American slowed just slightly to bring his weapon's red dot sight up to the area, and he found his target. The wide-eyed sentry was lifting his rifle up toward the men in the light in front of him.

Digger squeezed off a pair of bursts toward the man's position, but he was moving too fast to be certain he'd achieved any hits. He ran to the wall while Slapshot slowed to fire at a target to the south.

Kolt and Hawk had made it to the wall of the office building, and they were using it, and a line of cars and SUVs parked there, for cover as they headed to the warehouse.

They flattened themselves in front of the Mercedes S-Class sedan as a sentry passed by on the other side of the vehicle.

Kolt and Hawk hadn't heard the suppressed gunfire but did hear the radio call from Slapshot. "Contact!" Kolt knew the call meant one of his men had pulled the trigger on a bad guy, but the neighborhood had not started scrambling just yet.

Then loud bursts of automatic AK fire from the rear of the property echoed through the parking lot in the front.

"Shit," Raynor said. He knew it was going to go loud tonight, but he had hoped to make it farther than this before the lead started flying.

As the sentry on the other side of the car shouted into his radio for an update as to what was going on, Kolt pulled his black matte-bladed knife from his waistband. He started to rise to take down the sentry from behind, but Hawk squeezed him on the ankle. He looked back over his shoulder quickly, and found Hawk flat on the cement shaking her head no. She pointed ahead, to the north, and Raynor followed her finger. Two more sentries were standing by the front door to the warehouse, thirty yards away. Their weapons were at their shoulders and they were scanning the night.

If Raynor had stood and revealed himself, it was likely he and Hawk both would have been cut down by AK fire.

Kolt just lowered back flat in the shadow of the Mercedes and waited for all three sentries to run off to the north.

Over Kolt's earpiece he heard, "Boss, it's Digger."

"Go," said Kolt, his voice barely a whisper.

"We dropped two sentries back here, but we're pinned. We're behind an AC unit taking fire from the roof of objective Stone. We can't make it around to the loading dock until we suppress that position. Sounds like two shooters on the northwest corner of the roof."

"Roger that. We'll enter Stone and take them from behind. Will alert you when to check your fire."

Kolt turned to Cindy. "Into the building and up the stairs." He stood, drew a nine-banger flash-bang grenade from his duffel, and pulled the pin.

Cindy had no idea what he was going to do with the distraction device here in the open parking lot.

Raynor threw the grenade hard away from them, and then he turned around to the window of the office. As the flash-bang detonated, he smashed and raked the window with the muzzle end of his HK. The grenade's detonation masked the sound of the breaking glass, and it also set off the car alarms on the long row of luxury cars and SUVs. It would bring trouble in seconds, but it might help take some of the pressure off of his two mates battling it out with sentries on the other side of the property.

"Inside!" Kolt shouted as he took a knee and raised the other one. Cindy stepped on Kolt's right knee and climbed quickly but carefully through the broken pane.

Kolt followed close behind.

If Cindy had any issues with Raynor taking liberties with his mission orders from Webber and making entry on the office building, she kept those reservations to herself. She kept tight on her commanding officer's shoulder as they moved through a darkened office. They opened the heavy door and then advanced up a quiet linoleum-floored corridor. Ahead of them they heard shouting from multiple rooms.

Kolt held his suppressed Glock out in front of him with his right hand, but in his left he held on to the MP7. This way, if any single threat presented itself ahead he could, theoretically at least, eliminate it with his silenced pistol. But if several enemy appeared at once and he needed to rock and roll, he could get his short-barreled PDW up in half a second.

As they passed a door with a sign on it, Cindy nudged Kolt.

"Stairwell," she said softly, tipping her head toward the sign.

Kolt nodded and he let his MP7 hang from the sling around his neck as he opened the door with his left hand.

Just on the other side of the door, a man in a suit and tie leapt down the last three steps of the staircase, running toward the door. He held an unslung Kalashnikov with a folded stock in his right hand.

Kolt shot the surprised Saleh confederate three times in the chest with his Glock. Raynor still had to spin sideways and take the dead man's forward impact against his shoulder.

The Libyan dropped to the floor on his back. Hawk kicked the man's AK away from his body.

Kolt then kicked his attacker between the legs to make sure he was dead.

In the stairwell the suppressed .40-caliber rounds echoed off the steel of the staircase, but Raynor had been at this long enough to know that no one else in the building would perceive anything they might have heard as gunfire.

Hawk and Kolt closed themselves in the stairwell, and began heading up to the roof.

TWENTY-SIX

Digger fired a series of short bursts at the northwest corner of the warehouse. Twice a sentry leaned around the corner to fire his Kalashnikov at the two Delta men pinned down behind the large air-conditioning unit that protruded from the building's wall twenty meters away. Digger and Slapshot wanted to head in that direction, to make a right around the corner and enter the warehouse at the loading bay, but there was no way they could run across the parking lot along the wall without getting cut down from above and behind by the men on the roof.

"What about breaching this wall right here with C-4?" Digger shouted to Slapshot as he reloaded. "We can make a big enough hole to get inside the warehouse."

"No place to safely hunker down while we detonate it. Plus, what if there is a stack of Grinch rockets propped up against the other side of this wall?"

"Shit."

Slapshot stepped out from cover for a moment to fire at the roof. As he did so he saw a group of Saleh's men approaching across the parking lot of the office building. He directed his fire at them, sending them scrambling for cover.

He'd not fired more than a few rounds before asphalt in front of him kicked up in dusty, flying chunks, the result of a long burst from an AK three floors up firing down on his position.

Slapshot spun back behind the AC unit and dropped to a sitting position.

"We give Racer another minute to suppress the roof or we're going to have to try for the loading dock, one at a time while the other covers."

Neither man thought that was a tactic with a high probability of success, but the longer they stayed rooted to one position, the faster their chances here would spin down to zero. Just then Racer came over the interteam radio's headsets.

"Check your fire to the roof."

"Roger that," said Digger.

The sentry at the northwest corner was joined by a second gunman. One at a time they leaned out with their rifles and took undisciplined shots at the two men taking cover.

Slapshot said, "I'm gonna thin this herd," and he knelt on one knee and aimed his weapon carefully to the north. He kept perfectly still, waiting to place his red dot on the next piece of flesh to expose itself around the corner, not even flinching when one of the men stuck his AK blindly around and fired a three-round burst that clanged the steel machinery just above Slapshot's head.

Then the second sentry leaned out quickly for a better look.

Slapshot calmly broke the four-pound trigger on his weapon, and pink mist, shiny in the artificial light of the parking lot, erupted from the sentry's forehead.

The body fell from behind the corner into view and his AK-47 tumbled away from him.

"Sweet," Digger said, looking back over his shoulder. Then he leaned away from the protection of the green AC unit and fired again at the five men near the rear entrance of the office.

He struck one of the five in the leg.

As Digger tucked back in to reload, Kolt came over the headset. "The roof is clear."

"Thanks, boss," said Slapshot. And then to Digger, "Let's go!"

Hawk and Raynor had each shot one of the men on the roof, killing them both instantly. Now they were back in the stairwell, heading down to the third floor. Cindy was listening in on the transmissions between the different members of Saleh's organization. With their frantic shouted radio calls, the constant cross traffic, and her limited knowledge of a different dialect of the language, not to mention the adrenaline racing through her body, it was hard for her to make out much of the conversation.

But as they entered the third floor of the office area, she grabbed Racer by the shoulder. She whispered, "One guy sounds like the boss. He says he's called the police and they will be here in five minutes. He's saying something about the BMW. I think he's going to go for the BMW and escape."

"The hell he is," said Raynor.

The pair turned to head back for the stairs, but a door opened down the hall in front of them. Two men dressed in assault vests over white button-down shirts stepped out into the hallway. They were carrying their Kalashnikovs at the low-ready. Raynor and Hawk both lifted their short-barreled PDWs and opened fire, dropping one of the armed men before he was able to get a shot off.

The second man spun away and back into the office.

Raynor charged up the hallway, Hawk moving backward behind him, covering the stairwell and the doors to the other offices.

As Raynor moved closer he heard the sound of sirens approaching up the Kornish al Nile.

At the open doorway to the office Kolt dropped to his knees next to the dead man. He spun into the room low, and a burst of shots went well over his head. He found the shooter, the same man who had just escaped from the hallway, and Raynor shot him dead at fifteen feet.

But there was another man in the room. A silver-haired Arab in a wool sweater and slacks. The man stood behind a walnut desk at the far wall. He held a briefcase tight in each hand. A gold-plated .45 pistol rested on the blotter of the desk in front of him.

It was Aref Saleh.

Raynor rose to his feet, his HK held out in front of him like a pistol. "If you go ahead and reach for that gun, you'd make shooting you a little less complicated."

Saleh looked at the American dressed in black. Hawk backed up to the door now, still looking up the hallway. A woman with bare arms carrying a machine gun. Saleh could not process this strange sight before him.

The Libyan spoke with a quavering voice. "I offer no resistance. I will go quietly."

Raynor raised his weapon to shoot the man through the head. He'd love to take him for any intelligence value, but hauling those two briefcases that Saleh considered so important would probably be almost as good as hauling Saleh himself, and a hell of a lot less troublesome.

Just as Kolt was about to fire, his earpiece came alive with Slapshot's voice.

"Racer, it's Slap. You read me?"

"Go," said Racer.

"We are inside Rhine. No joy on the cargo."

Raynor lowered the gun slightly as he brought his hand to his earpiece. "Say again?"

"Got a few crates of RPGs. A shit ton of AKs and such. But negative on the SA-24s."

"You gotta be sure, Slap. No time to back-clear the warehouse," Kolt said.

"We're sure. Dry hole!"

Behind Kolt, Cindy heard the same message in her earpiece. "Dammit," she muttered.

Raynor looked at Saleh. "Okay. Change of plans. You're going for a boat ride."

By the time they'd tossed Saleh into the dinghy and climbed in behind him, the sound of shrill police sirens was deafening. There were choppers approaching, as well, which made crossing the open ground at the rear of the property more of a rush job than a controlled exfiltration. Kolt and Hawk pushed Saleh along the southern wall and then north along the fence to the hole in the gate, and Digger and Slapshot threw mini–smoke grenades before exiting the warehouse at a sprint, avoiding a few rounds fired in their direction from surviving security men around the property.

The wooden dinghy was designed for four, so they struggled to get all five aboard, but soon enough they were headed upriver, with Digger holding the outboard motor's throttle wide open as he piloted them close to the shoreline to help hide them from the skies.

Slapshot zip-tied Saleh's arms behind his back at the wrists and elbows, and then he used a small nylon sack he kept stored in the utility pouch of his chest harness as a hood, placing it over Saleh's head as they neared their destination. Hawk had already shoved a scarf in his mouth to keep him quiet.

It took them only fifteen minutes to make it back to their panel truck upriver at the launching point of the dinghy. Curtis was unconscious when they began loading up, but he awoke with the noise. When Slapshot pushed a man into the back of the truck next to him and then shut the door, Curtis looked up to Kolt.

With a voice even weaker than before he said, "Holy hell. Is that who I think it is?"

"Yes."

"So much for the covert hit, huh?"

"Didn't go exactly as planned," Raynor admitted.

"And the SAMs?"

"Gone."

"You guys blew them? How many were there?"

"No. *Gone* as in dry hole. Hence our visitor here."

Curtis's eyes narrowed as he looked at the man in the hood. "We need to find out where they are."

The truck began moving as Raynor said, "No shit. How's the leg?"

"Numb."

"Good. We're going to our safe house to the south. We can drop you at a hospital, or we can take you to our place and have a helo pick you up and get you to the embassy."

Curtis reached for his phone. "I've got to figure that black American spies probably will have a long wait at the local hospital, so I'll go to the embassy."

At the Delta safe house on Gamel Abd El Nasir, the panel truck rolled right into the single-vehicle garage and the door was lowered behind. While Digger stayed with Curtis in the vehicle, Kolt took a flex-cuffed and hooded Aref Saleh out of the truck and up the steps, then all but dragged him through the house and into an empty bedroom. He shoved him to the floor, and then stepped out into the hallway. Here he and Slapshot covered their faces with local kaffiyeh head wraps, and Hawk donned a hijab, a traditional head covering for women, which she drew across her face below her eyes.

All three stepped into the room with Saleh without any discussion beforehand. They knew they had no time to waist.

Kolt took the lead, storming across the room and yanking the hood from Saleh's head. The Libyan tried to scream in terror, and he shut his eyes tight.

Kolt yanked the scarf from Saleh's mouth and grabbed the prostrate man by the throat. He put his face so close to Saleh's that the fabric of his head wrap touched Saleh's nose. Kolt spoke in a low, angry voice. "Where . . . are . . . the . . . weapons?"

"I don't know what you are speaking about."

Raynor let go of Saleh's throat now. "You don't know?"

"No. I swear it."

Kolt shrugged. "Damn. He doesn't know. I guess we don't need him." He turned toward Cindy. "Hawk?"

"Sir?"

"Shoot him."

"Yes, sir." Cindy crossed the wooden floor without hesitation. She raised the barrel of her suppressed rifle to his chest—"

"Wait! I tell you!" he screamed.

Raynor reached out and pushed the barrel of Hawk's rifle away from Saleh. "Tell me!" he demanded.

"I . . . I know many things. We can negotiate. I will tell you—"

"The missiles that went to the Iranians. Where are they?"

Saleh hesitated, but only a moment. Then he said, "They left by barge this evening."

"By *barge*?"

"Yes, sir! I swear it to be true."

Dammit. "Where are they going?"

"Ras El Bar."

Kolt looked up to Cindy and then over to Slapshot. Both of them just shrugged. Looking back to Saleh, he said, "Where is that?"

"It is where the Nile reaches the Mediterranean Sea," Saleh answered quickly.

"*Then* where are they going?"

"From there? I . . . I do not know."

"Wrong answer. Hawk?"

"Sir!" Cindy said, and she brought the rifle to her shoulder again.

"No!" the man cried. "I—I am sure they must have a freighter waiting there. But those logistics were not part of the transaction."

"Slap?"

"Yo?" he called from his position at the window.

"Wrap this asshole up good for transport. He's coming with us."

"One pig in a blanket, coming right up."

Hawk lowered her weapon with a pronounced sigh. Kolt had known all along it was an act, and she'd done a damn effective job of it, but the last sigh was a bit over the top for his taste. While the last few minutes had been an Academy Award performance, she'd finished up with World Wrestling Federation dramatics.

Still, there was no question as to whether or not she had pulled it off. Kolt could see where Saleh had wet his pants in terror.

"How are you holding up, Sergeant?" Kolt said as he took his first swig of the icy cold beer five minutes later in the kitchen.

"I'm good, boss." She held her hand up in front of her and looked at it. "First combat and all. No shakes." She paused, then said, "Yet."

"However you react in the coming hours or days, know that it is normal. There is no one way that a soldier processes what he or she has to do."

"You sound a little like a shrink, but thanks."

Kolt laughed. "I am an experienced patient."

"For the record, boss, I was *not* going to shoot Saleh."

Kolt nodded. "And for the record, I *knew* you would not. You fooled him, though, and that's all that matters. You should have been an actress."

"I am an actress. It's a fucked-up stage I'm performing on, though."

Raynor chugged a gulp of beer. "Don't I know it."

TWENTY-SEVEN

Just after dawn at the village along Wadi Bana in southern Yemen, David Doyle knelt on his prayer rug, having finished his morning Fajr, the predawn prayer.

His obligation fulfilled, he thought about his day ahead. He would read his Koran for a few minutes for strength, then he would send an e-mail to his cutouts in Europe, who would forward them on again, and then finally they would reach his contacts. The Igla-S missiles should arrive at their destination within five days, and he did not want the container to spend one more second in control of customs inspectors than necessary. He would have his well-paid agents in the destination country retrieve the sealed container, and he would be there within a day to open it and begin his mission. His e-mail would confirm that his agents were ready to act in accordance with their duties.

After he finished with his message he would work with his men. Eleven of the twelve had passed both their identity legend exam and their aircraft recognition exam and were now working exclusively on fitness, marksmanship, hand-to-hand fighting, and the operation of the Igla-S launcher. The one young man who had not passed was being given another shot later in the day. David decided he would work with this man personally so that he would be ready for travel in three days' time.

David and his four subunit operators would spend several more hours practicing their aspect of the operation. They had shaved a few more seconds off of the time it took them to get out of the container and ready five weapons to fire, now averaging about thirty-four seconds for the entire process.

After a pleading knock on the door, David called out, "Yes?"

Miguel stepped into Doyle's room. The American closed his Koran and looked up. "As *salaam aleikum*," Miguel said with a slight bow.

"*Wa aleikum as salaam*. What is it?"

"We have a problem. Araf Saleh and his operation were taken down last night in Cairo."

"What do you mean, 'taken down'?"

"Either Egyptian intelligence or maybe the CIA. There was a gun battle in Maadi. Saleh was captured, several were killed. I just heard—"

Doyle interrupted his second-in-command. Miguel had switched to Arabic. "In English, please." Doyle commanded everyone to speak nothing but English in preparation for their journey, and he would not let Miguel get away with a breach in this rule even if he was rushed and stressed.

He would be plenty rushed and stressed where they were going.

"Sorry," Miguel said in English. "I meant to say that I just heard the news from our brothers in Cairo. They did not have much information, but did reveal that Saleh is missing. There was a second news story about American businessmen being killed in another part of southern Cairo. Four Americans."

Doyle nodded slowly. "CIA, then."

Miguel said, "Saleh knows us, David. He can destroy everything."

Doyle took a moment to collect his thoughts. With a confident voice he said, "What does he know? Saleh and his people were fools, but they were necessary to our mission. I insulated us from their foolishness. He only knows he sold Russian shoulder-fired surface-to-air missiles to men from al Qaeda in Yemen. He ferried them to a trader in Port Said. He might know that the shipper delivered them to Aden. Even if the CIA tortures Saleh and everyone who touched the weapons up until and including our people in Aden, none of them know the path the goods took after that." David smiled thinly. "I was careful. I was very careful. But still, we will leave immediately. It does not matter how careful I have been. The Americans will still fill the skies over Yemen with their drones. They will concentrate on this province and they will find evidence of this place. Every day we wait is another day when we can be stopped before our plan begins. Not by any error I have made, but only through bad luck."

Miguel understood. Helpfully he said, "Our men are ready."

"Almost all have passed their tests here, but whether or not they are truly ready to go undercover in America remains to be seen. I would have liked more time."

He thought some more before saying, "I will get in contact with leadership and arrange our transportation for today. Gather everyone in the meeting hall, I want to speak with them."

Miguel nodded, and started to turn away, but he stopped. Looking at his leader, he asked, "What about brother Harry? We were going to allow him more time to prepare for the mission."

Doyle looked at the floor. With a bit of sadness he said, "I am afraid time has run out for brother Harry." The man's name was Hussein, he was a twenty-two-year-old Iraqi, and, Doyle and Miguel surmised after a week of training, a severe concussion he received in battle in Mosul in 2008 had left him with an impairment in his memory.

Harry could not remember the different types of aircraft, he could not remember the colors of the airlines, and he could not remember specifics of his legend.

But there was always a chance he would remember this place, the faces he saw here, and the hints inevitably passed on about the tactics, targets, and timing of their mission ahead.

So Doyle decided he would have to kill him.

"Would you like me to do it?" Miguel asked.

"No. I will do it myself." David stood and hefted a Kalashnikov rifle from the table, and he headed out the door.

Eleven cell members were called into the meeting hall in the barracks, and they sat on the floor, shoulder to shoulder in the small room. A space at the end of the back row indicated that one man was missing from the cell, but no one commented on this.

Miguel entered and faced the men, then told them David would be along shortly to make an announcement. No one spoke while they waited for David to appear.

The cell all wore American ball caps and blue jeans and tennis shoes. Were it not for their stone-cold serious faces one might take them for a group of exchange students in a student union in any college in America.

The report of a Kalashnikov firing a single round tore through the air. It was a common sound here in the camp, but some of the men cocked their heads in surprise, as all of the cell members save for two were here in the room together. Yes, it could have been one of the guards, but the firing of a single shot was odd.

A minute after the crack of the AK, David entered the darkened room from the sun outside. He was dressed in local garb, and his men could see the shine from sweat on his forehead.

He spoke English, as he had done for the past nine days of training. "There has been an event in Egypt that threatens our security. For this reason we will begin leaving immediately. We will travel to the east, at first we will be together, but we will separate along the way. We will divide into three groups. Some of us will travel to Dubai, some to Doha, and some to Muscat. From these three locations we will then fly to Mexico City, but that is not our ultimate destination.

"Our destination, my brothers, is the heart of America. We will make our way through Mexico, and cross over the border into the United States on a route that has already been established by our brothers there. Once in the heart of America, we will break into cells, with each traveling in a different direction. One cell will head to the West Coast, one will go to the East Coast, and a third will operate in the interior of the nation.

"Each of these cells will have in their possession twenty surface-to-air missiles."

"Miguel will lead the cell to the west. Thomas will lead the cell into the interior. And I will lead the group to the east. At a predetermined time we will all fire at a departing aircraft. Three large passenger planes, each packed with over two hundred people, will fall burning from the sky."

"After this we will all relocate, and then engage targets of opportunity. I suspect we might each have one more chance to fire on an airplane before the Americans do what they did after the Planes Operation of September 11, 2001. They will shut down all air travel in their skies."

One of the men, a Pakistani who had lived in Wales, asked, "What will we do when the airplanes stop flying?"

"We will go underground while America turns itself inside out searching for us. None of the cells will have any idea of the location of the other cells. Not even I will know where the others are. If one team is captured they will not be able to compromise the mission.

"You all have training on how to live in the United States under deep cover. Even if the subcells need to split into two-man or even individual units, you will keep going.

"America will lose more than six aircraft. It will lose billions upon billions of dollars a day, money it must borrow from China or the Saudis. America will be frantic to put its planes in the air again. And when it can't find us because we have blended in perfectly with its society, it will be *forced* to fly again. But when aircraft venture again into the skies, we will be there, we will come out of the shadows, and we will shoot them down."

All the men were smiling now. David Doyle, Daoud al-Amriki, spoke like a preacher at the pulpit. "The second ground stop will be longer, more costly, destroying the economy completely. The American government will turn on its own people to root us out. This will violate the civil liberties for which the United States holds itself above other nations, and it will reveal to the citizenry that America is nothing but a lie. Armed but weak leaders oppressing the masses. Riots will break out, banks will fail, and institutions will burn to the ground.

"There are thirteen of us. Inshallah, we will succeed in launching all sixty of our missiles successfully, killing over ten thousand nonbelievers in dozens of fireballs across the United States. But our true success will be the fall of the American government.

"You see, my brothers, beyond all this beautiful mayhem we will create, there is my mission. It is in addition to your work, and my mission will ensure that Washington is rocked by the war waging in the skies across the nation."

The men cheered. Some wondered about Harry, but no one asked what happened to him.

They knew, and they understood.

The cell left the base within hours, heading to the east to catch planes that would ferry them to the West.

TWENTY-EIGHT

As the first hint of dawn softened the black sky over Fort Bragg, Kolt and his team arrived at the Delta Force compound. He, Cindy, Digger, and Slapshot had all slept on the long transoceanic flight from Qatar to Atlanta. There they had linked up with a Unit rep at a nearby mall and executed a discreet doc swap, exchanging their cover IDs for their real IDs. In Delta-speak, this was called turning into pumpkins.

With the Cairo AFO gig behind them, they had been wide awake for most of the drive back to Fayetteville. After a half hour to stow their gear and do a quick e-mail check on the Unit's secure local area network, they met up in the chow hall for some coffee and breakfast. They all grabbed a second cup before meeting with Webber in the Beckwith Room for the hot wash of the action in Cairo.

With Webber was a Unit intel officer named Joe. He brought them up to date on a few critical items. He had spoken with the CIA and had learned Myron Curtis had had surgery on his leg the day before, and he was expected to make a slow but complete recovery.

Hawk and Digger nodded at the good news. Kolt looked at the floor and sipped his coffee.

Then came the hot wash. Webber wanted details. Uncharacteristically, he wanted *every* detail. The team filled him in on each and every action of the past week while he sat quietly.

When they were finished, the colonel looked at Kolt. "You a doctor, Major Raynor?" Webber said in an obviously serious tone.

"No, sir!"

"Then can you tell me why you elected to disregard a CIA officer's potentially fatal wounds to conduct a hasty assault?"

"Say again, sir?" Kolt heard him, but was a little stunned by the obvious accusation that his decision-making process in a crisis situation had been flawed.

"Major Raynor, that CIA officer could have died while you and your team were conducting a hit that wasn't entirely time-sensitive. Why?"

Racer hesitated. He knew going on the offensive was a nonstarter, but becoming defensive would be equally damning. But before he could answer, someone else beat him to the punch.

Hawk said, "Sir, I think Major Raynor made the correct command decision based on the available information we had at the time."

Colonel Webber cocked his head slightly and practically looked right through her.

"Hawk, I got it," Kolt said, holding his hand up to signal her to shut the hell up. "Sir, for context, four CIA officers had just been killed in cold blood. Myron Curtis was treated, stabilized, and coherent when we moved on the target."

Webber cut him off and raised his voice. "And he could have died while you were on target!"

"Yes, sir, he could have. In my assessment, at that moment, knowing that the alternative might be letting the missiles get away . . . Curtis was expendable."

Webber raised his eyebrows and stared at Kolt for a few seconds before looking into the other three's eyes to gauge their reaction.

"Slapshot? Was the CIA officer expendable?" he asked.

"Racer made the call, sir. I can't say I disagree with his logic," Slapshot said.

"What about you, Digger? You're the medic."

"Sir, I assessed him. Curtis's vitals were within tolerance. Personally, I would have questioned Major Raynor's ability to serve the Unit as an officer if he would have aborted the mission, considering Mr. Curtis's condition and the nature of the opportunity at target location Rhine."

Webber could see he was losing the argument. The team was sticking together. He didn't like it, especially the part about Curtis being expendable, but he understood. A lot of good men had been lost over the years because commanders had to make tough life-and-death decisions in an instant.

"Okay, before we move on, let me be perfectly clear here. No American is expendable. The Almighty has no problem making those decisions for all of us. Why don't we leave that up to him?"

"Yes, sir." All four said this in unison.

Webber gave Raynor a few more seconds of stink-eye, then he turned to the Unit intelligence officer.

"Joe, fill us in."

The senior intel officer explained that U.S. satellites were tracking two barges heading north on the Nile, both within a day's travel of Ras El Bar, at the mouth of the river. The alert squadron from ST6 had arrived offshore in the Med, ready to get the go-ahead to take one or perhaps both vessels down so they could get the SAMs back.

Kolt was relieved to hear this. He would've liked to have been there, with a remote detonator in his hand, crouched at a safe distance, while pressing a big red button that would make the SA-24s go up in a mushroom cloud.

In a perfect world, Kolt thought.

Oh, well, some lucky ST6 commander was going to get that pleasure, and Raynor knew better than to begrudge him for that. It would be a dangerous mission, and Kolt had a unique understanding of all the worries and stresses that would be on that commander's mind.

Even hits that went off without a hitch were no picnic. He wished them all the luck they could make.

Kolt thought about something else he'd learned from Curtis. "There was an earlier shipment of missiles that went through Cairo. Do we know the location of that?"

Webber stepped in and shook his head. "The ship made port a week ago. We lost the cargo."

"Why the hell didn't we blow it out of the water?"

"Politics. It was a Finnish-flagged boat, so POTUS wanted to be certain of its final destination before allowing it to be taken down. It docked in Aden before the Pentagon got the info to the White House and the White House sent back the go-ahead."

"Damn!" Raynor shook his head in disbelief. "Curtis said there were fifty SAMs on board."

The colonel said, "That was his estimation. We do not know for sure, but we do think a number of SAMs are in play. Al Qaeda in the Arabian Peninsula would be the obvious recipient of these weapons, due to the location they were sent to. The intel community agrees that they may have them to target government-forces helicopters that approach their operational bases and hide-outs in the country. Nobody is assuming that these SA-24s will be used against U.S. or Western commercial aviation."

Kolt had packed his right jaw with chew and turned his Styrofoam coffee cup into a makeshift spittoon by now. He took a long spit and blew out a long sigh. "So . . . CIA says there's nothing for us to worry about."

Webber put his hands up in surrender. "Just passing on the message. Of course there is a hell of a lot to worry about. Langley is just basing their assessment on AQAP's focus during the past couple of years. They have been fighting a civil war, not an international war."

"But . . . boss. They didn't have fifty damn SAMs until a week ago. Who's to say their mission might not have changed?"

"Agree totally, Major."

Kolt did not need to say that AQAP was the organization David Doyle belonged to. "Does TJ know about this?"

"He knows."

"Is JSOC planning to get these SAMs back?"

Webber said, "The President knows how important this is and he is a little pissed. He told the Secretary of Defense to move quicker on any new intelligence."

"So, the gloves are off?"

"Kolt, if the gloves didn't come off after 9/11, they aren't off now. Not in this political climate. But the JSOC commanding general says we have been given a good deal of latitude in course-of-action development to get the missiles out of the hands of the terrorists."

Raynor's frustration bubbled over. "Not exactly a catchy battle cry, Colonel."

Webber shrugged. "It is what it is. The SEALs got the call last time, but keep your kit bags packed because the CG says we have the next one. If the intel folks can find those SAMs in the next forty-eight hours," he said, "then it's likely you will get yourself another hit."

"It's not necessarily about our squadron getting the hit, sir. It's about knocking those SAMs out."

Webber nodded. "It's about both, Kolt. I know you want to be there when it happens. Nothing wrong with that. It's why we do what we do and don't leave it to someone else."

Raynor thought it over. Yeah, it was about getting the SAMs dealt with, but Kolt wanted to be front and center while it happened. This was a big deal. He knew a lot could change in the world before his squadron was on alert again three months from now.

After the meeting, Kolt found Stitch in the Grimes Library. Stitch's hand wound was still bandaged, and the big operator was in the same chair as the last time Kolt saw him, again reading some hefty tome on warriorhood.

"You ever think about going home and watching a game on TV?"

Stitch smiled. "Yeah, but I figure I've got the rest of my life to do just that, so I'll just hang out here a little longer. How was Cairo? Heard you got hitched."

"Hitched by the Army. Then divorced by the Army."

"Trust me, Racer. Someday you will wish it was that easy."

Kolt laughed. He knew Stitch spoke from experience. "How's the hand?"

"Hurting less and less. I'm ready to get back in action. Hoping Doc Markham will release me this week."

"Great. Just in time for training cycle."

Stitch waved the book in his hand. "Beats reading about it. Any chance you guys will deploy again before Gangster and his boys take over?"

"Heading down to the SCIF now to check my sources. You up for a walk?"

Stitch slammed the book shut with a bang and shot to his feet.

Kolt pressed the red button and lifted the phone receiver outside the thick metal SCIF door. "Raynor, 2836."

An audible balanced magnetic switch disengaged and then Kolt opened the door. The SCIF was pretty empty at the moment. An imagery analyst was leaning over a laminating map machine by the door; he looked up and gave a bored nod to the two operators at they entered.

The faint sound of Jason Aldean's "Dirt Road Anthem" could be heard from the back cubicle.

Stitch and Racer made a beeline past the rows of sliding filing cabinets packed with intel folders toward a cubicle near the back wall.

In his two months back in the Unit, Kolt had been down here nearly every day he was in the building, to sniff around for rumors and insight from the experts. Racer always made a point of crediting the intel folks with the lion's share of the work. Without their expertise and unsung dedication, guys like Racer wouldn't have anything to do. Kolt also knew that these men who connected the dots were the same men who could keep Kolt and his men alive.

Kolt had the feeling that a few people in the facility thought him to be a bit of a pest. Some of his old SCIF buddies had moved on while Kolt was away for three years, so he had worked hard and fast to make friends with the new crop—perhaps a little too hard and fast. He knew that came with the territory, but he did his best to not dawdle too long or take too much time from the people working here.

But one man in the SCIF stood out to Raynor for his smarts and his instincts, so Raynor always sought him out and made him feel welcome and important around the building. Kenny Farmer was a young ex–Air Force Intelligence officer who was now a civilian contractor with Booz Allen Hamilton, a strategic intelligence-consulting firm with Defense Department contracts. JSOC had a few Booz Allen guys working with them. They had to endure the same security clearance vetting as anyone else when trying to get a position working for the Unit with access to classified data. Civilian intel augmentees were generally worked like dogs overseas, putting in long hours while the operators lounged around playing Xbox or trading copies of *Playboy* and *Penthouse*. Guys like Farmer would stare at the ISR feed on a flat-screen all night looking for triggers and indicators. Once those were found, the glory boys would roll out quickly, do the deed, and then come back to hot chow. Farmer and the other guys would wait till the assaulters had cleared the chow line, then settle for the cold leftovers, before getting back to the computer to analyze the information brought back from the hit. It was an ugly, continuous cycle for the intel folks, and Kolt very much appreciated all they did.

Farmer was young; Kolt put him no older than thirty. He was red-haired and portly, but his analytical skills were, as far as Major Raynor was concerned, second to none. Anytime Kolt had a question about an image from a UAV or a satellite, or even a question about some of the technology that had come along during the three years Kolt was out of the Unit, Kenny was his go-to man.

Kolt considered his charm offensive with the young geek a success, but in truth Kenny Farmer dreaded his impromptu meetings with the bearded major. Kenny was a bookworm and a computer nerd, as well as a bit antisocial. All the interest from Racer was disconcerting. No Delta officer had ever given him that much attention in the box. Even when he was smiling and cheerful Racer had intense searching eyes; he was a little high-strung for Kenny's taste, and he seemed to show up at Kenny's desk nearly every damn day. Each time Racer left the SCIF, Kenny Farmer breathed a long sigh of relief and wiped sweat off his cheeks with a paper towel from a roll in a drawer, put there for the expressed purpose of wiping off after chats with Major Raynor.

One could easily pick Kenny out of a room of military personnel due to his thick midsection, not uncommon among civilian employees. Racer had invited him to work out or go for runs with him, but Kenny had always managed to find a way out of what he considered to be a horrifying ordeal. Besides, Kenny knew, operators were paid to build their muscles, analysts were paid to build target folders.

Kolt and Stitch came up behind Kenny while he filed something into an upper filing cabinet drawer, and Raynor tapped him on the shoulder. Kenny turned to see the two bearded men looming over him, and Raynor watched the analyst's eyes grow to the size of fried eggs.

"Hey, brother. How's it going?"

The young man forced a smile. "Great, Racer. Welcome back." He then looked to Stitch, and gave him a tentative nod while trying not to stare at his bandaged hand that, everyone in the compound knew, was missing a finger.

"Thanks. Got a minute?"

Kenny always had a minute for Racer, principally due to the fact that he'd yet to think up a reasonable excuse to say no.

"Sure."

"Word is you are one of the team analyzing photos in Yemen looking for missing SA-24s."

"That's right . . ."

"Any luck yet?"

"No." Farmer relaxed slightly, partly because he was comfortable talking about his work, but mostly because he realized he was not about to be asked to run the O-course or negotiate the rat maze with these two jocks. He said, "We know the SAMs went to the port of Aden. And we know the date they landed, but pulled satellite imagery shows no indication of where they went after that. Other assets and resources in theater haven't helped with squat to give us a starting point."

"So . . . where *are* you looking?"

The thick redhead shrugged his shoulders. "Everywhere. Well . . . pretty much everywhere AQ has known territory in Aden."

"That's a big area."

Farmer nodded. "It is. AQ runs around all over southern Yemen. We're focusing on highways and population centers, of course. CIA and the Air Force have aerial collection working it twenty-four/seven."

"You think you'll find the shipment?" Kolt asked.

Kenny hesitated, then said, "I'm going to keep looking, we all are, examining every image the community feeds us of a vehicle or a suspected AQ location that's big enough to hide a MANPAD. But . . . truthfully? No, I don't think we'll find them. Lot's of folks think the SA-24s are staying in Yemen to help AQAP fend off government attacks to their strongholds. But my guess is the SA-24s went to port in Aden in one shipping container, then they got broken out into individual crates and sent right back out on other conveyances. Trains, planes, automobiles, or boats. Those fifty SAMs, plus or minus, could be anywhere on planet earth by now."

Kolt smiled and squeezed Kenny's shoulder. He thought he was being gentle and friendly, but Kenny thought he'd have to grab an ice pack as soon as these two guys left the room. As he squeezed, Raynor said, "Farmer?"

"Sir?"

"You may be right. The SAMs could be long gone. But you are the best analyst in JSOC. It's on your shoulders. Keep looking. Find us *something*. There are high-level AQAP assets cooking up something big, and there are a shitload of SAMs in their possession."

"Yes, sir."

Kolt said, "Eat while you work, don't sleep, piss your pants, time is everything. You understand me?"

"Ye . . . yes, sir."

Kolt nodded, squeezed Kenny's shoulder one more time in a friendly manner that made Farmer wince, then he headed out of the SCIF.

Stitch held back just a minute. "Farmer . . . the major had a point to get across, and I assume that you got his meaning, right?"

"Yeah. Totally."

"Outstanding. Just so you understand, he was speaking metaphorically. Work hard, but there is no need to piss your pants."

"Okay."

As Stitch left the room he wondered if Farmer already had pissed his pants.

TWENTY-NINE

Kolt went back upstairs and poked his head in at RDI, Research and Development Integration. This was TJ's department. There were several men at low cubicles in the room, some of whom Kolt had worked with in his first stint in Delta, and others he'd only known by rep. Kolt said hello quickly to an ex-assaulter named Bobo, who waved back with one hand while he held his desk phone in the other. Bobo had been Racer's teammate in their initial training but had gone to a sister squadron when they crossed the hall. Tragically, within a few months Bobo took a three-story fall during an explosive breach of a window while tethered to a nylon rope. The fall cost him a lower leg and his spot on an assault team.

Raynor then headed to TJ's desk but found it empty.

Tackle, the master sergeant from the other squadron, was sitting on a table shooting the shit with some of the old-timers.

As Kolt turned to leave, Tackle called across the room, "Colonel Timble took a week of leave. Kind of strange since he's only been back a month, but Webber let him go. He's due back the day after tomorrow."

"Did he leave town?" Kolt asked.

Tackle just said, "I wouldn't really know. He's *your* buddy."

There was an inference to that, Raynor knew. He and TJ weren't as close as they had been in the old days.

Before Pakistan.

Kolt looked at Tackle for a moment, but he wasn't in the mood to start anything. He just turned and left the room.

David Wade Doyle passed through customs control without issue at Mexico City's Benito Juarez International Airport. He had not expected problems, even though the passport he gave the officer identified him as a citizen of the United Arab Emirates and Doyle's Arabic was not completely fluid.

But the document was authentic, it had been acquired through al Qaeda agents in Dubai, and Doyle's baggage and person contained no contraband, religious writings, nor any hint whatsoever that he may be carrying radical thought in his head, so he received his entry stamp in short order and headed outside the airport terminal.

He looked through the crowd outside international arrivals and found a man standing there with a sign that read simply HASSAN. Doyle nodded to the man, as his documents identified him as Hassan, and he followed the man out front to a waiting minibus. Doyle climbed into the back while his driver managed his luggage, and soon they were leaving the airport grounds.

His driver was a member of Los Zetas, the most violent criminal cartel operating in Mexico.

Benito Juarez receives regular direct flights from over one hundred destinations around the world, and it serves over twenty-five million passengers a year. It is a huge cargo hub, as well, and dozens of shipping and receiving warehouses rim the airport and extend out into the sprawling hills.

The hills around Mexico City also contained dozens of neighborhoods and suburbs, over twenty million inhabitants, and thousands of opportunities for David and his men to disappear and operate. It was a near-perfect destination for a criminal operation such as a terrorist cell, but this was not the only reason Doyle chose the capital as the first waypoint of his route in the Western Hemisphere.

No, his organization's connections in the Zetas drug cartel had assets here that would help Doyle and his men get his weapons and then move them north through drug cartel country without interference from either a competing criminal enterprise or government military or police forces.

The Zetas did not control Mexico City, no one cartel did, but they brought men, weapons, money, and chemicals through Benito Juarez International

Airport on a daily basis, so they were experts on moving from Mexico City to the north in a clandestine fashion. And even though a formal alliance between al Qaeda and the cartels of Mexico had been exaggerated over the years, this particular cooperation had been arranged as a single transaction, and all parties were well motivated to see that it went off without a hitch.

The Zetas would receive a large quantity of heroin delivered from Pakistan for their work on this operation, and al Qaeda in the Arabian Peninsula would get a dozen men and sixty shoulder-fired missiles into the United States of America.

Yes, both entities were well motivated to make this happen.

They drove for forty minutes but remained within the borders of the massive city, ending up in a walled private house in the San Pablo Chimalpa subdivision to the west of town. Doyle was led inside by the driver, who quickly placed the bags by the door and drove off.

Over the next six hours this driver returned four more times from the airport to the home, each time delivering men from Doyle's cell. Miguel, Roger, and Steven came with the second load, Jerry and Tim and Peter and Andrew came with the third. In the fourth van from the airport Benjamin and Charles and Nick arrived, and George and Arthur were delivered by the fifth trip from the airport.

After half a day all the men's flights had arrived on schedule from Dubai, from Manama, from Bahrain, and from Doha, in Qatar. All thirteen al Qaeda cell members made it into the country without a single issue with passports, visas, or customs.

The men prayed together as a group, but this was their only acknowledgment of their true selves. Otherwise they wore Western clothing, spoke English, and watched baseball on television, all waiting for the next morning, for their mission in Mexico to begin.

Two days after returning to Bragg from his operation in Egypt, Kolt and his squadron were officially taken off alert status. After all the action of the past month, and the unfinished business, the turnover to their sister squadron was a letdown for Major Raynor and his men.

Anything that happened now, or for the next couple of months, anyway, would be handled by Gangster and his mates. Raynor could not help but think of the SAMs on the loose in Yemen, or the hunt for AQ commander David

Wade Doyle, or any one of a dozen hot spots around the world that could flare up at any time.

Gangster was an asshole, Kolt knew this as fact, but Gangster and Tackle and Monk and Benji and the rest of the men were badass operators and they would get the job done with every bit of the skill of Kolt and his team.

Though he was off alert, Raynor did not have any downtime to speak of. On the contrary, he and his mates were about to begin a long and arduous training phase, though Kolt knew he would spend most of this behind a desk. The assault teams would be traveling to exotic places like Key West for civilian boat training, or Jackson Hole for mountain climbing, or Nevada for an off-road driving course. Officers weren't always welcome and they had plenty of administrative tasks to handle back at the compound. Writing up awards, conducting evaluations of subordinates, and planning future troop- and squadron-level training were daily duties for Raynor and the other officers in the Unit. Any free time Kolt had was split between the gym and the range.

He'd planned on working late into the evening that first day off alert, but a surprise call from TJ and an invitation to dinner sent him to Huske Hardware House just after eight p.m.

As soon as they saw each other and grabbed a table by the bar, TJ said, "So, another alert cycle behind you. Sure that feels pretty good."

"It sucks. Our OPTEMPO was insane, but we left a lot of loose ends out there."

Timble shrugged. "You've been at the right place at the right time, or the wrong place at the wrong time, depending on how you look at it, for most of the past month. You could use some downtime, amigo. You look like shit. Don't worry. I'm going to go out on a limb and promise that the world won't be a perfect place by the next time you get called to bat. JSOC will put your talents to good use then."

Kolt smiled. He knew his friend was right. "Speaking of downtime, I heard you've been off the net for a week. Did you go home to see your folks?"

TJ shuffled in his chair while he sipped his beer. Kolt knew him well enough to see clearly that there was something he was hesitant to talk about.

Raynor smiled. "Oh, shit. You found yourself a woman?"

"Nothing like that. I went out to California."

"What, no women in California?"

TJ turned even more serious now. "I went to Kelseyville."

Raynor had heard the name, but he could not immediately place it.

"Did we do building training there years ago?"

"It's where David Doyle grew up," Timble explained.

Kolt put his beer down. "Okay. Why?"

"I don't really know. Just wanted to go. I stood outside of his parents' house. Went to his high school, the grocery store where he worked."

"Sounds like you are building a target folder, brother."

"No. He's not going back home. That's not his style."

"Then what the hell *are* you doing, bro?"

"I just wanted to understand the guy. I wanted to know how he thinks. I want to be able to figure out his next move."

"On your leave? You can get that from the SCIF."

"Yeah, of course." He shrugged. "The Feds have got profilers, but who knows if they really have a feel for him? Not like I do. I met the guy last year. I talked to him, I argued with him, I punched him in the damn face." He paused for a sip of beer and then said, "I got a buddy in the FBI to give me a copy of some of Doyle's stuff. High school term papers, letters home to family after he emigrated to Yemen. Shit like that."

"I think you need a piss test."

"I admit, it sounds weird."

Raynor thought that was an understatement. But still, he asked, "Did you learn anything?"

"I think so. I spend each and every night going over every scrap of paper that has anything to do with David Wade Doyle. His known and suspected contacts in Pakistan, the events of his hit against the Khyber Pass black site last year, the writings of the mosque in Aden where he studied the Koran. I'm getting this bastard down cold."

Kolt was taken aback. TJ had always been an intelligent and intense soldier, but this level of focus was obviously personal. He asked, "Do you really think you know stuff the profilers at the FBI, or the folks at Langley, haven't figured out for themselves?"

"I don't know. I just think I can—"

A shout across the restaurant interrupted the thought. Then several people hushed the crowd as televisions were turned up near the bar. A news story showed video of a burning boat, taken from a helicopter. TJ and Kolt both stood up to get a better look. The volume was increased to where the two operators at the table could hear the female newscaster read her copy over the video.

"Unnamed government sources say that SEAL Team Six, America's most highly trained commandos, executed a daring and, by all accounts, perfectly executed raid early this morning on a cargo ship in the Mediterranean Sea."

The restaurant erupted in cheers. Raynor leaned closer to the television to hear the rest of the report.

"Under cover of darkness, SEALs boarded a freighter in international waters and recovered twenty-two SA-24 Russian-built, shoulder-fired surface-to-air missiles. The ship was a Panamanian-flagged freighter en route to Lebanon.

"This brings to over two hundred the number of recovered SA-24s since the fall of Libyan dictator Colonel Muammar Gaddafi last year.

"In March of this year, an SA-24 took down a passenger flight in Jakarta, Indonesia, killing all two hundred sixty-six on board.

"Experts say as many as two thousand of the shoulder-fired rockets are still unaccounted for, and many are presumed to be for sale on the black market, where fears remain that they could fall into the hands of terrorists and rogue states."

A brief video played over and over throughout the report as a retired Army-general-turned-talking-head fielded questions from a satellite studio. File footage of a stack of SAMs in a warehouse in Tripoli. Kolt had seen the footage dozens of times before.

He would love to have seen video of the actual SEAL takedown of the boat.

When the piece was over, Kolt looked back across the table to find TJ smiling at him. "Watching that story while sitting on a barstool would have *really* pissed off the old Kolt."

Raynor raised his eyebrows. "He would be fuming. That is true."

"How are *you* handling it, though?"

TJ showed amusement in talking to Kolt as if he were two different people.

"The old Kolt would have had TJ there to cover for him if he said something stupid." He paused, then said, "I'm okay. But I wish you would hurry up and become operational again, so I can go back to being a dickhead."

TJ's eyes widened, but Raynor just burst into laughter.

Just then, Cindy Bird entered the bar, looked around for a moment, and saw Kolt. She smiled and headed over to his table.

"Hey, boss." She then nodded to Lieutenant Colonel Timble and said, "Sir."

TJ said, "You just missed the news about America's bravest warriors."

She giggled. "Same as ever, right? SEALs are keeping us all safe and sound. Yeah, just heard it on the radio."

Kolt had not seen Hawk since the hot wash. "Pull up a stool."

"Thanks." She sat down and ordered a Level-Headed German Blonde Ale.

"You doing okay?" Kolt was asking her about her feelings after the Cairo hit, specifically how she felt after shooting at least one man dead in the operation.

She picked up on this, and her smile drifted away a moment, unsure of what she should say in front of TJ. "I'm fine, actually. I feel like we did the right thing."

Kolt nodded. "Don't feel it. *Know* it. I do."

She nodded. "Right."

"You seen the psych yet?" Kolt asked.

"No, tomorrow morning," Cindy answered.

TJ knew he had no part in this conversation. He had not been there, on the ground, when the bullets were flying. He decided to give them some space. He grabbed his wallet and tossed some bills on the table. "I'm out." He looked at Racer. "Guess I'll be seeing more of you around campus."

"For the next couple months, you'll see a ton of me."

After TJ left, Hawk scooted her barstool over to face Racer. "TJ is looking better."

Kolt agreed. "Every time I see him."

"I've always wondered. How did a guy with the initials JT get the code name TJ?"

"Why didn't you ask him?"

Cindy smiled. "Because I thought maybe there was an embarrassing story behind it."

Now Kolt smiled, then sipped his beer. "Not his greatest moment, but could have been worse."

"Tell me."

"TJ has nothing to do with his initials. It's short for 'towed jumper.'"

"Oh, shit!" Cindy knew what a towed jumper was. "When was this?"

"Jump school at Fort Benning. Josh exited the aircraft but his main chute failed to deploy, so he hung from his static line fifteen feet out the door. The jumpmaster couldn't get him winched back in. Josh bounced around for a good thirty seconds before he was cut away. He deployed his reserve chute fine, landed with a few bumps and bruises."

"So JT became TJ," Cindy said.

"Beats DD."

"What's DD?"

"It's what they call the guys who don't get good canopy on their reserves in time. A 'dirt dart.'"

"Damn."

"The Army knows how to give you a thrill."

"Take us, for example. When I get married for real, the honeymoon is going to seem pretty bland compared to the one we just took."

"No shit," Kolt said as he drank.

Cindy laughed, but she stopped suddenly as she looked at a man approaching through the crowded bar. He was young and extremely muscular, and the hair products making his spiky black tufts stand straight up shone under the bright lights over the bar.

He wore an Ed Hardy muscle shirt to emphasize the amount of time he spent in the gym.

"Oh, shit," she said.

The young man walked up to the table, looking first at Cindy, and then regarding Raynor.

"Hi," said Kolt.

The young man did not respond.

Cindy spoke nervously. "Uhh, Kolt, this is Troy. Troy, this is Kolt."

Troy was Cindy's boyfriend, this much was obvious to Raynor. He stuck out a hand with no real expectation that the Green Beret would shake it. He did not, and Kolt retracted the hand.

"Okay," said Cindy, "I'll see you at work, Kolt. Have a good one."

Troy just sat down, right in front of Raynor. "Go get us a table. I'm going to talk to this guy a minute."

"Troy, let's just—"

"Do it," he said, and Cindy headed off to grab a table for two. Kolt just raised his eyebrows in surprise at what the tough girl was putting up with in her personal life.

"Thought you were going to get a little tail tonight?"

Raynor did not respond. He just held eye contact with Troy.

"How old are you, pops?" asked Troy.

Kolt smiled now. "How old are you, shithead?"

"I'm twenty-nine."

"I'm thirty-eight."

"Damn," Troy said in surprise. "That's been a rough thirty-eight."

"Tell me something I don't know," replied Raynor.

"I'll tell you something you don't know. Cindy is too young for you. And she's taken."

Kolt just shook his head. "Buddy, you need to relax."

"I don't know who you are or what you do. If you've got to work with her, then there's not a damn thing I can do about that. But if I catch you hanging out with her off post again, I'm going to kick your ass."

Kolt knew he should do his best to talk his way through this encounter for the simple reason that he wasn't much good in bar fights. He had little experience or success in administering black eyes and fat lips. No, when Kolt got into a hand-to-hand encounter, he had the habit of either putting the other man in the intensive care unit or in the morgue.

Kolt Raynor just smiled. "Troy . . . I hate to admit it, but I was a lot like you once."

"What the fuck is that supposed to mean?"

"You know exactly what that means. I was a jackass."

Troy stood up and started around the table, his fists balled in anger.

Oops, thought Kolt. *So much for talking this guy out of a fight.*

Raynor was at a distinct physical disadvantage sitting at the table with the muscular soldier looming over him. But he did not stand up and square off with him. He just eyed Troy as the Green Beret reached back with his right hand and then fired a right hook at Raynor's jaw.

The punch never connected. Josh Collins, the owner of the restaurant, grabbed Troy from behind by the biceps, then twisted the young man's arm behind his back and slammed his head down on the table. Collins pinned him there, face-to-face with Raynor.

Troy was obviously stunned by this turn of events and by the strength of the proprietor of the restaurant.

Collins said, "This is a family establishment, son. A street fight needs to be taken out into the street."

Raynor just smiled. Now he was the one looking down at Troy. He knew Collins had a sixth sense for trouble around his bar, and Kolt had seen the ex-Ranger move in behind the unsuspecting sergeant the moment the kid stood up from his barstool.

Kolt took a sip of his beer, placed his glass back on the bar, and looked at Collins. "Thanks."

Collins just nodded while he kept the pressure on the man's arm and the back of his head. "I see you haven't lost your touch for pissing people off, Major."

"This time it is a clear misunderstanding. Mind if I try and rectify it before you toss him?"

Collins shrugged, and Kolt leaned forward. "Okay, Troy. Number one, Sergeant Bird and I work together, that is all. Number two, she obviously sees something in you, otherwise she wouldn't give your mouth-breathing, knuckle-dragging dumb ass the time of day, so you might want to think about treating her with a little more respect before she wakes up and decides that you are not only ugly and stupid, but you are also an asshole, at which point she will hit the bricks and find someone worthy of a woman with her obvious beauty, intelligence, and poise."

"Look," Troy said with his face pressed hard into the tabletop. "I—"

"*You* look, Sergeant. I've got no problem with you at all. In fact, from what little time I've spent around Sergeant Bird, I've heard good things about you, and I do know her well enough to respect her judgment to some degree. All that said, if you want to go to war with me out of some misplaced need to compensate for some shortcoming, we can go outside, at which point I *will* fuck you up."

"I thought that you—"

"You and me and Bird have real enemies in this world, Troy. We are in the military because we feel the call to fight those enemies. I understand how shit can get turned around in your head to where you lose track of that for a minute. I was twenty-nine once myself, though back then the Krauts and the Japs required my full attention, so I never got the chance to court a young lady as lovely as Sergeant Bird."

Troy seemed to relax with the joke. Collins kept the pressure up in case the young man still tried to lunge at Raynor.

Kolt wrapped up his speech. "But you are a Special Forces man, which means you deserve my respect and you have it. It also means you have a hard job against hard enemies, so you would do well to make friends when you can."

Kolt looked up at Josh Collins and gave him a subtle nod, and Collins released his grip on Troy. The SF soldier stood up slowly.

Raynor reached out his hand again and, this time, Troy took it.

"I'm sorry, sir. Shitty day all around, I guess."

Kolt stood. "No problem." He looked over to Cindy, who was sitting alone in a booth and staring back at the two men, her eyes wide at the quick turn of events. Raynor slapped Troy playfully on the arm. "Got a feeling your evening is going to be just fine."

Kolt nodded to Cindy and headed out the door, shaking Josh Collins's hand on the way.

THIRTY

On the evening of their first night in Mexico, David Doyle and three of his cell members left the safe house in San Pablo Chimalpa and headed toward the airport in a van driven by a man working for the Zetas.

They pulled into the gated property of a shipping company on Ruiz Cortina, just off the airport grounds, and drove past armed sentries in blue uniforms, and through iron gates that locked again behind them. They were then ushered out of their van and taken into a large nondescript storage building set apart from the warehouse.

Along the wall of the building were three air freight containers, each one the size of a small car. Their doors were sealed, and a sticker affixed to each one showed the shipping point of the cargo. Even though all the goods had left the Middle East through Dubai, the shipping origins of these containers read Paris, Marseilles, and London.

The agent the Zetas arranged for the al Qaeda cell to use was accustomed to the importation of contraband. He and his people had taken care of everything on this shipment, including the bribing of Mexican officials, so the containers remained sealed and had not been X-rayed while in customs control. They had cleared customs the day before and had remained untouched, here in the receiver's storage building.

Also, as previously arranged, the Mexican agent had purchased four International TerraStar medium-duty work trucks, each a different color, and each with a covered bed that could carry fifteen crated Igla-S systems. The ample cab space allowed for four men, including the driver. The trucks were not new, but the agent followed his instructions from his mysterious Middle Eastern contacts to the letter, and he had each of the vehicles painstakingly checked and reconditioned.

These four vehicles were lined up in the warehouse next to the sealed containers, and next to these trucks sat several canvas bags. Each bag contained a Kalashnikov rifle with a folding stock and several loaded magazines.

Compliments of the Zetas.

The Mexican agent left the Middle Easterners to their work and they broke open the seals of the shipping containers and began loading the crates onto the trucks.

It was the first time any of the cell other than David and Miguel had seen a crated Igla-S MANPAD system in person.

It was backbreaking work for only four men, but Doyle did not want to expose his entire force in case the agent double-crossed them and sold them out to the authorities. It took over a half hour to load the cargo, and another forty-five minutes to return to the safe house. Here Doyle took the license plates off the trucks and handed them to four more of his men. Each of these men then left the house that night under cover of darkness, and returned later with a different plate. The truck plate they had placed on a parked vehicle somewhere in the neighborhood, exchanging it for the parked vehicle's plate.

It was not perfect tradecraft, but he expected it to get them through the next days in Mexico in case the agent turned them in down the road.

At eight a.m. on their second day in-country, David and his men stood in the large driveway of the home, their missiles and guns loaded onto the four trucks. As rain fell, a single black Jeep Liberty stopped at the edge of the drive, and a man climbed out of the passenger seat.

He was Hispanic, late twenties, and armed with a small Ingram MAC-10 machine pistol that swung from a strap on his shoulder, the black metal glistening wet on the outside of his green rain parka.

David and Miguel stepped up to him as he scanned the group of men by the trucks.

"You are Henrico?" David asked.

"Yes. David?"

Doyle just nodded. "I assume you have more men and vehicles?"

Henrico reached into his parka to his belt and pulled out a walkie-talkie. He handed it to David. "Take this to communicate. The total distance of our journey is thirteen hundred miles. We will have seven vehicles in the convoy in addition to your four. They will stay in traffic, mostly ahead of you, until we get out of the city, but as we head north we will be all around you. We have a bus, a minibus, some sedans, some SUVs. Twenty-eight men. We will drive all day and arrive at our first destination after nine p.m. Tomorrow we will go farther, and arrive at the border around midnight."

"You don't want to drive at night?" David asked.

Henrico shook his head. "On some of these highways, only a fool or an army drives at night. We are like an army, but we do not want anyone to know this. We will travel during the day."

"Fine," said Doyle. It was much the same back in Yemen.

Henrico said, "On the morning of the third day, we will take you to the final destination, where more vehicles are waiting for the crossing."

David nodded. He did not like depending on the Mexicans, though his organization had used them in the past in smaller-scale operations to test their competence and trustworthiness, and they had passed these tests with flying colors. These Zetas were coldhearted killers, but they did not kill for ideology or for honor. No, they were in it for the money. David's benefactors had paid them well with heroin and access to more heroin and, David knew, there was no way he could get his men and his munitions into the United States without making an alliance with these criminals whose expertise on the southern border would be crucial to his operation's success.

David said, "Your men. I assume they are armed?"

Henrico smiled. "*Sí, señor.* Rifles and RPGs. But we do not expect problems. The route we are taking should be safe. The Federales are patrolling more to the west, and our scout car in front will alert us of any police or Army roadblocks. If we run into bandits or other competition"—Henrico patted his MAC-10—"we will take care of it."

Doyle knew these men would be decent fighters. Not good, but good enough for most encounters.

"All right. Let's go."

Minutes later, Doyle and his four TerraStar trucks were rolling out of the driveway and toward the United States.

•   •   •

Kolt spent his morning at the rifle range with several of his mates, and then he showered, slammed some powdered protein from a blender in the squadron lounge, and had just sat down behind his desk to do some paperwork when his secure red line rang.

"Racer," he said.

"Hi, Racer. Kenny Farmer here, from down in the—"

Kolt interrupted him. "You got something?"

"I'm not sure what it is, but I did find something. Yes. If you want, I can—"

"Stay put. I'm en route," Kolt said, and he hung up the phone.

Racer leaned over Kenny Farmer, too close for the redhead's comfort, and he looked at the Booz Allen man's monitor. On it was a thermal overhead image of a simple village. Raynor's eyes flashed to the time stamp on the lower left portion of the photo, and saw that the shot was taken three nights prior.

"Where is this?"

"It's a no-name settlement in southern Yemen, about a hundred and fifty klicks south of Sana'a, just east of Wadi Bana."

"AQAP territory?"

"Most definitely, although we've never heard a peep out of this tiny speck. Al Masani, just to the east of this grid, is a hotbed. CIA has launched three Hellfire strikes there in the past year."

"So . . ." Kolt asked, "what am I looking at here?"

Farmer tapped a tiny building's roof with his pen. "See the heat signature off of this structure?"

Raynor did, and he'd spent enough time looking at thermal images in his career to get an idea of what was going on. He said, "It's uniform all over the structure. Not like warm bodies inside, or cooking fires." Kolt looked up to Farmer and spoke as if he were guessing the answer on a quiz in school. "It doesn't have central heat . . . Is this building made out of metal?"

Ken nodded. "Yes. Steel, by the looks of it."

Kolt looked back to the screen. He tried to get an idea of the size of it by comparing it with a donkey standing nearby. "Is it a shipping container?"

Farmer smiled and nodded, either impressed with Racer's analytical abilities or just faking it to be polite. "It's a twenty-foot standard dry goods intermodal shipping container."

Kolt knew these devices well. Although Delta operators did not find themselves working on or around ships as much as SEAL Team 6 crews, intermodal containers were carried by truck and stored in warehouses and ports and were therefore ubiquitous in locations where Delta might find themselves operating. He had trained on and around shipping containers many times over the years.

"I would have thought the heat register would have been higher," Kolt said. "I mean, this *is* Yemen in the summer."

"It *should* be higher," the younger man agreed. "What I think they have done, along with painting the walls the same color as the baked brick buildings all around, is cover the roof of the structure with burlap or canvas or something to mask the register. It helps, but the focal-plane-array thermal imagers on our collection assets can see right through them."

Raynor pulled up a chair and sat next to Farmer slowly. "So . . . so it looks pretty obvious that this is something they are trying to mask from UAVs overhead."

"No question about it. Whatever is in that container is something they are trying to keep under wraps."

"Does the rest of the village look quiet?"

"At first we thought it was quiet. No obvious militant presence. But . . ." Farmer said as he began clicking away on his keyboard. Kolt got the impression that the Booz Allen contractor was glad he'd been asked the question. "But after I found the intermodal container out here in the boonies, I double- and triple-checked everything we have on this vil." He took a few more seconds to bring up a set of overflight images in daylight. He moved to a picture of a highway bisecting low brown hills, and he enlarged it. He said, "It's only by chance that we caught this shot. UAVs overfly the village all the time, but with a regular overflight they never would have caught it. But these pictures came from a Reaper on station in a sector well to the south, looking at some traffic on the highway near Al-Sàfra. It looks, from the progression of the images, like the camera was just recording as the UAV circled around, when it caught this." He zoomed in again and enhanced the image.

Kolt Raynor cocked his head and leaned forward. On the screen he could make out two simple buildings, photographed at an angle shallow enough to show the walls, windows, and doors, instead of the roofs. Raynor saw some sort of covered walkway that led between the buildings, and two men walked under the covering, shaded against the sun and hidden from any UAVs flying overhead.

Kolt focused on the men, but Kenny Farmer used the tip of his ballpoint pen to point to the tops of the buildings. "Here and here," he said, referring to both structures.

Kolt said, "I see shadows, but it's too dark to see anything there."

"Exactly," confirmed Farmer. "But it's not what's there that is important. We can infer what is there."

Kolt was confused. He chuckled, admitting that he was lost. "We can? *You* can, maybe, you are the whiz kid. I'm just the dumb ROTC grad."

Farmer laughed at this. "What I mean is . . . I can tell that this is some sort of false roof on the building. On both buildings. It has been created by putting beams up at all four corners and covering them with canvas. Under the canvas, just like under the material covering up the intermodal container, lies something the people at this location do not want us to find."

Kolt nodded. "From the placement here at the tops of the buildings and overlooking the open ground to the south, I wonder if they could be gun emplacements."

Farmer said, "I guess you aren't just a dumb ROTC grad, sir. That's what I think it is."

"So this village is not just a little collection of houses. It's a fortress."

"A clandestine fortress," Farmer said. "I spent all day looking over the images we have of the vil, the vehicles coming and going, the tracks in the dirt around there, things like that. And I have found things."

"What things?"

"Motorcycle tracks down to the wadi, although I don't see any bikes in the village. They have a burn pile for their trash that looks like it's working about four times harder than one would expect for the trash accumulated by dirt-poor civilians in the quantity that we would expect to find living in a settlement of this size."

"You're pretty slick."

"Thank you, sir, but I'm not slick enough. I'm sure there's something I've left out. I wish I could get more overflights of this area from the north, maybe just to see if more of the structures there have false roofs."

"I'm sure you'll get it with this intel that you've pulled off of the images we have." Kolt was damn impressed, but nearly certain this fake village wasn't actionable enough for JSOC to commit to it. He knew how hard it was to get boots on the ground in Yemen. He asked, "Anything else? Anything at all?"

Farmer nodded, then brought a new image up on the monitor. It was a further enhanced shot of the two men under the covered walkway.

Kolt looked at it for a long moment. "Is that guy on the right wearing . . . No. No way."

Ken Farmer just looked at Raynor. "It's two males. One in garb traditionally worn in the area."

Kolt blinked hard and leaned forward. "And the other guy has on blue jeans and a baseball cap."

"And what look like tennis shoes," Farmer added. "I don't think this is a CIA base, though, just from the location."

"No way. We'd know." Kolt did not look away from the monitor to say, "I'll be damned."

The four TerraStar trucks full of Igla-S surface-to-air missiles pulled off the highway and into their first overnight destination just after eight p.m. Ahead of their arrival four of the vehicles driven by the Zetas gunmen had rolled up the long gravel drive and then parked, and the dozen or so men inside the vehicles had fanned out to guard the area.

David Doyle had been traveling in the third vehicle in the TerraStar convoy and as he climbed out to stretch his tight muscles he looked around at the location. Under a moonlit sky he could see the Sierra Madre Occidental all around him and, in his immediate vicinity, a cluster of large vacant buildings built on a rocky expanse of ground next to a mountainside.

As Doyle took in the view here in the dark, Henrico appeared next to him. "This is a vacant silver mine. We have used it many times in the past when we have convoys passing through this part of Coahuila. There is only access from one road, and I can put my men on the hills to see the highway from a great distance. There is some risk from helicopters, of course, but we will put men on higher ground to watch out for them."

Henrico continued, "We have twelve men on guard duty around the mine. I am in contact with them. If there is any trouble, we will be ready."

Doyle left the Mexican by his truck and walked back to the rear Terra-Star. Here, Miguel stood with Charles, Nick, and George.

David said, "I want two of our men awake all night. Everyone stays armed, even while sleeping."

Miguel said, "Very well, David. I will organize this."

Doyle then walked away from the group, made his way up a pile of black rock discarded during the mining process, and took out a mobile phone and battery set that he'd bought at a gas station that afternoon. He put the battery in the phone, then activated it with the prepaid card he'd purchased along with the phone.

It took a minute for the device to power up, but as soon as it did, David dialed a number that he'd committed to memory months ago.

The call was to the United States, and it took a moment to make the connection, but soon enough Doyle heard the ringing signal.

"Hello?" The voice was tentative.

"Hello," David said, his own voice lighter and more relaxed. "I wanted to let you know we will be in town soon. Not more than four days' time. Perhaps a little sooner."

"Good."

"Are you ready for our visit?"

A pause. "All is in place. We are ready. We are excited."

"Then I can't wait to get there." Doyle looked down to his watch. Only twenty seconds had passed since the man on the other end had answered. "Good-bye," he said. And he quickly ended the call. Then David took the battery out of the back of the phone, and smashed the device with his bootheel.

The discovery of the shipping container in the clandestine militant stronghold in al Qaeda territory sent a shock wave through the U.S. intelligence communities. Numerous satellites were diverted and more overhead flights of the area became an instant priority, and within thirty minutes of a directive being sent out to Langley assets in the area, an unarmed Predator drone's cameras were snapping tens of thousands of digital frames of the tiny settlement along Wadi Bana.

The video and still images were fed to Langley, and there, imagery analysts went to work.

They found women and children in the village, but they also found canvas-covered breezeways between freestanding homes, gun emplacements on the roofs of six of the buildings, armed men with binoculars on the hillside who, no doubt, served as lookouts for the village, and the telltale sparkle of spent rifle and pistol ammo in the dirt. Most telling, though, was that all the historical pulls of sat images couldn't find a single evening in the last two weeks when the occupants had slept on the roof. Prior to that, for the past seven months, there wasn't a night they hadn't slept on the roof. Something, for some reason, had forced a change in an age-old local custom.

This was no innocent settlement in the hills.

Just three hours and twenty minutes after Kenny Farmer pointed out the curiosities in the tiny village in Yemen to Kolt Raynor, Langley and JSOC had determined the village to be a clandestine training camp of al Qaeda in the Arabian Peninsula. Kolt thought that determination should have taken only about twenty minutes.

This information went straight to the Secretary of Defense, along with the CIA's admission that, without a well-placed HUMINT or human intelligence asset in the village, they could not know what was going on there without boots on the ground, kicking in doors and searching the homes, barns, corrals, and adjacent area.

They did not need to remind SECDEF that approximately fifty SA-24 Grinch man-deployable air-defense systems had disappeared in that area, and the President of the United States had demanded that the weapons be found before they could fall into the wrong hands.

The order to send the Delta alert squadron to Yemen came at 1700 hours. ST6 was still deployed in the Mediterranean after their operation to take down the SAMs purchased by Quds Force operatives, so they were much closer than Gangster and his men at Fort Bragg, but ST6 was also close to getting a high-probability hit themselves of a suspected cache of SA-24s and other munitions in Libya, near Sirte. There was plenty of work for everyone.

Gangster and his team were wheels-up at nearby Pope Field at 1930. They would be flying to Eritrea in advance of the mission into Yemen, although they would work on the details of the hit throughout the flight, just in case their timeline got pushed up and they had to do an in-extremis hit.

All this activity meant little to Kolt Raynor, other than the fact that he and his mates would have a little more room around the compound the next day. He planned on heading in early in the morning and sticking around, so he could be there to listen in to the radio chatter between the guys on target and the JOC.

Raynor knew he had been center stage almost constantly for most of the past month, but right now he felt incredibly left out. It was an operational imperative to rotate fresh guys into the fight, because killing is not an innate character trait. It can be in one's blood—in fact, after 9/11, most Americans would have argued it was in theirs—but it's not passed down from one generation to the next. Some are into it more than others, but after a while, after ten years of killing, even in the mind of a Delta operator, a switch flips. Everyone has limits.

Everyone needs a break.

He had been off the net for three years, but like Webber implied at Relook, the rules had changed. It didn't take him long to see it in his former teammates. One of his former assaulters even argued that guys with eight rotations to the box either sat the next one out or succumbed to extensive testing for post-traumatic stress disorder and traumatic brain injury. Raynor was moved by the humble admission that even America's most highly trained killers were not immune to the psychological impact of war. The Unit psych was arguably the busiest and most important member of the command.

Other than the chaplain.

Kolt knew the rules, and he understood he had to stand down for a while. He resolved himself to getting his entire squadron in the best shape, mentally and physically, that he could, before they returned to bat in three months.

THIRTY-ONE

By ten o'clock at the abandoned silver mine in Coahuila, Mexico, most of the al Qaeda operatives and the Zetas gunmen had formed into small groups, either sleeping in, on, or by their vehicles, or on sleeping mats inside the derelict buildings of the mine. A few flashlights scanned the distance and the occasional scratch of a walkie-talkie transmission or the scuff of a boot traveled quickly around the natural bowl next to the mountain that made up the mining site.

The eleven vehicles—four operated by al Qaeda and seven operated by the Zetas—were spread out over the several hundred yards of property. It had been decided that, on the off chance an aircraft flew overhead, stray trucks and cars parked around the facility in a haphazard fashion seemed less likely to be noticed than a big collection that looked suspiciously like a convoy bedding down for the night.

Doyle lay in the passenger seat of the green truck, his tennis shoes up on the dashboard. He struggled to find sleep. Two Iraqi brothers snored in the truck with him. Tim and Andrew would be backup for guard duty in a few hours, so David let them sleep.

He heard a shout in the distance, one of the sentries on the hillside to the south of the mine, and he hoped the noise would not be followed by other men yelling and shouting.

But it was, and David Doyle lifted his head off the headrest of the seat, then quickly rolled down the window next to him.

He reached for the walkie-talkie. He did not know which one of the eleven vehicles in the mining site Henrico was sleeping in, so he did not take time to look for him. Instead he just transmitted. "What's wrong?"

Henrico's voice came back over the radio seconds later. "Helicopter. State police. It is small, and not heading directly for us. Make sure all lights are off. Everything will be fine."

Doyle instructed his men to stay in their positions and to keep their lights off, and he heard Henrico shout orders on the radio to his men.

A minute later the flashing lights of a helicopter appeared over a ridge to the south. It was high in the sky, heading north, but Doyle imagined a police helicopter might well have the means to see through the darkness and the distance and find these odd cars and trucks parked in an abandoned mine.

But the chopper kept going. The lights were visible for three minutes or so, and then they disappeared behind some peaks to the northeast.

Doyle checked again with the leader of the Zetas security detail. "Do you think they saw us?"

Henrico replied, "I don't know. It is possible that they reported vehicles here at the mine. My spotters in the hills report no more aircraft in the area."

"Should we leave?"

"No. If we get back on the road we will be more exposed. We will stay right where we are, but I will double the guard force."

Doyle put the radio back on the dashboard and worried. He had known from the beginning he would be in constant danger of exposure here in Mexico, but there had been no alternative.

He closed his eyes to sleep, trusting in Allah to see him and his men through the night.

Doyle finally fell asleep with the volume on his walkie-talkie turned low, but not all the way down. Just after four a.m. he awoke to excited calls in Spanish from one of Henrico's men. He reached over and turned up the volume to try to get a feeling of what was going on.

Doyle then heard the low thumping sound of a helicopter echo off the hillside, identified it for what it was, and leapt straight up in the passenger seat of the truck. He lifted the walkie-talkie, but before he could depress the push-to-talk button, Henrico transmitted in English.

"David! Navy helicopters in attack formation!"

Henrico had screamed the order, and now Doyle shouted at his men. "Move away from the trucks!" His order was not to protect his men, it was to protect his missiles. If his men created some distance between themselves and the vehicles, then maybe the SAMs would be spared if the choppers opened fire on the men.

In the moonlight he saw a pair of helicopters appear over the ridge in the east. He did not recognize their make immediately, but within seconds he could see the pill-shaped fuselage, and he identified them as German-made Messerschmitt-Bölkow-Blohm BO105s. He'd seen these in Iraq, flying for various militaries. The BO105 could be equipped with either rocket pods or machine guns. They were not heavily armored, but they were small, light, and nimble.

And there was no question as to whether or not they were just passing by. Their outboard lights were off and their noses were pointed directly at the silver mine.

Doyle called Henrico on the walkie-talkie. "Don't do anything stupid. They don't know who we are. Tell your men to hide their guns."

But the Mexican had other plans. "No. There will be trucks of Marines here behind the helicopters. If we stand here and do nothing, then we just wait for capture. We attack now. Only by getting rid of the choppers will we have time to escape before the troops get here."

Doyle understood the logic of this, and he knew the Zetas knew the tactics of their adversaries better than he. He resigned himself quickly to the fact that they were not going to stay low-profile here in Mexico for much longer.

The two BO105s raced over the flatland to the east, toward the silver mine. When they were still three hundred meters out, small weapons fire erupted from two dozen positions in the buildings, hills, and rocks around the mine. An RPG raced away from the hillside on David's right, but it streaked through the air far above the approaching helicopters.

A second RPG, this one fired from behind one of the aluminum buildings, hit the hard earth and exploded in front of the attacking choppers.

David ran toward the relative safety of the pile of iron ore that he'd climbed to help him with his cell phone reception earlier in the evening. As he ran he saw sparks flash across one of the black helicopters. The aircraft pulled out of the formation and turned away from the gunfire, but the second helo continued on. Just when David and two of his men dove down behind the rocks, a pair of outboard cannons on the remaining BO105 opened up, raking the ground in front of it and everything on it with 20mm shells.

David kept his head low, but he saw a Zeta minibus explode in flames and several Mexican gunmen eviscerated by cannon fire.

The helo shot past his position, not more than one hundred feet above the roof of his truck. It fired at the source of a third RPG launch, up on the hillside, and while it did this, Doyle stood to empty his AK into the tail rotor of the craft. He fired a thirty-round magazine at the helicopter, not caring if his rounds hit Zetas on the hill.

But the chopper banked to the north and began circling around for another pass.

David reloaded his rifle with the single thirty-round magazine he carried in his side pocket, but as he chambered a round, he looked back over his shoulder at the sound of another explosion. The second Bo 105 had retreated several hundred yards back to the east, and from here it fired rockets toward the silver mine. The rockets struck the aluminum outbuildings of the mine, and flames and smoke burst forth from the structures, sending three men near them spinning into the air.

Doyle knew they would not be able to stop this attack without a perfect shot from an RPG into the BO105. His four TerraStars were still alive, parked in a gravel lot to the south of where the Navy was attacking, but the raking rocket fire would hit them as soon as the pilot took out the resistance near the buildings.

"Henrico?" David called into the walkie-talkie from his position behind a rock pile, just ten yards from the nearest TerraStar truck. "Henrico?"

There was no reply.

David dropped the walkie-talkie, looked up at the closest truck to his position, and then he made the decision. He leapt to his feet, leaving his AK on the ground, and he ran to the rear of his green truck.

Doyle did not want to use one of the Iglas. He knew that knocking down a Mexican Navy helicopter with a shoulder-fired missile would alert the United States that Libyan SAMs were in the hemisphere.

But he saw no other options.

He pulled a case out of the rear of the truck, and let it fall to the gravel drive. The wood smashed as he did this, and he dug through the broken crate to retrieve the launcher, the missile, and the power supply from its foam casing.

Around him the chatter of AK fire continued, along with the lower drumbeat of cannon fire from one chopper and the *whoosh-boom* sound of rockets fired from the other.

The screams of men were all but drowned out in the melee.

As Doyle seated the power supply, Miguel appeared behind him. He helped David finish the assembly, and then he slid the rocket into the firing tube. With Miguel's assistance, David got the forty-pound device on his shoulder, and he peered through the sights toward the attack chopper firing rockets.

An explosion close by knocked David off balance, but Miguel grabbed the weapon and held it up while his commander regained his composure.

As David's eye pressed back into the sights, he saw a third helicopter arrive on the scene. This was a huge Mexican Marine Black Hawk, and David knew it could be carrying a dozen troops or more. It hovered over the highway, nearly two kilometers south of his position, well out of range of the Zeta RPGs and rifles.

This chopper was not armed, but it was bigger and slower than the other two and as it crossed into his sights he thought it would make an easier target. He half depressed the trigger on the SAM to initiate the warhead's lock onto the Black Hawk.

It took only four seconds before he heard the tone that told him the warhead had picked up the heat register.

To his right cannon fire raked the men firing from behind the pile of ore, killing Mexicans and Middle Easterners alike.

David pressed the trigger on the launcher and he felt the same jolt he'd felt in Greece a few weeks before. The weapon sailed out of the launch tube and almost instantly its propellant ignited and it raced skyward. Behind it a wide spray of flame illuminated the night until it turned into a pinprick of moving starlight in the distance.

Doyle later wondered if the Black Hawk pilot two kilometers away had heard a warning from his machine that an infrared missile was inbound. He suspected the warning had come, but David also suspected the pilot would not have been expecting Mexican drug smugglers to be in possession of a surface-to-air missile capable of destroying his modern aircraft.

In any event, the pilot did not alter his flight at all, even as the missile raced down from above. No evasive maneuvers, no deployment of antimissile chaff or flares.

It was like he never saw it coming.

The pilot just held his hover while Mexican Marines in the cabin dropped ropes that they planned on using to rappel to the road, where they could set up a hasty blocking position by the highway to prevent the drug smugglers' escape.

But the missile slammed into the Black Hawk from above before even the first Marines could slide down the ropes. The black craft spun on its center axis and then jacked hard to the side. Its rotor disintegrated in sparks and electric flashes just a fraction of a second before the aircraft pounded the hard earth next to the highway, instantly killing all on board.

The Igla-S also ruptured the fuel lines of the craft, and a fire broke out that would glow until dawn.

Two kilometers to the north in the derelict silver mine, a moment of quiet enveloped the scene. The Zetas had all seen what had happened. None of them, not even Henrico, had any idea they were helping al Qaeda transport antiaircraft missiles into the United States. All of the fifteen or so surviving members of the cartel's security force had combat experience, but not one of them, not even those who came from the military, had ever seen anything like a missile launch against a helicopter full of men.

David and Miguel did not stop to admire their work; they were already back on their knees behind the truck, pulling a second weapon out of its crate. There were still two helicopters in the attack and, as far as Doyle was concerned, there would be no more damage to the security of his operation by using a second missile.

His first launch had destroyed any chance that they would remain undetected to the U.S.

Doyle rose with the weapon, Miguel helped him up, and he searched for a target. He found an attack helicopter, centered his sights, and prepared to depress the trigger.

But the chopper was clearly in full retreat. It shot to the east at high speed, pulling to the left and right, in a clear attempt to avoid any missiles on its tail.

Miguel then turned Doyle around to the second helicopter, but it, too, was getting the hell away from the site of the SAM launch.

After making certain the BO105s were not just circling around for another try, Doyle lowered the weapon from his shoulder and put it back in the truck.

Zeta fighters and al Qaeda operators cheered, the natural exaltation of surviving a deadly battle, but Doyle was all business. He turned from the truck, and then ran past the burning wreckage of the buildings and vehicles. Some one hundred yards away he found Henrico, shoving his men toward their cars. Blood from a cut above the Mexican's left eyebrow stained his entire face.

Doyle grabbed him by the collar of his jacket. "Who set us up?"

"I don't know!" he screamed back. "Maybe the helicopter that passed by earlier had thermal. Maybe they saw men and trucks here, maybe the—"

"Maybe your people sold us out to the government!" David answered back.

Henrico shook his head. "I . . . I don't think so. Even if they did, you know I was not involved. I lost eight men, and I almost got blown to shit myself!"

"What are we going to do?"

"I've told my men to collect our dead. You should do the same. We will go to a ranch I know about twenty kilometers away. We can hide out for a few hours. There we can get more support before continuing on."

"Will there be cops on the road?"

Henrico barked orders in Spanish in his radio. While he did so he nodded to the American al Qaeda man. He switched back to English to say, "Yes. Federal police, state police, municipal police. Marines, too. I will contact the regional commander of my organization and try to clear a path for us ahead. Maybe we will take a different route. I don't know." The Mexican shouted another order in Spanish, then turned back to Doyle. "Hombre, that missile you fired will put us all in danger."

"I had to fucking fire it because your secret hide location was discovered by the fucking Navy!"

Henrico turned away and climbed into the back of one of his cars. David ran back to his men and their trucks, desperate to get out of here before more choppers arrived.

When he returned to his men he discovered that Arthur and Roger, two of his three Turks, were dead. Miguel had ordered them both loaded into the back of the yellow truck. Benjamin, from Saudi Arabia, was wounded in the arm and face, but he was still on his feet and seemed to be stable.

David would assess the man's wounds when they made it to the next safe house. For now he ordered everyone into their trucks, and within moments they were racing back down the drive to the highway.

Kolt arrived at the compound just after six a.m. He went to the gym for an hour, got a light upper-body workout with the vertical ropes and caving ladders, and worked his grip strength on the climbing wall mockups. Nothing that would put too much stress on his weeks-old thigh injury. Then he showered, slipped into his OD green flight suit, and walked back into the squadron lounge for some coffee. He caught the last half of a news-flash story on the squadron flat-screen as he entered the bay. A gun battle between Mexican forces and narcos in the country's interior had led to the deaths of thirteen Mexican Marines.

There was no mention of a missile shooting down a helicopter, and violence in Mexico had long been so commonplace that Raynor did not give it another moment's thought.

Kolt went to his office, checked his e-mail quickly, then headed down to the SCIF to see if there was any news from either Yemen or Libya.

Kenny Farmer had worked straight on through the night, helping to prepare the target folder for the impending hit in Yemen. Webber and the Delta alert squadron, led by Major Rick "Gangster" Mahoney, had landed at their secure staging base in Eritrea just an hour earlier at 1700 local time, and Kenny and others here in the SCIF had just updated them with the latest in real-time information pulled from a Global Hawk UAV flying fifty-nine thousand feet above the AQAP training facility.

Farmer was confident that Gangster and his boys had all the pieces they needed to plan the hit, and even though he had initially wished they had let him deploy with the headquarters section, the thirty-year-old analyst was satisfied with his contribution, and now just wanted to put his head down on his desk and crash.

"Morning," came a chipper voice behind him. Farmer turned to find Racer standing there with a cup of coffee and a dry whole-wheat bagel on a napkin. "Brought you breakfast, brother."

"Thanks," said Farmer, wondering if the major would actually make him take a bite of that nasty bagel.

"So . . . what's going on with Gangster and the boys?" Kolt asked, and

Farmer took the bagel and the coffee, placed both on the desk, and gave Racer a quick rundown of the situation in southern Yemen.

"Live G-Hawk feed on screen three right there."

Farmer explained that the hit would take place at midnight local. It was several hours off, but Gangster and his squadron would leave their staging base soon.

"Would love to be in Eritrea," Kolt said as he looked at screen three.

"Yes, sir. Me, too."

Kolt changed the subject. "Any word on ST6 in the Med?"

Farmer updated Kolt on what he knew about the SEALs' operation in Tripoli. As it stood, ST6 was still offshore on the USS *Kearsarge,* a helicopter carrier, waiting for final approval to launch an attack against a farm just west of Sirte, where intelligence from Aref Saleh himself had indicated a weapons cache was protected by ex-members of the Libyan military. Farmer explained that the intel was anything but absolute, and years ago the target would have just been another NAI—a named area of interest—that would receive intermittent attention from aerial collection platforms.

But missiles scared POTUS, and he'd given SECDEF the mandate to root them out wherever he could find them, so chances looked good for an ST6 hit in Sirte within the next few hours.

Kolt headed back down the Spine to his squadron a few minutes later. He had a ton of work to do today, and he wanted to get it over with before the Yemen hit so he could sit and listen to the action over the radio.

THIRTY-TWO

Fifty-five-year-old United Nations investigator Dr. Renny Marris stood on the edge of the highway, shielding his eyes from the afternoon sun and wiping his forehead with a towel. The heat here reminded him of Libya, but the dust floating through the air was of a different makeup than the dust he'd experienced in North Africa.

More powdery dirt and less gritty sand.

He turned away from the sky and looked back to the flat scrub-strewn dirt just east of the highway. On it, the wreckage of the downed Black Hawk helicopter lay twisted and burned. Charred human remains were visible both inside and outside the twisted black metal.

Around Dr. Marris, Mexican federal police officers, Mexican naval personnel, and investigators from the AFI, the Agencia Federal de Investigación, stood around, waiting to hear what he had to say.

He wiped his brow again.

If he had his choice he would say nothing. He did not normally make on-scene preliminary reports, but these Mexicans had been insistent that he give them his initial assessment.

Marris had been to the scene of many skirmishes in his life, and he knew he was looking at the remnants of a major incident. In addition to the burned and charred helicopter, as he and his Mexican minders had flown into the area they'd passed over a deserted silver mine a couple of kilometers away. There, buildings had burned to the ground and vehicles had been blown to bits. Bullet holes, as well as the telltale scorch marks of RPG strikes, indicated that an engagement had taken place between forces on the ground and forces in the air.

It was also clear that the Mexican Navy had lost. Their body count had been high, some thirteen dead. The surviving government forces had claimed that many of the enemy had also been killed, but no bodies had been recovered, and local hospitals reported no more patients with gunshot wounds had arrived during the night than on a normal evening in this part of Mexico's interior.

Marris had flown in from Toronto, getting on a flight at nine-thirty in the morning, just six hours after the incident itself. He'd been asked to come down because he was the foremost expert on the Igla-S missile and, according to reports from two other helicopter crews involved in the battle, it seemed extremely likely that an Igla-S missile had been used to down the Black Hawk helicopter.

Marris hoped this was not the case. He hoped like hell some dumb gunman for the narcos had gotten a lucky shot off with an RPG-7, and the Black Hawk had caught it just right, sending the craft and its men into the dirt before the pilot had time to properly react.

But now, as Marris inspected the impact point of the strike on the fuselage of the helicopter just behind the engines, it was abundantly clear to him that a SAM had indeed knocked the big helicopter out of the sky. The warhead of the SA-24 was larger than any of the other MANPADs on the market, and he could see the effects of the bigger blast in the metal and the scatter path of debris along the highway.

"Damn." Marris said it to himself so that the Mexicans who spoke English would not hear and understand. Marris knew much of the Mexican leadership hoped that this was, in fact, an SA-24 shoot-down. That would mean, they all assumed, that the Mexican cartels had purchased weapons from Libya. While horrifying news for Mexican military and police flight crews, for the leadership in Mexico City this meant more money from the United States to combat the narcos.

Marris had no patience for such bureaucratic cynicism. He was here to find out if "his" weapons had been used, and he had established this with just a quick inspection.

But what was he going to do about it? He knew good and well that the moment he announced definitively that an Igla-S had, indeed, brought down the Black Hawk, the United States of America would know that Libyan weapons were in their hemisphere and this would raise the stakes precipitously.

He could not well hide this information from the world—he knew this, but he didn't like it. If he had his way he would go straight to New York, to the United Nations, and he would tell the leadership of his organization in secret. They would redouble their efforts and, sooner or later, Renny Marris would find the rest of the missing SAMs.

Getting the United States even more involved in the hunt than they had been over the past year would do nothing but raise the level of bloodshed even higher.

Another brush of the towel over his brow, and another look at the sun in the afternoon sky, helped the Canadian doctor organize his thoughts.

"Damn." Renny Marris had no respect for the Americans, even less so after the incident in Tripoli with the CIA man and the goons Marris assumed were Navy SEALs. But he did have respect for the truth and he knew he could not cover up what he knew to be true.

He turned to the Mexicans on the highway.

With a reluctant nod he said softly, "Yes. This is clearly the work of a missile smuggled from Libya."

Marris walked away from the wreckage, back toward his helicopter, his heart heavy with worry about what was now to come.

Raynor sat with his mates in the briefing room at 1630 hours, picturing the scene in Yemen, filling in the details from the transmissions coming through the speakers. Gangster and eighteen of his men had hit the village just after midnight local time, approaching from the ocean, flying nap-of-the earth in Black Hawks flown by the 160th Special Operations Aviation Regiment, also known as the Night Stalkers.

AH-6J Little Birds took out the gun emplacements on the roofs of the buildings, and Monk, Tackle, Benji, and Gangster led the ground assault on the target.

Raynor found himself gritting his teeth with tension as he listened to the action over the radio and watched the heat signatures on the live feed as the assaulters flowed effortlessly to multiple external breach points. Operator and air crew transmissions cracked and hissed, gunfire and thumping chopper rotors filled the dead air between the words.

It was not long into the mission before a "wounded eagle" call came, a code for an injured operator. The men around Racer sat silently; they'd all been in ops like this where mates had been wounded, and some of the men in the room, including Raynor, had themselves been wounded eagles in the past. They all wished they were there, helping to take down the target while making certain the enemy paid for their mate's blood with blood of their own.

Kolt listened to Gangster command and control his operators during the hit. He sounded a little amped up, but was so far getting a passing grade. It was evident Monk was in charge of the clearing of the village itself, and Benji controlled the perimeter. Tackle breached a small building and met resistance, and another wounded eagle call was broadcast in the briefing room.

One of the Black Hawks circling the perimeter of the target area took several rounds from an AK fired from inside the village, and the radio transmissions indicated that two of the air crew were wounded, but the helo remained airborne and on station.

Kolt and the rest of the men at the compound sat quietly through an attack that lasted less than twenty minutes. When it was over, Gangster called Webber, who was back at the staging base in Eritrea, to give his sitrep. These comms were broadcast in the briefing room as well.

"Wrangler Zero One, this is Gangster."

"Go for Wrangler Zero One."

Gangster's voice was clipped and professional. "Target secure. Numerous EKIA, still counting. Status of friendly—door gunner on one of the Black Hawks is dead. Copilot on the same helo took a round in the arm. I've got four WIA eagles. Two of them critical."

"Roger. Send call signs of the criticals, over," Webber said over the radio.

Kolt had not expected it to go down clean, but watching the ISR feed as several people were loaded onto a helicopter made his stomach tighten and the back of his neck sweat.

"Tackle caught an AK round to the stomach. Lost a lot of blood. He's on a helo now. We're working on him. Kingfish ate frag from an RPG. He's stable but not out of danger, over."

"Roger all," said Webber. "Good job."

Gangster continued, "Can confirm now one-four EKIA. Several more bugged out to the hills. We've got another two dozen or so women and children here in the vil, as well. Looks like we hit a family reunion. Over."

The assault phase of Gangster's operation now over, the operators began the SSE, the sensitive site exploitation phase. Now they would tear the place apart looking for any items of intelligence value.

Gangster had been ordered to first head to the twenty-foot container that Farmer had found there in the middle of the settlement. It was hoped by all that it would be filled to the brim with the missing SA-24s, so everyone could go home happy.

"Wrangler Zero One, Gangster, over."

"Zero One, go."

"We're at the container. It's up on blocks. Just about four feet off the ground. We'll pop the door and climb up in it. Wait one . . . Okay . . . I've got a stack of wooden crates here," he said before a long pause.

The pause lasted several seconds. Then, "Negative. These boxes are all empty. Only thing in here are some bedrolls and some water bottles lying loose on the floor."

Kolt and the others in the briefing room looked at one another. No one was sure of the significance of this, or even if it was significant.

Then Gangster's voice came back up on comms. "Wrangler Zero One, something else interesting here. It's a device that seems to be made out of expended ordnance and a piece of an RPG. It's not a functioning weapon, but it looks like a SAM launcher."

"But it's *not* a SAM launcher?" Webber asked.

"Negative. No way. But it looks like it could be a model. For training purposes."

"It's in the container?"

"Affirmative."

"Okay. Get some video and wrap it up."

"Roger that. Gangster out."

Kolt and the others said a silent prayer for Tackle and Kingfish, then they speculated about the potential intel haul. There was much still to learn about what was going on at the target location, so Kolt decided he'd drop in on Ken Farmer at the SCIF later in the afternoon to see what news had made its way back to the SCIF from the CIA or other channels.

Kolt left the conference room with a group from his squadron who would be heading to Wyoming early the next morning for alpine training. With the target area in Yemen being a semi-permissive environment, they figured the op was a wrap. They all went together to the squadron bar and passed around some cold ones to celebrate Gangster's squadron's success.

Kolt had just offered up a toast.

"Here's to Tackle and Kingfish and a speedy recovery."

Just as the cold beer hit Kolt's upper lip his beeper went off. As he reached for it he heard the Unit PA buzzer. Webber's secretary came over the PA. "Major Raynor call 4005. Major Raynor, 4005."

Kolt killed his beer, finished a short story about something that had happened when he was a young troop commander, and wished the guys well on their trip before heading to the command group. He wasn't on alert anymore. No hurry.

He was close enough to Webber's office, so he just walked in. As he did so, Joyce stood quickly from behind her desk. "Major Raynor, I have Colonel Webber on the phone for you. I can send it to his extension. Head right on in."

Raynor looked down at his watch in confusion. It had only been thirty minutes and a tallboy since he'd left the briefing room. Even if Gangster and his men had left the target, they would still be in Yemeni territory. Kolt could not fathom why Webber would be calling him here at Bragg, essentially during a hit on the other side of the globe, while the other squadron was still in harm's way.

He stepped into Webber's office, grabbed the phone off the colonel's desk, and sat down in one of the chairs in front of it. As much as he would have liked to sit in Webber's seat, he fought the urge.

"Raynor here, sir."

Webber's voice was stressed. "I just got a call from Langley. There is a situation developing."

"Send it, sir."

"There was an engagement last night in Mexico between suspected members of the Zetas cartel and military forces."

This was odd. Why the hell would Webber be calling about that? "Yes, sir. It was on the news this morning."

"An SA-24 took down a Navy Black Hawk with thirteen on board," said Webber.

"Holy shit," Raynor said softly. "*That* was not on the news."

"There have been reports of SA-7s and SA-16s, and maybe even some Stingers on the loose in Mexico, even though none of them have turned up. But this has been verified by your old friend Tripwire as a Grinch strike, and the only missing Grinches are out of Libya."

"Did it come from the shipment that went to Yemen?" Kolt asked.

"No way to know that yet. But if they traveled by air they could have made it into Mexico with time to spare. The SECDEF wants JSOC down on the border and ready in case there is an opportunity to get the munitions back."

"Of course," said Raynor, slowly understanding the reason for the call from Webber.

"Six is still in the Med, and Gangster and his squadron won't be on U.S. soil for twelve hours minimum. SEALs from Coronado are going to predeployment locations to the west, in California, Arizona, and New Mexico, but the commanding general has given us the hit if the SAMs are found in the east."

"Are you putting us back on alert, sir?"

"Yes, I am. Recall your teams still in Fayetteville. You're wheels-up in ninety minutes. You're going straight to McAllen, Texas, for right now, but Langley has assets in Mexico searching for the Zetas with the missiles, and UAVs over the border looking for any signs of them."

Kolt asked, "How do we know they were Zetas? What if they were AQAP and they are heading to the U.S.?"

Webber said, "If this AQAP camp was training terrorists how to fire the SA-24, then I think you are asking a great question. We will double-time the analysis of the intel haul at the target in Yemen, and push the details to the White House. You just get everyone available in your squadron on the C-17 ASAP. The deputy commander will get everybody there to help push you guys out."

"Yes, sir. By the way, any update on Kingfish and Tackle?"

"Kingfish is critical. Tackle didn't make it. His wife hasn't been notified yet, so close hold."

Shit, thought Kolt. *Son of a bitch.*

"Focus on the task at hand, Raynor, and watch yourself down there," added Webber. "The Zetas may not be jihadists, but they've been fighting a two-front war down there in Mexico for over five years. They have fought off other cartels and they've fought off the military and federal police. I want you to give their potential for danger to you and your men your full attention and respect. They are as bad a bunch as you've come up against over here and we certainly don't need any more fallen eagles' names engraved on the wall."

"Yes, sir."

Seconds later, Major Kolt Raynor ran through Webber's outer office on his way to the staff duty to initiate the squadronwide recall, passing Joyce by at a sprint.

Raynor stood behind his desk in his office. In front of him, a half dozen of his men sat on the other desks and leaned against the wall. These were the first group of squadron members to make it in, as they had been down at the range working some evening CQB—close quarters battle—training. The coded page went out to the entire squadron, of course, but many of the guys had already departed for team training across the country or signed out on leave.

But those available had come running or come calling. Even though they weren't on alert anymore, when a Unit member's beeper shows the real-world recall code, he is expected to drop what he is doing and make his way directly back to the compound.

They would not all be here in the next hour, so some would miss the movement and the aircraft taking the first group down, but Kolt hoped he could get a second plane of men down to McAllen posthaste, should the need come to cross the border.

To the six men already in front of him, Raynor said, "Word just came down from the colonel. We're heading to Mexico."

Slapshot had been leaning against the wall in the back. Although he knew from his boss's demeanor that this meant there was trouble, he made a joke anyway. "Margaritas and nachos?"

Kolt did not laugh. "SAMs. Libyan SAMs."

Slapshot pushed off the wall and said, "I'll have a margarita when I get back. Let's go get those SAMs."

Raynor clarified, "We've got confirmation that a helo owned by the Mexican Navy was shot down yesterday by an SA-24. You may have seen something about it on the news today. We don't know if these are the MANPADs that went to Yemen, or if AQ is involved at all. JSOC already pushed every available resource down there a few hours ago looking for them. When they are found, either the SEALs or us will go after them."

"The SEALs?" One of Raynor's men asked with a tinge of irritation.

"Yes, but white SEALs out of Coronado. Not Team Six. JSOC is doing the best they can working multiple ops and the SOUTHCOM commander must have pushed for it. We're lucky as hell our sister squadron is already in Berlin at building training. That leaves only us."

Nobody said anything; they just nodded in unison, letting Kolt know everyone understood the stakes. The group dispersed immediately to their team rooms to quickly repack their kit bags and into the weapons vaults for their weapons, contingency ammo, and secure radios.

Raynor then rushed down to the SCIF to talk to Kenny Farmer. He knew he could have called him from his office, but he felt he could make more of an impression if he showed up in person.

He found the redhead bleary-eyed, looking at his monitor in front of him. On it, real-time video feed showed roads and flat scrubland.

Kolt looked over his shoulder. "It that Yemen or Mexico?"

"Mexico," Farmer said without looking up. "We've got a couple of Homeland Security MQ-1 UAVs out of Brownsville searching the highways north of where last night's engagement took place."

"No luck?"

"None. It's low-probability. Big-ass area and, you already know, doesn't take much to hide a shoulder-fired launcher. The J2 is working with the Mexicans to try and get some intercepts of known Zetas commander's phones, which would be a better bet than just cruising overhead at twenty-five thousand feet, but still . . . these cartel bosses won't be chatting on open lines."

Kolt patted Farmer on the back. "Keep at it, brother. If anyone can find them, you can. I need to grab my kit. You need coffee?"

Farmer shook his head. "My bloodstream is ten percent Colombian dark roast already."

THIRTY-THREE

David Doyle and Miguel rode together in the back of a red Ford Econoline van as they headed northeast on Mexico's Federal Highway 85. With them in the back of the van were fourteen Igla-S systems. On the right-hand side of the highway, a huge reservoir, Presa Rodrigo Gómez, shimmered in the late afternoon sunlight, forcing Doyle to push the visor to the side to shield his eyes from the glare while he drove. David and Miguel just turned away from the blue water's shine, and continued their conversation.

The three other vehicles hauling surface-to-air missiles through Mexico were spread out along Highway 85 over a swath of twenty-five kilometers. Interspersed throughout the small convoy of AQAP operatives were five SUVs full of armed security men from Los Zetas.

It was not in the original plan for the vehicles to be spread so far apart, but David and Miguel had been calling audibles all day, knocking the Zetas' plan off-kilter and also, they hoped, preventing any double-crosses from their supposed allies here in Mexico.

After the shoot-out in Coahuila State early that morning they had all re-treated to a ranch Los Zetas owned, and there they buried their dead in shallow graves, and stayed off the roads while the inevitable search began. At the ranch they'd found out that one of their trucks had taken some battle damage, and its radiator had leaked dry, so they dumped the truck in lieu of the van, fitting the fourteen weapons and three men in the Econoline.

David and Miguel discussed their new plans while Jerry drove. They had decided to divert from their original crossing point in Agua Prieta, just south of Arizona on the nation's border with the United States, and instead head northeast, where the border with Texas was much closer. This would get them out of Mexico and into the U.S. much more quickly than their original plan, although they knew the Zetas would have to scramble to find a suitable location in which to hide them out tonight so that they could cross the following morning along with the regular flow of NAFTA-approved commercial traffic.

To that end they were heading up Highway 85, passing Santiago now, and soon enough they would be in Monterrey. By dark they planned on being out of Monterrey, still on 85, and, barring any major hazards, they would reach Nuevo Laredo by ten p.m.

Nuevo Laredo was the home base of Los Zetas. The cartel came closer to controlling the territory around it than any cartel controlled any major city in the nation. Henrico and David and Miguel had agreed that would be their destination this evening. There the Federales and the Navy and the Army and even the Americans could not reach them without being prepared to lose a lot of men.

It was not a perfect plan. If they were seen on the road to Nuevo Laredo it would be hard to slip away. The roads here were straight and flat and the options to get off the road and into cover were few and far between. But if they made it into Nuevo Laredo, David was confident they could remain undetected for a day or two until the Zetas could bribe border guards and they could slip into the United States.

Doyle looked at his watch. Three hours more and they would be on the border with America. He leaned over and asked Jerry to drive faster.

Kolt Raynor sat in a seat he found very familiar: a soft black fold-down bench bolted onto the cabin wall of a C-17 Globemaster. Heavy-strapped to the D-rings on the floor were four Little Bird helicopters, a pair each of MH-6Js and AH-6Js, from the 160th Special Ops "Night Stalker" Aviation Regiment out of Fort Campbell, Kentucky. Around Kolt were the eight pilots, along with nineteen men from his squadron—Twelve assaulters, five snipers, a medic, a communicator, and a dog handler with Roscoe, a Belgian Malinois.

A second wave of seven more assaulters and snipers would arrive in

McAllen a few hours later, feeling like shit for missing the initial deployment and, Kolt also knew, hoping like hell that they had not missed their opportunity for a hit south of the border.

The Globemaster pilot had just reported they were over East Texas, having crossed over Alabama and then a piece of the Gulf of Mexico, and soon they would be landing at Randolph Air Force Base in San Antonio, Texas. There the C-17 would taxi to an obscure end of the runway and the men would help the helo crews off-load and build up the Little Birds, and then they would climb aboard two vanilla UH-60s flown by the Texas Air National Guard. The Little Birds would fly slick on to McAllen and remain separated from the Black Hawks carrying Delta to minimize the signature and prevent being compromised by an alert and curious cattle rancher.

Using the National Guard helos had been no one's first choice, but they were here and they were ready. There would be no 160th MH-60J Black Hawks for this op, as they had all been deployed overseas to support the alert squadron's ops.

If the hit into Mexico was authorized, however, the Black Hawks would not be involved. Instead the men would load up on the skids of the Little Birds and head over the border.

At roughly the same time as all this, SEALs from California would be staging along the border to the west, no doubt following similarly chaotic and rushed procedures.

Even though his squadron was off alert status, Raynor felt good about the team he had with him, and proud that, within three and a half hours of Webber's call, he was approaching Texas with a potent force of operators. And even though he knew the chance was low that his team, and not one of the several white SEAL teams deploying, would get the call to shoot over the border, he did not let that affect his thinking for one second. Major Raynor would prepare for this op as if it were a certainty that he and his men would be heading into harm's way.

Operate any other way in a Tier One unit, Raynor knew, and he'd find himself in the black Chinook and heading home.

As he and several of his sergeants looked at a map of northern Mexico on a tablet computer, one of the C-17's loadmasters appeared above him and handed him a headset connected to a long green cord. "We've got traffic for you."

Kolt put his headset on and gave the loadmaster a thumbs-up. A moment later, Kolt heard the hissing and cracking of a satellite phone connection.

"Racer, this is Webber."

"Yes, sir?"

"Understand you are twenty minutes from Randolph."

"Affirmative."

"All right, listen up. The SAMs have not yet been detected in Mexico, but we've gotten a lead over here."

"A lead?"

"One of the crows Gangster rolled up ID'd Daoud al-Amriki as the cell leader running the training of one dozen AQAP operatives."

Kolt took a moment to process this information. "Rolled up? I thought they smoked all the fighting-age males."

"All but one, fortunately. Long story," Webber answered.

"Hot damn! Any word where al-Amriki and his men are now?"

"Negative, but they left in a hurry six days ago."

"That's the day after we took down Saleh in Cairo. Did the crow say if al-Amriki had the SAMs with them?"

"He said they did not, but they trained on the system with some pretty elaborate mock-ups. This guy who's singing is just a guard. He doesn't seem to be dialed in. Didn't know squat about the shipping container, or al-Amriki's plans. They are still working him."

"Sounds like we need to squeeze Saleh a little harder to see if he knows anything about David Wade Doyle."

"Yep. I expect Langley is doing just that."

"So are we linking all that to the SA-24 launch in Mexico?"

"No one has drawn that conclusion definitively just yet, but it could be the case."

Kolt felt the C-17 begin its descent into San Antonio. "Sir, if Doyle has a dozen guys with SAM training, some of whom are dressing up in Western clothing, and AQAP has SAMs, and we know SAMs are in Mexico . . . it's not going too far out on a limb to say Doyle is in Mexico, too. And if he's in Mexico, he's going to try to get himself and his boys into the USA."

"Preaching to the choir, Racer. We are doing everything we can to find the missiles down there, so that you or the SEALs can go in and blow them, and whoever's got them, to kingdom come."

"Who's the main effort down here? Us or the white SEALs?"

"SOUTHCOM is pushing hard for the mission. The CG is working it though with the SECDEF. Too early to tell, but it will depend on where the SAMs are."

"Sounds a little political to me."

"It always is," confirmed Webber.

David Doyle's red Ford Econoline pulled off Federal Highway 85 and onto a flat blacktop two-lane road. The van's headlights illuminated little but blowing dust, hovering and leaping bugs, and brown-green scrub that ran off into the dark on either side of the track. Jerry drove east, following the directions he'd been given by Henrico, but he did not really know where he was heading.

They knew from the bright lights just to the north that they were near the southern suburbs of the dangerous and gritty metropolis of Nuevo Laredo, which meant they were just a couple of miles west of the U.S.-Mexico border. They also knew that they were heading out here, off the main highway, to hunker down for the night.

All the men in the van hoped there was something out here to protect them other than grasshoppers and rattlesnakes.

Soon Jerry saw the taillights of another vehicle ahead, and as they closed on it they were happy to see the yellow TerraStar. In front of that was the blue truck, and a pair of SUVs David and the men with him recognized as those belonging to Los Zetas. All the men in the Econoline breathed a quiet sigh of relief that they had exited the highway at the correct side road.

The Econoline followed the others through a gate in a high chain-link fence. Doyle saw a sign that read ARROYO DEL COYOTE SUBESTACIÓN, and inside the fence his van's lights illuminated a massive field of metal towers, power lines, transformers, and outbuildings. They followed the Zetas past guards in black uniforms with ball caps with CFE above the bills. The guards wore pistol-gripped shotguns around their necks and, more important to Doyle, they did not look surprised by the new visitors to their facility.

They all drove to the back of this electrical substation, idling their vehicles under cover of long awnings that ran the length of the two largest buildings on the property. A large garage sat next to the buildings, and men opened the garage doors, then began driving green and white trucks marked

CFE out of the garage. After a minute of this, the two TerraStars were waved into the garage, and the Econoline was directed around the side to a small parking lot.

Doyle climbed out of his vehicle, holding his AK-47 in his arms, and he went looking for Henrico. The air was hot and dusty, and Doyle had to use the lights coming from the outbuildings to guide him.

He found Henrico in front of the control building near the garage. In the light coming from the building's windows, Doyle could see exhaustion in the Mexican's eyes and face. The wound above his eye was just a fat black knob now. Nothing serious. But the effort of the last thirty-six hours, along with the stress of their predicament, was clearly taking its toll.

It was often like this with infidels, Doyle thought. Their bodies were not sufficiently refueled by their faith in their mission. Doyle knew he and his cell would continue on, no matter the hardships.

Miguel spoke wearily. "I just heard from one of our *halcons* back at the highway."

"What is a *halcon*?"

"They are falcons. It's what we call watchers. Informants on the street who tell us what is going on. We have them all over the place around Nuevo Laredo. They say the last of your vehicles will pull in the driveway in a few minutes."

"Excellent." David looked around in the dark; he could barely make out the metal towers that ran for over a hundred meters in either direction. "This is some sort of electrical substation?"

"*Sí.* CFE is the national electrical company here in Mexico. We control them in Nuevo Laredo. We will be safe here as long as we stay inside the buildings. Follow me."

Henrico led Doyle into the control building. There was an open reception area, and two floors of hallways, offices, a control room, a kitchen, and a machine shop. The Mexican explained that the other outbuildings around were storage facilities for the equipment here at the station.

"What about tomorrow morning, when everyone gets to work?" Doyle asked.

"Sunday. It is a skeleton crew. We put our people here all the time. The employees who are here will not say a word." He paused. "They all know the penalty for that."

"What is your security situation here?"

Henrico said, "We have a force of twenty-five men with us, all armed with rifles and RPGs. There is some added security from the guards here protecting the substation, but not much."

Doyle looked at his watch. It was ten-thirty p.m. "And the plan for tomorrow?"

Henrico shrugged. "I talked to my bosses. They are going to try to have one of our men at the border crossing, and one of our paid members of U.S. Customs on the other side. Neither man was scheduled to work, so it is difficult to say if it will happen tomorrow. Since you changed the operation this morning, we are doing our best to catch up."

Doyle shrugged. "I made us all safer. Yourself included. I'm certain my organization's leadership and your organization's leadership can work out a fair trade for your services."

Henrico just said, "We will find a way for you across the border."

The American walked back to the garage, where now all four of his trucks and the fifty-nine missiles they carried were parked. Miguel and the others all stood near the vehicles.

Doyle addressed the group. "We may not be here very long, but I want four of you to take an Igla from its crate and carry it, along with your rifles, to the four corners of this property. We will stay in contact by radio. Keep your eyes open for any threats from above." Doyle looked off to the north. There, a small plane was taking off from Nuevo Laredo's one-runway airport. Laredo, Texas, had an airport as well, but it was at least fifteen miles away.

To the south a small police helicopter flew across the night sky.

David said, "Make sure you only target something that is attacking us. Not any plane or chopper that is just flying by."

The men understood and agreed.

Next Doyle said, "Everyone leave your keys in the trucks. Drivers stay behind the wheel. Miguel and I will be in the control building with the Mexicans, waiting to hear when we will cross the border."

At 0300 hours, Kolt Raynor sat in the cabin of a closed-door UH-60 Black Hawk helicopter that raced over moonlit South Texas scrubland a thousand feet below. Seated with him were eight of his men, including Slapshot, Roscoe the Malonois and his handler, and half of the gear they brought with them from Bragg. The other Black Hawk flew just behind them with its load of operators. They were still twenty minutes out of McAllen, and they still didn't have a clue what, if anything, they'd be doing when they got there.

The Little Birds were back at Randolph AFB, still being assembled and prepped for flight. One of the helos was having engine problems, and this would delay them at least an hour.

Just then, the pilot slowed the Black Hawk and began banking to the west. Kolt looked around for some explanation, but in the cabin of the helo, eight sets of goggled eyes and one furry face just looked back at him.

The pilot came over Kolt's headset seconds later, his Texas drawl pronounced. "Is this the ground force commander?"

"Call me Racer."

"Chief Bartow in the cockpit. Just got a change of orders. I've been told to take you to a location south of Laredo, with further instructions to come. We're thirty-five minutes out."

"Roger that, thanks," Kolt said, as he scribbled the words *FRAGO— Laredo* on a white wipe board and passed it around to his men. The men nodded, and they all hoped the fragmented order to change the landing zone meant some critical intel had been received that would get them the hit over the border.

THIRTY-FOUR

The two National Guard Black Hawks landed on a soccer field at an abandoned middle school well off the beaten path, a couple miles north of Rio Bravo, Texas. Here, the helos shut down their engines to save fuel. Racer and his men climbed out of the two birds, bringing with them guns and gear bags. They set up a hasty command post near the wobbly bleachers, and Raynor laid the sat phone down delicately. He prayed it would ring soon with Webber sending them a sit rep along with execute authority. They pulled up FalconView on a couple of laptops to familiarize themselves with the area, even though they had no way to pinpoint any targets.

Shit, Kolt thought. He was amped up about getting the SAMs and Doyle in one fell swoop. He needed to check his emotions on this. He told himself that the hit still could end up going to a team of SEAL studs in New Mexico, and he was getting way ahead of himself.

Colonel Jeremy Webber called within minutes. He was still in Eritrea at the Assab airport working some details out with the U.S. ambassador to Yemen, although he'd sent all the operators in the alert squadron back home on the double with a pair of MH-60Js in a C-17.

There was no greeting. "Are you on the ground?" Webber asked. Kolt could hear from his boss's voice that the SEALs in New Mexico would *not* be getting the action this morning.

"Yes, sir. We are waiting for the Little Birds to get here. They had a problem cranking the flight lead's MH and then have some weather on the way down to contend with. Do you know anything about the change of plans that brought us to Rio Bravo?"

"Yes, I pushed you there. ISR sighted a group of vehicles converging just south of Nuevo Laredo, directly to your west. One of the vehicles, a green medium-duty truck, matches a vehicle reported leaving a Zetas stronghold in Coahuila early this afternoon along with several more vehicles. They passed through Monterrey earlier in the evening, and now they are at an electrical substation complex ringed with two-dozen-plus armed security."

Webber gave Raynor the coordinates, and Kolt found the Coyote Sub-estación on his FalconView map. He was only six miles away. Kolt said, "They are right on the border, boss. Is anyone besides me assuming that Doyle and his MANPADs have a plan to make it into Texas?"

"I agree with you. So does the White House. We need to stop him on the Mexico side."

"Why doesn't the Air Force just flatten the place?" Kolt asked.

There was a pause on the line. "Shit, Racer. Guess you won't be working for the State Department when you get too old to kick doors. The United States is not going to fly bombers over the border to bomb Mexico, especially not at a facility that controls the electrical power for over half a million citizens."

"I know, boss. Stupid question. If we *don't* get them before they get into the States, is the Border Patrol or some SWAT team ready to stop them inside the border?"

Webber just said, "They are being warned as we speak, but . . ."

Kolt got the inference. "Best we stop them before it comes to that."

"That would be best." Now the colonel cleared his throat. "The White House has cleared you for action inside Mexico. You have execute authority to destroy the suspected cache of SA-24s and eliminate any resistance you encounter to this objective. The White House is trying to work it out with Mexican authorities so that you don't have to worry about federal forces as well as the Zetas targeting you."

"I recommend against that, sir," Kolt countered. "That would be like telling the Pakistanis that the SEALs are coming for bin Laden. This is already about as hasty as it gets. Let's not turn this into a flash mob and a high-speed chase across the desert."

"Sorry, Raynor. The White House has to be able to say they notified the

Mexican government before we took action, and you guys wasting a bunch of Federales would be problematic."

To Kolt this was all politics, and politics got in the way of his job.

The old Kolt would have bitched about this for a few seconds more. But the new Kolt just said, "Understood."

"Stand by, Racer."

As Kolt waited for Webber to get back on the line, he caught himself pacing back and forth in a ten-foot space near the south end soccer goal. He stopped, knowing that he must be looking awfully amped to his men watching from the bleachers.

"Raynor?"

"Go ahead, sir, still here."

"You will have real-time UAV feed on your laptop within moments. There is fresh movement of vehicles at the substation right now."

"Understood."

"Not yet, you don't. The SECDEF is concerned the missiles might be moving again within minutes. It has been decided that they are too close to the border and too close to the city of Nuevo Laredo, where our ISR will probably lose them, to risk waiting for them to leave their current location. They're nervous at the highest levels, Raynor. Nobody wants to lose a jumbo jet on U.S. soil."

"What are you saying, sir?" Kolt asked, confused.

"You have to go." He paused, then said, "*Now.*"

Raynor's eyebrows rose. "Little Birds are thirty-five minutes out, boss. We swimming the Rio Grande?"

"Negative. The two helos on scene will insert you to the target."

Raynor's voice rose as he said, "The National Guard air crews, sir? Are you fucking kidding?"

"The J3 is on their net now briefing them up. Make it happen. This is in extremis. The Little Birds can catch up later. No time to wait on them. And no time to infiltrate the area on foot and find a perfect opportunity."

Kolt Raynor did not back down. "Sir, with all due respect. This is a total soup sandwich."

"I understand, Major. It's less than ideal. But the enemy gets a vote, and they just voted to hit the road, so you need to stop them."

"Sir, where is the intel dump? How many bad guys? How many Mexican guards? What does the guard uniform look like? This is probably the most important mission we've had in the last ten years and we are assaulting with a troop minus, flying in on big, slow helos flown by the fucking Texas Air National Guard?"

"Racer, I can confirm you are outnumbered three to one. Kill the foreigners and spare the local guards, unless they engage you. Your country is counting on you guys to get this done."

"Please, sir, don't patronize me. You know we're going in, but for the record, this is suicide."

"Make your own luck, Kolt!" Webber said. "And for the record, I'd give anything to be hitting that target with you and your Tier One Wild boys tonight."

Kolt thought, *Well, come on down,* but he did not say it.

"Racer out."

The pilots of Racer's National Guard Black Hawks had been getting their orders while Kolt was bickering with Colonel Webber, but as soon as they were done they climbed out of their helos and walked over to the scrum of men in goggles and black Nomex. Raynor walked the men away from the Delta assaulters and back over to their helos. Here, the three men shook hands.

Kolt looked the pilots over. In the long shadows from the lights of the helos and under cover of the full helmets on the men's heads, it was hard to see much of either pilot, but he could tell one was much older than the other. The younger man's name tape identified him as Wilkins, and the older was Bartow. Bartow was the pilot of Racer's aircraft.

Kolt said, "I imagine you guys heard what's up?"

Both men nodded. The younger man spoke quickly. "Guess this ain't just another repositioning flight to Waco."

Kolt shook his head. "Not hardly."

Bartow had a slow Texas drawl. He asked, "You guys Navy SEALs?"

"Yes," Kolt lied. He then asked, "Guys. No offense, but do either of you have any experience with hot insertions?"

Wilkins shook his head, but said, "Did a tour in Afghanistan. Took some fire, but I'm not going to claim I've ever done anything like this."

Kolt looked at Bartow. The older chief warrant officer said, "Did four tours in Iraq. Based mostly at Camp Victory. I'm no shit hot Night Stalker, but I put boys like you down in Sadr City at high noon more than once. Didn't much care for it, but I got them all in and out. Chief Wilkins will follow me, we'll get you down in one piece, and then we will stand off until recalled. It would be damn handy if you guys could do us the favor of shooting any son of a bitch you see shouldering one of those damn SAMs."

Kolt knew he had the right man on the stick. "We'll do our best. Sorry I questioned you, Chief."

"No biggie. You just go back to worrying about everything else, and let us drive the buses."

"You got it."

Within a minute Raynor, Digger, Slapshot, and two other veteran sergeants in Raynor's squadron were in the back of one of the Black Hawks, hunched over the laptop, watching real-time feed from a Homeland Security Predator high overhead. Together the men worked on their plan of attack.

The substation was surrounded by wires, which made the helicopter insertion even more difficult. Primary power lines, ground wires, and overhead lines ran all over the property inside the ten-foot-high security fence, and outside the fence, primary and secondary power lines ran north to Nuevo Laredo and west to the highway.

To the south the land was mostly flat and covered with trees and brush, and to the east it was much the same, with the only differing feature being the Arroyo del Coyote, Coyote Creek, a small, shallow, wooded, and winding creek that ran from the northwest all the way to the Rio Grande, two miles east of the substation.

Inside the security fence Kolt and his men counted twelve men armed with AKs, shotguns, and AR-15s in static sentry positions outside, and several more moving around a small complex of buildings in the back of the property.

At least a dozen vehicles were visible from the air, several of which looked like they belonged to the electric company. Of the others, Raynor saw no large trucks, although there was a van near the largest building on the property, and there were several SUVs.

Slapshot said, "Looks like a minimum of twenty-five crows. It's going to be tough on the helo crews due to the high-tension wires."

Rocket, the senior recce team leader and one of Racer's snipers, added, "Look, who are we kidding? These National Guard guys don't do wires at night. And it's kinda dumb to be in these things when we know they have SAMs."

Kolt said, "Rocket is exactly right. This is a cluster fuck in the making. But we need ideas, guys."

"Are the Black Hawks fast-rope capable?" Slapshot asked.

"No."

It was quiet for a second, then Digger asked, "What if one of the helos took us a few miles up the highway, and we commandeered a couple of vehicles? Just drove up to the gate. The other helo can come in low to mask sound and insert at the back of the compound."

Kolt thought that sounded like a decent plan, but just then, on the UAV feed from over the border, the thermal images of three of the civilian SUVs at the substation began moving, heading toward the exit.

"Are those the target vehicles moving?" Slapshot asked quickly.

"Shit," said Raynor. "Let's load up. We can talk it over with the helo crews in the air."

THIRTY-FIVE

Doyle had managed thirty minutes of sleep, but now Henrico had him up and walking down the stairs of the control building, and heading back out into the night.

The Mexican said, "We will reposition inside the city. There is a truck there with a trailer that is cleared for NAFTA crossing. They might X-ray it, but the truck is lined with goods that will not allow the X-ray to pass through. Your cargo will go down the middle of the trailer, and the truck will be in line as one of the first to pass through when the crossing opens in the morning."

"Excellent," said Doyle. "When do we leave?"

"Immediately. We need to load the cargo under cover of darkness, and it will be dawn in a half hour. I have some of my men leaving now. They will position themselves along the route into the city to make sure there are no roadblocks by the police."

Doyle cocked his head. "And if there *are* roadblocks by the police?"

Henrico shrugged. "Then we kill a few police. The rest will leave."

"Very good," said David, and he headed outside with Henrico to move the trucks out of the garage.

He called the four men with the SAMs back from their positions so they could recrate the systems and get them back in the trucks, and then they fired up the vehicles.

A few minutes later, just as Doyle climbed inside the red Econoline, he heard one of Henrico's men shout, "*Helicóptero!*" into the radio. A second later he heard, "*Dos helicópteros!*"

He heard rotor noise just after this, and he wasted no time shouting orders of his own. Miguel, Jerry, and Tim were with him in the van. He said, "Jerry and Tim! Each of you get an Igla out of the back and fire on the helicopters!"

The two men slid open the side door and pulled crates out onto the parking lot. Frantically, they began unpacking and assembling the big weapons.

"Texas two-one is over the border and one minute out," Chief Warrant Officer Bartow announced as he gorilla-gripped the cyclic and fat-footed the peddles of his UH-60 Black Hawk. Behind him, Chief Warrant Officer Wilkins flew forty meters behind at his five o'clock. The crew chiefs of both helos manned .30 caliber miniguns on the starboard side of their aircraft.

Kolt replied in his headset. "Roger, one minute. Just stay as low as possible and put us on the biggest roof you see. And watch those wires."

Kolt then reached down and found his radio knob, turned it three clicks to the right to switch from helo common to his assault net, and he keyed the mic near his left shoulder. He communicated with Rocket in the other aircraft, Texas two-two. "Rocket, you've got the squirters. Your helo will head to the road to the highway and land there so that no missiles escape."

"What if they split up?" Rocket asked.

"Then go after any truck that looks like it could be hauling missiles." Kolt was surprised he answered that quickly. He wasn't trying to be a smartass, but it may have come out like that.

Rocket responded, "Sounds like a plan, boss. We'll load back in the helo and follow the trucks that can shoot us down before we can tell what color they are." Rocket made no attempt to hide his sarcasm.

Moments later, with both doors open and a door gunner in the port-side window, Texas two-one crossed the outer chain-link fence, passed a massive silver-and-rust-colored water tower on the right, and headed straight for the long two-story building bookended by large transformer power lines.

The operators unhooked their safety belts and slid on their rear ends to the edge of both doors, letting their boots and calves hang over the end and catch the powerful wind blast. At thirty seconds out, Kolt removed his headset and moved into a kneeling position to exit quickly behind his men.

"Shit! That's them!" Kolt yelled as he saw three big International TerraStar trucks hauling ass for the front gate. Three SUVs led the trucks by fifty meters. Raynor felt certain he was looking at the AQAP cell with the missiles, all heading toward the blocking position being set up by Texas two-two and eight operators.

Kolt neither wanted nor needed to stay on the roof engaging Zetas if his targets were heading out the front gate.

But Chief Bartow was lowering Texas two-one's three rubber wheels down to the roof, concentrating on missing the high-tension wires all around, just like Racer had instructed him to do.

Kolt grabbed his wipe board and frantically scribbled, *Stay on helo!* He tried to pass it around, but everyone was focused on the hard landing to come.

They slammed down hard and the assaulters unassed the bird in two seconds, going prone on the roof. Kolt fought with the headset, trying to get it back on to tell Bartow not to take off just yet. He wanted to reload the helo to chase the fleeing convoy.

On the roof Slapshot fired his HK416 in short bursts at a group of men near an open garage. He dropped two, but a third spun around the corner of the building and aimed an RPG at the helo above him. The master sergeant screamed, "RPG!" as the weapon fired.

But his scream was lost in the thunderous engine noise from the Black Hawk.

The smoke trail raced just over Slaphshot's head, and he turned to look behind him just as the finned grenade sailed straight through one open door of the helo and exited through the other open door, missing Major Raynor by a foot and a half.

A perfect shot and a perfect miss.

As he knelt in Texas two-one, Kolt's eyes widened like softballs as the grenade passed. He dove out of the chopper, onto the roof, as Chief Bartow lifted back up into the dark sky, clipping two high-tension wires that snapped and sparked.

The Black Hawk raced off to the south.

"Somebody find the stairs!" Kolt yelled. He wanted his men off the roof and out of the line of fire before recalling Texas two-one.

Chief Warrant Officer Wilkins brought Texas two-two to a hover above the road halfway between the substation and Highway 85. Utility poles holding power lines ran along the south side of the road, so he brought his craft a touch to the north before landing just off the blacktop. Rocket and Digger and six other men leapt out of the helo and found cover in the greenery on either side of the road, as the headlights of the lead Los Zetas SUV closed on them from the east.

Wilkins lifted back into the air and rose to a hundred feet above the earth.

Kolt and his team moved down the stairs to the second floor and smashed windows that gave them a view to the substation's grounds. A few Mexican sentries opened fire at the building now, so Racer and his men took aim on each and every muzzle flash in sight.

Canine, a thirty-year-old assaulter, took an AK round to the side of his helmet that knocked him flat on his back. He lay stunned in the substation's control room, shaking the blur out of his eyes.

A medic crawled over to assess him, but Canine sat up, feeling his face for blood around his goggles and forehead. Finding nothing but a hot crease in his ballistic helmet, he climbed back to his feet and hefted his HK.

He returned to the fight within seconds.

Kolt thought he and his men were getting control of the resistance down below them. He got the idea that most of these Los Zetas gunmen who'd not left with the convoy had either tossed their rifles to the ground and jumped into vehicles to make a run for it, or else they were running off into the surrounding brush on foot.

To his right Raynor saw a pair of cars crash through a small rear gate of the substation and bounce out toward the lightening sky to the east. Kolt doubted the little two-door beater vehicles would be carrying SA-24s, so he kept his focus on the hostiles inside the grounds.

"Racer, this is Rocket."

"Go for Racer!" Kolt said as he fired.

"Multiple hostile vehicles. Plus or minus seven in all. The three target trucks are in sight. Engaging dismounted enemy."

"Roger that," said Raynor. "We're going to try to get a lift over to your position to help out."

Kolt then leaned into his mic and tried to raise Chief Bartow. "Texas two-one, Texas two-one, over."

"This is Texas two-one, over."

"Chief, the missiles are leaving the compound in a seven-vehicle convoy. I need you to come pick us up immediately so we can assist."

"Roger, inbound, one minute."

So far, Kolt was pleased that his radio worked, that many of the Mexicans seemed to be surrendering, and that Chief Bartow was willing to come back so soon after almost eating an RPG on the roof.

Kolt ran to a window near Slapshot to begin moving everyone back to the roof. As he began shouting in Slapshot's ear, both men watched as Texas two-one approached the building. Without warning, the door gunner in the Black Hawk opened up on a position behind a cluster of transformers on the north end of the facility. Two seconds later, a burst of AK-47 rounds rose up from another position near the transformers, piercing a hydraulic line behind Texas two-one's thin skin. Heavy black smoke started to pour out, swirling above the rotor blades.

Kolt keyed his mike and yelled as he watched, "Texas two-one, abort, abort, abort."

"Aborting," said Bartow, and his Black Hawk peeled off to the south, away from the target area.

Kolt knew things didn't look good for Bartow and his aircraft. Kolt wasn't in a position to help him, and as much as he wanted to, there was still the problem of Doyle and the missiles. He keyed his mic again. "Texas two-two, Texas two-two. Lame duck, divert to service two-one with SAR, over."

"Texas two-two is on the way."

Kolt and his men rained fire on the position from where the AK rounds had come, sending several dozen 5.56 rounds into a twelve-foot-high substation transformer there. The transformer exploded, knocking two men from behind it, blinded and stunned.

All over the facility the lights went out. Kolt and his men had night-vision goggles on their helmets, but before any of them could flip them down over their eyes, from behind the garage ahead on their right a huge flash erupted, and a missile screeched into the predawn sky. Racer's heart sank, knowing one of the Black Hawks was about to go down.

Chief Warrant Officer Wilkins, his copilot, and his crew chief/door-gunner were alone in Texas two-two, turning back to the east, when Wilkins's headset came alive with the warning of an inbound infrared missile. The UH-60's infrared countermeasures engaged automatically, and Wilkins banked hard to try to avoid the incoming warhead.

But the missile was on him in just seconds, and there was no time to avoid it. It slammed into the tail rotor of the Black Hawk and sent the big craft spinning clockwise. Wilkins and his crew lost all control and they lost altitude; the windscreen in front of them showed a high-speed revolution of dawn to the east and then darkness to the west, of city and country and city and country again.

Texas two-two crashed hard on its belly just one hundred meters north of the Delta men on the road.

Raynor had seen the helo take the hit a kilometer to the west, but he did not wait around in the window to watch it go down. He and his team now ran out of the front of the control building, bounding and covering for one another as they headed for the garage from where the SAM had launched. They passed Zetas who had dropped their weapons and raised their hands in the air, terrified of the fast-moving men in black who swarmed around them.

But Kolt and his men had time neither for prisoners nor for getting bogged down outside, so they kept moving to the next large structure, leaving only one of their operators behind to flex-cuff the Mexicans. The rest converged on the garage, shone the lights of their weapons into the big space to find it empty, and then closed on the far corner of the building.

Suddenly a vehicle's engine fired and tires spun on gravel. Kolt and Slapshot ran forward and spun around the side of the garage, just in time to see a red van drive away. In the passenger-side window Kolt saw the unmistakable face of a Caucasian with short brown hair.

David Wade Doyle.

Raynor raised his weapon to fire, but a burst of rounds kicked up around his feet, fired from a position in the dark near the security fence. Kolt dove back behind the corner of the garage.

When he stuck his head back around, the van had passed behind the garage and shot out the back gate of the substation property.

Near where the van had been parked, a man stood with an SA-24 launcher on his shoulder. Raynor raised his weapon and fired a half dozen rounds into the man, who fell backward. The heavy launcher broke apart on the cement drive.

Kolt looked back to his men. "We need wheels!" he screamed.

Slapshot ran to a blue Dodge Durango parked under the awning next to the garage. A heavyset Mexican lay dead next to it, a shotgun still cradled in his arms. Slapshot opened the passenger door and looked in. "Keys in this one!"

Kolt ran around to the other side and jumped in, while behind him the rest of his men kept up the fire on the Zetas' position out near the security fence.

Kolt and Slapshot drove out of the gate to the east, in pursuit of Doyle and his missiles.

With the rotor of the crashed Black Hawk still slowly spinning to their left, Rocket, Digger, and the rest of the men from Texas two-two were in the middle of a heavy firefight with an unknown number of enemy just up the road. All three TerraStar trucks had stopped in the road, along with three other vehicles. Men had poured out of them and they all scrambled to get off the blacktop and into the brush. Some made it. Many did not.

Digger reloaded his HK and moved up the southern side of the road. He'd killed two Zetas here and, along with the three men behind him, he closed on the wrecked-out convoy in front of him.

Rocket was on the northern side of the road. Two of his men had been hit and were being treated by a third, so he kept up the fire on the trucks in front of him.

Roscoe, the Belgian Malinois, was with them as well. His handler wrapped a field dressing quickly on the biceps of a wounded recce operator, while Roscoe barked.

As Rocket turned to check on the status of his injured mates, he heard someone shouting in Spanish, not far away in the low bushes. He turned back and shone his light, catching a single Zeta, obviously wounded in the stomach, stumbling out of the foliage. The man saw Rocket and raised his empty hands, so the Delta operator just motioned for him to drop to his knees and then onto his face.

The wounded and disoriented man complied.

Now Rocket looked to the sky. The lights of Nuevo Laredo were bright in the north, and in these lights he saw four Little Bird helos coming in low and fast. He hoped like hell the 160th pilots would be able to identify all the different gaggles of armed men out here in the dust, but he did more than hope. He immediately activated an infrared strobe on his helmet, and he ordered his men to do the same.

On the southern side of the road Digger had moved to within fifty feet of the TerraStars by the time the Little Birds swooped down from overhead. He and his men activated their IR strobes, and then Digger reengaged the fighters around the trucks. The shooters in the brush near the SUVs threw down their weapons and threw up their hands as soon as they saw the helos. Two of the four Little Birds were armed with rocket pods and machine guns, and the copilots on each bird held M4s out their doors toward the threats below.

The four helicopters hung like bees in the air, not twenty feet above the earth, and they covered everyone still alive from the convoy.

Kolt and Slapshot were a mile southeast of the substation now, still in hot pursuit of Doyle and the van. They found themselves on a disused gravel road that ran straight to the east.

"Looks like they are running for the border," Raynor said.

"Roger that."

Kolt felt certain that they would continue on this road all the way to the Rio Grande, which wasn't much more than a wide bubbling brook here, especially during the summer. He thought Doyle would try to make his way across in the truck or else dump the truck and the SAMs and cross over himself.

But when the dust ahead of him drifted away, he realized Doyle had turned to the south. He saw the red van head into a brush-covered field off to his right, bouncing over the heaviest foliage as it raced on.

Kolt turned the wheel hard to the right and followed, just as a man leaned out of the van's passenger window and fired a burst from an AR-15.

Raynor pulled farther to the left to shield himself and Slapshot from the van passenger's field of fire.

Within another minute of hard off-road driving, Kolt and Slapshot realized that they were on an old track that ran along a dry creek bed that went to the southwest.

Kolt called out to Slapshot, "This is Arroyo del Coyote, it heads straight to the border."

Even though the track was bumpy, Kolt pushed the accelerator all the way to the floor. The Durango shot forward. Rocks kicked up by the tires banged the undercarriage of the truck and it sounded like the vehicle was taking sustained fire from a belt-fed machine gun.

"Contact front!" Slapshot shouted, surprising Kolt, who looked forward to see a bend in the creek, and the road that ran alongside it, some one hundred yards ahead. Standing on a rise at the turn was a small group of men, and they seemed to be armed. The van passed them by at high speed.

"Who the hell . . ." Kolt began to ask, but as soon as the last word left his mouth he understood. Doyle had led him right to the Zetas who'd squirted out of the substation in the two beater cars. Now they were parked here at the creek, and they were ready to fight.

Before he could hit the brakes on the Dodge SUV, a plume of smoke appeared behind the man on the rise, faint in the glow of the dawn, but then it grew into a bright plume of fire. Kolt knew a rocket-propelled grenade was on its way. The finned rocket shot over the hot dry earth and raced toward his vehicle at an initial speed of 115 meters a second.

Slapshot saw it, too. He screamed, "RPG!"

Kolt wasn't sure if the rocket was going to miss or pass by, but he knew he could not wait to find out. He jacked the wheel to the left to get out of its path, sending the black Durango off the track and down a steep hill toward the creek bed. The grenade impacted the dirt road right behind them and the explosion smashed the rear windows out of the truck and filled the interior with dust and flying glass and rock.

Raynor and Slapshot both held on as the truck careened out of control. Kolt tried to hit the brakes but the Durango was already tipping over as he did so. It slammed onto its left side and slid down the hill farther, then flipped onto its roof. Broken glass and small river stones assaulted the men as they rode the truck farther down into the gulley.

The SUV came to rest on its right side at the bottom of the creek bed.

It took Raynor several seconds to regain his wits. He felt blood streaming across his face, and his rib cage hurt like hell. On top of this, his seat restraint was all but cutting off the blood supply to his brain. He fought for several seconds to get the belt off his neck.

Then he looked down at Slapshot, below him as the truck lay on its passenger side. He could barely make out his friend in the low light.

"Slap! You okay?"

Slapshot was not okay. His face was covered in blood, and his right arm was broken cleanly just below the elbow. It hung in a grotesque fashion, like he had an extra joint in the appendage. The big operator's eyes were closed and his mouth hung open.

He was either unconscious or dead.

The passenger side of the vehicle was now embedded in the river rock and broken earth. Fast drips of blood ran down from Racer's face and hit Slapshot below him, where it mixed with Slapshot's own blood, creating a constant rivulet of red that drained onto the white stones.

"Slapshot! Sergeant! Jason!" Kolt kept shouting at his mate, trying to get a reaction.

But between his shouts he heard multiple sets of footsteps racing toward him.

He jacked his head from side to side, looking around the vehicle for either his or Slapshot's HK416, but he could not find either weapon anywhere. He pulled his Glock 23 pistol from the holster on his chest. He knew that, unless the Zetas crossed directly in front of his smashed windshield, he would not be able to defend himself until he could get out of his seat.

Then low thumping of a rotary-winged aircraft caught his attention. Raynor could tell a helo was approaching from behind where he lay.

Gunfire erupted from multiple points around him. He tried again to get his seat belt off, but he could not. He just hung there, his eyes spinning left and right, looking for threats, while he continued to yell at Slapshot. "Wake up, brother!"

Just moments after the shooting stopped and the sounds of the helo rotors blocked out even his own shouts, he heard the sound of someone climbing up onto the Durango. A man leaned over, looking down into the driver's window.

"Boss?" it was Digger.

Kolt spoke, his voice tinged with the pain in his side. "Slap's bad! Get him out through the windshield and then worry about me!"

"Right." Several operators moved into view now, slung their rifles behind their backs, and started pulling on the broken windshield of the Durango to begin extracting Slapshot.

A minute later Kolt found himself on his back in the creek bed. Digger was crouched next to him, working on Slapshot on the dry stones by the SUV. Steam poured from the vehicle into the morning, obscuring Raynor's view of the helicopters circling overhead.

Kolt tried to sit up but the pain in his ribs stopped him.

Digger began CPR and chest compressions on Slapshot.

Raynor lay on his back, his men around him. His rib cage hurt; from the agony he felt with each breath he was certain he'd broken two or three ribs low on his right side.

"Where is Doyle?" Kolt asked.

Rocket had arrived in the creek now. He said, "He's gone. He didn't go for the border. His van made it to Highway 2. He could be back in Nuevo Laredo, or heading the other way. We've lost him."

Kolt struggled back up to his elbows. "He can still get over. We need to alert Homeland Security!"

"Already done, boss."

"Divert the ISR."

"Done, too. We've demo'd forty-six SA-24s. The rest must be with Doyle."

"We have Little Birds?"

"Yes."

"We're going after them in the city." Raynor said this with a wince, and he grabbed his side.

"Negative, sir," Rocket answered back. "Slapshot needs immediate medical evac. The Texas two-two crew needs immediate medical evac. We've lost both Black Hawks. One ate a SAM and the other crashed-landed over in Rio Bravo. And Digger hasn't checked you out yet, so you need to lie your ass back down. You could have internal injuries. We've been recalled back over the border. We'll have to ferry in the Little Birds, make two trips."

Kolt shook his head. It hurt to do so. "We have to get the Little Birds up to search for—"

"They're gone, boss! We don't have the assets to track them in the city now."

A Little Bird landed in the creek bed on the other side of the Durango. Kolt turned his head back to Slapshot. The dust kicked up by the rotors swirled between Kolt and the badly wounded master sergeant, but Raynor could make out Digger frantically performing mouth-to-mouth on the big man.

THIRTY-SIX

Four days after fleeing Nuevo Laredo in the red van, David Doyle, Miguel, Jerry, and Tim sat in the bowels of a semi-trailer waiting to make the crossing over the border from Agua Prieta, Mexico, into Douglas, Arizona. With them were twelve Igla-S missiles, interspersed in a shipment of Buick Regal radiators from a GM factory in Hermosillo.

Agua Prieta was hundreds of miles from Nuevo Laredo, and to get there Doyle and his men first drove blindly back into the interior of Mexico, where they stole a new van at gunpoint from a commercial driver, and then shot him dead by the side of the road so that he could not talk later. They then found a place to hunker down in Hermosillo, and here David spent two days on his satellite phone, frantically working his contacts over the border in the United States as well as back in Yemen and Dubai. He urged his masters in AQAP to pay the Zetas as much Pakistani heroin as they wanted to help him get into the United States, even though the loss of sixteen of their gunmen and worldwide attention to their defeat by American military forces in Nuevo Laredo had seriously hampered AQ-Zetas relations.

At first Doyle's masters were reluctant to continue supporting his mission. He had, after all, lost more than three-fourths of his surface-to-air weapons, and all but three of his original thirteen operatives. But David persisted, insisting that, if he could only receive help from the Mexicans to get him into the U.S., then there he could use sleeper agents that he was already in contact with to help him achieve his main objective.

He would not need sixty weapons to bring down the American government. No, he could do it with twelve.

Ultimately the leader of al Qaeda in the Arabian Peninsula was persuaded to do as Daoud al-Amriki asked by the simple fact that he said he would try it anyway, with or without the support of the Mexicans. AQ could work with him a little more, lose a little more heroin, to ensure his success in getting over the border. Or they could give him no support and risk suffering the incredible negative publicity of failure if the remaining cell members and their weapons were caught or killed trying to make it over the border.

AQAP contacted the Zetas, acquiesced to their demands, and then Doyle, his three men, and his twelve Iglas were picked up in Hermosillo and driven to the border.

In the little conversation he'd had with the Zetas, David had learned that they had paid agents working at both border crossings, and the truck they were in was cleared under NAFTA rules to enter the U.S. and continue into the nation's interior.

In the end, the crossing into the U.S. went off without a hitch. The men in the hot trailer felt the truck crawl up the line of commercial vehicles heading over the border, then it stopped for a while, just long enough for the four men to get nervous.

But then it rolled on, driving for another half hour, until it stopped and the engine was turned off.

The back gate opened and a Mexican stood there, looking in on the sweat-soaked Middle Eastern men. In a heavy accent he said, "Welcome to United States, my friends. We are in Tombstone, Arizona."

A Ford SUV and a Toyota minivan, purchased by the Zetas, sat in an empty parking lot of an office building that had a large FOR RENT sign on its front window. Four Mexicans off-loaded the crates into the two vehicles, six in each, and the Mexicans drove off to the south, leaving American David, Kuwaiti Miguel, Pakistani Jerry, and Iraqi Tim, all alone. Each man had a driver's license, though they were not their own. Weeks earlier, an AQ cell in the United States stole identification from men attending a mosque in Dearborn, Michigan, taking the IDs following orders from David himself. He had sent a list of ages, heights, weights, and skin colors corresponding to the members of his cell, and the thieves followed this list as they targeted their victims. Some of the faces were more of a match than others, and none were anywhere near perfect, but David felt reasonably certain they would all pass quick scrutiny.

Other than these IDs, the weapons, and the cash each man carried with him, the four men had nothing else other than mobile phones and the clothes on their backs.

David and Miguel shook hands in the parking lot of the vacant building. Tim and Jerry had already moved into the back of the Ford SUV.

Miguel asked David a question he'd been thinking about for the past day. "Why don't you take one of the men? I do not need them both. You should not travel alone."

David was in a somber mood, but he managed a smile. He did not like going alone, either. But he thought it would give his plan the best opportunity for success. "It is as Allah wills it," he said. "The three of you will go to the west, and I will go to the east."

"But why alone?"

Now Doyle's smile was real. "I will not be alone."

"But—"

"Remember, Miguel, it is best that we do not know what the other is doing. We have our missions, and they will work best if they are not coordinated."

Miguel acquiesced. "Yes, David. I understand."

"We will not see each other again, my friend," David said.

"In paradise."

"Yes, in paradise. But there is still so much work here for us to do. Do not be in a hurry to leave this earth before your work is done."

Miguel found strength in David's words; the American al Qaeda commander could see this in the improvement in the Kuwaiti's body language.

They shook hands again, and then they walked to their vehicles.

Just after ten the next morning David Doyle walked the aisles of a Walmart in Phoenix, Arizona, looking at all the incredible choices.

He was a wanted man. If he was not the most wanted man in America now, he expected he would be before the day was out. But no one took any notice of him.

With a face shaved clean and his brown hair cut and died white-blond in a north Tucson hotel the evening before, and his rugged all-American looks,

David was not going to be recognized either through his junior high year-book photo or any pictures taken of him in Yemen, where his full beard and long matted hair covered his face.

It had been his plan all along that, once he got into the U.S., he would make his way to a discount store somewhere, and he would buy clothing and accessories that would make him fit in perfectly with the men shopping there.

Of course, his original plan did not have his force of operatives whittled down to only three men.

But it did not matter. His first plan had met with resistance, incredible resistance in the form of, as near as he could guess, the same unit of men that had thwarted his attempt to steer the outcome of the Afghanistan war the previous year.

But now David Doyle and a dozen of his missiles were in the United States. He had a few men left to help him with his plan, and he would soon get a few more.

And the United States military could not fucking touch him here.

Doyle knew all about the Posse Comitatus Act. He was comforted in the fact that, once in U.S. territory, he would have law enforcement, municipal and state and federal and Homeland Security, after him. But he would not be up against the Army, the Navy, the Air Force, or the Marines. Those Navy SEALs or whoever the hell they were who had been after him since the attack on the black site in the Khyber Pass the previous fall, would have to slam on the brakes once he crossed over the border.

And he'd done it.

All along David planned on buying a cowboy hat once in the U.S. so he would fit in. But as he looked around the Walmart at the customers, he saw a few cowboy hats on the heads of Hispanic-looking men, but the Caucasians wore ball caps if anything at all.

He found a Caterpillar ball cap with some sort of phony grease stains and weathering on the bill. It would be perfect, almost as if Walmart were complicit in his disguise. He next picked up a new pair of blue jeans; these also came off the rack looking like they'd been taken from a grease monkey at an auto repair shop. It was early August, so a few rustic and worn T-shirts were thrown into Doyle's cart, along with tennis shoes and socks.

He next walked past the sporting goods department and eyed the rifles, shotguns, and pistols lined up and ready for sale. Doyle himself did not need a firearm; he had a Kalashnikov and a Beretta pistol in his minivan. But looking over the powerful small arms available for purchase by the general public gave him some concern. The prevalence of weapons in the hands of the citizenry here in the United States was going to have to color his every action. Although U.S. Special Forces could not touch him here inside America's borders, some do-gooding housewife with a snub-nosed revolver could shoot him dead if she thought he was a danger to her little yard-ape kids.

Infidels, Doyle thought. He could not wait to bring every last one of these Americans to their knees.

He passed by the guns and purchased a large hunting knife with cash, and in minutes he was out the door and back on the road.

Kolt spent four days in the hospital at Fort Bragg, suffering from three broken ribs and a severe concussion that required observation. He'd been out of it for much of the time, but each time TJ or Digger or Stitch or any of his other mates visited him, the first question he asked was the status of Slapshot. He'd learned little about Slap's injuries, but everyone assured Raynor that the big man had survived his wounds.

It was not until day three that Digger helped Kolt out into the hall and then down an elevator into the ICU. There they looked through a window at Slapshot, lying unconscious on his bed while Doc Markham finished an examination.

The doctor came out of the room a moment later.

"How's Jason?" Kolt asked. He never called Slapshot anything other than Slapshot, but looking at him lying there in his hospital bed in his gown, covered with the bandages and with a tube down his throat, he did not look like a tough-as-nails Delta operator.

Markham said, "He's got seven broken bones, a concussion, contusions, internal bleeding, but he's hanging on. We've got him in a medically induced coma till the swelling on his brain goes down. Probably another day."

"But he'll make it?"

Doc Markham replied, "He won't die."

"Meaning?"

"Just that, Racer. Anything else that happens is out of my hands."

Kolt and Digger had both experienced severe injuries with long recoveries. It would be tough on Slapshot, but he was as tough as them, if not tougher.

Before Kolt left the hospital he'd learned that Chief Warrant Officer Wilkins and his crew chief had survived the crash of Texas two-two, but the copilot had been killed on impact. Three other of Raynor's operators had been wounded in the hit as well, but none seriously.

Kolt was released with instructions to go home and stay in bed until his dizzy spells and headaches went away, but as soon as TJ picked him up at the hospital they drove over to the compound. Here Kolt and TJ both went straight in to see Webber.

Colonel Webber had been dealing with the fallout of the mission on the border constantly since his return from Eritrea, and he barely had time for his wounded major and his nonoperational lieutenant colonel this afternoon. But the two officers slipped by Joyce and knocked on Webber's open door.

"Do you have just a second, sir?" TJ asked.

Webber invited the men to come in and sit down. "Thought you were sent home, Racer," he said as he slid back into his chair.

"We wanted to drop in and see what's going on with the search for Doyle."

Webber shrugged. "We'll deal with the hot wash when you get better. For now I'll say that I'm proud of you for taking forty-five missiles and eight AQ operators out of commission. Especially with all the curveballs you were thrown on that op." He paused. "But this is not over. Assets are searching Mexico high and low, but if it's just a couple of guys and a van, we won't find him. If he's here in the States, we are out of the hunt. Posse Comitatus Act. They are looking for him here. FBI, Homeland Security, state and local cops on the border."

"Nothing, then?" Kolt asked.

"Not a sound. The White House is putting out fires with the Mexicans and telling everyone else that there is nothing to worry about, but it won't be long till it comes out that the skirmish on the border did not totally neutralize the threat. And if a plane goes down in Cincinnati, then word will get out even faster."

"Anything we can do, sir?" Kolt asked.

"Yes. You can go home, take your meds, and get better. There are other battles for you to fight, just not this one. It's out of all of our hands now."

TJ drove Kolt back to his trailer. There was no conversation between the two men. Kolt suspected TJ was disappointed in the opportunity lost. Raynor had had David Doyle right in front of him, and he'd not been able to drop the hammer.

Kolt suspected this, but he did not bring it up with his old friend. Raynor did not want to get into an argument with TJ; he was too worn out from his first day out of the hospital.

He just wanted to go home and get some sleep.

THIRTY-SEVEN

At ten on their second night in the United States, Miguel, Tim, and Jerry pulled into the parking lot of the Algin Sutton Recreation Center in South-Central Los Angeles. The park was closed, but there was no gate at the lot, so Jerry parked the Ford and kept it in idle, while Miguel climbed out of the passenger side and stood in the darkness.

His eyes to the sky.

Los Angeles International Airport was four miles to the west, and tonight's departure aircraft were flying directly over South-Central L.A. within a couple minutes of takeoff from Runways 7L and 7R.

The park Miguel had chosen was not exactly out of the way—homes and apartments lined the other side of Hoover Street. But traffic at this hour was light to nonexistent, and Miguel knew he could have his vehicle on Interstate 110 sixty seconds after he climbed back into the passenger seat, so he was not terribly worried about being caught.

Still, his heart pounded in his chest and his hands perspired.

Inside the back of the SUV Tim had already opened a case and prepped an Igla to fire. He now sat crouched in the back, pressed tightly between the weapon's crates and the wall of the vehicle, peering through a hole in black cardboard the men had taped in the windows to mask the view inside the vehicle.

Outside the SUV Miguel watched a massive 747 rise into the air to the west, its lights shimmering in the warm summer night, and he reached behind him and opened the rear door of the Explorer.

A police car rolled by, but took no notice of the vehicle or the man standing by it.

The aircraft was nearly overhead now. Miguel's training back in Yemen helped him identify the craft as belonging to United Airlines. He had no idea where it was going or how many people were on board, but as a target he found it suitable for his needs.

He turned and opened the rear door fully now, and Tim slid him the big shoulder-fired missile system.

With one last look around the park and the street, Miguel hefted the device, then turned to face the departing jumbo jet.

Witnesses all over the greater Los Angeles area reported what came next: an arc of fire, rising up out of South-Central L.A. and heading directly toward the departing 747, then a flash of fire under the wings of the aircraft. The United flight continued on to the east for several seconds more, but then a massive explosion at the center of the plane's fuselage illuminated the sky. The crack of an explosion was heard at different times in the different portions of the city, depending on the distance to the catastrophe, but by this time even those who had missed the missile launch stared in horror as the massive jumbo jet turned upside down and broke apart as it fell, sending fire and metal and fuel and bodies twelve thousand feet down.

It was only by some miracle that the vast majority of the wreckage missed the greater Los Angeles population center and instead impacted the desolate terrain in Whittier Hills, killing only eleven on the ground, a tiny fraction of the potential death toll.

By the time the airplane crashed, and the resultant brush fire began scorching Whittier Hills, Miguel, Tim, and Jerry were on Interstate 110, heading north to their next target.

San Francisco.

Kolt opened his eyes at one-thirty in the morning. He'd spent the day popping over-the-counter pain meds for his broken ribs and headaches and it had kept the worst of both injuries at bay, but after a few hours' sleep his bloodstream had been drained of the painkillers, so he awoke now in extreme discomfort.

He sat up with difficulty, using a chair he'd placed by the mattress on the floor to help him get up and down without using his torso, lest the pain in his side get the better of him. He felt his way into the bathroom and found his ibuprofen, swallowed four pills, and washed them down with tap water that he scooped into his mouth with his hand so he didn't have to lean over to get it out of the faucet.

The effort of all this left him exhausted, so he made his way back to his mattress and then gingerly lowered himself down to it by using the chair.

"I need a fucking bed," he said to the dark and empty room.

Just as he relaxed back on the mattress his mobile phone rang. He found it lying on the floor and he looked at the readout on the screen: *TJ.*

Raynor almost didn't answer it. He would do anything in the world for his best friend, but he figured TJ was just down in the dumps about David Doyle, and since Kolt felt every bit as depressed about letting Doyle slip away in Mexico as Timble had about missing his semi-opportunity in Pakistan, Kolt figured he would be the last person TJ needed to help buoy his spirits tonight.

But on the fourth ring Raynor reluctantly answered the phone.

"Hey, bro," Kolt said wearily.

"Turn on the TV!" TJ said, and Kolt quickly reached for the remote.

"What channel?"

"*Any* fucking channel."

Kolt flipped it on, and even before the old big screen came to life, he knew. There was no doubt in his mind that somewhere in the United States an aircraft had been shot down.

"Where?" he asked softly while he waited for the picture.

"L.A.," came the reply.

Now the screen showed a black landscape of hills with a grass fire raging in the center of them. Fire trucks raced up a street and the crawl under the video feed said a United Airlines flight to Taipei had crashed on takeoff at 10:05 p.m.

Kolt looked at his watch and saw this was only a half hour ago.

As he continued to watch the chaotic scene, he spoke into his phone. "How many dead?"

Timble was obviously watching the news as well. "CNN says two hundred eighty-six, plus God knows how many on the ground."

Raynor thought about the number of casualties, and then he thought about the number of missiles left in play. He said, "CIA estimated they took fifty SAMs from Libya. He launched one in central Mexico against the Navy helo, one at the National Guard helo, and one tonight. We found forty-six at the scene. One more plane is coming down unless the cops stop them."

TJ responded bitterly, "You don't know that. Fifty SAMs was just a CIA guess based on the size of the container that left Benghazi. Could have been fifty-one, fifty-five, or even sixty-five. Be careful with your assumptions."

Kolt knew his friend was right. This could be just the beginning.

Timble and Raynor sat quietly in their own homes and watched the televised success of their enemy into the morning hours, like two beaten men.

THIRTY-EIGHT

In the early afternoon of the next day, Miguel, Tim, and Jerry watched aircraft take off from San Francisco International Airport's two Runway 28s—28L and 28R. The planes flew north, rising over the city, before departing their runway heading and banking to the east toward Oakland or to the west, which took them out over the Pacific Ocean.

The three terrorists had positioned themselves on the northern side of Golden Gate Park. They'd parked their Explorer alongside North Lake, and they had taken an Igla launcher, wrapped in a large blanket, into the trees at a secluded section of the park near Chain of Lakes Drive, where foot traffic was light this hot afternoon.

At 1:40 p.m. Miguel decided the time was right. He would take the next wide-body jet that flew overhead. He sent Jerry back to the Explorer to wait behind the wheel, while he and Tim readied the weapon to fire.

A steady procession of smaller aircraft took off, frustrating both Tim and Miguel. Finally, just before two p.m., an American Airlines Boeing 777 wide-body aircraft rose skyward over the southern half of San Francisco. "Inshallah, we will kill three hundred more infidels," Miguel said with a determined smile.

Miguel shouldered the missile launcher while still deep in the trees, and he put his hand on the grip to hold it steady. He knew he'd have to step out into the open to launch, but he wanted to wait until the last possible moment.

Tim stood at his side; his Kalashnikov rifle had been hidden in a garbage bag, but he brought it out and to his shoulder.

As the 777 passed overhead, Miguel waited a few seconds more, and then stepped out into the bike path rimming North Lake. All his senses were focused on the aiming reticule of his iron sights as he centered them on the jet above.

The aircraft was still too close for Miguel to fire; he'd need to wait a few more seconds to be certain his missile would have time to acquire its target's heat register after launch.

"Hurry," said Tim next to him.

"One moment. Yes. Now is good," Miguel said confidently.

Just then, from behind, Miguel heard shouting.

"Hey! Hey!"

Miguel took his eye out of the sights for an instant, just as Tim spun around, raising his rifle toward the shouting. There on the bike path, not fifty feet away, two San Francisco Police Department bike patrol officers leapt off their still-moving bicycles and began drawing their sidearms. They shouted in English as they drew their guns.

"Drop the fucking weapon!"

Tim fired his AK, missing with his first two rounds, but his second burst hit the nearest bike cop in the thigh and spun him to the ground.

The second officer got his gun out of its belt holster and he raised it to fire. A long spray from Tim's rifle cut him down, but not before he'd squeezed off two rounds from his .40-caliber Smith & Wesson service pistol.

Shouts and screams came from the road to their left and from across the tiny lake. More police on bicycles hurried around the path to come to the aid of their friends. Miguel looked up again at the aircraft, but he knew he would have to start the targeting sequence over, and he did not want to wait around for the ten seconds or so necessary to accomplish this.

The white Explorer screeched to a stop on Chain of Lakes Drive, just twenty feet from the two men. Miguel shoved the forty-pound launch system off his shoulder and let it fall to the bike path, and he and Tim ran for the safety of the vehicle.

Jerry pushed the barrel of the AK out of the driver's window of the SUV and fired a burst at a group of people running toward the wounded policemen, killing a young woman, and Tim spun around to spray the remainder of his magazine indiscriminately across the lake at the traffic on John F. Kennedy Drive.

Both men were back in the Explorer in seconds, and the big vehicle spun out of the park, turning right on Fulton Street, heading across the city for the Bay Bridge.

"Dammit!" Miguel screamed, furious for failing to knock down the jet, but even more angry with himself for leaving the Igla behind. He pounded on the dashboard with his fist.

Jerry shouted back at him, "Calm down and help me navigate!"

"Keep going east! East to the bridge!"

Behind them, in the back of the SUV, Tim shouted, "Police! Following us!"

Miguel looked back over his shoulder and saw several patrol cars, their lights flashing, racing through the afternoon traffic on Fulton in hot pursuit of the Explorer.

"Dammit!" Miguel said again. He handed his rifle back to Tim, who wasted no time in opening fire out the back windshield, firing past the four crates of missiles stacked next to him.

Twice the three men in the Explorer managed to lose the police in traffic, but soon a California Highway Patrol helicopter appeared overhead and began overtly tracking them as they made their way east across the city toward the Bay Bridge.

The three men had not anticipated the amount of traffic they encountered getting across San Francisco in midafternoon. Multiple times Jerry was forced onto the median in order to keep moving, and twice he had to stop completely before bumping other vehicles to encourage them to get out of the way.

All the while Tim bounced around in the back of the vehicle, desperately trying to unpack and assemble another SAM. The CHP chopper flew directly behind them, and Miguel ordered Tim to shoot the cursed thing down, hoping it would keep other eyes in the sky off their tail.

They made a series of turns, desperate to avoid traffic as well as dodge police coming at them from the other direction, and this turned them to the north and then back again to the west.

Miguel realized where they were from the quickly moving GPS device he kept attached to the windshield. He also realized the folly of trying to make it back around to the Bay Bridge. He'd studied the street map of San Francisco to some degree in Yemen, but they were already traveling in an area he had not studied, as his plan had been to head to Oakland.

But the GPS showed him another escape route out of the city. The Golden Gate Bridge was just to the north, so he ordered Jerry to take the next right. The Pakistani driver swerved across two lanes of traffic to do so, causing a multicar collision on Geary Boulevard and a near-miss with a gas truck on Park Presidio.

Within a minute they had made their way into the MacArthur Tunnel, over a dozen police lights flashing in the traffic behind them. They shot out the other side of the tunnel onto Doyle Drive, and passed the Presidio on their left at speeds approaching eighty miles an hour, the helicopter and the police cars still tracking their every move.

Tim had been beaten and battered by Jerry's evasive driving, and he still had not managed to assemble the Igla-S launcher. Miguel looked back and saw the futility of his efforts, so instead he said, "Pick up the rifles and fire at everything behind us. Make them back off!"

In seconds Tim had opened fire on civilians and police alike. As they raced up Doyle Drive, the vehicles around them skidded left and right to avoid the flying lead.

A minute later they shot through the FasTrak lane onto the Golden Gate Bridge. Tim reloaded and dumped another magazine into the traffic.

They made it a fourth of the way across the bridge before Jerry screamed, "Roadblock on the bridge!"

Miguel looked ahead and saw a line of SFPD squad cars, CHP cars, and even an armored vehicle, along with dozens of armed police, completely blocking traffic in both directions.

He knew there was no way they could escape. "This is the end, my brothers. Prepare yourselves for martyrdom." His voice was solemn. He lifted the Beretta pistol from the center console of the SUV and he slid it into his jeans.

Jerry hit the brakes and turned the wheel, and the Ford Explorer swung violently to the left. As it came to a stop, Miguel opened the passenger-side door, away from the roadblock ahead, and he rolled into the street. Behind him, both Tim and Jerry elected to remain in the SUV. He heard the booming fire of their rifles chattering in unison, as together they raked the police cars ahead of them.

The cops must have known that behind the terrorists' vehicle were dozens of civilian cars, and they would all be in the line of fire. As the two al Qaeda operatives dumped 7.62 rounds into the police cars fifty yards ahead on the bridge, the return fire was hesitant. But when the first cop fell, dropping his pistol and falling dead on his back, his brothers- and sisters-in-arms poured more and more fire into the SUV ahead of them.

Miguel crawled away from the SUV, keeping himself shielded behind the vehicle and his body low to the ground to avoid the bullets whizzing overhead. He was heading for a bright red four-door full of college-aged adults who were huddled down in their seats and screaming in terror.

Behind him he heard the Kalashnikovs of his fellow jihadists fall silent. He did not know if the men were just pausing to reload or if Tim and Jerry were dead.

It did not matter, he told himself, as the fear of his impending death tightened the muscles in his back and squeezed his heart nearly shut. Tim and Jerry had fought bravely in Yemen and Mexico and now here in the United States. They were lions, and they would be rewarded in paradise.

Just then the Explorer's tires squealed. Miguel looked back as he ran away, and he saw the big truck fire across the bridge, slam into the pedestrian rail, and smash through. The truck hit the side of the bridge itself at speed, and the force of the impact sent the Explorer headlong over the side. The truck tumbled from view, leaving smoke and dust and metal and glass behind as it fell hundreds of feet down into San Francisco Bay.

Miguel turned away and kept running.

Though the thirty-four-year-old Kuwaiti was fleeing, he had no illusions about surviving this. Along with the roadblock that stopped him, the police who had chased him here were still on the bridge as well. He was surrounded and there was no way he could commandeer one of these vehicles and punch it through the traffic jam between here and freedom.

No, the al Qaeda operative was running from the roadblock, toward the red car, because he wanted to pull out his pistol and shoot the infidels there. One last act of defiance against the Great Satan just as he was cut down.

The shooting behind him slowed as he arrived at the college students covering their heads with their hands inside their car. Miguel pulled the 9mm pistol from his jeans and lifted it toward the windshield, and he rose with it, standing erect as he slipped his finger on the trigger and shouted, *"Allahu Akhbar!"*

He fired twice, the gun cracked and jolted, and his bullets pocked the windshield and struck the driver in the chest. He started to pull the trigger a third time, but instead he felt himself spinning, out of control, the gun toppling out of his grasp, and he saw the asphalt roadway rushing to meet him.

He'd been shot in the stomach, he felt the burn there, and somehow he knew it was a fatal wound.

He fell to his side, reached out frantically for his gun, and found it with his fingertips. He brought it back into his grip and sat up quickly, keeping the weapon on the ground in his hand. As Miguel looked around, he found himself surrounded by too many policemen to count. They had closed to within ten meters, holding their guns on him and screaming bloody murder in all directions.

Waleed Nayef, aka Miguel, looked at the policemen for a brief moment. Then he lifted the Beretta off the roadway and every man and woman in sight with a gun and a badge shot him dead.

THIRTY-NINE

While members of the California Highway Patrol and the San Francisco Police Department stood over Miguel's bullet-ridden corpse, David Doyle parked his car in an empty lot at Barr Lake State Park, just north of Denver, Colorado. He'd been driving for nine hours straight, and he wanted to take a nap, but he did not allow himself the luxury. He knew all about Los Angeles the night before, and he also knew Miguel would be heading up the West Coast with his men now, so Doyle wanted to act here, many hundreds of miles away, as soon as possible, in order to take a small measure of the heat away from his partner. If America knew there were two missile crews loose in the country, they might worry there were three, or ten, or more. It could remove some of the focus from California.

David knew it would be many hours before he could rest easily. He might get an hour somewhere between here and his intermediate destination, but only there would he be able to call himself safe enough to sleep for any significant amount of time.

It would be another day at least before comfort. Now was time to work.

He climbed in the back of the minivan, and took his time readying a missile for launch. When he was finished, he cracked the back door, slid the Igla-S system to the edge of the door, and then crawled back into the front seat.

He climbed out of his Toyota minivan, taking his backpack with him. He pulled his high-powered binoculars out of the bag, and looked off to the southeast. There, five miles across the flat landscape of farmland laced with straight roads and dotted with simple farmhouses, lay Denver International Airport.

Through his binoculars he saw a plane, a big fat Delta Boeing 757, begin its takeoff roll. David knew that, depending on the variant, the aircraft in front of him could carry somewhere up to 250 passengers and crew.

It would be perfect.

The 757 raced down the runway, picking up speed, though through his optics and the heat coming off the ground between his position and the airport, to David it looked almost as if the huge machine in the distance were moving like a gentle wave.

Farther down the runway now, seconds from takeoff, and David lowered his binos and opened the rear hatch of the minivan. He checked the area around him, found it clear, and hefted the big weapon.

He labored to get it on his shoulder, then he turned back around toward the airport.

The plane was still there. Still on the runway, although it was down near the end of the runway now. It had slowed to a crawl, and soon it taxied off the runway at the last taxiway.

David lowered the weapon back to the rear of the Toyota and closed the door.

Why did it not take off?

Doyle grabbed his binoculars and waited for the next aircraft in line for takeoff at the far end of the runway, but it just sat there.

For ten minutes Doyle watched through his binoculars as first one, and then three, and finally all of the aircraft on the long taxiway rolled slowly down the runway, taxied back onto the taxiway, and then returned to the gate.

He had his suspicions early on as to what was happening, but it was not until he climbed back into the Toyota and headed back to the highway that he knew for certain. He turned on the satellite radio in the car and listened to the news.

A complete ground stop over the entire United States of America had just been enacted following a second terrorist attack involving a shoulder-fired missile, this time in San Francisco.

Doyle listened as early reports were broadcast about the event in San Francisco. Fragmented half-truths and wild assumptions were espoused by the news anchors, but one thing was certain. A group of men with a shoulder-fired missile had dropped their weapon before launching, and then led police on a twenty minute chase through the city.

Although the reporter said no planes were actually struck by SAMs, and it was likely the terrorists had been killed or captured by the authorities, the ground stop would go in effect and last until the FBI had determined that there was no continuing threat to aircraft in the United States.

Doyle wished he could pull over somewhere to watch raw footage of the scene on television, but instead he kept driving to the east. He looked out his passenger-side window at the airport as he passed to the north a few minutes later, and marveled at the dumb luck of those 250 infidels on that 757.

Raynor's first day back at the compound since Mexico was supposed to include nothing more than a visit to Doc Markham, followed by a drive to the hospital with some mates to look in on Slapshot.

Instead, he, and most everyone else who could fit, sat in the briefing room, watching the television reports from the West Coast.

It was a somber and angry mood in the briefing room, in the entire Delta Force compound, as news report after news report broadcast each and every facet of the ongoing terrorist threat to the nation. The operators and support personnel all felt a sense of responsibility for the loss of the aircraft and the nationwide shutdown of air traffic. Even more than this, they all felt an incredible sense of impotence, knowing they were now out of the hunt. U.S. military forces would not be operating on U.S. soil, so all these men and women could do was sit and watch.

Gangster and his alert squadron were still in the hunt for more MAN-PADs, of course. ST6 had successfully recovered a dozen shoulder-fired missiles in Sirte, but all intelligence indicators had pointed to that cache being three or four times as large, so it seemed quite likely that another big shipment had made its way out of Libya. The Delta alert squadron, like ST6, was literally crawling the walls waiting for intel that would earn them an opportunity to go find the munitions, get them back, and smoke anyone who tried to stop them.

But Kolt and his squadron could do nothing now but train for their next time at bat. Raynor had sent much of his force off for training around the U.S., but Kolt himself was in no condition to do much more than walk up and down the Spine from his office to the briefing room with a constant grimace on his face while he fought through the pain from the injuries received in Mexico and the anguish he felt about the failure of his mission.

He was just about to leave the briefing room and head to the SCIF when CNN went live to the President of the United States. POTUS was out of the country, in Australia for a conference with the Asia-Pacific Economic Cooperation, a free-trade organization that was meeting in Sydney this year. He opened his comments about the events in California by saying he was cutting short his trip to the Pacific Rim and would be heading back to Washington as soon as the Secret Service determined it was prudent to do so.

He was subdued and reflective in his comments about the loss of life and the attack on the fabric of American society, but he was also upbeat in his assessment of the ongoing threat. He said that his attorney general would be holding a press conference regarding the case within the hour, and he was confident in the Justice Department's ability to bring the perpetrators to justice swiftly.

Kolt thought the President hit all the right notes in his comments. He grabbed another cup of coffee, washed down four more ibuprofen, and stuck around the briefing room for the AG's press conference.

The attorney general appeared live from his office in D.C. He said, "Authorities are searching the waters in San Francisco Bay near where the terrorist vehicle went under the waves. We do expect to find the body of David Wade Doyle and his remaining confederates. It is also our belief the terrorist threat to the United States has passed, and we anticipate reopening America's skies within the next twenty-four to forty-eight hours."

There were audible groans in the briefing room.

Monk sat in back with Benji, Gangster, and a few other men from the alert squadron. Monk said, "So the bad guy is dead, but there's no body. Doesn't that sound a little like every shitty horror movie you ever saw?"

Men chuckled without smiling.

Raynor spoke the consensus of the room. "If I don't see a body, then that bastard isn't dead."

Kolt pushed himself out of his chair and headed back up the Spine toward his office.

David Doyle pulled into the driveway of an old home on East Seventy-fifth in Chicago's South Side just after midnight. A man lifted a manual garage door and David drove his Toyota straight in, and the man in the drive shut the door quickly behind him.

Doyle followed the man through the dark and into the back kitchen door of the house. A group of women were there in the kitchen, but they just looked away as the stranger entered, and he passed them by without speaking.

Doyle was led into the living room, and he found himself face-to-face with five men, all seated on a long wraparound sofa. David was handed a cup of instant coffee, and he took a chair placed in front of the television set.

"As salaam aleikum."

The five men answered back as one. *"Wa aleikum as salaam."*

Months ago, when Doyle chose his resources for this mission from the thumb drive brought by the six AQ operatives from western Pakistan, he carefully selected confederates already in the United States who could help him hide out if he ran into trouble. These sleeper cell agents needed to be as committed to the cause as he was, and they needed to be prepared to martyr themselves for the cause if David ordered them to do so.

He found a suitable group in Chicago. They were Saudis who had lived in the U.S. for over a decade, and the five men ranged in age from nineteen to thirty-seven. Three of the five men had trained at AQ camps in Pakistan, and all five had expressed a willingness to commit jihad against their adopted nation.

Doyle decided they would be perfect for his needs, even though they knew nothing about the mission they would undertake. He had contacted them in Mexico knowing that he would use them in some capacity, but now was the moment of truth, the point when they would learn their role in the coming event.

"The Americans have stopped flying all their aircraft," said the oldest in the room, Abdul Rahman.

Doyle just nodded. "I knew they would do this. It serves our purpose. Each day the skies over the United States are empty, Americans lose billions of dollars. They will do everything they can to find us and end the threat to their planes."

"They say on the news that they think you died in San Francisco."

Doyle smiled at this. "Another benefit for our operation. This means they will resume flights shortly, and they will lower their guard. Our success is all but assured, my brothers."

"So . . . what will we be doing?" another man asked.

"We are going to go to the one place where there will still be air traffic."

"Where is that, Daoud?"

"Washington, D.C."

The men looked intelligent and resolute, and this was good. Doyle needed to teach them in short order how to fire missiles, and even though this did not take much in the way of skill or talent, it would take their concentration. Still, Doyle knew, the hard part was getting men who would point the missiles at aircraft full of live humans and pull the trigger. Doyle needed these five Chicagoans to help him with that.

"I need to know that I can trust you."

"You can, Daoud. All of us have been waiting for years for our martyrdom operation. We have rifles and ammunition buried in the backyard. We can dig them up tonight."

"Very well. We will need them," David said. "But first it is time for your lessons. Let us begin."

Doyle left the room, and then returned with a single Igla launcher. He placed it on the oak table, and then put a rocket alongside it. The five men stood around the table as the al Qaeda operational commander showed them the basics of the weapon. He loaded the missile into the tube and attached the power supply, and then he hefted it onto his shoulder.

After a moment he passed it around to the four other men. Each one held it, looked through the round sights, squeezed the hand grip with a sweaty and shaky hand, and then passed it on around the room.

After an hour David felt the men had a perfunctory knowledge of the weapon and how to fire it.

Doyle next went into his explanation of the mission. All five men found it both audacious and brilliant.

When he was finished he asked, "Any questions?"

"Yeah," said a thickly built man in his early thirties. His voice was more Chicago than Saudi Arabia. Doyle had already identified the man as the leader of the cell, but he gave equal respect to all five of the operatives. "When do we leave?"

"We will leave in the morning. I will rest for a while, and then we will travel in two vehicles. Inshallah, we will arrive at our destination with time to spare."

FORTY

Kolt Raynor lay in his dark trailer and listened to the sound of gentle rain on the metal roof. He cursed the mattress under him. He'd lived like this for years, and it had never bothered him before, but now that he was sporting a couple of broken ribs he found himself missing the added support of a box spring. Moving around on the mattress was hell.

He sat up with a wince, and found his way to his feet. He headed into his tiny kitchen toward the coffeemaker, but the sound and lights of a vehicle pulling up outside stopped him in his tracks.

He looked at his watch and saw it was not yet 0500.

Kolt rarely received visitors to his trailer, and never at this hour.

As he opened his front door, TJ came jogging in from the rain. "How you feeling?"

Kolt shut the door behind him. "I feel like I spent a couple hours in an industrial washing machine on the spin cycle."

"Anything new on Jason?"

"Slapshot is recovering," said Raynor. It was the word the doctors used, so Kolt had used it himself, though he knew it could mean virtually anything short of dead.

"That's good to hear." TJ just stood there in the little trailer.

"Were you just in the neighborhood?" asked Kolt jokingly.

Timble hesitated before saying, "I have a proposition for you."

"Okay."

313

"How 'bout you and me take a couple days' leave?"

"And?"

"And we go on a little trip."

Raynor had no idea where this was going. "A trip? A trip to where?"

TJ sat on the couch, and Raynor lowered slowly and painfully to the recliner.

"Kolt, David Doyle is out there. He's not dead. He's not running from this. He's out there and he's getting ready to act."

"Where do you think he is?"

"Not on the West Coast. The West Coast cell was just a ruse. He planned on them getting killed so that the heat would be off him and his main objective."

"Shooting down passenger jets wasn't his main objective?"

"I don't think so. It's something else. Something big and nasty." He paused. "I know how this guy thinks. He is not going to lie low, and he damn well knew we would initiate a ground stop. It was part of his plan."

"So what does this have to do with our trip?"

"I want us to go find him."

"Don't tell me JSOC has talked the White House into rescinding Posse Comitatus." Kolt knew Webber had been seeking a waiver on Posse Comitatus to allow JSOC forces to operate within the U.S. borders. It had been waived on rare occasion, and, in the thinking of many in the military, it should be waived now. But the White House had been vehemently against the practice even before they had convinced themselves the threat had passed.

"Posse Comitatus is still in effect," Josh said flatly.

Raynor looked into his friend's eyes for a long moment, trying to decide if TJ had lost his mind. But his eyes seemed as sharp and intelligent as ever. "You don't think the Feds are going to find him?"

TJ just shook his head. "Shit. I don't know. Maybe so. But if they don't and he does something, then I won't be able to live with myself for not trying to put a stop to him."

Kolt nodded slowly. "I feel responsible for letting him slip away in Mexico."

TJ just nodded. He offered Kolt no comfort. He was using Kolt's guilt to push him forward.

"I don't know, man, what if we get alerted again?" Kolt asked.

"Dude. You know damn well that last hit in Mexico was a fluke. Your squadron isn't on alert. If anything, pops, Gangster has it."

"Where do you want to go?" Raynor asked.

"Someplace where a guy with a missile might go to shoot down an aircraft."

"There aren't any planes flying."

"Haven't you seen the news? A plane is landing tomorrow morning."

Kolt cocked his head. "The President?"

"I figure it's worth a shot. I think Doyle might be thinking the exact same thing."

Kolt just sat there for a moment. "Andrews Air Force Base will be protected. Surrounded like Fort Knox."

TJ said, "I know. Doyle knows, too. I don't have any answers yet, brother. Just questions. But I am going to go to D.C. and try to get some answers."

Raynor thought it over for a few more seconds. Then he said, "I'll talk to Webber."

"I'll be in his office at 0800," TJ said. "Best you pop in after that."

Kolt entered Webber's office at 1000 hours, and sat in one of the chairs in front of Webber's desk. It was a Saturday, but Webber was there.

"What's on your mind?" Webber asked.

"Sir, I was wondering if POTUS was going to waive Posse Comitatus."

"He hasn't yet, why?" Webber asked.

"What's your feeling, sir? Do you think he will?" Kolt pressed him.

"Major, the President is nervous about that, as you can understand. Right now it seems the SECDEF's biggest hurdle is convincing him that the threat is not over. POTUS will be back in the States tomorrow and flights will resume on Monday. They think this is behind them."

"Sir. I would like to request leave."

"Sure. I've cracked ribs myself and I know how inconvenient it can be when it hurts to breathe. Take a few days. If you need more, just—"

The colonel stopped himself in midsentence. After looking at his major for a long time, he said, "TJ asked me for leave today. You planning on a little vacay together?"

Kolt nodded.

"What's up?"

"It might be better if I don't go into it."

"You guys are going after Doyle, aren't you?"

Raynor hesitated for a moment, but finally said, "Josh seems to think he's got a line into the guy's psyche. I don't necessarily believe it, but I feel like I owe him. I'd like to go along."

"Kolt, you can barely move with those broken ribs."

"I'll cinch them up tight. I'll be fine."

The colonel sighed. "Timble is a very intelligent man. Pakistan shook him up, but I am of the opinion that, long-term, it will only make him stronger. He is *not* crazy, Racer."

"No, sir."

"You are service members. Active-duty service members."

"We aren't operating with the Army or JSOC, sir. We're just two guys going for a drive. If we happen to run into a wanted terrorist . . ."

"You'll make a citizen's arrest?"

Raynor did not answer.

"If TJ thinks he can find Doyle, he might be able to do just that. The question remains, though."

Kolt asked the question. "What are we going to do with him if we find him?"

Webber paused, as if he were choosing his next words carefully. "Kolt, David Doyle is an American citizen. If you find him on U.S. soil, it might be . . . problematic."

"Problematic, sir?"

"Yes. I am speaking about the complications involved with taking him alive."

Raynor recognized that Webber was trying to tell him something very important. He asked, "Are you saying we should *not* take him alive?"

"Hell, son, I'm not saying you should even go looking for him. I'd rather you didn't get yourself mixed up in a capital murder charge."

Raynor had not considered this, but he honestly did not care. If shooting David Doyle in front of fifty federal judges meant ending Doyle's reign of terror, then Kolt knew he would gladly do this and then suffer the consequences. But he had no intention of making Webber complicit in his plan. He just said, "I understand, sir. We will do everything in our power to call in law enforcement if we get close to Doyle or his men."

"Right. I have a pristine mental image of that happening." Webber cleared his throat again. "What I am saying is this: if you should happen to take him in alive, as a United States citizen, he will get the full treatment from our laws. Fancy lawyer, day in court, jury of his peers—as if he had any peers here in America. If Doyle should be captured and not killed . . ."

Kolt understood. He thought back to the conversation he had with Webber just before his reinstatement into Delta. The colonel asked him, in effect, if he had any problem dropping the hammer on some crow who might otherwise end up on *60 Minutes*. Kolt had said no.

And now Webber was telling him, in a roundabout but certain manner, that if he caught David Doyle in the field, then he should not allow him the chance to surrender.

"I understand, sir."

Webber said, "This is a bad idea. But I know what you guys can do. And I know Doyle is not in the bottom of San Francisco Bay. So get out of here and good luck."

"Thank you, sir."

As Raynor left the room, Webber said, "Enjoy your vacation."

TJ parked his Ford F-350 pickup outside Kolt's trailer at noon. Raynor came out a moment later with a backpack and a Remington pump-action shotgun.

TJ said, "Great minds think alike. I've got a Mossberg stowed under the seats. A Glock in an ankle holster. You have your 1911?"

"Don't leave home without it."

"You aren't using Unit ammo in it, are you?" TJ asked to be sure. "Remember, no comebacks on Delta if something goes down."

"No shit. No, my ammo is from my personal stash, bought from Jim's Pawnshop."

"That'll do."

In minutes they were on the road. It was a five-hour drive into D.C. from Fayetteville, and they spent most of the time heading up I-95 listening to the news on the radio and speculating about Doyle's location and his next move. The news droned on and on about how the President's plane was due to land at Andrews at eight the next morning, and security would be extra tight around the White House.

TJ said, "We are listening to Doyle's intelligence agents. The damn media is going to give him every detail about POTUS's return to the U.S."

Kolt said, "I wish he'd just sit overseas until Doyle was caught."

"He can't do that if his AG is telling people they think they've got a handle on the threat. Plus, it's all politics. He's flying back to Washington to look presidential, like he's in control of the crisis."

Kolt shook his head. "The SA-24 is the most advanced MANPAD out there, and it can defeat many infrared countermeasures. But Air Force One has countermeasures out the ass. Plus he will fly into Andrews, and security there will be incredible. You said it yourself—Doyle is smart. He would know that."

TJ looked at Raynor, taking his eyes off the interstate in front of him for more time than Kolt found comfortable. He said, "*Not* Air Force One! *Marine One!*" The President's helicopter. "If POTUS lands at Andrews, he'll take Marine One to the White House."

Kolt shook his head. "With loose SAMs and terrorists? He'll probably take a motorcade."

"The terrorists are dead, remember? How is he going to avoid taking his helo after his Justice Department told everyone there's nothing to worry about? No, he'll take Marine One, despite the Secret Service's protests. They will very quietly and very thoroughly canvass the entire flight path with cops and Feds, but he *will* fly home from Andrews."

"Marine One has countermeasures, too, Josh. It flies with decoy aircraft and has chaff and flares and IR jammers that can—"

"I know all that. But Doyle has a plan."

Kolt looked off in the distance for a moment. "You know, there might be a way he could do it. What if you and your asshole buddies fired two SAMs, or four SAMs, or ten SAMs, all at the same time?"

"Would that work?" TJ asked.

"I don't know. But it's the only thing that makes sense at this point. And the Grinch has a range of ten klicks or more. That's a twenty-klick death zone that the Secret Service will have to cover for the duration of the flight to the White House. No way they can do that."

Josh replied, "They'll get help from FBI, DC Metro, Maryland state troopers, park police, poultry inspectors. Shit, anybody who's got a badge and jurisdiction in the territory under the flight path is going to be there combing the ground. It won't be perfect, but they'll try."

"Sorry to break it to you, TJ, but a pickup truck with two good ole' boys slinging shotguns is not going to be able to cruise through that gauntlet you just described."

TJ smiled. The first time Kolt had seen him do so in a while. "Leave the talking to me. I'll get us close to the action."

"And then? What, we're just going to stumble onto Doyle with a SAM on his shoulder?"

Now TJ's smile morphed into a frown. "I know how he thinks, Kolt. That's important."

"We'll have to do better than that." Kolt thought it over. "Back at his training camp in Yemen, there was an anomaly that no one understood. A twenty-foot shipping container."

"Empty?" TJ asked.

"It had empty crates in it, as well as a mock-up SA-24 launcher."

"Maybe they store the SAMs there?"

Kolt said, "There were water bottles and bedrolls, too. Maybe they stored themselves there."

TJ was energized by this intel. "We need to check docks and boats on the Potomac under the flight path."

Kolt wasn't as sure as his friend. He just said, "Got to start somewhere, I guess."

FORTY-ONE

David Doyle and his five Chicago cell members sat in the living room of a small apartment in Woodmore, Maryland, just a half mile from Six Flags. This was the home of their local contact, a sixty-two-year-old truck driver named Ali.

Ali seemed overwhelmed by all the young men in his simple home, but he wanted to prove to Daoud al-Amriki that he had executed the orders he'd received months earlier to the letter.

"I have the truck outside. It is full of palletized cans of soft drinks. I am to deliver it this evening. All is prepared like you asked."

David just nodded. "Then you have done well. What can you tell us about the Americans' arrangements for tomorrow morning?"

Ali said, "The Secret Service, the FBI, and the Maryland State Police will be all over the area. They said this on the radio. They will be on rooftops and at intersections. They are saying all vehicles are subject to search."

The others sat around the living room, most drinking tea and smoking nervously. More nervously after Ali's report about the local situation.

But Doyle was not concerned about lifting their spirits at the moment. Instead he asked, "How long will they be doing this?"

"They say the security measures will only last until the President is back in the White House. They say everyone can go to church tomorrow after nine a.m. with no delays."

Doyle smiled. "Yes. They *will* all go to church tomorrow. They will be in mourning."

This earned smiles from his jittery men.

"You have been on the news, David," Ali added. "Old photographs of you."

"I am famous." Doyle smiled as he said, "You all are in the presence of a celebrity. But tomorrow, tomorrow you all will be famous, too."

The men laughed, a little nervously still, and they prayed together, and then they went outside, downstairs to the parking lot.

Doyle and his five Chicago cell members climbed back into their vehicle, and Ali climbed behind the wheel of a Peterbilt tractor-trailer with the words BUY-RITE in blue on the side of the fifty-three-foot trailer.

Together both vehicles drove to a U-Stor-It mini-storage facility in Walker Mill, Maryland, and they backed the trailer up between a pair of ten-by-ten storage lockers. Quickly Ali and the Chicago cell leapt into the back of the fifty-three-foot trailer and began off-loading cases of orange soda, placing them in the rented storage rooms. They had to break the cases out of the pallets to do so, and this took time, but they finally emptied twenty feet of space in the back of the semi.

They closed the lockers and returned to the house near Six Flags, and Ali parked his trailer in the lot of his apartment complex. Doyle and his men climbed into the back and began moving the cases of soda around. They lined the walls the length of the trailer with cases of soda, floor-to-ceiling, but they left the center of the space open. Here they loaded the six SAM crates from the back of the minivan.

It took a full hour, but finally they created a nest for themselves, their six SAMs, their rifles, and several duffel bags of gear, food, and water.

At seven in the evening, with David and the five members of the Chicago cell inside the trailer, Ali prepared to close them in. Before he shut the door Doyle knelt down over the older man. "Everything depends on you, my friend. Back in Yemen they told me you were very brave, very intelligent, and very strong. They told me you were in Lebanon in the 1980s, and the infidels took everything from you."

Ali nodded, his eyes filled with sadness, but then they gleamed with pride. "My family died when the USS *New Jersey*'s shells hit my neighborhood.

I have spent the last quarter century waiting for the opportunity to get my revenge. Thank you for this chance, Daoud al-Amriki."

David smiled broadly. "Thank *you,* brother. Now close us in and go in peace."

The door shut on David and the Chicago cell, and within seconds the engine started in the truck.

Raynor and Timble drove through Washington, D.C., at 1930, after spending over an hour in Beltway traffic and then stopping for gas and provisions in nearby Alexandria. They parked their vehicle near the mall and walked to the White House. Both men could see the heightened security all over the place as they did their best to look relaxed and nonthreatening.

TJ looked up at the Willard InterContinental, a stately hotel adjacent to the White House, and he leaned over to his friend. In a whisper, lest any tourists misconstrue the meaning of his comment, he said, "You could rent a room over there, arm your SAM on your bed, and then smash out the window as Marine One came in for a landing. The pilot wouldn't have a chance in hell to get away."

Raynor looked at the hotel. "I hope like hell we aren't the first people to think of that and there is some sort of security glass on those windows."

TJ just shrugged. "Don't be so sure. Lots of people thought about hijacking planes to turn them into missiles before 9/11. When it happened the authorities just shrugged and said nobody could have imagined it."

Raynor turned to walk back to the truck. "Dude, we *are* the authorities. Doyle's not at the Willard. Too many cameras and too much security. If he's around here at all, he's in some out-of-the-way place on the route from Andrews."

"I agree."

"It will be dark soon. Let's head down to the water to start looking for a shipping container."

"A shipping container," TJ said. It was an overwhelming task. "There might be thousands."

Kolt said, "It's gonna be a long night, brother."

The Peterbilt pulled the fifty-three-foot semi-trailer into the lot of Buy-Rite, a big-box discount store on Southern Avenue, just after eight p.m. Ali backed his rig into a space in the lot across from the store's loading bays. He lined his trailer up alongside three other fifty-three-foot semis, and then he set his parking brake and began decoupling his rig.

The parking lot was officially in Maryland, although just barely. On the opposite side of Southern Avenue was the start of the District of Columbia.

As Ali had expected, the stock manager came out upon seeing the new semi in his lot. He was a heavyset black man and he wore dungarees and black work boots.

"Evening, Ali."

Ali had liked Larry since he'd started delivering trailers for Buy-Rite two months earlier. "Good evening, Larry."

"Once again, you are too late to get unloaded. It's Saturday, everybody's leaving for the night."

"Yes, I know. I will leave the trailer and be back by noon on Monday."

"Sounds good. You want some coffee before you take off?"

Ali shook his head. "Not tonight, Larry. Maybe next time."

"Take it easy."

Ali drove his Peterbilt out of the Buy-Rite parking lot, leaving his fifty-three-foot trailer behind.

The trailer sat in the lot as the store closed at eight, and as the last hues of daylight left the sky at nine. It was third in a line of four nearly identical trailers. Four times during the evening Maryland State Police cruisers came through the lot, and each time shined their window light on the trailers as they passed, looking for anyone who might be hiding under or between them.

Doyle had cut three small holes in the bottom of the semi so that they would have fresh air to breathe, but he did not dare chance a look outside the semi. He did not need to orient himself, he had spent many hours over the past two months looking at the scene on Google Earth. He knew that he was in the rear parking lot of the Buy-Rite. He would only need to jump out of the semi and walk around the side of the container to see the green hills and trees of Cedar Hill Cemetery. Beyond the cemetery the sprawling grounds of the Office of Naval Intelligence ran for several acres.

And beyond ONI were the low suburbs of Suitland—Silver Hill and Morningside and, beyond all this, Joint Base Andrews Naval Air Facility.

Andrews Air Force Base.

The President would be landing at eight a.m., and he would fly overhead minutes after that. With this incredible field of view in this location, they would see the President and his helicopters coming for five kilometers. Plenty of time to ready themselves to knock his helicopter out of the sky.

As he pictured the morning to come in his mind's eye, a whisper of doubt came in the hot dark from one of the men. "Daoud. If the authorities will be everywhere, how can we expect to succeed?"

"They will not be in the parking lot of Buy-Rite at the moment we come out of the trailer. I believe God wills us to succeed, and he will not let that happen.

"But if they *are* there . . ." Doyle reached for the AK. "There are six of us. We will be fine."

He put the gun back down. "We will need forty-five seconds to get out of the trailer, and to take a weapon and fire it at a helicopter. Forty-five seconds." Doyle smiled ruefully in the dark. In Yemen he'd gotten that time down to twenty-seven seconds with his operatives. They were all dead now, his new cell members were not well trained, but the lessons David had learned about how to position the men and ready the weapons would serve him when the time came.

"We will have forty-five seconds, and that will be enough. After that it does not matter what they do to stop us. We will have succeeded."

The men praised Allah in their hot, tight hiding place.

David added, "There will be many helicopters. They will all look the same. The Americans send them along with the President's helicopter so that an enemy does not know which aircraft to target."

"How many?"

"Sometimes there are three, sometimes four. But with the current situation . . . there may be five. I don't know. When we see the flight, I will give everyone a number, and that is the helicopter you attack."

"Which one will the President be in?"

"I only know it will not be the first helicopter. Not today."

"How do you know?"

"Americans are cowards. And the President is the biggest coward of them all." Doyle said it as if the answer were obvious.

He then pulled a tablet computer out of his bag, turned it on, and used the 3G connection to check the Internet for news of the President's arrival the following morning.

By 0500, Raynor and Timble were exhausted. They had spent the previous seven hours driving up and down the roads near the Potomac River, doing their best to avoid the police as well as to look for a twenty-foot intermodal container that they were not even sure existed.

They had done well staying away from the cops, but they had gotten nowhere with their objective of finding Doyle. They had seen shipping containers, yes. But many were behind fences or in the backs of private property. They had wasted hours getting into and out of these locations to find nothing more than empty or sealed containers.

They'd also seen containers hauled by trucks on the highway, and this worried them greatly. Highway 295 ran right through the middle of the area Marine One would cross in just a few hours, and traffic there would not be blocked off. Yes, the highway would be crawling with state police, but Josh and Kolt both knew it took next to no time to operate a MANPAD.

To fight their exhaustion the two men decided to take a break. They sat in their truck at a gas station in Anacostia, sipping coffee and taking a few minutes to rest their brains.

Daylight would arrive in an hour and a half, and with it more police. They knew it would be harder for them to move around the closer it came to time for the President's plane to land, so they were desperate to find Doyle long before then.

TJ spoke wearily. "What if the container doesn't have anything to do with it?"

"Possible," said Raynor. "I don't know why he'd truck a container up here anyway. Seems like he and his buddies could just hop out of the back of a truck or a van or a—"

TJ sat up, causing Raynor to stop talking.

"You said the container was up on blocks."

"Yeah. So?"

"Like the same height as truck tires?"

Kolt thought for a moment. "Yeah. They said it was four feet off the ground. Sounds about right."

TJ nodded. "About right for a semi-trailer."

"Trailer rigs are longer, though."

"Yeah. Like fifty-three feet for a full-sized semi. But they wouldn't need all the space in the trailer to stow themselves and some SAMs." Timble shut the door of the pickup and turned over the engine. As he left the parking lot of the gas station, he said, "Maybe the container was just a stand-in to practice getting out of a semi with a missile quickly and quietly."

Kolt just shrugged. "Could be, but we're grasping at straws."

"I told you, brother. I know how he thinks. We need to start driving the route looking for semi-trailers parked overnight. I don't think he'd move into the area right when the cops are concentrating their search. He's already here, somewhere, waiting to attack."

FORTY-TWO

At eight a.m. all six of the Al Qaeda operatives in the semi-trailer had donned their chest harnesses, passed a few water bottles around to either drink out of or urinate into, and stood to stretch their legs.

Each man carried four thirty-round magazines of Kalashnikov ammo. This, plus the magazine already in each man's gun, gave the cell nine hundred rounds to fight off any police or security men if necessary.

They went over the procedure once more for firing the weapons. Everyone was comfortable shouldering the Igla, even in the darkness of their hide.

"And after we fire?" one man asked.

David said, "We pick up our guns and head for the road. The police will descend on us, it is unavoidable. But we will kill many men on the ground before we enter paradise."

David sat back down and checked his tablet computer. It was open to CNN, and he watched live streaming video of Air Force One as it descended through thin clouds on final approach to Andrews, just a few miles to the southeast of where he sat sweating in the dark.

Doyle said, "Soon, my brothers. Very soon."

Raynor and Timble could not believe the intense law enforcement presence over the route the helicopters would take in minutes. Although traffic was allowed on the streets, roadblocks had popped up at every major intersection.

Four times in the past half hour Kolt and Josh had been slowed while police just looked in the cab of their truck before waving them on again.

In the skies a half dozen police helicopters were visible, although they were spread out at great distance.

The two Delta men were waved through a roadblock for the fifth time just north of Andrews. Kolt said, "If anybody pulls us out and finds our guns, we're going to be in some serious hot water."

But TJ wasn't listening. Instead, he pulled over into the parking lot of an automated car wash, and looked out toward the northeast.

"High ground."

"What do you mean?"

"I mean, look over there. That spot in the distance. Where there are no buildings, the rise over there. I can't make it out. What is that? A golf course?"

Kolt looked. Squinted. "It's a cemetery. It might be Washington National."

TJ said, "Pass me your binos."

Kolt did so, and TJ scanned the area for a long time.

Josh lowered his binoculars slowly. "We're going over there."

"What do you see?"

"I see high ground, a great view toward Andrews, and a Buy-Rite. You can't tell me they won't have semis on their lot."

"This whole area is pretty flat, though. Why do you think he'd need high ground?"

"He wouldn't *need* it. But . . . like the black site hit the previous year, he took his time, he obsessed over every little bit of the operation, he studied the location of the event. Doyle would have been holed up in some building in Yemen for months planning this day, and you know he picked his terrain carefully. He would have found the highest point on the President's route, with the fewest buildings to block his view, and he would have picked that as the place to set up."

Kolt looked back over his shoulder. "Shit. POTUS is landing."

It took ten minutes for Timble and Raynor to make it off Suitland Parkway and onto Southern. Once on Southern, TJ did his best to keep his speed in check as he passed a police cruiser at every intersection. The two bearded men looked like craftsmen or laborers heading off to work early on a Sunday morning. Since the bed of their pickup was empty and there was no way they could have stashed an SA-24 missile with them in the cab of the vehicle, they did not garner much interest as they passed the checkpoints and roadblocks.

As they approached the entrance to the Buy-Rite, though, flashing lights around them had them both looking into the rearview.

Behind them a Maryland State Police patrol car approached quickly. It squawked its siren, and the lone officer spoke into his PA. "Pull over to the right."

"I wasn't speeding!" Timble said to Raynor.

"Just pull over before every cop in the county drops what they're doing and heads over here."

Timble slowed and turned on his blinker, but he kept moving forward, heading to the Buy-Rite parking lot. The trooper squawked the siren again.

TJ pulled into the parking lot and turned off the engine.

Raynor and Josh both looked at the several unattended semi-trailers in the back of the lot, a hundred meters from their position. They could not see the roll-up doors at the back of the semis, only the front portion of the big containers where the legs and the kingpin were.

"Son of a bitch," Kolt said.

"We have to get over there," Josh said.

"We going to run from the cop?"

TJ seemed to consider it for a moment, then he deflated with a long, frustrated sigh, and said, "No."

One hundred meters away, David Doyle watched the live feed from CNN streaming onto his tablet. Over a caption of "President Returning to White House," Doyle counted five Sea King black and white helicopters rising into the air above Andrews Air Force Base.

He looked at his men, who were nearly hidden in the dark, and said, "It is time, my brothers." He used the light coming off the tablet, and he pointed at each man in turn. "You fire at number two, you at number three, you at number four, you at five." Doyle had decided that the first helicopter would not be carrying the President, so he had two more missiles than he had targets. He decided he would have his fifth cell member fire a second missile at helicopter number three, and David himself would fire a second shot at chopper four.

In just minutes six powerful warheads would be streaking over Maryland and, inshallah, one or more of those warheads would decapitate the American government.

As it turned out, Lieutenant Colonel Timble had overestimated his ability to talk his way through any law enforcement they encountered in D.C. When the officer approached the driver's side of the vehicle, Josh rolled the window down and tried to talk to the young policeman, but Officer Weizer just held his hand up. "You gentlemen weren't speeding, but you passed me a couple of stoplights back and I couldn't help but see your North Carolina tags. You sure looked agitated for a couple of tourists."

Josh told the officer he and his friend were military officers in town for the weekend, but the beards on their faces and their nonregulation haircuts only created more suspicion in Weizer.

"Why don't you boys step out of the truck for me?"

Timble gritted his teeth. "Is that absolutely necessary, Officer?"

Weizer replied, "I'm not going to tell you again."

A minute later, Raynor and Timble stood with their hands on the hood of Josh's truck. They'd handed over their IDs, and Weizer looked them over slowly and carefully.

The two men had stowed their guns under the seat of the truck, so they did not expect trouble from the officer, a young man who seemed, to both men, to be a little too amped up.

Josh lowered his hands and turned to the officer, desperate to be sent on his way either with or without a ticket, but the movement spooked the Maryland State Police officer. He took a few steps back in the street, ordered Timble to put his hands back on the hood, and used his radio to call for backup.

When he heard a low thumping in the distance, Raynor looked over his right shoulder. There, to the southeast, he saw two, and then three, and finally a total of five VH-60 Sea King helicopters in the presidential colors. They were four klicks away, maybe a little more.

"Shit!" said Kolt.

Josh now looked back over his shoulder. When he saw the helos he lifted his hands from the hood and stood up again.

"Hey! Hey!" said the trooper. "Hands back on the fucking truck!"

The door of the semi-trailer rolled up, and two men leapt out onto the concrete parking lot. Once they hit the ground they turned back and each grabbed a launcher that was lying on the trailer's wooden floor. As they did this, two more men leapt to the ground, turned, and grabbed SAM launchers that Doyle, still in the container, slid forward to them.

When all four men in the parking lot had a weapon, Doyle and the last member of the Chicago cell slid their launchers to the front of the trailer, then climbed over them and leapt to the ground.

Now the six al Qaeda operatives spread out, moved around the side of the trailer as a unit, and began forming in a line, each man no more than five to eight feet apart.

All this took forty-one seconds. His first unit of four men had managed it in twenty-eight.

The first helicopter was just passing to the southwest of their position now, heading to the north.

"Wait for my order to fire," David said.

But on the far end of the line of SAM-armed men, one of the Chicago Saudis struggled with the weight of the launcher on his neck. He pushed the grip stock forward to reposition his weapon and, in doing so, he accidentally pressed the trigger on the Igla-S.

The long missile ejected from the launch tube, a champagne cork from a bottle, and then its propellant ignited and it streaked into the sky.

Doyle took his eye out of the sights of his weapon, his face a mask of shock and fury.

The missile streaked skyward away from the far end of the parking lot, on the other side of the semi-trailers from TJ and Racer.

TJ saw this, then jacked his eyes to Officer Weizer, who stood there with his mouth open.

"Don't you fucking shoot us!" TJ shouted to the trooper, and then he turned and reached back into the truck, pulled his shotgun and his Glock

.40-caliber from under the seat. Kolt ran around to the other side and grabbed his weapons.

In seconds they were running toward the site of the missile launch.

A stunned Officer Weizer reached for the radio on his shoulder.

Kolt was more physically fit than Josh, but Kolt's injured ribs made TJ a faster runner. They sprinted toward the location of the launch and almost immediately they saw movement around the trailer. Two men with rifles hanging from their backs shouldering SAMs stepped just slightly around the front of the semi.

Even though Kolt and TJ were too far away to effectively engage the men with the shotguns, they could hear the helicopters in the distance, and they knew the enemy might get another shot off in seconds. Without speaking and without breaking stride, both men aimed their shotguns in the general direction of the men and fired. They were still ninety meters away; their guns would spread a pattern of small-caliber buckshot over several square feet. This was hardly the optimal way to fight men armed with powerful rifles.

But they had no choice.

After each fired off a shell of double-aught buck, they simultaneously racked their slides and chambered another cartridge as they ran on.

David was furious with the Chicago cell member for launching early. The missile was wasted, as the young man had not even managed to acquire his target before he fired. Doyle screamed at him, told him to get his rifle up to protect the rest of them, and then he asked the man which target he had been given, so David could attack that helicopter himself.

The man said, "Three!" as he lifted his AK to his shoulder.

David found the third helicopter in the formation, received the tone from his weapon that told him his target's heat register had been found, and he gave the command order to fire.

But as he began pressing down to launch, he felt an impact on his right shoulder, and another in his right calf. The blows were so startling that he spun away, and nearly lost control of the forty-pound system. Almost instantly he heard the booms off to his right, and he knew it was gunfire. His sights were well above and to the south of his target as he pressed the trigger of the Igla-S. The exhaust exploded out the back of the launch tube and the missile fired into the air. Its second stage erupted and it raced into the sky faster than the eye could track it up.

He knew he had missed.

A second volley of booming gunfire came within a second, and out of the corner of his eye he saw one of his men fall backward to the ground, and he heard a second scream out in agony.

"Fire!" Doyle shouted to his remaining men.

Doyle pushed his Igla off his shoulder and reached behind him to pull his Kalashnikov off his back.

One of the Chicago cell did get a positive lock and a good launch, and this missile arced into the sky after a Sea King just two kilometers to the southwest.

More booms from big rifles came; there were two distinct reports this time, and Doyle turned back to find one of his cell members clearly dead, and two more had fallen to the ground and dropped their weapons.

Now he heard a new sound, so while he knelt at the corner of the trailer with his rifle to his shoulder, he tracked the noise to the choppers in the distance. There, the line of helicopters seemed to be involved in some sort of aerial ballet. As flares fired from both sides of the choppers they banked left and right.

A puff of smoke appeared just behind the second helicopter. It had taken a hit.

Doyle looked for the threats in the parking lot, and he saw two men with shotguns running across open ground.

Doyle sprayed 7.62 rounds from the hip toward the men approaching. Both men dove for cover.

Raynor and Timble scrambled behind a cement staircase that led to a back door of the Buy-Rite. They checked each other for wounds and found, thankfully, that neither had been hit. Raynor's broken ribs were killing him. He had to take short, fast breaths to keep the pain intensity bearable.

Both men reloaded their shotguns from shells stored in sidesaddles on the receivers of the weapons. As they did so they saw a white-topped helicopter corkscrewing in the distance ahead of an arc of fire and a haze of black smoke.

They did not know if the President was on board or not. They did know, however, that there were four other VH-60s in the sky, and they knew they had to prevent more SAM launches.

Both men stood up and pointed their shotguns at the semi-trailer just twenty-five yards away.

"Go!" TJ shouted at Kolt, and Raynor began running forward while Timble fired shell after shell to keep the terrorists' heads down.

Kolt ran across the open parking lot, his weapon out in front of him. He saw the effects of TJ's buckshot closer now. Four men lay dead or dying on the cement. He ran wide around the trailer, his shotgun high on his shoulder, but there was no one there. Several SAM launchers lay around the parking lot, but Kolt didn't take the time to see which launchers had been fired and which still contained missiles.

"Clear!" he shouted, and within seconds he heard TJ approaching in a sprint. Timble had dropped his empty Mossberg and he now held his Glock 23 pistol.

He and Raynor moved to the rear of the semi to look inside. They swept around the back at the same time, and found a man with an AK there. Both men fired on the terrorist, knocking him back into the trailer.

"Is that Doyle?" Kolt asked.

TJ pushed himself up into the trailer and immediately leapt back down. "Negative." He looked around now. Just to the south of them was a line of trees, and off to the left was the back of the Buy-Rite.

"He's running," TJ said.

"How do you—"

"I know!"

And with that, both men took off at a sprint, Raynor around the corner to the loading docks of the store, and Timble into the trees.

David Doyle ran through the trees at the south end of the Buy-Rite parking lot, and here he found an eight-foot-high security fence. He climbed it as quickly as he could, but once he got to the top, he realized the injury in his leg and shoulder had weakened him. His limbs gave out and he slipped, his chest crashed onto the barbs, and then he rolled over the top of the fence and fell to the ground.

As he stood he realized his AK-47 had fallen down on the other side of the fence. He had no sidearm with him, only the survival knife he'd purchased in Arizona inside his waistband.

"Fuck!" he shouted. There was no time to climb back over for the rifle.

He turned and ran off toward the cemetery, desperate to put distance between himself and the men who had ruined his operation.

Behind him he heard the fence rattle with the weight of someone climbing it.

TJ holstered his pistol, leapt onto the fence, and scaled it effortlessly. He dropped down on the other side, pulled his Glock 23, and ran through some more woods, his eyes scanning for any sign of David Doyle.

Officer Weizer pulled up next to Raynor in his squad car. They were at the back of the Buy-Rite, and Kolt was reasonably sure no one had come this way. He told Weizer to continue on around to the other end of the building, and he retraced his steps, feeling certain that TJ would be closing in on Doyle at the cemetery.

TJ ran across the green lawn, sprinting between headstones and crypts. He saw a lone vehicle parked on a road in the grounds two hundred yards away. He thought it possible that this was Doyle's getaway vehicle, so he focused all his attention on the car as he ran, trying to see if anyone was inside. While doing this he passed a large marble crypt at a sprint.

David Doyle dove out from around the marble structure as TJ passed.

In the terrorist's hand he held the long survival knife.

Timble reacted to the movement, but too late to avoid the knife. Doyle plunged the blade into Timble's chest; it sank hilt-deep into the running man's lung.

TJ and Doyle crashed together into the dewy grass and the Glock fell out of Timble's hand.

Doyle rolled to his knees quickly, straddled the man with the knife still in his chest, and looked down at his face. David's eyebrows rose in shock. Even though it had been nine months since they'd last met, the al Qaeda man recognized the American military officer immediately. With surprise he said, "*You?*"

TJ's eyes blinked weakly and blood ran down his lips.

Four miles north, Marine One passed over the National Mall on its approach to the White House. The South Lawn was ringed by Secret Service agents, ready to rush the President of the United States inside to safety.

• • •

Raynor sprinted as fast as his broken ribs would allow, out of the cover of trees and onto the manicured lawn at the northern edge of Cedar Hill Cemetary. In the blue sky ahead of him he saw the black smoke where a helicopter had been hit by an SA-24 and then crashed in a neighborhood in the Hillcrest Heights subdivision of Prince George's County.

Kolt's .45-caliber pistol swung with each stride, and his head swiveled back and forth, searching for either Doyle or TJ.

Just in front of Raynor, a wide marble crypt stood in the green grass. Kolt went wide around it to check the other side and there, twenty feet down a slight decline toward a road, David Doyle sat astride Josh Timble. The terrorist had a pistol in his hand and he leveled it, point-blank, down at TJ's face.

"No!" Kolt shouted, and he fired a single round from his .45. The bullet nailed Doyle in the shoulder and he spun off TJ and tumbled down onto the damp grass. The Glock fell a few feet from TJ's head.

Kolt walked forward, his pistol still pointed at Doyle. "TJ! TJ!" But he saw the hilt of the knife, and he watched Timble grab it with both hands and pull it out of his chest.

"Don't move!" Raynor screamed, speaking to both men simultaneously. He ran forward and dropped to his knees.

Blood spurted from the sucking chest wound. Raynor's years of training told him instantly that the injury was not survivable. Still, he put pressure on the hole in TJ's chest. With all his strength he pushed his left hand down on the wound.

Blood pumped through his fingers.

TJ's eyes were glassy. Unfixed.

"I surrender," Doyle mumbled from the grass lower on the hill.

Kolt ignored him and spoke to Timble. Blood had trickled out of both sides of the lieutenant colonel's mouth.

"I'm sorry, brother," Kolt said, his voice cracking. "Shit! Just hang on. Help is on the—"

"Sir! I surrender!"

Kolt turned away from his friend now, and toward David Doyle. "No, you don't."

The bleached-blond man had sat up in the grass, clutching his left shoulder with his right hand. Slowly he rolled to his knees and stood up fully.

"I . . . I just told you, I give up."

"You give up?"

"Yes. I know my rights, Officer."

"Do I look like a fucking cop?"

Doyle shook his head slowly. "No. No, you don't. You are . . . you are from the same unit as Captain Timble. You are in the Army. You have no jurisdiction here inside the U.S."

Kolt stood now. "What does that tell you?"

Doyle thought it over. "You are committing a crime. You are a criminal!"

Raynor smiled angrily. "You ain't seen nothing yet, asshole." Kolt divided his attention between TJ and the man standing a few feet away. He pushed his knee into the wound now, but he could already tell the blood flow was slowing.

In the distance, Raynor heard a helicopter approaching.

Doyle said, "If you kill me, soldier . . . you will be committing a *capital* crime."

"Like I give a shit right now." Raynor motioned toward the Glock with his .45. "Go for the gun."

"No. No! I told you, I surrend—"

Kolt shot Doyle in the left shin. The American al Qaeda operative fell facedown to the grass, his right hand just feet from the black pistol.

"There! It's closer now! Pick it up!"

Doyle screamed. Raynor had taken enough battle damage in his life to know that the scream was from terror, not from pain.

Pain of that magnitude took time to register, for the mind to accept it.

And time was something Raynor had no intention of giving Doyle.

"Go for the gun!" Raynor demanded again. He purposefully did not look down into the eyes of his friend now. He focused every bit of his attention on Doyle and the Glock 23.

"Please! Take me in! Arrest me! Don't do this! I am unarmed!"

"Last chance to arm yourself before I execute you!" Raynor barked.

Kolt felt movement from TJ below him. He looked down, away from the threat, and he saw that Josh had turned his head to face Doyle now.

As soon as Kolt looked away, Doyle lunged forward in the grass, his hand reaching for the weapon. As he got his fist around the grip and swung it toward Raynor, he screamed, "*Allahu Ak—*"

Kolt fired a .45 round into David Doyle's forehead. The thirty-year-old was dead before his face hit the grass.

Sirens filled the air now, and their volume increased by the second. Helicopter rotors beat in the sky, but they were much farther off.

Kolt Raynor took his knee off of TJ's chest. No more blood drained from the massive knife wound.

"We got him, TJ," Kolt said. His eyes filled with tears. "*You* got him."

With his fingertips covered in his friend's blood, Kolt closed TJ's eyelids. He then placed the pistol in his best friend's outstretched hand.

"Medals for the dead, brother. Medals for the dead."

Kolt Raynor stood and walked back into the trees.